THE LAST MAGICIAN

ALSO BY LISA MAXWELL

Gathering Deep
Sweet Unrest
Unhooked

7th july,

THE LAST MAGICIAN

BY LISA MAXWELL

SIMON PULSE

NEW YORK LONDON TORONTO SYDNEY NEW DELHI

SIMON PULSE

An imprint of Simon & Schuster Children's Publishing Division
1230 Avenue of the Americas, New York, New York 10020
First Simon Pulse paperback edition July 2017
Text copyright © 2017 by Lisa Maxwell
Front cover title typography and photo-illustration
copyright © 2017 by Craig Howell
Back cover photo-illustration copyright © 2017 by Cliff Nielsen
For information about special discounts for bulk purchases, please contact
Simon & Schuster Special Sales at 1-866-506-1949 or business@simonandschuster.com.
The Simon & Schuster Speakers Bureau can bring authors to your live event.
For more information or to book an event contact the Simon & Schuster Speakers
Bureau at 1-866-248-3049 or visit our website at www.simonspeakers.com.
Cover designed by Russell Gordon
Interior designed by Brad Mead
The text of this book was set in Bembo Std.
Manufactured in the United States of America
2 4 6 8 10 9 7 5 3 1
This book has been cataloged with the Library of Congress.
ISBN 978-1-4814-3207-8 (hc)
ISBN 978-1-4814-3209-2 (eBook)
ISBN 978-1-5344-0531-8 (export pbk)

For Harry, who is proof that magic is real

~

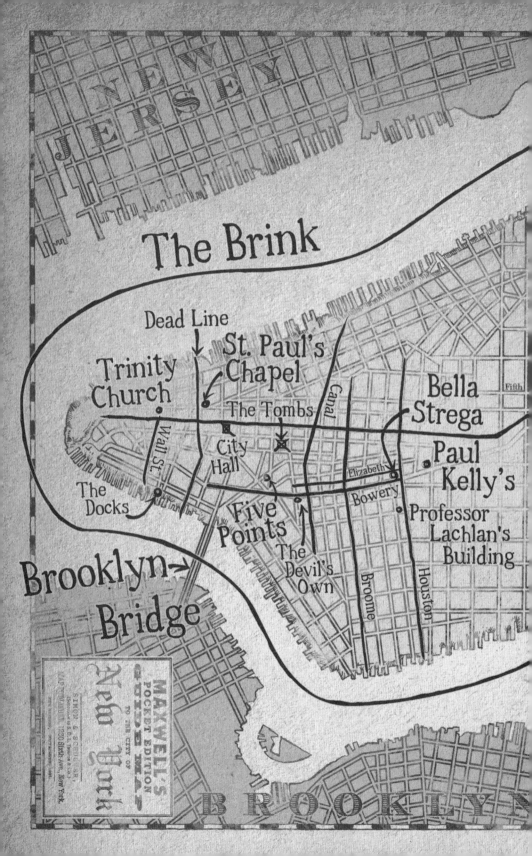

HUDSON RIVER

Schwab Mansion

Wallack's
Theatre

Haymarket

Broadway

CENTRAL
PARK

Satan's
Circus

J. P. Morgan
Mansion

Khafre
Hall

Park

Third

59th

BLACKWELL'S ISLAND

EAST RIVER

QUEENS

THE MAGICIAN

March 1902—The Brooklyn Bridge

The Magician stood at the edge of his world and took one last look at the city. The spires of churches rose like jagged teeth, and the sightless windows of tumbled buildings flashed in the rising sun. He'd loved it once. In those lawless streets, a boy could become anything—and he had. But in the end, the city had been nothing but a prison. It had borne him and made him and now it would kill him just the same.

The bridge was empty so early in the morning, a lonely span reaching between two shores. Its soaring cables were lit by the soft light of dawn, and the only sounds came from the waves below and the creaking of the wooden planks beneath his feet. For a moment he let himself imagine that a crowd had started to gather. He could almost see their tense faces as they stood in the shuffling silence and waited for his latest attempt to cheat death. Raising one arm in the air, he saluted the invisible audience, and in his mind, they erupted into cheers. His forced his face into the smile he always wore onstage—the one that was little more than a lie.

But then, liars do make the best magicians, and he happened to be exceptional.

As he lowered his arm, the silence and emptiness of the bridge wrapped around him, and his stark reality came into focus. His life might have been built on illusions, but his death would be his greatest trick. Because for once there would be no deception. For once it would be only the truth. His ultimate escape.

He shivered at the thought. Or perhaps that shiver was simply from the icy wind cutting through the fine material of his dress jacket. A few weeks later and there wouldn't have been any chill to the air at all.

It's better this way. Springtime was all fine and good, but the rank stink of the streets and the sweltering, airless buildings in the summer were another thing. The feeling of sweat always dripping down his back. The way the city went a little mad because of the heat. He wouldn't miss *that* at all.

Which was, of course, another lie.

Add it to the pile. Let them sort out his truths once he was gone.

He could still leave, he thought with a sudden desperation. He could walk across the remaining span of the bridge and take his chances with the Brink.

Maybe he *would* make it to the other side. Some did, after all. Maybe he would simply end up like his mother had. It wouldn't be any worse than he deserved.

There was a small chance he would survive, and if he did, maybe he could start over again. He had enough tricks at his disposal. He'd changed his life and his name before, and he could do it again. He could *try*.

But he knew already that it would never work. Leaving was just a different kind of death. And the Order, not bound by the Brink as he was, would never stop hunting him. Not now, at least. Destroying the Book wouldn't be enough. When they found him—and they would—they'd never let him go. They'd use him and use him, until there was nothing left of who he'd once been.

He'd take his chances with the water.

Pulling himself up onto the railing, he had to grip the cable tightly to keep balanced against those gusting spring winds. Far off in the direction of the city, he heard the rumble of carriages, the cry of wild, angry voices signaling that the moment for indecision had passed.

A single step is such a small thing. He'd taken countless steps every day without ever noticing, but this step . . .

LISA MAXWELL

The noise at the mouth of the bridge grew louder, closer, and he knew the time had come. If they caught him, no amount of magic or tricks or lies would help. So before they could reach him, he released his hold on the cable, took that final step, and put himself—*and the Book*—in the one place the Order could never follow.

The last thing he heard was the Book's wailing defiance. Or maybe that was the sound tearing from his own throat as he gave himself over to the air.

PART

THE THIEF

December 1926—Upper West Side

It wasn't magic that allowed Esta to slip out of the party unseen, the bright notes from the piano dimming as she left the ballroom. No matter the year, no one ever really looks at the help, so no one had noticed her leave. And no one had noticed the way her shapeless black dress sagged a bit on one side, the telltale sign of the knife she had concealed in her skirts.

But then, people usually do miss what's right in front of them.

Even through the heavy doors, she could still faintly hear the notes from the quartet's ragtime melody. The ghost of the too-cheery song followed her through the entry hall, where carved woodwork and polished stone towered three stories above her. The grandeur didn't overwhelm her, though. She was barely impressed and definitely not intimidated. Instead, she moved with confidence—its own sort of magic, she supposed. People trusted confidence, even when they shouldn't. Maybe *especially* when they shouldn't.

The enormous crystal chandelier might have thrown shards of electric light around the cavernous hall, but the corners of the room and the high, coffered ceiling remained dark. Beneath the palms that stretched two stories up the walls, more shadows waited. The hall might have appeared empty, but there were too many places to hide in the mansion, too many chances someone could be watching. She kept moving.

When she came to the elaborate grand staircase, she glanced up to the landing, where an enormous pipe organ stood. On the floor above, the private areas of the house held rooms filled with art, jewels, priceless vases, and countless antiques—easy pickings with everyone distracted by the loud, drunken party in the ballroom. But Esta wasn't there for those treasures, however tempting they might have been.

And they were *definitely* tempting.

She paused for a second, but then the clock chimed the hour, confirming that she was later than she'd meant to be. Tossing one more careful glance over her shoulder, she slipped past the staircase and into a hall that led deeper into the mansion.

It was quiet there. Still. The noise of the party no longer followed her, and she finally let her shoulders sag a bit, expelling a sigh as she relaxed the muscles in her back from the ramrod-straight posture of the serving girl she'd been pretending to be. Tipping her head to one side, she started to stretch her neck, but before she could feel the welcome release, someone grabbed her by the arm and pulled her into the shadows.

On instinct, she twisted, holding tight to her attacker's wrist and pulling it forward and down with all her weight, until he let out a strangled yelp, his elbow close to popping.

"Dammit, Esta, it's me," a familiar voice hissed. It was an octave or two higher than usual, probably because of the pressure she was still exerting on his arm.

With a whispered curse, she released Logan's arm and shook him off, disgusted. "You should know better than to grab me like that." Her heart was still pounding, so she couldn't manage to dredge up any remorse for the way he was rubbing his arm. "What's your deal, anyway?"

"You're late," Logan snapped, his too-handsome face close to hers.

With golden hair and the kind of blue eyes that girls who don't know better write poems about, Logan Sullivan was a master of using his looks to his advantage. Women wanted him and men wanted to be him, but he didn't try to charm Esta. Not anymore.

"Well, I'm here now."

"You were supposed to be here ten minutes ago. Where have you been?" he demanded.

She didn't have to answer him. It would have pissed him off more to keep her secrets, but she couldn't suppress a satisfied grin as she held up the diamond stickpin she'd lifted from an old man in the ballroom who'd had trouble keeping his hands to himself.

"Seriously?" Logan glared at Esta. "You risked the job for *that*?"

"It was either this or punch him." She glanced up at him to emphasize her point. "I don't do handsy, Logan." It hadn't even been a decision, really, to bump into him as he moved on to grab some young maid, to pretend to clean the champagne off his coat while she slipped the pin from his silken tie. Maybe she should have walked away, but she hadn't. She *couldn't*.

Logan continued to glower at her, but Esta refused to regret her choices. Regret was for people who dragged their past along with them everywhere, and Esta had never been able to afford that kind of deadweight. Besides, who could regret a diamond? Even in the dimly lit corridor, the stone was a beauty—all fire and ice. It also looked like security to Esta, not only because of what it was worth but also for the reminder that whatever happened, she could survive. The heady rush of adrenaline from that knowledge was still jangling through her blood, and not even Logan's irritation could dampen it.

"You do whatever the job requires." He narrowed his eyes at her.

"Yeah, I do," she said, her voice low and not at all intimidated. "Always have. Always will. The Professor knows that, so I'd have thought you would have figured it out by now too." She glared at him a second longer before taking another satisfied look at the diamond, just to irritate him. Definitely closer to four carats than she'd originally thought.

"We can't afford any unnecessary risks tonight," he said, still all business. Still clearly believing he had some sort of authority over their situation.

She shrugged off his accusation as she pocketed the diamond. "Not so much of a risk," she told him truthfully. "We'll be long gone before the old goat even notices it's missing. And you *know* there's no way he saw me take it." Her marks never did. She leveled a defiant look in his direction.

Logan opened his mouth like he was going to argue, but she beat him to it.

"Did you find it, or what?" Esta asked.

She already knew what the answer would be—*of course* he'd found it. Logan could find anything. It was his whole reason for being—at least it was his whole reason for being on the Professor's team. But Esta allowed him his triumph because she needed to get him off the topic of the diamond. They didn't have time for one of his tantrums, and much as she hated to admit it, she *had* been later than they'd planned.

Logan's mouth went flat, like he was fighting the urge to continue harping about the diamond, but his ego won out—as it usually did—and he nodded. "It's in the billiards room, like we expected."

"Lead the way," she said with what she hoped was a sweet enough expression. She knew the floor plan of the mansion as well as he did, but she also knew from experience that it was best to let Logan feel helpful, and maybe even a little like he was in charge. At the very least, it kept him off her ass.

He hesitated for a moment longer but finally gave a jerk of his head. She followed him silently, and more than a little smugly, through the dim hall.

All around them, the walls dripped with paintings of dour noblemen from some bankrupt European estate or another. Charles Schwab, the mansion's owner, wasn't any more royal than Esta herself, though. He'd come from a family of German immigrants, and everyone in town knew it. The house hadn't helped—built on the wrong side of Central Park, it was an entire city block of overdecorated gilding and crystal. Its contents might have been worth a fortune, but in New York, even a fortune wasn't enough to buy your way into the most exclusive circles.

Too bad it wouldn't last long. In a handful of years, Black Friday would hit and all the art lining those walls, along with every bit of the furnishings, would be sold off to pay Schwab's debts. The mansion itself would sit empty until a decade later, when it would be torn down to make way for another uninspired apartment building. If the place weren't so obviously tacky, it might have been sad.

But that was still a few years off, and Esta didn't have time to worry about the future of steel tycoons. Not when she had a job to do and less time than she'd planned.

The two turned down another hallway, which ended at a heavy wooden door. Logan listened carefully before pushing it open. For a second Esta worried he would step into the room with her.

Instead, he gave her a serious nod. "I'll keep watch."

Grateful that she wouldn't have Logan breathing down her neck while she worked, she slipped into the scent of wood polish and cigars. A thoroughly masculine space, the billiards room wasn't filled with the over-fussy gilding and crystal that adorned the rest of the house. Instead, tufted leather chairs were arranged in small seating groups and an enormous billiards table anchored the space like an altar.

The room was stuffy from the fire in the hearth, and Esta pulled at the high neckline of her dress, weighing the risks of unbuttoning the collar or rolling up her sleeves. She needed to be comfortable when she worked, and no one was there but Logan—

"Get a move on it," he demanded. "Schwab's going to start the auction soon, and we need to be gone by then."

Her back still to Logan, she searched the space as she forced herself to take a deep breath so she wouldn't kill him. "Did you figure out where the safe is?"

"Bookcase," he said before closing the door and sealing her into the stifling room. The silence surrounding her was broken only by the steady ticking of a grandfather clock—*tick . . . tick . . . tick*—a reminder that each second passing was one closer to the moment they might be discovered. And if they were seen—

But she put that fear out of her mind and focused on what she had come to do. The wall opposite the massive fireplace was lined with shelves filled with matching leather volumes. Esta admired them as she ran her fingers lightly over the pristine spines.

"Where are you?" she whispered.

The titles glimmered softly in the low light, keeping their secrets as she felt along the underside of the shelves. It wasn't long before she found what she was looking for—a small button sunk into the wood, where none of the servants would hit it accidentally and where no one but a thief would think to look. When she depressed it, a mechanism within the shelves released with a solid, satisfying *click,* and a quarter of the wall swung out enough for her to pull the hinged shelves forward.

Exactly as she'd expected—a Herring-Hall-Marvin combination floor safe. Three-inch-thick cast steel and large enough for a man to sit comfortably inside, it was the most sophisticated vault you could buy in 1923. She'd never seen one so new before. This particular model was gleaming in hunter-green lacquer with Schwab's name emblazoned in an ornate script on the surface. A beautiful vault for the things a very rich man held most dear. Luckily, Esta had been able to crack more challenging locks when she was eight.

Her fingers flexed in anticipation. All night she'd felt outside of herself—the stiff dress she was wearing, the way she had to cast her eyes to the floor when spoken to, it was like playing a role she wasn't suited for. But standing before the safe, she finally felt comfortable in her own skin again.

Pressing her ear against the door, she started to rotate the dial. One click . . . two . . . the sound of metal rubbing against metal in the inner cylinders as she listened for the lock's heartbeat.

The seconds ticked by with fatal certainty, but the longer she worked, the more relaxed she felt. She could read a lock better than she could read a person. Locks didn't change on a whim or because of the weather, and there wasn't a lock yet made that could hide its secrets from her. In a matter of minutes, she had three of the four numbers. She turned the dial again, on her way to the fourth—

"Esta?" Logan hissed, disrupting her concentration. "Are you finished yet?"

The last number lost, she glared over her shoulder at him. "I might be if you'd leave me alone."

"Hurry up," he snapped, and then ducked back into the hall, closing the door behind him.

"Hurry up," she muttered, mimicking his imperious tone as she leaned in again to listen. Like the art of safecracking could be rushed. Like Logan had any idea how to do it himself.

When the final cylinder clicked into place, she felt an echoing satisfaction. Now to try the combinations. Only a minute more and the contents would be open to her. A minute after that and she and Logan would be gone. And Schwab would never know.

"Esta?"

She cursed. "Now what?" She didn't look at Logan this time, keeping her focus on the second, incorrect, combination.

"Someone's coming." He glanced behind him. "I'm going to distract them."

She turned to him then, saw the anxiety tightening his features. "Logan—" But he was already gone.

She thought about helping him, but dismissed that idea and instead turned back to the safe. Logan could take care of himself. Logan would take care of both of them, because that was what they did. That was how they worked. She needed to do her job and leave him to his.

Two more incorrect combinations, and the heat of the room was creeping against her skin, the scent of tobacco and wood smoke burning her throat. She wiped her forehead with the back of her sleeve and tried to ignore the way her dress felt as though it would strangle her.

She tried again, dismissing the trickle of sweat easing its way down her back beneath the layers of fabric. Eight. Twenty-one. Thirteen. Twenty-five. She gave the handle a tug, and to her relief, the heavy door of the safe opened.

Outside the room, she heard the low rumble of male voices, but she was too busy scanning the vault's contents to pay much attention. The various shelves and compartments were packed with canvas envelopes filled with stock certificates and bonds, file folders stuffed with papers, stacks of neatly bound, oversize bills. She eyed the money, disappointed that she couldn't take even a dollar of the odd-looking money. For their plan to work, Schwab couldn't know that anyone had been there.

She found what she was looking for on a lower shelf.

"Hello, beautiful," she crooned, reaching for the long black box. She barely had it in her hands when the voices erupted in the hallway.

"This is an outrage! I could ruin you with a single telegram," Logan bellowed, his voice carrying through the heavy door. "When I tell my uncle—no, my *grandfather*—how abysmally I've been treated here," he continued, "you won't get another contract on this side of the Mississippi. Possibly not on the other, either. No one of any account will speak to you after I—"

It must be Schwab, Esta thought, pulling a pin from her hair and starting to work on the locked box. Schwab had been trying to make his mark on the city for years. The house was one part of that, but the contents of the box were an even more important part. And it was the contents of the box that Esta needed.

"Be reasonable, Jack." Another voice—probably Schwab's. "I'm sure this is a simple misunderstanding—"

Panic inched along her skin as her mind caught up with the man's words. *Jack?* So Schwab wasn't the only one out there.

However good Logan might be, it was never optimal to be outnumbered. In and out fast, with minimal contact. That was the rule that kept them alive.

She wiggled the hairpin in the lock for a few seconds, until she felt the latch give way and the box popped open.

"Get your filthy hands off me!" Logan shouted, loud enough for Esta to hear. It was a sign that things were escalating too quickly for him to contain.

She set the box back on a shelf so she could lift her skirts and remove the knife hidden there. Even with the scuffle in the hall, Esta felt a flash of admiration for Mari's handiwork as she compared the knife from her skirts to the jewel-encrusted dagger lying in the black velvet of the box. Her friend had done it again—not that she was surprised.

Mariana Cestero could replicate anything—any material from any time period, including Logan's engraved invitation for the party that night and the six-inch dagger Esta had been carrying in the folds of her skirt. The only thing Mari couldn't completely replicate was the stone in the dagger's hilt, the Pharaoh's Heart, because the stone was more than it appeared to be.

An uncut garnet rumored to be taken from one of the tombs in the Valley of the Kings, the stone was believed to contain the power of fire, the most difficult of all elements to manipulate. Fire, water, earth, sky, and spirit, the five elements that the Order of Ortus Aurea was obsessed with understanding and using to build its power.

They were wrong, of course. Elemental magic wasn't anything but a fairy tale created by those without magic—the Sundren—to explain things they didn't understand. But misunderstanding magic didn't make the Order any less dangerous. Just because the stone didn't control fire didn't mean there wasn't *something* special about the Pharaoh's Heart. Professor Lachlan wouldn't have wanted it otherwise.

Even in the soft light thrown by the fire, the garnet was polished so smoothly it almost glowed. Without trying, Esta could feel the pull of the stone, sensed herself drawn to it, not like she'd been drawn to the diamond stickpin, but on a deeper, more innate level.

After all, elemental magic might be a fairy tale, but magic itself was real enough.

Organizations like the Order of Ortus Aurea had been trying to claim magic as their own for centuries. Schwab had purchased the dagger and arranged the night's auction in the hopes of buying his way into the Order, but since the only magic the Order possessed was artificial and corrupt ceremonial magic—pseudoscientific practices like alchemy and theurgy— they wouldn't be able to sense what Esta could. They wouldn't know that Mari's stone was a fake until much later, when they were running their experiments and trying to harness the stone's power. Even then they would assume it was Schwab who had cheated them . . . or that Schwab couldn't tell the difference to start with. Schwab himself would believe that the antiquities dealer who'd sold him the dagger had swindled him. No one would realize the truth—the real Pharaoh's Heart had been taken right out from under them.

Esta made the switch, placing the counterfeit dagger into the velvet-lined box and tucking the real dagger back into the hidden pocket of her skirt. It was heavier than the one she'd been carrying all night, like the Pharaoh's Heart had an unexpected weight and density that Mari hadn't predicted. For a moment Esta worried that maybe Schwab *would* notice the difference. Then she thought of the house—his overdone attempt to display the number in his bank account—and she shook off her fears. Schwab wasn't exactly the type to understand which details mattered.

Outside the room, something crashed as an unfamiliar voice shouted. More quickly now, Esta locked the box, careful to put it back on the shelf exactly as it had been, and closed the safe. She was securing the bookcase when she heard Logan shout—an inarticulate grunt of pain.

And then a gunshot shattered the night.

No! Esta thought as she sprinted for the door, the crack of gunfire still ringing in her ears. She needed to get to Logan. He might be a pain in the ass, but he was *their* pain in the ass. And it was her job to get them *both* out.

At the other end of the hall, Logan lay on the floor, trying to pull himself up, while Schwab attempted to wrestle the gun away from a balding blond man in a tuxedo that bulged around his thick middle. Struggling against Schwab, the blond leveled the gun at Logan again.

Esta comprehended the entire scene in an instant and immediately took a deep, steadying breath, forcing herself to ignore the chaos in front of her. She focused instead on the steady beating of her own heart.

Thump. Tha-thump.

As regular as the cylinders of a lock tumbling into place.

Thump. Tha-thump.

In the next beat, time went thick for her, like the world around her had nearly frozen: Schwab's wobbling jowls stilled. The angry sweat dripping from the blond man's temple seemed to be suspended in midair as it fell in excruciatingly slow motion toward the floor.

It was as though someone were advancing the entire world like a movie, frame by painstaking frame. And *she* was that someone.

Find the gaps between what is and isn't, Professor Lachlan had taught her.

Because magic wasn't in the elements. Magic lived in the spaces, in the emptiness between all things, connecting them. It waited there for those who knew how to find it, for those who had the born ability to grasp those connections—the Mageus.

For those like Esta.

She hadn't needed magic earlier that night, not to escape the party or to pick the lock, but she needed it now, so she let herself open to its possibilities. It was almost as natural as breathing for her to find the spaces between the seconds and the beating of hearts. She rushed toward Logan, stealing time as she darted through the nearly frozen tableau.

But she couldn't stop time completely. She couldn't reverse the moment to stop the blond's finger from pressing the trigger again.

She wasn't quite to Logan when the sound of the gun shattered her concentration. She lost her hold on time, and the world slammed back into motion. For Esta, it felt like an eternity between the door of the billiards room to where she was standing, exposed, in the hallway, but for the two men, her appearance would have been instantaneous. For members of the Order, it would have been immediately recognizable as the effect of magic.

The men froze for a moment, their eyes almost comically wide. But then the blond seemed to gather his wits about him. He jerked away from Schwab, lifted the dark pistol, and took aim.

ON THE BRINK

August 1900—East 36th and Madison Avenue

olph Saunders was born for the night. The quiet hours when the city went dark and the streets emptied of the daylight rabble were his favorite time. Though they might have been criminals or cutthroats, those out after the lamps were lit were his people—the dispossessed and disavowed who lived in the shadows, carving out their meager lives at the edge of society. Those who understood that the only rule that counted was to not get caught.

That night, though, the shadows weren't a comfort to him. Tucked out of sight, across the street from J. P. Morgan's mansion, he cursed himself for not being able to do more. His crew was late, and there was an uneasiness in the air—it felt too much like the night was waiting for something to happen. Dolph didn't like it one bit. Not after so many had already disappeared, and especially not when Leena's life was at stake.

It wasn't unusual for people to go missing in his part of the city. Cross the wrong street and you could cross the wrong gang. Cross the wrong boss, and you might never be heard from again. But those with the old magic, especially those under Dolph's protection, knew how to avoid most trouble. A handful of his own people disappearing in the span of a month? It couldn't be an accident.

Dolph didn't doubt the Order was to blame, but they'd been quiet recently. There hadn't been a raid in the Bowery for weeks, which was unusual on its own. But even with their Conclave coming up at the end of the year, his people hadn't heard a whisper to hint at the Order's plans.

Dolph didn't trust the quiet, and he wasn't the type to let those loyal to him go without answers. So Leena, Dolph's partner in absolutely everything, had gotten herself hired as a maid in Morgan's house. Morgan was one of the Order's highest officials, and they'd hoped someone in the household would let something slip.

For the past couple of weeks, she'd polished and scrubbed ... and hadn't found out anything about the missing Mageus. Then, two nights ago, she didn't come home.

He should have gone himself. They were his people, his responsibility. If anything happened to her ...

He forced himself to put that thought aside. *She'll be fine.* Leena was smart, strong, and more stubbornly determined than anyone he knew. She could handle herself in any situation. But her magic only worked on the affinities of other Mageus. It would be useless against the Order.

As though in answer to his dark thoughts, a hired carriage pulled up to the side of the house. They weren't expecting a delivery that night, and the arrival only heightened Dolph's apprehension. With the carriage obscuring his view, he wouldn't be able to see if there was trouble.

Before he could move into a different position, angry male voices spilled out into the night. A moment later, the door of the carriage slammed shut and the driver cracked his whip to send the horses galloping off.

Dolph watched it disappear, his senses prickling in foreboding as the sound of fast footsteps approached. He gripped his cane, ready for whatever came.

"Dolph?"

It was Nibsy Lorcan. A castoff from the boys' mission, he had shown up in Dolph's barroom a few years back. Slight and unassuming, he would have been easy enough to overlook, but Dolph could sense the strength and tenor of a person's affinity from ten paces. He'd thought Nibsy would be a valuable addition to his crew, and he'd been right. With Nibsy's soft-spoken demeanor and sharp wit, the boy managed to win the respect of even the surliest of Dolph's crew, and with his affinity for predicting how different decisions might pan out, he'd quickly earned a place at Dolph's right hand.

As Nibsy came into sight, the lenses of his thick spectacles glinted in the moonlight. "Dolph? Where are you?"

Dolph stepped out of shadows, revealing himself. Despite the heat of the night, his skin felt like ice. "Did you find her?"

Nibs nodded, trying to catch his breath so he could speak.

"Where is she, then?" Dolph asked, his throat going tight as he searched the house again for some sign. "What happened?"

"The Order must have been expecting us," he said, still wheezing for breath. "They got Spot first, right off. Knife to the gut without any questions. And then Appo."

"Jianyu?"

"I don't know," Nibsy gasped. "Didn't see where he went. I found Leena, though. Morgan had her in the cellar, but . . . I couldn't get to her. They'd created some kind of barrier. There was this foglike cloud hanging in the air. When I got close, it felt like I was dying." Nibsy shuddered and took another gulping breath. "She's pretty weak. I couldn't have dragged her out of there. But she tossed this to me," he said, holding out a small object wrapped in muslin. "Told me to leave her. And there was more of them coming, so . . . I did. I'm sorry. I shouldn't have—" His voice cracked. "They took her."

Dolph took the object from Nibs. A bit of cloth had been wrapped around a brass button—one Dolph recognized from the maid's uniform Leena had worn. The scrap weighed no more than a breath between his fingertips. It was ragged on one side. It must have been torn from one of her petticoats. She'd used what looked like blood to scrawl two words in Latin across its surface. *Her blood*, he realized. The message had been important enough to bleed for. But at the sight of the smeared letters, already drying to a dark rusty brown, a feeling of cold dread sank into his very bones.

"We'll get her back." Dolph refused to imagine any other outcome.

He rubbed his thumb across the scrap, feeling its softness along with the familiar echo of Leena's energy. He pressed his own magic into the scrap, into the traces of her blood, trying to feel more and understand what had happened. While he could sense a person's affinity if they had one, could even tap into it and borrow it if he touched them, reading objects hadn't ever been his strength.

Still, Nibs was right—what little trace of Leena he sensed felt off, weak. He tossed the button aside but tucked the scrap of fabric into his inner coat pocket, the one closest to his heart.

"There's still time," he said, already heading toward the place where their carriage waited.

With the streets empty of traffic, they caught up to the other coach quickly. But as they followed it south through the city, he had a sinking feeling about where the carriage was headed. When they finally turned onto Park Row, Dolph knew for sure.

He directed their carriage to stop at the edge of the park that surrounded City Hall. Beyond the night-darkened gardens stood the great, hulking terminal that blocked the view of the bridge to Brooklyn. Steel and glass, it loomed almost like a warning in the night. Beyond it stood the first bridge of its kind to cross such a great span of water. And bisecting the bridge was the Brink, the invisible boundary that kept the Mageus from leaving the city with their magic intact. From corrupting the lands and the country beyond with what the Order—and most of the population—believed was feral, dangerous power.

Leena, like Dolph himself, had been born to the old magic. For the Order to bring her to the bridge meant only one thing—they knew what she was. And they were going to use the Brink to destroy her affinity. To destroy *her*.

He wouldn't let that happen.

Dolph watched as the hired cab carrying Leena turned beyond the terminal, toward the entrance for vehicles crossing the bridge. "I'll go on foot," he said. "You stay here. To keep watch."

"You sure?" Nibs asked.

"We can't chance alerting them." There would be no way to hide if they followed by carriage, but on the walkway above they might be able to surprise them, maybe have a chance to save Leena. "They'll have to wait to pay their toll. It will be easy enough for me to catch up."

"But with your leg," Nibs said. "I could—"

He cut Nibs a deadly look. "My leg's never stopped me from doing what needs done. You'll stay here, as I said. If I'm not back before their carriage appears again, go warn the others. If this goes badly, the Order may be coming for them all." He stared at Nibs, trying to convey the weight of the moment.

Nibsy's eyes widened a bit. "You'll be back," Nibs told him. "You'll bring Leena back."

Dolph was glad for the assurance, but he wasn't going to depend on it. Pulling his cap low over his eyes, he began to walk in the direction of the terminal. He ignored the stiffness in his leg, as he always did, and lifted himself up the wide steps that led to the entrance of the bridge. Once he was above, he kept away from the thin columns of lamplight on the planks of the walkway. Using the shadows for cover, he moved quickly despite his uneven gait—he'd lived with it for so long now that it was part of him.

The hired carriage was pulled to a stop before the first tower of the bridge—just beyond the shoreline. Below, three figures emerged. One reached back to pull out the fourth. Even from that distance, he knew it was Leena. He sensed her affinity—familiar, warm, *his*. But she was hanging limply between her captors. He felt the weakness of her magic, too, and when he got closer, he saw what they had done to her, saw her bruised face and bloodied lip. Saw her flinch with a ragged exhale and struggle against the men as they started to pull her toward the tower, toward the Brink.

His blood went hot.

Dolph, like every other Mageus in the city, knew what would happen when a person with the old magic crossed that line. Once they stepped across the Brink, it drained them. If the person was lucky and their affinity was weak—closer to a talent than a true power—they might survive, but they'd be left permanently broken from that missing part of themselves and would spend the rest of their life suffering the loss.

But for most, the Brink left them hollowed out, destroyed. Often, dead. So he understood what it would do to Leena, who was one of the most powerful Mageus he'd ever known.

Keeping to the shadows, he calculated his chances of getting Leena away from the men. He could take one down easily enough, even with his leg as it was, and the poisoned blade in his cane could do well enough on the other, but the third? There wasn't time to go back for Nibs, not that the boy would be much help in a fight.

"Hold her up, boys," the leader of the three said. "I want to see the fear in her eyes—filthy maggot."

The two men pulled Leena upright and one gave her a sharp smack across the cheek.

Dolph's blood pulsed, his anger barely leashed. But he forced himself to stay still, to not rush in and ruin his one chance of freeing her.

Still, seeing another man touch her, harm her . . . His knuckles ached from his grip on his cane. *To hell with destroying the Brink.* He would destroy them all.

He crept through the shadows until he was almost directly above them. Already he could feel the cold energy of the Brink. Unlike natural magic, which felt warm and alive, the Brink felt like ice. Like desolation and rot. It was perverse magic, power corrupted by ritual and amplified by the energy it drained. And like all unnatural magic, it came with a cost.

This close, every ounce of his being wanted to turn and flee. This close, he could feel how easily everything he was could be taken from him. But he wouldn't let anyone touch her like that again.

The man who spoke lifted Leena's head by her hair. "There you are," he said with a laugh when she opened her left eye to look at him. Her right eye was swollen shut. "Do you know what's about to happen to you, pigeon? I bet you do. I bet you can feel it, can't you?" The man laughed. "It's what maggots like you and your kind deserve."

Leena's eye closed. Not a betrayal of weakness, Dolph knew, but to gather her strength.

That's my girl, Dolph thought as Leena muttered a foul curse. Then she opened her unbruised eye and spit in the man's face.

The man reacted instantly. His hand flew out, and Leena's head snapped backward at the force of the blow.

Dolph was already moving. He hoisted himself up onto the railing and busted the streetlamp with the end of his cane. Like prey that sensed a hunter nearby, the men below went still as the light went out, listening intently for the source of the disturbance.

"What are you waiting for?" the leader shouted, breaking their wary silence, but his voice had an edge of nerves to it that wasn't there before. "Drag her over."

The men didn't immediately obey. As they hesitated, their eyes still adjusting, Dolph switched his patch, so he could see with the eye already accustomed to darkness. The bridge below now clear and visible to him, he dropped soundlessly from the walkway above. He ignored the sharp ache in his leg as he landed on the leader, knocking him to the ground and plunging the sharp blade concealed in the end of his cane into the man's calf. The man let out a scream like he was being burned alive.

That particular poison did have a tendency to sting.

As the leader continued to scream, Dolph turned to the next man, but he was already struggling against some unseen assailant. With a sudden jerk, he went still, his eyes wide as he slumped to the ground. Jianyu appeared, seemingly materializing out of the night, and gave Dolph a nod of acknowledgment as they turned together to face the third man.

The only one left seemed too paralyzed by fear to realize he'd be better off running. He was holding Leena in front of him like a shield.

"Leave me be or I'll kill her," he said, his voice cracking as he blinked into the dark.

Dolph stepped steadily toward them as Jianyu circled around the man's other side.

"You were already dead the moment you touched her," Dolph murmured when he was barely an arm's reach away.

The man stumbled back, and Leena took the opportunity to struggle away from him. But he was too off-balance and his hold was too secure. Instead of letting her go, the man pulled her with him as he stumbled back, away from Dolph and toward the cold power of the Brink.

Without thought for his own safety, Dolph reached for them, but his fingers barely grasped the sleeve of the man's coat. The fabric ripped, and the man—and Leena—fell backward into the Brink.

Dolph knew the moment she crossed it, because he felt her surprise and pain and desperation as keenly as if it were his own. The night around them lit from the magic coursing through her, draining from her. She screamed and writhed, her back arching at a painful-looking angle. Her arms and legs went stiff and shook with the terrible power that held her.

The man holding her screamed as well, but not from the Brink. When she began convulsing, he dropped her and ran, disappearing into the night of that other shore, where Dolph couldn't follow.

But Dolph's eyes were only for Leena. He watched in helpless horror as her body shook with the pain of her magic being ripped from her. He moved toward her, pushing past his own bone-deep fear of the Brink, but when his fingers brushed against the icy energy of it, he couldn't make himself reach any farther.

"Leena!" he shouted. "Look at me!"

She slumped to the ground, drained but still moaning and twitching with pain. He could no longer feel her affinity.

"Leena!" he screamed, fury and terror mingling in his voice.

It was enough to distract her for a moment, and even as her face contorted, she tried to turn toward the sound of his voice.

"That's it," he said when their eyes finally met.

Her expression was wild with the pain and shock of the Brink's devastating effect, but she wasn't dead yet. As long as her heart beat, there was a chance, Dolph told himself, pushing away the truth.

People didn't come back from the Brink.

Still, Leena was different, he told himself as she tried to focus on him. Dolph thought for a moment he saw her there, his own Leena, somewhere behind the agony twisting her features.

"I need you to come to me, *Streghina*. I need you to try," he pleaded.

And because she was the strongest person he'd ever known, she *did* try. She forced herself to move, reaching for him, her limbs trembling with effort as she pulled herself back to safety.

"That's it, my love. Just a little more," he told her, struggling to keep his voice from breaking into the animal-like wail he felt building within him.

With the last of her strength, she inched along. Her face was drawn tight, but she kept going. His Leena. His own heart.

"You can make it. Just a little farther."

But she looked up at him, her once-beautiful eyes now a lurid bloodred. Her expression was determined as she tried to whisper something, but before she could finish, she collapsed beyond his reach.

"No!" he screamed. "You can't leave us. You can't give up now." He knelt as close to the Brink as he dared get, willing her to keep moving.

But Leena only blinked up at him, barely able to focus with her unbruised eye.

No, he thought wildly. He wouldn't accept her fate. *Couldn't* accept it. Not his Leena, who had stood by his side since they were children. Not the woman who had been his partner in every way, despite all the mistakes he had made. He couldn't leave her there. No matter what it meant for him.

Dolph forced himself to reach out to Leena, to press through the searing cold bit by bit. To ignore the excruciating pain. Breaching the Brink was like putting your hand through glass and feeling the shards tear through skin and tendon. Or like dipping yourself in molten metal, if liquid steel could be colder than ice.

But even that pain didn't compare to the thought of losing her.

Finally, he grabbed Leena's hand. She blinked slowly, vacantly, at the pressure of his grasp, but with his fingers now wrapped securely around hers, he found that he didn't have the strength to pull her back. The Brink was already wrapping its icy energy around his wrist, burrowing deep beneath his skin to seek out the heart of who and what he was.

Then, suddenly, he was moving. Jianyu had taken him by the legs and was pulling him and Leena both back, away from the invisible boundary. With the strength he had left, Dolph took Leena into his arms and settled her across his lap, barely aware of the numbness inside his own chest.

"I wasn't fast enough," Jianyu said. "I tried to get her before they took her, but . . ."

Dolph wasn't even hearing him.

"No," Dolph whispered, tracing the lines of her face. Her breath rattled weakly from her lungs as he clutched her to him, rocking and pleading for her to stay with him. "I can't do this without you."

But she didn't respond.

"No!" he screamed when he realized her body had gone limp in his arms. "No!" Again and again, he wailed into the night, hatred and anguish hardening him, sealing him over, like a fossil of the man he'd once been.

A SLIP THROUGH TIME

December 1926—The Upper West Side

Esta froze as the blond trained the gun on her. His expression was a mixture of disgust and anticipation as he shifted his aim between her and Logan.

"I told you," he growled at Schwab. "I *warned* you something like this would happen."

"Jack!" Schwab yelled, grabbing for the man's arm again. "Put that gun down!"

Jack shook him off. "You have no idea what they are, what they're capable of." He turned to Esta and Logan. "Who sent you? Tell me!" he screamed, his face red with fury as he continued to swing the gun back and forth, alternating between the two of them.

Esta glanced at Logan and noticed the dark stain creeping across the white shirt beneath his tuxedo jacket. His eyes flickered open and met hers. He didn't look so cocky anymore.

"I won't be ruined again," the blond said as he cocked the hammer back again and steadied his aim at Logan. "Not this time."

Never reveal what you can do. It was one of their most important rules. Because if the Order knew what she was capable of, they would never stop hunting her. But they'd already seen her. And the stain creeping across Logan's shirt was growing at an alarming rate. She had to get him out, to get him back.

It seemed to happen all at once—

She heard the click of the gun being cocked, but she was already pulling time around her.

"Noooooo!" Logan shouted, his voice as thick and slow as the moment itself had become.

The echoing boom of the pistol.

Esta rushing across the remaining length of the hallway, putting herself between Logan and the gun.

Grabbing Logan tightly around the torso, she reached for safety . . . focusing all of her strength and power to reach further . . . and pulled them both into an empty version of the same hallway.

Daylight now filtered in through an unwashed window at the far end of the hall, lighting the dust motes they'd disturbed in the stale air of the completely silent house.

Logan moaned and shifted himself off her. "What the hell did you do?"

She ignored her own unease and took in the changed hallway, the silent, unoccupied house. "I got us out of there."

"In front of *them*?" His skin was pale, and he was shaking.

"They'd already seen me."

"You didn't have to come barging in like that," he rasped, grimacing as he shifted his weight. "I had it under control."

She should have been irritated that he'd reverted to his usual pain-in-the-ass demeanor so quickly, but Esta was almost too relieved to care. It meant his injury probably wasn't killing him. Yet.

Esta nodded toward his bloody shirt. "Yeah. You were doing great."

"Don't put this on me. If you hadn't gone after a diamond, you wouldn't have been late meeting me. We could have already been gone before Schwab showed up," he argued. "None of this would have happened."

She glared back at him, not giving an inch. But she knew—and hated—that he was right. "I got you out, didn't I? Or maybe you'd prefer being dead?"

"They're going to know."

"I *know*," she said through gritted teeth.

To Schwab and the other man, Esta and Logan would have seemed to disappear, and people *didn't* just disappear. Not without magic—*natural* magic. Old magic. Even Schwab would have understood that much.

"The Order will have heard about it," Logan said, belaboring his point. "Who knows what that will do. . . ."

"Maybe it won't matter," she said, trying to will away her uncertainty. "We've never changed anything before."

"No one has ever seen us before," he pressed.

"Well, we don't live in the 1920s. It's not like they're going to keep looking for a couple of teenagers for the next hundred years."

"The Order has a long memory." Logan glared at her, or he tried to, but his eyes still weren't quite focusing, and the dizziness that usually hit him after slipping through time was having a clear effect. He fell back on his elbows. "When are we, anyway?"

Esta looked around the musty stillness of the hallway. All at once she felt less confident about her choices. "I'm not sure," she admitted.

"How can you not be sure?" He sounded too arrogant for someone who was probably bleeding to death. "Weren't you the one who brought us here?"

"Yeah, but I'm not sure *exactly* what year it is. I was just trying to get us out of there, and then the gun went off and . . ." She trailed off as she felt a sharp pain in her shoulder, reminding her of what had happened. She touched the damp, torn fabric gingerly.

Logan's unfocused gaze raked over her. "You're hit?"

"I'm fine," she said, frustrated that she'd hesitated and ended up in the bullet's path. "It's barely a scratch, which is more than I can say for you." She pulled herself off the floor and offered Logan her hand.

He allowed her to help him up, but he swayed, unsteady on his feet, and put all his weight on her to stay upright.

"We're not any later than forty-eight. Probably sometime in the thirties, by the look of the house. Can you walk at all?" she asked before he could complain any more.

"I think so," he said, grimacing as he clutched his side. The effort it had taken to stand had drained him of almost all color.

"Good. Whenever this is, I can't get us back from in here." Pain throbbed in her shoulder, but the bullet really had only grazed her. She'd heal, but if she didn't get Logan back to Professor Lachlan's soon, she wasn't sure if he would. "We need to get outside."

The fact was, Esta's ability to manipulate time had certain limitations, mainly that time was attached to place. Sites bore the imprint of their whole history, all layered one moment on top of the other—past, present, and future. She could move vertically between those layers, but the location had to exist during the moment she wanted to reach. Schwab's mansion had been torn down in 1948. It *didn't* exist during her own time, so she couldn't get them back from inside the house. But the streets of the Upper West Side were still basically the same.

Logan stumbled a little, but for the most part, they made it through the empty house without much problem. As they reached the front door, though, Esta heard sounds from deep within the house.

"What's that?" Logan lifted his head to listen.

"I don't know," she said, pulling him along.

"If it's the Order—"

"We have to get out of here. *Now*," she said, cutting him off.

Esta opened the front door as a pair of deep voices carried to her through the empty halls. She tugged Logan out into the icy chill of the day, and they stumbled toward the front gates of the mansion.

Traveling through the layers of time wasn't as easy as pulling on the gaps between moments to slow the seconds. It took a lot more energy, and it also took something to focus that energy and augment her own affinity—a stone not unlike the Pharaoh's Heart that she wore in a silver cuff hidden beneath the sleeve of her maid's uniform.

Against her arm, her own stone still felt warm from slipping through time a few minutes before. The pain of her injury and everything else that had happened had left her drained, so trying to find the right layer of time was more of a struggle than usual. The harder she tried, the warmer the stone became, until it was almost uncomfortably hot against her skin.

Esta had never made two trips so close together before. She and the stone both probably needed more time to recover, but time, ironically enough, was the one thing that neither of them had if she wanted to avoid being seen again.

The voices were closer now.

She forced herself to ignore the searing bite of the stone's heat against her arm, and with every last ounce of determination she had left, she finally found the layer of time she needed and dragged them both through.

The snow around them disappeared as Esta felt the familiar push-pull sensation of being outside the normal rules of time. Schwab's castlelike mansion faded into the brownish-red brick of a flat-faced apartment building, and the city—*her* city—appeared. The sleek, modern cars and the trees full with summer leaves and other structures on the streets around them materialized out of nothing. It was early in the morning, only moments after they'd originally departed, and the streets were empty and quiet.

She let out a relieved laugh as she collapsed under Logan's weight onto the warm sidewalk. "We made it," she told him, looking around for some sign of Dakari, Professor Lachlan's bodyguard and their ride.

But Logan didn't reply. His skin was ashen, and his eyes stared blankly through half-closed lids as the modern city buzzed with life around them.

LIBERO LIBRO

November 1900—The Bowery

Dolph Saunders sat in his darkened office and ran his finger across the fragile scrap of material he was holding. He didn't need light to see what was written on it. He'd memorized the single line months ago: *libero Libro.*

Freedom from the Book.

At least, that's what he thought it said—the *e* was smudged. Perhaps it was better translated, *from the Book, freedom?*

"Dolph?" A sliver of light cracked open the gloom of his self-imposed cell.

"Leave me be, Nibs," Dolph growled. He set the scrap on the desktop in front of him and drained the last of the whiskey in the bottle he'd been nursing all morning.

The door opened farther, spilling light into the room, and Dolph raised his hand to ward off the brightness.

"You can't stay in here all the time. You got a business to run." Nibs walked over to the window and opened the shades. "People who depend on you."

"You don't value your life much, do you, boy?" he growled as the brightness shot a bolt of pain through his head.

Nibs gave him a scathing look. "I'm almost sixteen, you know."

Dolph gave a halfhearted grunt of disapproval but didn't bother to look up at him. "If you keep using that mouth of yours, you won't make it that far."

"If you drink yourself to death, I'm not gonna last the month anyway," Nibs said calmly, ignoring the threat. "None of us will. Not with Paul Kelly and his gang breathing down our necks. Monk Eastman's boys have been making noise too. If you don't get back to work and show them you're still strong enough to hold what's yours, they're going to make their move. You'll lose everything you've built."

Dolph thumped the bottle onto the desk. "Let them come."

"And the people who'll get hurt in the process?"

"I can't save them all," he said with a pang of guilt. He'd sent Spot and Appo to their graves, hadn't he? And he hadn't even been able to protect Leena, the one person he would have given anything—*everything*—to protect.

"Leena wouldn't have stood for you acting like this," Nibs told him, taking the risk to come closer to the desk.

"Don't," Dolph warned, meaning so many things all at once. *Don't speak of her. Don't remind me of what I've lost. Don't push me to be the man I'm not any longer. Don't . . .*

But Nibs didn't so much as blink at his tone. "That's the message she gave me that night, isn't it? You're still trying to figure it out?"

Instinctively, Dolph picked up the fabric and rubbed his fingers across the faded letters. "Leena would have wanted me to."

"Can I see?" Reluctantly, Dolph handed the fragile scrap over to Nibs, who studied it through the thick lenses of his spectacles, his face serious with concentration as he tried to decipher the Latin. "Have you figured it out? What book do you think she means?"

"I can't be sure, but I think she means *the* Book."

Nibs glanced up at him over the rims of his spectacles, confusion and curiosity lighting his eyes. "*The* Book?"

Dolph nodded. "The Ars Arcana."

Surprise flashed across Nibsy's face. "The Book of Mysteries?" He handed the scrap back with a frown. "That's only a myth. A legend."

"Maybe it is, but there are too many stories about a book that holds the secrets of magic for there not to be some truth to them," Dolph said, accepting the scrap with careful fingers.

"There are?"

Dolph nodded. "Some stories claim the Ars Arcana might be the Book of Toth, an ancient tome created and used by the Egyptian god of wisdom and magic, lost when the dynasties fell. Others say it was a record of the beginning of magic, stolen from a temple in Babylon before the city crumbled. They all end with the Book's disappearance." Dolph shrugged. "What's to say that someone didn't find it? What's to say the stories aren't true? If the Ars Arcana is real, what's to say the Order doesn't have it? Look at the devastation the Brink has wrought. . . ."

"But the Order—"

"The Order's power had to come from something," Dolph said irritably. "They aren't Mageus. They don't have a natural affinity for magic, so how did they come to have the power they wield now, even defiled as it is?"

Nibs shook his head. "I've never really thought about it."

"I have. Who's to say that this book isn't *the* Book? What else would Leena have been willing to sacrifice herself for?"

Nibs hesitated. "What will you do?"

"I don't know." Dolph let out a tired breath and placed the scrap on the desk before him. "Leena was no green girl. If anyone could handle themselves against the Order, it would have been her. Even you didn't see how badly it would turn out."

"I'm sorry. . . ."

"I don't blame you. It was her choice, and mine. But I don't know if I can make that choice for anyone else."

"But Leena's message . . ." Nibs frowned. "What if this book—the Ars Arcana, or whatever it is—what if it *is* the key to our freedom?"

"I don't know if I can ask anyone else to put themselves at that kind of risk for a hunch."

"They're already at risk," Nibs said. "Every day more come to this city, believing they've found a haven only to find themselves in a prison instead. Every day, more and more Mageus arrive and become trapped by the Brink—by the Order."

"You think I don't know that?" Dolph grumbled, tipping the bottle up again and frowning when he found it empty.

"They need someone to protect them. To lead them." Nibs took the bottle from Dolph.

It can't be me.

Dolph rubbed his chin, and the growth of whiskers there surprised him. Leena would have hated it. She liked his face clean and smooth and often ran her fingers over his skin, leaving trails of warmth behind.

She *used to* run her fingers over his skin, he corrected himself. But she'd been gone for months now, and Dolph hadn't felt anything since then except for the ice lodged in his chest. And the emptiness that filled his very soul.

"I can't lead them, Nibs. Not anymore."

The boy cocked his head, expectant, but didn't push.

"It's gone."

An uneasy silence grew between them as Dolph wondered if he'd ever been so young. By the time he was sixteen, he'd already put together his own crew. He'd already started on this mistake of a journey to change their fortunes. He had just over a decade on Nibs, but those years had aged him. And the past few months had hardened him more than an entire lifetime of regrets could have.

"*Everything* is gone?" the boy asked carefully.

Dolph licked his dry lips. "Not everything, no. But when I reached through to get Leena, the Brink took enough."

"The marks?"

"I can't feel them anymore. I won't be able to control them either." He met Nibs' questioning eyes. "They won't fear me if they know."

"So we don't let them know." Nibs gave him a long, hard look. "Control doesn't have anything to do with fear. Control is all about making them think following you is their idea."

"If they find out, they'll turn, and without Leena—"

"Even without Leena, you still have Viola for protection. You're not defenseless."

Nibs was right. Leena's ability to defuse the affinities of anyone around him who meant to do them harm had helped him build his holdings, but Viola could kill a man without touching him. He was making excuses, running scared, and that was something he'd never done before.

"Do it for her," Nibs urged. "If she sent you this message, it's what she wanted. Going after the Book, going after the Order, don't you think it's what she intended for you to do?"

"Fine. Put some people on it—people we trust. But I don't want word getting out about what we're looking for. If anyone else found out that the Ars Arcana exists . . ." He didn't finish the thought, but they both understood how dangerous it could be if others knew that he was after it. A book that could hold the secrets of magic? Whoever had it could be as unstoppable as the Order.

Which meant that Dolph had to be sure to get it first.

"I'll get on it," Nibs said, "but would you do me a favor?"

"What now?" Dolph asked, furrowing his brow in irritation.

"Get yourself a bath or something. The gutter out back smells better than you do."

ISHTAR'S KEY

Present Day—Orchard Street

The first indication that something was wrong was the entrance to Professor Lachlan's Orchard Street building. When Dakari got them back, the building looked the same from the outside, but inside, things had changed. There was a new, ultramodern lobby, complete with a security desk and a guard she'd never seen before. And extra security measures on every floor, at every door.

The building had always been something of a fortress, an odd place to call home, but now its austerity made the unseen threats outside its walls seem that much more foreboding.

But that wasn't the worst of it.

The brightly lit workroom in the basement of their building, where Mari once had produced everything the team needed, was nothing more than a dusty storage closet. Esta had returned from 1926 to find Mari was gone.

It wasn't just that Mari was no longer part of their team. Mari no longer even *existed*.

Esta had used every skill she'd learned over the years from Professor Lachlan to look for her friend. She'd searched immigration records and ancestry registries for some sign of Mari or her family, but instead Esta had found the unsettling evidence that her world had somehow changed.

It was more than Mari's disappearance. Small shifts and subtle differences told Esta the Order of Ortus Aurea had grown stronger and become emboldened in the late twenties and beyond, when they hadn't before. Waves of deportations. Riots that hadn't existed before. A change in who had been president here and there. All the evidence showed that the Order was more powerful now than they had been before Esta and Logan went to steal the Pharaoh's Heart.

With shaking hands, Esta did the one search she'd been dreading—the night of the heist. She had to know if that had been the source of the changes. She had to be sure.

She wasn't surprised to find herself inserted in the historical record where she never should have been. Not by name, of course. No one there that night could have known who she was. But she found a small article that talked about the break-in and the theft of the Pharaoh's Heart.

They knew she'd taken the real dagger.

And from the sparse two inches of print, it was clear they knew that Mageus were behind it.

She'd underestimated the danger they faced. She'd been raised to defeat the Order, trained since she was a young girl in all the skills necessary to do just that. Esta had read the history—public and private—and spent her childhood learning about the devastating effects the Order had on Mageus in the past. She trained daily with Dakari so that she could fight and defend herself against any attack, and still she hadn't truly understood. Maybe it was because the Order of Ortus Aurea and all they'd done so long ago seemed more like myth than reality. The stories had been so monstrous, but in actuality, the Order itself had always been little more than a shadow haunting the periphery of Esta's vision, the boogeyman in her unopened closet. It had been so easy to slip through time, to take things from right under their noses, that she'd never understood . . . not really.

Yes, the Order had created the Brink, and yes, that invisible barrier had effectively stripped the country of magic—and Mageus—over the years. Maybe there had once been a time when everyone knew magic existed, and certainly there was a time when people feared and persecuted those who had it, but by the end of the twentieth century, old magic—*natural* magic—had been mostly forgotten. A fairy tale. And as the public forgot magic, they forgot their fears. The Order had gone underground. It was still a threat to those few Mageus left, of course, but without public support, it operated in secret and its strikes were limited.

The changes in the Professor's building, the small differences in the history books, and, most personally, the erasure of Mari's very existence made Esta think that might no longer be the case.

She had caused this.

In the choices she'd made, she had somehow traded Logan's life for Mari's, traded the relative safety that had been her life for this other, unknown future. She hadn't even realized that was possible.

She had known that traveling to other times carried risks, but Professor Lachlan had taught her that time was something like a book: You could remove a page, scratch out a word here and there, and the story remained the same except for the small gaps. He had always believed it would take something monumental to change the ending.

Apparently exposing her powers to save Logan had been enough.

Three days after she brought Logan back, Esta found herself sitting at the end of his bed, watching his slow, steady breathing. He'd lost a lot of blood, and Dakari's affinity for healing hadn't been strong enough to stave off the infection his body was fighting. He still hadn't come to.

It wasn't that she'd ever been particularly close to Logan, but he was a part of the Professor's team. They needed him. And seeing him pale and so very still shook her more than she would have expected.

She knew the moment Professor Lachlan entered the room, his soft steps punctuated by the click of the crutch he used. Esta didn't turn to greet him, though, not even when he took a few steps through the door and paused as he often did when he had something to discuss with her.

"Don't say it. Please—don't even say it."

"Perhaps I was going to thank you for saving him."

"Bull." She did turn then. Professor Lachlan hadn't moved from the doorway. He was leaning, as usual, on his silver crutch.

She wasn't sure exactly how old he was, but despite his advanced years, the Professor was still fit and slender. He was dressed in the same uniform of tweed pants and a rumpled oxford shirt he'd worn when lecturing to scores of undergraduates at Columbia over the years. He was a small man, not much taller than Esta herself when he straightened, and at first glance most people overlooked him, often dismissing him as too old to be worth worrying about.

Most people were idiots.

The cataracts that had plagued him for years clouded his eyes, but even so, they were astute, alert. Three days ago, when she'd told him what had happened and tried to explain about Mari, he'd simply listened with the same impassive expression he usually wore, and then he'd dismissed her. They hadn't talked since.

"You were going to tell me I broke the most important rule," Esta said. She'd been waiting for this lecture for three days now. "I put us all at risk by blowing our cover and exposing what we were to the Order. I already know that," she said, feeling the pang of Mari's loss more sharply.

"Well, then. It's good of you to save me the trouble." He didn't smile. "We need to talk," he said after a moment. "Come with me."

He didn't wait for her agreement, so Esta didn't have much choice but to leave Logan and follow the Professor down the hall to the elevator. They rode the ancient machine in silence, the cage vibrating and rattling as it made its way to the top of the building he owned. It had once been filled with individual apartments, but now Professor Lachlan owned all of it. She'd grown up in those narrow hallways, and it was the only home she could remember. It had been a strange childhood filled with adults and secrets—at least until Logan arrived.

When the doors opened, they stepped directly into the Professor's library, its walls lined floor-to-ceiling with books. These weren't like the unread, gilded spines of Schwab's books, though. Professor Lachlan's shelves were packed with volumes covered in faded leather or worn cloth, most cracked and broken from years of use.

No one had a collection like his. He'd purchased most of the volumes in his personal library under false names. Others, he'd had Esta liberate from reluctant owners over the years. Many of his colleagues knew his collection was large, but no one knew how extensive it was, how deep its secrets went—not even the members of his own team. In truth, no one dead or alive knew as much about the secrets New York held as James Lachlan did. Esta had spent almost every day of her childhood in that room, studying for hours, learning everything she needed to blend in during any time in the city's history.

She'd hated those hours. It was time she would have rather spent on one of their daily walks, the long, winding strolls that Professor Lachlan used to teach her the city, street by street. Or better, prowling through the city herself, practicing her skills at lifting a wallet, or sparring with Dakari in the training room. The long hours she'd spent learning in that room had served her well, though. That knowledge had gotten her and Logan out of more than one tough spot.

But it hadn't helped at Schwab's mansion. She made a mental note to do more research on the blond—Jack—whoever he was. If their paths crossed again, she'd be ready.

Professor Lachlan made his way slowly into the room, straightening a pile of papers and books as he went. Clearly, he was in no hurry to get to his point.

It was a test, she knew. A familiar test, and one she was destined to fail.

"You said we needed to talk?" she asked, unable to stand his silence any longer.

The Professor regarded her with the expression he often wore, the one that kept even the people closest to him from knowing his thoughts. He might have made an excellent poker player, if he'd ever cared to gamble. But he never did anything unless he was already sure how it would turn out.

"Patience, girl," he told her, his usual rebuke when he thought she'd acted impulsively—which was all too often, in his opinion.

He took a few more labored steps toward his desk, his lined face creasing with the effort. When his cane slipped and he stumbled, she was at his arm in an instant.

"You should sit," she said, but he waved her off with a look that had her stepping back.

He hated it when anyone fussed. He never wanted to admit that he might *need* some fussing every so often.

Never expose your weaknesses, he'd taught her. *The minute someone knows where you're soft, they can drive in the knife.*

"I don't have time to sit." He leveled an unreadable stare in her direction. "You allowed a member of the Order to see you." His tone made it clear that the words were meant to scold as much as to inform.

"What was I supposed to do?" she asked, lifting her chin. "Leave Logan? I saved his life. I brought him back to you. I kept our team together."

Professor Lachlan's expression didn't so much as flicker, but something in the air between them changed. "You lost sight of your assignment."

"I got the dagger."

His mouth went tight. "Yes, but that wasn't the only thing you took, was it?"

"I tried to give you the diamond."

"I didn't send you to steal diamonds. If you had been on time, as was planned, none of this would have happened."

"I can't say that I'm sorry," she told him, forcing herself to meet his eyes. "I saw an opportunity, and I took it. Just like you taught me."

"You did, didn't you?" He studied her. "You've always been a good student, possibly even better than Logan—though not as disciplined—but your impulsiveness had consequences this time."

She'd learned long ago not to flinch under the weight and expectation of the Professor's stare, so she didn't now. But the reminder of her mistakes hit its mark.

Her throat went tight. "What do you want me to do? I can go back, fix it."

"What would you do? Try to stop yourself?" Professor Lachlan shook his head. "I don't know if it's even possible. And I won't risk any more damage to the stone for a fool's errand." He pinned Esta with his steady, patient stare just as he'd done since she was a small girl. "What's done is done. We go on from here. As always."

"But the Order," she reminded him. "You said yourself, they've seen me now." She looked up at him, forcing herself to meet his eyes the way he had taught her when she was a girl. "The whole point of stealing from the past is so the Order can't see me coming, but now they'll know. They might even be waiting for me." *I'm useless to you,* she couldn't stop herself from thinking.

And if that were true, what role could she play in the Professor's world? If she couldn't do the job he had groomed her for, where would she belong?

"They saw you in 1926, true. But that only means they'll know who and what you are *after* that point." He gave her a look that said she should have figured that much out on her own.

Understanding hit. "But not *before*," she whispered.

"No, not before," he agreed.

"There *has* to be plenty to take from the years before the twenties."

Professor Lachlan leveled another indecipherable look in her direction that had her falling silent as he made his way steadily past the stacks of old newspapers and books to the large wall safe at the far side of his office.

He placed his hand against the sensor, and when the lock released, he took a large box from the recesses of the vault. Esta kept quiet and didn't bother to ask him if he needed help with it, not even when it was clear he did. Finally, he managed to make his way to the large desk that stood at the midpoint of the room.

The heavy oak table was covered in piles of papers and stacks of books. Setting the box on one of the smaller piles, he sank into a straight-backed chair and set the crutch aside before he bothered to speak.

"Back when I found you wandering alone in Seward Park, I wasn't in the market for a child. But when I discovered what you could do— your affinity for time—I realized you could be the key to my plans," he said, leaning forward in his chair. "It's why I've spent the last twelve years training you, teaching you everything you would need to know to go to any point in the city's past and take care of yourself.

"I didn't adopt you because I wanted to steal shiny baubles and old journals," he said, his voice twisting with his annoyance. He stopped short then, as though realizing he'd let his emotions get away from him, and then started again, more measured this time. "This has never been about getting rich, girl. Each of the jobs you've done has had a purpose." He opened the box. "I needed information, and that information led me to the various treasures you've managed to bring me."

One by one he took the objects out of the box.

"You're familiar with the Pharaoh's Heart," he said as he removed the newly stolen dagger from the bag. "But your first real piece was the Djinni's Star."

He took out a heavy necklace that Esta remembered taking from an Upper East Side jeweler four or five years back. In the platinum settings was a rare turquoise that seemed to hold an entire galaxy within its blue depths.

"And I'm sure you'll remember the Delphi's Tear," he said, holding out an agate ring with a stone so clear and pure it looked almost liquid.

Of course she remembered. She was barely thirteen when she'd slipped it off the finger of a socialite sometime in the 1960s. It had been the first of the pieces she'd taken from the past and the first piece she'd stolen with Logan's help. He'd been an unexpected—and not altogether welcome—addition to the Professor's crew. Esta hadn't been happy when Professor Lachlan had introduced Logan, the nephew of one of his contacts. She'd seen it as a sign that she wasn't trusted enough, that Professor Lachlan didn't think she was ready to go out on her own. She'd been even less happy when they'd all gone together, with each of them taking one of her hands to slip back through to the midcentury city. Logan had found the ring, and she'd taken it. And she'd hated him a little for being so necessary.

He'd won her over, though—too fast. She'd been young and didn't have much experience with anyone outside the Professor's small circle, so she didn't know at first to look beyond his charm. She'd fallen for it, until she realized that everything was a game to Logan. It wasn't that he was heartless or uncaring. He was as dedicated and loyal to the team—and to Professor Lachlan—as she was. But whether it was a shiny jewel or a never-been-kissed girl, he was only interested in the chase. And once the chase was over . . .

"Then there's the Dragon's Eye," Professor Lachlan said, bringing Esta's attention back to the present moment as he removed a glittering tiara from the box. At its center was a large piece of amber so flecked with gold that it practically glowed.

She'd found that piece in Chinatown sometime in the forties. She'd been fourteen, and it was the first big job they'd done without Professor Lachlan escorting them. By then she'd accepted what Logan was and had forgiven him for making her think he was something more. She'd even formed a begrudging friendship with him. Professor Lachlan needed and trusted Logan, and she trusted Professor Lachlan. So that was that.

"And then there's the Key." Finally, he pulled out the most familiar treasure of all—Ishtar's Key. The rock was a strange, dark, opal-like stone that glimmered with a deep rainbow of colors. Set into an arm cuff that fit perfectly against Esta's own biceps, it was the stone that allowed her to slip vertically through the layers of time. Her stomach sank when she saw the jagged line bisecting its smooth surface, the reminder of yet another consequence of her mistakes.

When they'd finally gotten back to their building on Orchard Street, Esta had discovered the crack. The only explanation was that she'd used it too much without giving it time to cool, but they didn't know what it might mean for the stone's power. She hoped it was a positive sign that even from across the room, its familiar warmth and energy still called to her.

Looking at the objects on the table was like looking at her own history, but she understood that there was more to the display than a walk down memory lane. Seeing the five objects there on his desk, she could tell there was a pattern she hadn't previously understood.

Professor Lachlan ran his finger over the crack in Ishtar's Key, pausing thoughtfully before he spoke. "These five stones were once in the possession of the Ortus Aurea. Back when the Order was at the very pinnacle of its strength, it kept them in a secure room called the Mysterium, a vault deep within their headquarters in Khafre Hall. Only the highest circles ever had access to them, but their existence was the very source of the Order's power, until they were stolen."

She looked up at him. "Stolen?"

Professor Lachlan opened one of his notebooks and flipped through it until he found a page with a yellowed piece of newsprint taped onto it. He turned the book so Esta could read the story.

"Back in 1902, a group of Mageus attempted to take down the Order," he explained, pointing at the clipping. "They broke into the Mysterium and stole the Order's most important treasures. But one of the crew double-crossed the rest, and the job went off the rails. The crew scattered, and the artifacts disappeared."

She scanned over the faded column of print. "This is a story about a fire," she said, confused. There was no mention of a robbery.

"Of course it is. The Order couldn't let anyone know what had really happened. If word got out that they'd been robbed of such important treasures—by the very people they were trying to control, no less—they would have looked weak. It would have put them at risk for more groups to try retaliating. They hid their losses. They hid their failures. They pretended nothing had happened, that everything was the same.

"It worked, for a while at least. I've already taught you about the early years of the last century. You know how dangerous this city was for anyone with the old magic—the fires, the raids disguised as simple policing to protect the city. And there was always the Brink. Stealing the Order's artifacts didn't change any of that. But as the years passed, the old magic began to fade and be forgotten. New generations were weaker than the ones who had come before, and the city began to forget its fear.

"The Order never forgot, though. For years the highest members of the Order tried to find these pieces and bring them back together, but because of the work we've done, they've never managed to. Occasionally a piece would pop up at an auction, like the one at Schwab's mansion, or rumors of another would surface, but since that original theft, these pieces have never been in the same room." The Professor smiled, his old eyes sparking. "Until now."

He didn't have to tell Esta that there was something about the various stones that made them more than they appeared. Just as Ishtar's Key called to her, the artifacts together seemed to saturate the entire space with a warm, heady energy.

"You see," he continued, "there has been a method to what we've done these past years. One by one, I discovered the fate of the stones. One by one, I've collected them and kept them safe. But it's not enough. Everything we've done has only been a prelude to one item, the last of the artifacts." He leaned forward. "I've been more than careful, or haven't you noticed? Each job has been a little farther back, each one a little more challenging. I was getting you ready for the one job that means everything."

Esta straightened a bit. Professor Lachlan was still willing to trust her. He still *needed* her.

"What's the mark?" she asked, her voice filled with a bone-deep desire to prove herself to him.

He smiled then. "We need the final item that was stolen that day. A book."

Esta couldn't hide her disappointment. She'd stolen plenty of books for him over the years. "You want me to get another book?"

"No, not *another* book." His old eyes gleamed. "You're going to get *the* Book—the Ars Arcana."

Even with all her training and the many, *many* hours she'd spent learning about the city and about the Order, Esta had never heard that particular term before. Her confusion must have shown.

"It's a legendary book, a text rumored to be as old as magic itself," he explained with a twist of impatience. "For years it was under the Order's control, and I believe it can tell me how to use these stones to topple the Order once and for all. Imagine it, girl—the few Mageus left wouldn't have to hide who we are anymore. We'd be *free*."

Free. Esta wasn't sure what that word even meant. She loved her city, had never really thought about or yearned for a life outside it. But Professor Lachlan was looking at her with an expression of hope and warmth. "Tell me where it is, and it's yours," Esta said.

"Well, that's where it gets tricky." Professor Lachlan's expression darkened. "The Book was lost. Probably destroyed."

"Destroyed?"

Professor Lachlan nodded. "One of the team double-crossed the rest. He took the Book and disappeared. If the Book still existed, I would have found it by now. Or Logan would have." His eyes lit again. "That's why you have to stop the traitor before he can disappear. If you can save the Book and bring it back here, it would change *everything*."

Anticipation singing in her blood, Esta kept herself calm, determined. "Who is he? Where do I find him?"

Studying her a moment longer, Professor Lachlan's mouth turned up ever so slightly. It wasn't a real smile, but it was enough to tell her that she'd started to win back a measure of his approval. "The spring of 1902, when the heist happened," he said, tapping the news clipping. "You're going to have to go back further than you've ever gone before. The city was a different place then."

"I can handle it," she said.

"You don't understand. . . . *Magic* was different back then. Now the city is practically empty of magic. Now people think magic is a myth. But back then the streets would have felt electric. People knew that the old magic existed, and they feared those who held it. Back then there was still the feeling in the air that something was about to start. Everyone was picking sides."

"I know," she told him. "You've taught me all of this."

"Maybe I did." He sighed as he lifted Esta's cuff from the table and examined it, frowning as he studied the crack in the stone. "But I'm still not sure you're ready. This last job makes me wonder . . ."

Esta wanted to reach for the cuff, but she held back. It wasn't exactly hers—the Professor only permitted her to wear it when he needed something from the past. Otherwise, he kept it safe in his vault. Still, the cuff had always *felt* like hers, ever since the first time he'd slipped it onto her arm a little more than six years ago, when she was eleven years old, and shown her that she was meant for more than lifting fat wallets out of tourists' pockets.

"I won't disappoint you again," she promised.

He didn't offer her the cuff, though. He was still punishing her, however gently. Teasing her with the promise of the stone but reminding her who Ishtar's Key—and the power that came with it—really belonged to.

"We can't afford to wait for Logan to heal. You'll go after the Book now, and you'll go alone."

"Alone?" Esta asked. "But without Logan, how will I find it?"

"You'll get yourself on the team that steals it."

Confused at the change in their usual way of working, Esta frowned. "But if we waited for Logan to heal, we could get there before them. In and out quick, like you've always said. We don't have to take the risk of it disappearing."

"No," Professor Lachlan said sharply. "It won't work."

"But with my affinity—" she started.

"It isn't enough," he snapped, cutting her off. "Do you think you could simply waltz into the Order's stronghold and lift the Book? You're a gifted thief, but it took a team to get in, to get past their levels of security. And the person who eventually double-crossed them was essential to that."

"There has to be another, easier way," she argued.

"Even if there were . . ." Professor Lachlan shook his head. "Every one of our jobs has been carefully designed so that the Order never knew when they were actually robbed. Every time you've taken an artifact, I've planned it so the theft was invisible, so they couldn't trace it to us. I did that for a reason. But look what happened this last time—you *changed* something by being exposed. How much more of our present might be affected if you mess with the events of the past?"

He tapped again on the news clipping. "The heist has to happen *exactly* as it happened then. You can't risk changing anything. Think about it—if the heist doesn't occur or if the Order knows who was behind it, there's no telling what that might do to the future. To *our present*. The only difference can be who gets the Book. Otherwise, think of what repercussions there might be."

She thought of Mari and knew too well what the effects might be.

"Besides," he said, examining the crack in the surface of the stone, "I'm not sure that Ishtar's Key could handle taking two through time again. You put a lot of pressure on the stone with what you did at Schwab's mansion. You'll have to do this alone." He still wasn't smiling as he held out the silver cuff. "Unless you don't feel up to the challenge?"

Esta hesitated before she reached for it. This, too, seemed like a test, but if she failed this time, how much more damage could she do? How many more lives might she be putting in danger?

But if she succeeded . . . Maybe by getting the Book, she could make everything right again. Maybe she could get Mari back.

She thought of the uncounted others who might still live in the shadows of the city, their affinities weak and broken from years of disuse and generations of forgetting. If one mistake in the future could have caused so many changes to her present, what might destroying the Order do?

If she succeeded, she could do more than simply fix the mistakes she'd made and make her present right again. Maybe she could rewrite her own future. Reclaim magic.

There would be no more hiding—for any of them.

She took the cuff. The silver was still cold from being in the vault, but she slid it onto her arm without so much as a shiver. Again, she felt the pull of the stone, like something was warming her from within. Something that felt like possibility . . . and the promise of power. "Tell me who betrayed them," she said, determined. "Who is it I need to stop?"

Professor Lachlan's mouth curved into a smile, but his eyes held nothing but cold hate. "Find the Magician," he told her. "And stop him before he destroys our future."

THE DEVIL'S OWN

August 1901—The Bowery

Harte Darrigan cursed himself ten times over as he pushed his way through the crowd of The Devil's Own, a smoke-filled boxing saloon on the Lower East Side named for the gang that ran it. The sound of bones crunching as fist met face caused the crowd to surge with an eagerness that made Harte's pulse race and turned his resolve to mush.

The dive was filled with the type of people Harte had done everything he could to avoid becoming. They represented the most dangerous parts of humanity—if you could even call it that—south of Houston Street, the wide avenue that divided the haves from the have-nots and probably-never-wills. Harte himself might have been a liar and a con man, but at least he was an honest one. Or so he told himself. He'd risked everything to get out of Paul Kelly's gang three years ago, and he didn't want the life he'd managed to build for himself since then to get muddied by the never-ending war between the different factions that ruled lower Manhattan.

Yet there he was.

He shouldn't have come. He was an idiot for agreeing to this meeting, a complete idiot to let Dolph Saunders goad him into being drawn back into this world with an impossible promise—freedom. A way out of the city. It was fool's dream.

Harte must be a fool, because he knew what Dolph Saunders was capable of and, still, he had agreed to meet him. He'd seen Dolph's cruelty with his own eyes, and if Harte were smarter, he'd turn tail and leave before it was too late. . . .

But then a familiar voice was calling his name over the crowd, and he knew his chance had passed.

The kid approaching him was probably the skinniest, shortest guy in the room. He wore a pair of spectacles on the tip of his straight nose, and unlike most of the crowd that populated The Devil's Own, he wasn't dressed in the bright colors or flamboyant style that characterized the swells of the Bowery. Instead, the kid wore suspenders over a simple collarless shirt, which made him look like an overgrown newsboy. Unlike the barrel-chested men curled around their drinks after a long day of hard labor, Nibsy Lorcan had the air of someone who spent most of his time indoors poring over books.

"Harte Darrigan," Nibsy said, giving a sharp nod of his head in greeting. "It's good to see you again."

"I wish I could say the same, Nibs."

The kid tucked his hands into his pockets. "We were beginning to think you wouldn't show."

"Your boss made it sound like I'd be an idiot not to come and at least listen to what he had to say."

Nibsy smiled genially. "No one could take you for an idiot, Darrigan."

"Not sure I agree with you, Nibs, seeing as I'm here and all. Where's Dolph anyway? Or did he send you to do his dirty work for him like usual?"

"He's in back, waiting." Nibsy's eyes flickered over the barroom. "You know how he is."

"Yeah," Harte said. "I know exactly how he is. Just like I should have known better than to come here."

He turned to go, but Nibs caught him by the arm. "You're already here. Might as well listen to what he has to say." He gave an aw-shucks shrug that Harte didn't buy. "At least have a drink. Can't argue with a free drink, now, can you?"

He glanced at the doors at the back of the barroom.

Harte might have been an idiot, but he was a curious idiot. He couldn't imagine what would have made Dolph desperate enough to ask for his help after the falling-out they'd had. And he wanted to know what would possess Dolph—a man much more likely to hold his secrets close—to make such wild promises.

"I'll listen to what he has to say, but I don't want any drink."

Nibs shifted uneasily before recovering his affable-looking smile. "This way," he said, leading Harte toward the back of the bar and through double saloon doors to a quieter private room.

It might have been years since Harte had seen him, but Dolph didn't look all that different. Same lean, hard face anchored by a nose as sharp as a knife. Same shock of white in the front of his hair that he'd had since they were kids. Same calculating gleam in his icy eyes. Or at least in the eye Harte could see—the other was capped by a leather patch.

There were four others in the room. Harte recognized Viola Vaccarelli and Jianyu Lee, Dolph's assassin and spy, respectively. The other two guys were unknowns. From their loud pants and tipped bowler hats, Harte guessed they were hired muscle, there in case things went south. Which meant that Dolph trusted Harte about as much as Harte trusted Dolph.

Fine. Maybe they'd been friends once, but it was better this way.

"Good to see you again, Dare," Dolph said, using an old nickname Harte had long since given up. Harte didn't miss that Dolph hadn't offered his hand in greeting, only gripped the silver gorgon head on the top of his cane more tightly.

"Can't say the feeling's mutual."

The two peacocks in the corner scowled, but Viola's mouth only twitched. She didn't reach for her knives and he wasn't dead yet, so he must be safe for the moment.

"You want something to drink?" Dolph asked, settling himself back in his chair but not offering a seat to Harte.

"Let's cut the bullshit, Dolph. Why'd you want to see me? You know I'm out of the game."

"Not from what I've heard. Whatever freedom you pretend, Paul Kelly's still got you on a leash, doesn't he?"

"I'm not on anybody's leash," Harte said, his voice a warning. But he wasn't surprised that Dolph knew the truth. He always did manage to find out the very things a person wanted to keep hidden. "And I know there's no way you can do what you hinted at. Getting out of the city? I wasn't born yesterday."

"Then why *did* you come?" Dolph asked.

"Hell if I know," Harte said. He realized he was crushing the brim of his hat and forced himself to relax his fist.

Dolph's eye gleamed. "You never could resist a challenge, could you?"

"Maybe I wanted to see if the rumors about you were true," he said coldly. "If you'd really lost it after Leena, like everybody said."

"I don't talk about that." Dolph's expression went fierce, even as his face went a little gray. "*Nobody* talks about that if they want to keep breathing."

"I bet they don't," Harte said. He shook his head. "This was a mistake." He turned to go, but Jianyu stepped in front of the door, blocking his way. "Call him off, Dolph."

"I've got a proposition for you," Dolph said, ignoring Harte's command.

"I'm not interested." He turned his attention to Jianyu. "I bet your uncle's real proud of you right about now, isn't he? He must love you being a lapdog for that one there."

Everyone knew that Jianyu Lee was the nephew of Tom Lee, the leader of the On Leong Tong over in Chinatown. The kid could have had his own turf, maybe even run his own crew, but here he was working for Dolph. That was the thing about Dolph Saunders—he had this way of pulling people in. Even people who should've had some brains.

Jianyu just smiled darkly, an expression that warned Harte not to push.

"I said *call him off*, Dolph," Harte said again, trying not to let his nerves show. He might be a fool, but he wasn't stupid enough not to realize how dangerous his position was.

"I think you'd be interested if you gave me five minutes," Dolph said. "Or I can always have one of my boys convince you."

"Threats?" Harte glanced up at the two rough-looking boys still looming behind Dolph. "That isn't usually your style, old man."

Dolph couldn't have been older than his midtwenties. But with the streak of white hair and the way he'd been born to lead, Dolph had always seemed even older. Once, "old man" had been a term of endearment between friends. Not anymore. Now Harte slung the nickname like an insult.

Dolph's mouth curved to acknowledge the slight, but he didn't otherwise react. "Never used to be," he admitted. "But it turns out you *can* teach an old dog new tricks." His mouth went flat. "Sit. Give me five minutes before you go off half-cocked. Or haven't you grown out of your temper yet?"

The two puffed peacocks behind Dolph shifted, like they were getting ready for their boss's next order. Harte eyed them warily and measured the inconvenience of a black eye if he left against the sting of his wounded pride if he gave in. It was damn hard to charm an audience when you looked like a common thug, so he went back to the table and took a seat.

"Five minutes. But I'll tell you straight off, I'm not interested in any of your scheming. Never was."

"I won't call you on that particular lie, but getting out of the city isn't a scheme," Dolph said, signaling to Nibsy to pour Harte a glass of whiskey. "It's a real possibility."

The fine hairs at the nape of Harte's neck rose in warning. There was only one way out of the city—through the Brink—and it was a trip Harte had no interest in taking. Not by choice. Not by force, either.

He shifted in his seat. "More threats?" he asked, cautious.

"Not a threat. A proposition. A way out."

"None of us can get out of the city," Harte said carefully, wondering what Dolph was up to. "Not without paying the price. Every Mageus in town knows that."

Dolph took a long, slow drink from the glass in front of him and then motioned for Nibsy to pour another before he spoke. "The Brink hasn't always been there, Darrigan. Did you ever stop to think that if the Order was able to make it, then there has to be a way to *un*make it?"

"Now I *know* you're wasting my time." Harte shook his head. "If you knew how to punch a hole out of this rattrap of a city, you'd have already done it and then started charging admission for the crossing." He started to push his chair back to go, but Jianyu had moved behind him and pressed his shoulders down. Jianyu's thumb was firm against a tender spot at the crook of Harte's neck, keeping him in his seat. "Get your lackey off me, Dolph. I have somewhere else to be."

"The Ortus Aurea doesn't have any real magic," Dolph continued. "Everything they have, everything they can do—it's counterfeit power. It all comes at a cost. The Brink isn't real magic, but it's destroying real magic just the same."

"It seemed real enough when it took everything my mother was and left her a shell of what she used to be."

"I'm not saying the Order isn't powerful. What I *am* saying is that they can be stopped," Dolph said. "The men in the Order see magic as some kind of mark of the divine. They can't bring themselves to believe that the poor, wretched masses who come to these shores could possibly have a stronger connection to divinity than they themselves do. But we both know that magic isn't anything to do with angels or demons. Old magic, the kind you and I know intimately, is a connection with the world itself. You can't split affinities into neat categories or elements any more than you can separate fire and air. One needs the other. When the Order tries to divide up the elements and control them through their rituals and so-called science, there's a cost. It weakens magic as a whole."

"Funny for you of all people to say that," Harte said flatly, without so much as blinking. He tested the pressure against his shoulder and found he still couldn't move.

Dolph frowned, but he didn't respond to Harte's implied challenge. "You know I'm right. The power they wield isn't a natural part of the world, like ours is, and I believe the Brink can be destroyed if we take away the source of their power."

"You're talking about taking them head-on," Harte said. That was a stretch, even for Dolph.

"I'm talking about destroying the one tool they have to control us."

"You're talking about a fairy tale."

Dolph didn't blink. "Every day people come to this country—to this city—because they believe their children will be safer here than in the places they're from. They're lured by the promise of a life away from the superstition and hate in their own countries. All lies. Any Mageus that enters this city is snared like a fish in a net. Once they land on these shores, they can't leave without giving up the very thing that defines them, and trapped on this island as they are, they're at the mercy of the Order. Held down, held back, always kept in their place by those in power."

"I know all that already, Dolph," Harte said. His stomach churned. Of course he knew. "But there *are* ways to make a life here, even in this city."

Dolph gave him a mocking look. "You mean like you have?"

"I've done well enough for myself."

"Sure you have. You've managed to get yourself some smart new clothes, a safe apartment in the good part of town, and money in your pocket. You've even managed to find yourself some well-connected friends. But do you think you'd last a day in your new life if those new friends of yours knew who you actually are?" Dolph leaned forward. "*What* you are?"

Harte refused to so much as flinch. "You plan on outing me and destroying the life I've built for myself? I've lived through worse."

"No, Darrigan," Dolph said. "I'd prefer to use that new life of yours to our advantage."

"I'm not interested in helping your advantage."

Dolph ignored his rebuff. "It's good you've managed to do what you have, but you always were scrappier than most. There's plenty who aren't. And even scrappy as you are, you can only get so far in this city. You and I were friends once, so I know how it must chafe to always have to hide what you are. As long as the Order has power over our kind, it will always be a liability. But if the Order's main tool for controlling us was destroyed, you could have a different life. The Brink *can* be undone, I'm convinced of it."

"You can't know that," Harte challenged. "And I like my life well enough. I'm not about to get myself killed over one of your mad theories."

"It's not a theory." Dolph nodded to Jianyu, and the pressure on Harte's shoulders eased. Then he pulled a small scrap from his pocket and set it on the table so Harte could read the faded writing on its surface. "Leena died getting that to me."

Harte read the smeared letters on the scrap and then glanced up at Dolph. "I don't speak Italian."

"It's Latin," Dolph corrected.

"What's it mean?"

"Libero Libro. It means that the Order has a book—"

"I'm sure they have lots of books."

"Probably," Dolph said, not taking the bait. "But there's one book in particular they protect more than any other, and getting this book means freeing our kind."

Harte gave him a doubtful look. "A single book couldn't do all of that."

"The Ars Arcana could."

This gave Harte pause. "You think the Order has the Ars Arcana?"

Dolph tapped his finger against the scrap of fabric. "I do."

Harte shook his head. "Even if you're right, even if the Order has the Book of Mysteries, you'll never be able to get it. Everyone knows that Khafre Hall is built like a fortress. You couldn't even get through the front door, much less get your hands on any book—Ars Arcana or otherwise."

"I think you're wrong," Dolph said. "With the right team, we can get in *and* get the Book. Think of it, Dare. . . . We could change *everything*. No more slums. No more scraping by. Without the Brink standing in your way, you could walk out of this city a free man to go make your fortune. You could do *anything*, go *anywhere*, and keep your affinity all the while."

Harte ignored the lure of that promise. "The only people who can get into the front door of Khafre Hall are members of Ortus."

"So we'll have a member let us in," Nibs said.

For a moment all Harte could do was gape at the boy. "*You're* insane too," he said. "Did you forget that they *hate* us? There's no way one of their members is going to help one of us."

Dolph pinned Harte with a knowing glare. "That life you've made for yourself has introduced you to some interesting people. Word is you've been seen with Jack Grew, one of J. P. Morgan's nephews, I believe?"

"So what of it?" Harte said, even more wary than before.

"Morgan's one of the highest-ranking members of the Order."

"No," Harte said, shaking his head as he pushed away from the table and stood. "No way in hell. *No*."

But Jianyu's strong hands sat him back down roughly and held him in his seat.

"It's like you said, you've managed to make a whole new life for yourself. New name. New suit. New address on the right side of town. If you keep rubbing elbows with the right people, you could get us in."

Harte choked out a hollow laugh. "I'm not in the market for suicide. Besides, even if what you're proposing is possible, even if you and your crew could get in and get this book, the Order wouldn't simply accept defeat. They'd hunt down every Mageus in this town. You'd get hundreds of innocent people killed. Thousands, maybe. No one with magic—or with connections to people with magic—would be safe."

"We're *already* not safe," Dolph countered. "We already live like rats, fighting each other for whatever the Order leaves us. Everyone's so worried about getting a little bit more for themselves, they don't even realize they're killing one another over the garbage.

"The Order of Ortus Aurea *depends* on that, Harte. They want us lining up along old divisions, clinging to what we know so that we can't imagine a bigger future. But I've already imagined it. Look at the people in this room right now—Viola, Jianyu. I've started putting together a team that could take down the Order once and for all. I need someone to get us in, though. Someone with the right talent for it." His jaw tightened. "Someone like you."

Harte knew what it must have cost Dolph to say those words, but it wasn't enough. Not considering how dangerous the Ortus Aurea was and how much he had to lose.

"You've had your five minutes."

Dolph studied Harte a long minute before lifting his hand and gesturing vaguely for Jianyu to release him. "I'm not taking your answer now," Dolph said, dismissing him. "You listened and maybe you'll think about it. We'll talk again."

The pressure no longer on his shoulders, Harte stood. "No, we won't. I'm not interested now, and I won't be interested ten days from now, so you can just leave me the hell alone."

He maneuvered through the still-crowded barroom, cursing himself again for his own curiosity, his stupidity for coming in the first place. Because damn if Dolph wasn't right—he had listened, and now he *was* thinking. He was thinking about the possibility of getting out of that godforsaken city. Of being free once and for all.

Dolph Saunders might need him, but Harte certainly didn't need Dolph. He'd find a way to do it on his own.

Harte pushed his way through the crowd and out into the night. He never once looked back, so he didn't see the knowing smile curve at Dolph Saunders' mouth.

BENEATH THE EPHEMERAL
MOMENT OF NOW

Present Day—Orchard Street

The next evening, Esta sat on the edge of her bed reading over the yellowed news clipping yet again, as though the century-old scrap could tell her something more about what had happened the night of the heist. She probably shouldn't have taken it from Professor Lachlan's office, but she hadn't been able to help herself. He was sending her back, alone this time and for longer than she'd ever been in the past before, and it was all happening too fast. She didn't feel nearly as confident as she wanted to.

Someone rapped on the door to her room, and she jumped at the sound of it.

"Just a minute!" Her fingers shook as she folded the clipping into a small waxen envelope and shoved the packet as far down into her corset as she could manage.

The knock came again. "Esta?" The voice was muffled by the heavy door.

Relieved that it wasn't Professor Lachlan, she opened the door to reveal Dakari on the other side. She looked up into his familiar face. "Is it time?"

"Not quite. I came to check your arm again." Dakari had been with Professor Lachlan longer than any of them. The Professor had found him in an illegal fighting club more than twenty years ago. After he made his share of the pot by winning his fights, he'd charge his opponents for the privilege of being doctored by him, so they could go back to their lives without the bruises he'd left on their bodies.

It wasn't work he would have otherwise chosen for himself, so when the Professor offered him a position, he took it. Part bodyguard, part healer, Dakari was over six feet of pure muscle, but when he smiled—and he often smiled at Esta—he looked exactly like the kind soul he was.

"It's fine," Esta said, not letting him into the room. He'd already checked it that morning anyway.

"Humor me." He gave the door a gentle push and stepped into her room.

With a dramatic sigh, she unbuttoned the neckline of her dress enough to show him her shoulder. She'd taken off the bandage the day before, and now the wound from the bullet wasn't anything more than a spot of new pink skin that would one day barely be a scar.

Dakari took her arm in his hands and pressed his thumb over the spot as he studied it with careful concentration. Her own skin wasn't exactly pale, but his was darker. His palms were rough from years of fighting, but his magic came as a soft pulse, the warmth that characterized most of her childhood. Those hands could kill a man in 532 different ways, but they had also healed every one of her scrapes and bruises—mostly after he'd put her through a punishing training session. Because of Dakari, she could take care of herself, and because of him, she'd always felt like she had someone to take care of her.

If she'd lost him the way she'd lost Mari . . .

"You'll do," he said after he was done examining her. "It's healed well enough that you won't have to worry about infection. You ready?"

She nodded.

"Then why do you look so unsure?" He frowned at her. "You're never unsure before a job."

"I'm fine," she said, turning away, but he took his hand and lifted her chin, forcing her to look him in the eye.

"Tell me. Before your worries become the distraction that gets you killed."

Esta hesitated, but finally she said, "You really don't remember Mari?"

Dakari frowned. "That's what's bothering you?"

She nodded. "Messing up the way I did, it changed things. She was my friend, and she doesn't even exist now."

"You can't know that your actions were what erased her life."

"What if they were? What if I make another mistake? What if, when I come back, other people are gone? Other lives are erased?"

He thought for a minute before reaching into his boot and pulling out a small pocketknife with an ornately carved bone handle. He offered it to her, and when she took it, he gave her a serious look. "That was my father's. He gave it to me before I left my country. I would only give that to someone I trusted. Whatever happens, I trust you with my life."

The knife was warm from having been snug against Dakari's leg, and though it was small, its weight was reassuring.

"Thank you," she said, her throat tight with emotion as she tucked the knife safely into her own button-up boots. "I'll bring it back to you. No matter what."

"I know you will," he said, and gave her a wink. "And I'll be here waiting for you."

Esta took a deep breath. "Let's get this over with."

By the time Esta was in the back of Dakari's car and heading toward their destination, it was nearly four in the morning on a Tuesday, long after most of the bars had closed. People should have been home, asleep in their tiny apartments, but even this deep in the night, the city glowed. The streets still teemed with life as the car crawled upward, past the low-slung buildings of the village, toward the towers of Midtown.

Esta rolled down the window, letting the hot breath of summer rustle across her face. With it came the familiar smells of the city, stale and heavy with the metallic choke of exhaust and the ripeness of too many people sharing one tiny piece of land. But it was also enticing—the scent of danger and possibility that lived and breathed in the crowded streets. Dirty and frantic though it was, the city—*this* city—was home. She'd never wanted to be anywhere else.

Dakari turned onto Twenty-Eighth Street and then pulled into a narrow parking lot that spanned the block between two streets. The lot had been an alleyway a century before, one of the countless places in the city that hadn't been built over and changed beyond recognition. A place where she could slip into the past without being seen.

He stopped just inside the lot and shut off the engine before turning to her. Draping his large forearm across the passenger seat, he looked at her. "You ready?"

She gave him what she hoped was a sure nod, and they both got out of the car. He leaned against the back of it, eyeing her. "See you in a few?" he asked, turning his usual farewell into a question.

Despite the heat of the summer night and her layers of linen and velveteen, Esta felt a sudden chill. She made herself shake it off. This was only a job, she reminded herself. It was *her* job.

"You always do," Esta told him, giving her usual wink. She didn't let the confidence fall from her face until her back was turned.

Dakari's voice came to her as a whisper: "Keep yourself safe, E."

She glanced over her shoulder. "You doubting me?"

"Never in a million." His eyes were still solemn as he raised his chin in a silent salute.

For a heartbeat, Esta imagined getting back in the car and telling him to drive. *Just drive.* Dakari had always had enough of a soft spot for her. He'd probably do it, too, no questions asked.

It wasn't that she wanted to run from the responsibility the Professor had given her. She didn't even need that long . . . just another jog around the block to settle her nerves. Another few minutes with the bright lights and the hurried pace of *this* city. *Her* city.

But she didn't want Dakari to know she was nervous. It was bad enough admitting it to herself. Wrapping her hand more securely around the smooth handle of her carpetbag, Esta started walking toward the center of the lot, away from the car and from Dakari's reassuring presence.

She didn't let herself look back again.

The parking lot was quiet, and it smelled like that combination of piss, garbage, and exhaust that only New York could smell like in the summertime. Something scuttled beneath one of the sleeping cars, but Esta ignored the noise, and as she walked, she let her doubt fall away.

Or, rather, she shoved it away.

Trying to find the right layer of time was a little like riffling through the pages of a book. Sometimes she could catch glimpses of what each layer held—the flash of chrome, a bright swirl of skirts. It took all her concentration to find a single image to latch on to, a single date to focus on, before she could slip through to it. And, of course, it took the power held in Ishtar's Key.

As she looked past the present moment, the stone in the cuff answered by warming itself, almost humming against her already-heated skin. The tumble of trash and debris along the edges of the buildings, the pallid glow of a yellow security light over a door—all of it went blurry as she searched down through the layered moments of the past. Back, back, back . . . until she found what she was looking for.

A single day. A single moment waiting beneath her modern world.

She reached for it, preparing herself for the unsettling feeling of slipping out of her own time. Her destination was there, well within her ability to reach it, but just as she started to feel the energy of her own magic tingling along her skin, her foot froze in midair and her breath went tight in her chest as an unexpected feeling of absolute dread rocketed through her.

The image in her mind faltered, and her own world came into focus again.

"Shit." Esta dropped her bag and took an actual step backward, away from the glimmer of the past and from what she had to do. Her fingers felt clammy and damp inside the smooth leather of her gloves, but the stone was hot against her skin.

Above her, the brightly lit top of the Empire State Building looked down, mocking her inability to erase it. To find a time before it had defined the skies of the city.

Esta didn't do nerves, but there she was, struggling to shake off her trepidation, forcing herself to gather the courage to do what she'd done a hundred times before. She knew the city, its streets and secrets. Its people, and especially its past. Professor Lachlan had made sure that every minute of her childhood had been devoted to preparing her for this. She was ready.

So why did it feel so impossible?

"You okay?" Dakari called.

She took a breath to steady herself but didn't look back at him. "I'm fine," she lied.

She had to focus. *This* was what Professor Lachlan had saved her for. *This* was why he'd rescued her, kept her out of the system, and had given her the only home she remembered. If she couldn't do this one thing he asked of her, where would she go? Who would she be?

Esta picked up her bag again and, teeth clenched in determination, expelled another a deep breath through her nose. Her head was pounding, but she adjusted the smooth handle of the bag in her gloved grip and started again.

There . . .

The time she was seeking was there, just beneath the ephemeral moment of now. She found the date Professor Lachlan had directed her to waiting for her beneath the layers of years and memories. In that moment, her fear receded a little, and the rightness of what she was about to do wrapped around her.

Lifting her foot to take a step, Esta could feel the familiar push–pull sensation of simultaneously flying apart and collapsing in on herself. But then the bewildering dread spiked through her again like a warning.

Something's wrong.

But Esta didn't do nerves. She forced herself through the feeling, through to the past.

Every cell in her body was on fire as the brick walls on either side of her began to blur and the cars around her began to disappear. The lights of the city dimmed, the tip of the Empire State Building started to fade, and as she began to feel the cold blast of winter from that other time, a barrage of shouts came from the mouth of the lot where Dakari's car waited.

Esta hesitated, her body screaming with the effort of keeping hold of her present as the past pulled at her. Her vision cleared, and she saw Dakari struggling against a trio of hooded figures, his expression determined as he fought free of them.

I have to help him. . . .

"Dakari!"

"Go!" he shouted, looking at her with such determination that her hold of the present slipped.

"Dakari!" she screamed again as gunfire erupted and she watched his large body jerk and slump to the ground. The shock of it knocked her backward, far past the place where the dirty pavement should have caught her.

Esta couldn't stop. She lost her grip on her own city, her own time, and was falling into light itself, barely catching herself before she landed hard, in a deep drift of snow.

PART

II

SIREN'S CALL

February 1902—Wallack's Theatre

Harte Darrigan brushed a piece of lint from the front of his crimson waistcoat before checking his appearance once more in the cloudy dressing room mirror. Lifting his chin, he examined the edge of his jawline for any place the barber might have missed during his regular afternoon shave, and then he ran his fingertips over the dark, shortly cropped hair above his ears to ensure it was smooth and in place. Stepping away from the footlights didn't mean he'd stepped offstage. His whole life had become a performance, one long con that was the closest thing to freedom he could ever have.

A knock sounded at his dressing room door, and he frowned. "Yes?"

The stage manager, Shorty, opened the door. "You got a minute?"

"I'm heading out to meet someone in a few—"

"Good. Good," Shorty said, closing the door behind him. He had the nub of a thick cigar between his teeth, and as he talked, ash from the still-smoldering tip fluttered to the floor. "Here's the thing—the management has been talking lately, and—"

"This again?" Harte let out an impatient breath to hide his nerves. He knew what was coming, because they'd had a similar conversation last week. And the week before. There were too many theaters in the city, and it didn't matter how good your act was; people got bored too quickly.

"Yes, this again." Shorty took the cigar from between his teeth and used it to punctuate his point, jabbing it into the air and sending more ash floating to the floor. "They run a thee-ate-er here, Darrigan," he said, snapping out the word to emphasize the second syllable. "This is a business, and a business has to make money."

"They make plenty of money, and you know it," Harte said, shrugging off the complaint as he turned to fix the knot in his cravat. "The house was decent this afternoon, and even pretty good tonight."

"I know. I know. But decent and pretty good ain't enough anymore. The owners have been talking about maybe switching some things up . . . changing the acts a little." Shorty gave him a meaningful look.

His fingers stilled and the silk around his neck suddenly felt too tight. "What are you trying to say?"

"I ain't *trying* to say nothing. What I *am* saying is that you've gotta do something to get more people in the seats. Something new."

Harte turned back to Shorty. "I did add something new, or weren't they watching? The escape I did tonight was new. Two sets of handcuffs, shackles, and ten feet of iron chains—"

"Yeah, yeah. You got yourself out of a locked box. Big deal. Houdini's been breaking out of things for years now. Nobody cares anymore. You want top billing? You need something bigger. Something with some more flash." Shorty put the cigar back between his teeth.

Harte clenched his jaw to keep from saying something he'd regret. "Is that all?"

"Yeah, kid. I guess that's it. Just wanted to tell you what's what. Thought you'd want to know."

Harte didn't thank him. He stood silent and expressionless as Shorty shrugged and took his leave. Once the door was closed and he was alone, he cleaned up the fallen ash.

Still unsettled, he turned to the mirror and took a deep breath before giving himself a smile, his clear gray eyes searching his reflection for any indication that his old life was showing through. There wasn't room for a misstep or a crack in the carefully cultivated facade he presented to the world. That night, nothing could be left to chance.

Finally satisfied, he let the smile fall from his face, as heavy and sure as a curtain falling between acts. He pulled on his gloves and coat and took up his hat from where it rested on the dressing table before extinguishing the lamp and letting himself out of his dressing room.

It was barely past midnight, and already the theater was empty and silent. Playing this house was nothing like the rough-and-tumble theaters of the Bowery, which remained open at all hours of the night, their drunken audiences roaring for more—more skin, more laughter, more of the brittle pieces of self-respect Harte had tried to hold on to night after night.

Harte had escaped those beer-stained halls well over a year ago, but Shorty's warning was one more reminder that it wouldn't take much for him to find himself back there again. With nowhere to go but farther down.

He wouldn't let that happen.

Far-off sounds echoing through the cavernous building told him there were still a few stragglers left. No doubt they were gathered in the chorus girls' dressing room, drinking Nitewein to burn off the excess energy brought on by the crowd. Or to numb the constant ache of hiding what they were.

The theater world was filled with Mageus. The stage was a good place for those with magic to hide in plain sight, but for many in the business, using their affinity onstage made them crave it that much more. The rumbling approval of the crowd only amplified that yearning to answer the old call of magic, to embrace what they really were. Many resorted to using the opium-laced liquor to stop the resulting ache. Usually it was enough to get them through to the next performance.

For Harte it was exactly the opposite—the applause was the only thing that made the ache any better.

He'd been invited to their after-hours gatherings plenty of times before, but he hadn't been invited that night. Actually, he hadn't been invited for quite a while, come to think of it. At some point the others must have given up on their well-meaning attempts to bring him into their circle.

It was probably for the best, he thought, brushing aside any regret like the lint from his coat. He had too many secrets to risk entanglements. Especially now.

"Sneaking off without even a good-bye?" The voice came to him through the darkness, smoky and warm.

His hand tightened on the brim of his new silk hat. He was already on edge from Shorty's warning, but he pasted on his usual charming smile. "Would I ever sneak away from you, Evelyn?" he asked as he turned to face her.

"You're always sneaking away from me," she purred, "but I can never tell why."

The woman stepped forward into a beam of light, her ruby mouth pulled into a sultry pout and her eyes glassy from the drink. It didn't matter that every night he passed within inches of her when he exited the stage and turned the spotlight over to her. Familiarity did nothing to mute the effect of Evelyn DeMure because every ounce of her attraction was calculated, manipulated, and most of all, imbued with magic.

In her act, she and her two "sisters" wore flesh-colored bodysuits beneath Grecian-inspired gowns that barely covered their most scandalous parts. With their legs visible almost to the thigh and the risk that at any moment the gowns might unravel completely, the three performed a series of songs filled with double entendres and bawdy jokes that kept the audience—male and female alike—on edge, hoping for more.

Evelyn wasn't wearing the bodysuit now. Her eyes were still ringed in kohl and her lips were stained by bold paint, but her embroidered emerald robe hung low to reveal one creamy, bare shoulder and the slope of her full chest. Her henna-tinted hair, a red too vibrant to be real, was soft and untamed around her face.

An effective display altogether, he admitted. Even with her age showing at the corners of her eyes, she would have brought any man to his knees.

But Harte wasn't one of those who filled the theater eager for a glimpse of thigh—or something more—and who fell at her feet at the stage door. He knew her appeal came from something more than simple beauty. Even drunk as she was on Nitewein, whispers of magic betrayed her attempt to entangle him.

Ignoring the tightening in his gut, he gave her a formal nod. He wouldn't be taken in, especially not by the tricks of a siren like Evelyn.

"Where *are* you running off to so fast?" she crooned, taking another few steps toward him. Cat and mouse.

Desire coiled in his gut, but he held his ground, pretending his usual indifference to her many charms. "Urgent business, I'm afraid." He gave her a roguish grin that promised his destination was anything but.

Evelyn's expression flickered, and Harte thought he saw the hurt behind the pride she wore like armor. But for all he knew, that was also part of her act, another effect perfectly calculated to slay him.

He could find out, of course. It would be easy enough to strip off a glove, pretend that he was lured into her too-obvious seduction. It would only take a touch. . . . Harte took a step back instead, placing his hat on his head at a rakish angle and touching the brim in a silent farewell.

"You're really not going to tell me where you're going?" She crossed her arms, hitching the robe back up over her bare shoulder as her mouth went tight.

He'd upset her, not hurt her. "Sorry, love. I never kiss and tell." And with a wink, he left her standing in the back of the empty stage as he stepped out into the night.

For a moment he permitted himself the luxury of letting go. There, in the shadows of the stage door, he allowed himself to breathe, imagining a future when he could be more than his starched lapels and expertly tied cravat. More than this mask he wore.

Just how much more, he wasn't sure. . . . That depended on how well the evening went.

Adjusting his hat again, he tucked his cane beneath his arm and checked his pocket watch to see how much later he was than planned. *It could be worse,* he thought, glad to be away from the pull of Evelyn's magic and the weight of Shorty's warning.

Tonight things would start to change. Tonight he'd finally take his first steps toward true freedom. He started walking, making his way toward the part of the city called Satan's Circus, and his certain destiny.

A STAR-BRUSHED SKY

Twenty-Eighth Street near Fifth Avenue

Esta stumbled to her feet, stark fear coursing through her. She didn't notice the icy shock of the snowbank or the searing pain on her upper forearm where the silver cuff burned against her skin. The echo of the gunshot still rang in her ears.

Dakari.

She turned to where the entrance of the parking lot had once been, open and waiting, but now the street beyond was lit softly by an antique streetlamp. Unsteady on her feet, Esta took a tentative step forward, knocking the wet snow off her skirt as she went. Above, the sky was empty, completely devoid of the skyscraper that had been there moments before.

No . . .

Even with the snow drifting around her skirts, she staggered toward the street. Her muscles and bones ached as they always did after slipping through time. *No,* she thought as she came to the entrance of the alley.

But no amount of denial could change what was.

She stepped onto the wide, cobbled sidewalk and took in the changed city. A few minutes before, the tall shoulders and flat faces of uninspired, boxlike buildings had lined the streets. Now the structures were shorter, squat with rows of windows like watching eyes. A couple of the buildings hadn't changed that much, but now their street-level shops were capped with faded awnings rolled back to protect them from the heavy weight of the snow. Where a canyon of buildings once stood, now barely a gully of shops remained, as though life in the city was the reverse of nature, time building up instead of washing away.

She took it all in, the silence of the streets and the swath of stars—she could see *actual stars*—above her. Marveling at how different and familiar everything looked all at once, she barely heard the muffled clattering of hooves. It was a sound so rare in her own city that it didn't register as a danger, and she glanced back barely in time to avoid being run down by a horse-drawn carriage.

The driver gestured angrily and cursed her as he passed, and the wheels of the carriage caught at her skirts, making her stumble back. The heel of her boot slipped on the icy road, and she went down hard, landing in the slush-filled gutter.

Shaking from the adrenaline still pulsing through her, she stood up and brushed herself off—again.

A high-pitched whistle sounded, and Esta looked up to search for the danger. Instead, she found a red-faced old man, his filthy shirt open at the collar to expose the hairs climbing up from his chest. He was leaning far over a second-story fire escape, his eyes squinting at her like he was having trouble focusing.

"Süsse!" he called, grabbing at the front of his unbelted pants as he leaned drunkenly over the edge of the rickety railing. "You're missing your brains tonight, ja, Süsse? I can help you to find them." His words were slurred, his German oddly accented to Esta's ears.

Some things never change, she thought as disgust swept away her panic. She made a rude gesture and cursed back at him in his own language. The man doubled over laughing and almost fell from the fire escape. By the time he'd caught himself, Esta had already retreated to the relative safety of the alley.

But her bag was gone. The only evidence that remained were the footprints in the snow leading off to the other end of the street.

"No," she whispered. It was a stupid, rookie mistake that she never would have made if she hadn't been so distracted by the attack and so shaken by the memory of Dakari's body jerking and falling. The bag had contained everything she needed—

Except none of that mattered anymore. She had to get back. She had to help Dakari. To make sure he wasn't . . .

She couldn't even think the word.

Blinking back tears, she took a breath and focused on finding her own time—layers marked by brighter lights, blaring car horns, and the glow of the city stretching far above her.

But nothing was there.

No shimmers of past or future. Nothing at all but that present moment in an unfamiliar city filled with the cold scent of winter and a night so quiet it chafed.

Her chest was tight, her whole body shivering as she worked to unfasten the tiny buttons at her wrist. Finally, the last one came free. The icy air bit against her exposed skin as she pulled her sleeve up as far as it could go and reached beneath it.

As she pulled the cuff off, she let out a hiss of pain. She hadn't noticed the injury before, but now her upper arm throbbed and ached where the top layer of skin had peeled away with the metal. But the shock of the pain was nothing compared to the shock of what she saw when she examined the cuff.

The burnished silver had turned black and the iridescent stone was covered in what looked like black soot. Confused by its appearance, she touched it gently with her fingertip, and the stone crumbled on contact, disintegrating like ash until only the empty, burned-out setting was left.

Ishtar's Key was gone.

At first she couldn't process what she was seeing. Her stone couldn't be gone.

Had it burned up because she'd hesitated between present and past? Had she put too much pressure on it, cracked as it had already been?

As the reality of its disappearance began to set in, the loss hit her like the ache of a missing limb. Or maybe like something even more vital, like her heart. Without the stone, she couldn't find the layers of time. Without the stone, she wasn't anything more than an exceptionally good thief stuck in a city that wasn't her own.

Panic emptied out her chest, leaving her breathless and panting.

She was trapped. In the past.

She would never again argue with Logan about who was in charge on a job or enjoy the surprise in Dakari's eyes when she bested him on the mat. She would never again see the city she knew and loved, with its dizzying speed and clattering rush and brilliant buildings that erased the stars. She would die *here*, in this other city, not even a footnote in the history books. Alone and out of time.

She sank to her knees in the snow, laid low by the truth of her situation. But as the cold dampness began to seep through the layers of her skirts, a thought occurred to her: *Her* stone was gone, yes. But *the* stone wasn't gone. Ishtar's Key was still here, in this time, with all the other artifacts. With the Book she'd been sent to retrieve.

Was that it, then? Had Professor Lachlan been right about the stone's properties? He said they were unique—*singular*. Maybe Ishtar's Key had disintegrated because it was already there, waiting for her in the past.

But if that were the case, had he known this would happen, that she might be trapped here? And if he had, why hadn't he warned her?

The whole situation felt like another one of the Professor's tests, which meant it was another chance to prove herself to him. Only this time, her life—her very future—was at stake.

The thought only made her that much more resolved. If she could get the Book, she could get the earlier version of the stone as well. Once she had it in her possession, she could return to her own time. She could make sure Dakari was okay.

Another wagon clattered past the open mouth of the alley, the wooden wheels rattling and the muffled *clip-clop* of hooves disrupting the stillness of the night. In theory, she had been trained with all she needed to fit into the past, to blend with the people there and do what she was meant to do. But theory and reality felt like such different things from where she stood now, alone in a dark alley, listening to horse-drawn carriages clattering down streets that should have held the soft rumble of engines and blaring horns of automobiles.

But worrying about her fate wasn't doing anyone any good. The city might have changed dramatically, but she hadn't. She could still put the plan into action. She would make her way to the Haymarket and find Bridget Malone, as Professor Lachlan had instructed. She helped girls with magic find places to use their skills, places that weren't the back rooms of brothels. If the rumors were right, the madam worked for Saunders specifically. Esta just had to get Bridget's attention.

The only way to go was forward, as always.

Looking up and down the street, Esta got her bearings. Even though the streets looked so different, her own city was still there, pulling her in the direction she had to go and, with a little luck, toward Bridget Malone.

A SMART MOUTH

The Haymarket

By the time Harte turned onto Sixth Avenue, he could see the glow of the Haymarket ahead. It was the best-known—and most notorious—dance hall in the city. Inside, those who lived above Houston Street rubbed elbows with waiter girls from the slums, music played long into the night, and for the right price, the private stalls on the upper floors could be used for any entertainment a paying customer wanted.

Not that he needed any diversions of that type. He knew well enough what attachments like that could do to people. He'd seen what it did to his mother and knew firsthand how love and infatuation had made her desperate enough to throw everything away—including him.

He wasn't that little boy anymore, though. If the evening went to plan, he might be able to leave all those memories and regrets far behind him.

Stepping out from the shadow of the elevated tracks that ran above the entrance of the dance hall, he climbed the three steps and passed through the narrow entryway. Even before Harte was completely inside, the bright notes of a newly popular ragtime tune and the discordant buzz of the crowd assaulted him.

The moment he stepped through the door, a girl with white-blond hair took his overcoat. She was so young, not even the paint on her face could cover her greenness. She was eager—new, perhaps. But he knew the innocence beneath the powder and paint wouldn't last for long. Not in a place like the Haymarket.

Harte gave a tug to straighten his sleeves. "Mr. Jack Grew is expecting me," he said, imbuing his soft voice with the same compelling tone that made his audiences lean forward to listen. He gave over his hat—but not his gloves. Those he tucked into his jacket.

"He's not arrived yet," the girl told him, her cheeks burning scarlet. Another mark of her doomed innocence.

"Let him know I'm at the bar when he does?" He slipped the girl a few coins.

He made his way through the crush of bodies, hating the too-potent spice of perfumes that were barely able to hide the stale odor of sweat beneath. It reminded him too much of how far he'd come, of those mornings his mother would stumble home smelling the same.

Shaking off the memories, he found a space at the crowded bar and ordered, tipping the woman who poured his drink more than necessary when she served him. Her eyes lit, but he turned from her, making it clear he wasn't interested.

The first floor of the dance hall was already crowded. Women in brightly colored silk gowns with painted smiles clung too closely to the men who led them across the floor. The minutes ticked by as he nursed his drink. When it was gone, he didn't order another. Half an hour past when they were to meet, Jack Grew still hadn't shown.

The hell with it.

He wasn't staying. He probably shouldn't have come in the first place. Ever since Shorty had given him the warning, nothing about the night felt right, and Harte hadn't survived so long by ignoring his instincts. He'd go back to his apartment, run a steaming-hot bath in the blessed silence, and wash off the grime of the day. He could deal with Jack some other time.

Harte placed the empty glass back on the bar, but as he made to leave, he felt the unmistakable warmth of magic nearby.

Impossible. No one would be stupid enough to use their affinity in the Haymarket, not when many in the room had ties to the Ortus Aurea.

Not when the entire hall was monitored by the watchful eyes of Edward Corey's security guards. Corey, the owner of the Haymarket, played both sides. He had close ties to the Order, but it was rumored that he also used Mageus as guards, people who were willing to rat out their own in exchange for a fat paycheck each week.

But there it was again—the rustling of magic calling out to him and anyone else nearby with an affinity.

Harte scanned the crowd. On the edges of the room, it was clear Corey's men had sensed it as well. Already, they were on the move, searching for the person who'd brought the contraband power into the ballroom.

In the periphery of Harte's vision, a flash of deep green caught his eye at the same time that he felt another flare of warmth. He turned and found the source of it—a girl smiling up at her much older dance partner, while her fingers dipped nimbly into his pocket.

Harte was halfway across the dance floor before he realized she didn't look like the other girls. She was young, which wasn't unusual in her line of work, but her face wasn't covered in the usual powder and paint, and her eyes didn't have the weariness of a woman who'd already given up. Her clothes, a gown in deep hunter velvet, fit her slender figure too well to have been ready-made. Clearly, she came from money, but from the way she was maneuvering her right hand into her dance partner's pocket without him noticing, she was no novice dip. It was an intriguing combination.

By the time her partner looked up at him, Harte had already taken hold of the girl's wrist, effectively drawing it out of the man's pocket and stopping the couple's dance.

"May I help you?" the old man sneered.

Harte smiled pleasantly, letting his eyes go a little glassy and soft as he turned to the girl. She tried to pull away, but he had her secure. "I've been looking for you, darling," he said, allowing the words to slur together a little.

"I'm sorry, but this one is already taken," the old man said, attempting to wrestle the girl back from Harte. "Go find one of the others."

"But I *love* her," Harte told him, refusing to relinquish control. He swayed a bit on his feet for effect.

The old man's thick brows bunched in a scowl. "Then perhaps you should have kept better watch of her."

"You're right," Harte told him, turning his attention to the girl, who was glaring at him with eyes the color of whiskey and with just as much fire. He gave her a besotted smile. "I should have never let you go, not after you *stole* my heart," he said, enjoying the way the girl's eyes widened slightly when he emphasized the word.

"I don't believe I know you," the girl said, her voice shaking a little. Her words were well formed, her voice soft, cultured, but then, so was his. Considering his own beginnings, her lack of accent didn't mean much. The more interesting question was where she'd learned to pick pockets. And why her teacher hadn't warned her about using her magic in the Haymarket.

"You couldn't have forgotten so soon." Keeping in character, Harte lifted his free hand to his chest dramatically, as though struck. "Why, it was only last Friday we met here. The band was playing this very song when your eyes found mine across the room. I was reluctant, but you were"—he lowered his voice conspiratorially—"*convincing.*" He gave her a teasing wink before he turned to her partner.

"It was nothing at all to overlook her little affliction for such beauty." Harte leered at the girl, who was still trying to pull away from him. He felt a pang of conscience at the fear lurking behind the anger in her golden eyes, but Corey's men were too close. Better she fear him than meet with them.

Why he had decided to help her was beyond him, though. He was no white knight, no one's protector.

"Yes, well . . ." The old man looked uneasily at the girl as he relinquished her to Harte. "Who am I to stand in the way of young love?"

Harte pulled her closer to him as the old man backed away into the crowd. "Easy now," he whispered, his head close to hers. She smelled faintly of flowers and something soft and musky, like sandalwood. It was what a summer day should smell like, he decided, instead of the stink of the streets.

She was still struggling to get away from him, but he tightened his hold, a subtle adjustment that to any other dancer would look like an embrace. "Go along with me and don't make a scene."

"I'll show you a scene," she hissed.

She wasn't small. She was nearly as tall as he was, and her features were more interesting than classically pretty. On anyone else, the wide mouth with such a sharp nose might not have worked, but on her it was striking. Her eyes were bright with fury, and damn if it didn't make her that much more attractive.

Or maybe that was the whiskey talking. . . .

The girl wriggled again, settling into his arms, and then suddenly, she twisted, trying to knock him off-balance. But Harte had been in his share of dirty fights. He countered her attack easily, wrapping her in his arms to secure her again as he drew them both into the swirl of men and their women on the dance floor.

"Impressive," he murmured, leading them into the first turn of a waltz.

The girl's golden eyes narrowed at him, her cheeks flushed from the exertion of trying to get away. He'd been right—her skin was clean of paint. Unlined, it looked smooth and soft as a petal.

I should let her go. . . .

Over the girl's shoulder, he saw one of Corey's men prowling the dance floor, still searching for the source of the magic. The man turned, looking in the girl's direction.

"Dance with me," Harte told her, leading her away from the man and toward the center of the crowded dance floor.

Energy spiked around her again as she struggled to get free from him. "I wouldn't dance with you if—"

LISA MAXWELL

Corey's men were getting closer. Without thinking through the consequences, Harte covered her mouth with his own, locking her in his arms as he brought her close.

The kiss did exactly what he'd intended—the warmth of her magic went cold as she stiffened, pressing against his shoulders with her hands. Corey's men were right next to him now, so he deepened the kiss and pulled her against him, away from them.

She smelled clean as a prayer beneath the soft scent of her soap, and it had been so long since he'd been that close to a girl—to anyone, really—that it took everything he had to keep his own wits about him. He was barely able to keep track of the two guards as they began to move away.

Without warning, her body went pliant in his arms, and he reacted instinctively. He couldn't have stopped himself if he had tried. But he didn't try. Instead, he drew her closer, the velvet of her gown soft beneath his fingertips, as she kissed him back.

Maybe he'd been wrong, he thought as her mouth moved in heady rhythm with his. Maybe she wasn't so innocent after all.

His brain felt heavy, numb, and he didn't know what to make of her. . . .

But even that thought was distant and obscure as her lips slid against his. He wasn't thinking at all when he parted his lips slightly, seeking to taste her. He wasn't considering how bad an idea it was when she opened her mouth for him. He was simply lost.

In that moment, the danger Corey's men posed didn't exist. Nor did the crush of bodies around them. He couldn't think of anything at all but the feel of her mouth against his, the scent of her filling his senses . . . until her sharp teeth bit down hard enough on his tongue to draw blood.

He released her and grabbed his mouth with a surprised yelp. *You bit me,* he wanted to say, but by the time he opened his eyes the girl was already gone. The only trace she left was the tingling energy from her sudden burst of magic and the taste of blood in his mouth.

It wasn't that she'd ducked away into the crowd. *No.* She'd been there one second and in a blink—in *less than a blink*—she had simply vanished.

He'd spent years working on illusions, and he'd never seen anything quite like it before.

He needed to go before Corey's men returned.

Instead, he stood stupidly in the middle of the swirling bodies, his tongue smarting, his head muddled by the whiskey, and his entire body electrified by the memory of her mouth against his. Impressed by her in spite of himself.

"Darrigan?" A voice was calling his name through the haze. "Harte Darrigan, is that you?"

His mind still spinning, Harte turned to find Jack Grew making his way across the dance floor. Too late to make his escape, he swallowed the blood that had pooled in his mouth and waved a greeting to Jack. He hardly felt any satisfaction at Jack's appearance. All he could think of was the girl.

"I thought that was you," Jack said with a smile that told Harte he'd already been drinking. "Well, come on, then. I have a table in the corner." Jack pointed across the crowded room.

"Lead the way," Harte said amiably. He tentatively checked his still-tender tongue as he forced himself to forget about the girl and focus on the situation before him. She wasn't his problem anymore, but Jack Grew might be his solution.

A WASTE OF GOOD BOOTS

Esta ducked farther back into an alcove on the second floor and tried to force herself to calm down. She unfastened the top two buttons of the heavy velvet dress to dispel the heat that had climbed up her neck.

He'd kissed her.

She could still feel him on her lips, still taste the whiskey that had been on his breath. She didn't know who he was or why he'd picked her, but she hated him for it.

First he'd ruined her chance at lifting the old man's wallet—and her chance of getting Bridget Malone's attention right along with it—and then, of all things, he'd kissed her like he had a right to.

As his head had bent toward her, it felt like time had gone slow, like the room had dimmed around them and she was frozen. It wasn't that he had any power to *actually* stop time, not like she had. It was simply that she—who had spent her whole life training for attacks, who was an expert at getting out of tough situations—knew what was about to happen and somehow *still* couldn't make herself move away or put a stop to it.

Worse, she'd kissed him back. *Like an idiot.*

When his lips finally touched hers, she'd been braced for an attack, so she was too surprised by how gentle he was to even think. She'd felt the warmth of his mouth, the scent of him, like soap and fresh linen and citrus, and something inside of her had split open. It wasn't that she'd never been kissed before. Of course she'd been kissed. By Logan, by men she'd needed to distract on various jobs. She might have even gone as far as saying she liked it, the tangle of breath, the push-pull excitement of desire.

But she hadn't realized how much she craved gentleness. How susceptible she still was to a yearning for human contact that was more than the physicality of her sparring matches with Dakari. For *warmth*.

His mouth had offered her that, and for a moment she'd fallen into the kiss as easily as breathing. She hadn't even tried to stop herself. It was like the mistakes she'd made with Logan all over again.

If she was honest, that bothered her more than the kiss itself.

Luckily, she didn't have time to be honest with herself any more than she had time to think too much about the kiss. *Or* how stupid she'd been. Thank god she'd finally come to her senses and given it all back to him, and then some.

Too bad that only made her feel marginally better.

From her vantage point in the alcove, she could see the entire ballroom, including the boy. He'd been so commanding on the dance floor, she'd assumed he was older, but now that she looked closer at him, she realized he didn't have any more than a couple of years on her.

She couldn't help but watch him. It was important to understand your enemy, she told herself. It didn't hurt that he was nice enough to look at. His suit fit perfectly over his broad shoulders. She knew firsthand that there wasn't any padding in his coat—she'd felt his strength as he'd gripped her wrist and held her in his arms. Still, there was something about him that bothered her. Something more, that is, than the way he kissed.

Maybe it was simply that the old adage was true—you really can't con a con—but after a few minutes of studying him, she realized all his confidence and swagger was an act. Or at least part of one. Just like Logan's easy charm was a way to manipulate and Dakari's fierce features were only a cover for the softness beneath.

The longer she watched, the more she noticed how uncomfortable he was. He fidgeted. The small tugs at his sleeves, the way he touched his temples to make sure every hair was in place, the way he arranged the gloves on the table, lining up the fingertips so they matched—he couldn't seem to stop checking himself. The longer she watched, the more she wondered what he was hiding. Or what he was hiding from.

Then something struck her—the other man at the table was familiar. It took her a second to place him, but once she realized that he'd been older the last time she'd seen him, she easily recognized the blond as the man who'd shot Logan in Schwab's mansion.

She pulled herself back from the railing. She wouldn't steal the Pharaoh's Heart for another twenty years or more, and in that past, he hadn't known her. She was probably safe enough now, but it was too much of a coincidence that the man who had ruined everything at Schwab's mansion was here as well.

She needed to find Bridget Malone before anything else happened. . . .

"Well, what have we here?" a voice said from behind her.

Esta jumped and turned to find a large man with whiskers like a goat leering at her, his belly preceding him into the small alcove. With him came the stale reek of sweat and beer and too much cologne.

"Corey said he had a treat for me tonight." His heavy gold signet ring flashed as he flexed his fingers in what was clear anticipation. "I see you've anticipated my arrival," he said, gesturing to her open collar.

At first Esta thought the man had made a mistake or had confused her for someone else, but his eyes traveled over her, lingering on her chest, her corseted waist and hips. She remembered suddenly where she was, in one of the semiprivate areas the girls who worked the hall used to entertain their clients. The man clearly thought she was there waiting for him on purpose, and before she had a chance to correct him, he'd already moved closer, blocking her in with his wide body.

She *really* hadn't wanted to injure anyone else tonight, she thought, as the man took another step forward. Backing up until she was pressed against the railing, she considered her options.

"Now, now," the man slurred, stumbling toward her. The smile curving his lip exposed his yellowed teeth when she lifted her hands, preparing for his attack. "None of that," he said, the excitement clear in his voice.

The man grabbed for her, and he was lighter and faster on his feet than Esta expected. She barely had a chance to focus on the moment, to find the spaces between the seconds, so she could create a path through it and away from him. The room stilled, the bright cawing laughter and tinny notes of the band dimmed to a low drone, and the man went almost comically slow, as though he were moving through air as thick and solid as sand.

Relief flooded through her like quicksilver. It was almost too easy to slip past the man's massive body. She caught the laugh bubbling up in her chest at the confusion in his eyes as she slipped out of the alcove, beyond his grasp. The second she let go of time, the world slammed back to life, and the man stumbled heavily to the floor with a groan.

In her relief, she didn't realize how alert he actually was. Before she could get away completely, he caught her by the ankle.

"Let me go!" Esta growled under her breath. She didn't want to draw attention to herself, not here in the middle of this overcrowded room. She had to get away and find Bridget. She needed to get back to what was important—the Book, the stone. The job she had been sent to do.

But the man seemed to be enjoying himself. "That how it's to be, is it?" He laughed, tugging on her with his ironlike grip, and hauled her along the floorboards, back toward the alcove.

In that moment, what she wouldn't have given to be able to do anything else—to be able to call up a wind or send a jolting shock. But all she could do was manipulate the present. A powerful-enough affinity when she was nicking a diamond stickpin, it was useless if someone had ahold of her, unless she wanted to slow time for them as well.

"I'm not here for you," she hissed at him again, trying to pull away.

"You were waiting for me," the man said, his eyes bright with the chase.

"Corey, whoever he is, didn't send me." She gave him a few sharp kicks as she tried to get her ankle free.

The man simply laughed and dug his fingers into her ankle. His eyes were alert and more clear than they had been seconds ago, and before she could brace herself, he gave a sharp, unexpected jerk that brought her to the floor. Nearby, a group of people glanced over their shoulders at her struggle and then promptly averted their eyes.

The man laughed and kept tugging, causing Esta's skirts to climb higher as he dragged her, exposing her legs as she fought against him. But it was no use. He had one ankle and was reaching his sausagelike fingers up her skirts, pinching her bare thigh above her petticoats, up farther. . . .

Not caring who saw her now, she let out a vicious kick that caught the man directly in the face. She felt the crunch of bone collapsing through the thin sole of her boot, and then blood spurted from the man's broken nose. He roared like an injured bear but still didn't let go of her ankle. His fingers tightened as he twisted her leg painfully, his eyes bright with some lurid excitement, and she felt her own bones ache under the pressure.

Desperate, she kicked him again. And again. Exactly like Dakari had taught her. Until the heels of her button-up boots were coated with the man's blood. Finally, his fingers released their grip, and he slumped unconscious to the floor.

Esta scurried away from him, vaguely aware of the group of people who had surrounded her. The man's face was a broken mess as he lay sprawled on the floor, but he was still breathing. For now, at least.

The group around her had grown silent. She met the eyes of one girl with too-pink cheeks whose skin had gone an ashy gray beneath the paint.

"I didn't mean . . . ," Esta started, but her words died as the girl let out a ragged scream at the same time that two men from the crowd took a step toward Esta.

She could tell by their expressions that pleading would get her nowhere.

Esta stood on shaking legs. She would try to find Bridget later. For now she needed to get as far away from the crowded hall and the snub-nosed bouncers as she could. But suddenly she couldn't breathe. Her lungs seized, her chest went tight, like the oxygen had drained from the room. In a panic, she searched the still life around her for some sign of an attack, but her vision was already going fuzzy around the edges. Desperately, she struggled to pull in air that seemed to be missing from the room.

Before she could even begin to focus on the seconds ticking past her, before she could find the spaces between them to escape, a sharp pain erupted across the back of her head. And then everything went black.

THE APPROACH

J ack glanced up at the commotion in the balcony, but he dismissed it without another look. Harte, though, had felt the spike of magic, the telltale energy jolting through the room that only someone who had an affinity to the old magic would recognize. He wondered what the source of it had been, and whether the girl had been the unlucky recipient of the attention from Corey's security.

If so, it was partially his fault for chasing her away. He should never have kissed her. He should have found a different way. His stomach tightened with guilt, but there wasn't anything he could do for her now.

He turned his attention back to Jack, who was taking two glasses of whiskey from a waiter girl's tray. The prodigal nephew of J. P. Morgan, Jack Grew was one of the sons of the city. His family was deep into the political machine and were known members of the Order of Ortus Aurea, so no one was more surprised than Harte when Jack had shown up at his dressing room after a show months ago, wildly excited about the act and desperate to know everything about Harte's skills.

Harte had kept Jack at arm's length . . . until the night Dolph Saunders summoned him to propose that suicide mission of a job. After that, Harte saw Jack in a different light and had started cultivating a careful friendship with him, all the while figuring out how he could best use him. And how he could keep Jack away from Dolph.

"It's been a few weeks since I've seen you," Harte said, accepting one of the glasses. "I was surprised to get your message earlier."

"Sorry about that." Jack grimaced. "I haven't had time to do anything lately," he said before taking a long swallow of his drink. "My uncle's been on my case all week to help with a reception for an exhibition he's planning at the Metropolitan. Opens Friday, though, so at least it'll be over with at the end of the week."

"Oh? I hadn't heard about it. . . ." Harte let his voice trail off, as though his not hearing was some mark against the reception itself.

"Some big fund-raiser," Jack said sourly into his nearly empty glass. "It's a waste of everyone's time."

Harte gave him a wry smile. "Kind of you to help with it."

Jack snorted at the joke. "Kindness has nothing to do with it. I would have found a way to get out of it, but there are a couple of things I wanted the chance to examine."

"Oh?" Harte asked, his voice breezy and his expression disinterested, because he'd learned over the past few months that it was the easiest way to egg Jack on. At first Jack had been careful and closed off in their conversations when it came to his family or the Order, but Harte knew how to work an audience. It wasn't long before Jack was willingly handing over information in an attempt to prove his own importance and win Harte over.

"He's got quite the collection of art from the Ottoman Empire, but some of these pieces are fairly unique. He tends to keep his most valuable and rare pieces to himself, but with the Conclave at the end of the year, he couldn't resist showing off."

"Anything I'd be interested in?" Harte asked, careful to keep his tone easy and light.

Jack nodded. "Maybe. A couple of the seals and tablets go back to ancient Babylon, and there's at least one manuscript owned by Newton himself." Jack smiled. "It won't exactly be a burden to take a close look at those. Especially since they haven't granted me access to the collections at Khafre Hall."

"Still holding you off, are they?" Harte asked with a disapproving shake of his head.

"Of course," Jack grumbled. "Only the Inner Circle has access to the records, and until I prove myself, my uncle's not going to sponsor me. If this event goes well, though, maybe I'll be a step closer. It's not as if they can hold me off forever." He glanced at Harte. "They know as well as I do that they're all basically fossils. They don't want to face facts—it's only a matter of time before they're completely obsolete. The world's changing too fast to stay in the past."

"It's a damn disgrace," Harte murmured, pretending to take another drink. "And they're damn fools to underestimate you, Jack. You're the best of the lot of them." He raised his glass. "Here's to it being over quickly, so you can get back to more important endeavors."

"I'll drink to that." Jack lifted his glass, but he stopped before he could return the toast. "Speaking of damn fools," he muttered as a trio of young men in well-tailored coats approached.

When they stopped at the table, three pairs of eyes appraised Harte with the kind of bored indifference that only the truly rich could affect.

"Gentlemen," Jack said, reluctance tingeing his voice as he stood to greet them.

Harte followed suit. He recognized the three easily. Considering how often they were in the society columns, anyone would. One was a Vanderbilt, another was Robert Winthrop Chandler, who was a cousin of the Astors, and the last was the younger J. P. Morgan, Jack's own cousin. These men were the sons of the city, kings of their world—or they would be when their fathers finally decided either to hand over the reins of their empires or die.

"Fancy meeting you here, Jack," Chandler said with a cold gleam to his eyes. "Though I can't say I know your friend."

Jack made the introductions, but if any of the three recognized Harte's name, they didn't show it. They also didn't bother to extend their hands in welcome.

"It's an honor to meet you all," Harte said, not letting his pleasant, impassive expression falter as he gave them a small bow, an answer to the insult of them not greeting him properly.

"Aren't you going to invite us to join you?" J. P. Morgan, Jr. said, lifting one brow in challenge.

Harte could practically feel the reluctance rolling off Jack, but there was nothing for it.

"Please," Jack said, waving at the empty chairs at the table. "Why don't you join us?"

The men traded cool glances with each other and then, seemingly in amused agreement, took the offered seats. The three men were all older than Jack, closer to thirty than twenty. Harte immediately understood that they viewed Jack as a joke and Harte himself as an intrusion.

Not that they would say anything outright. Jack wasn't the richest or the most powerful person at the table, but he was still one of them—even if his family had recently dragged him back home, humiliated, after he'd almost married a Greek fisherman's daughter on his grand tour.

But their good breeding would only get him so far.

A waiter girl brought an extra chair for the table. She gave Jack a drunken smile and draped herself over his shoulders to whisper something close to his ear that made him roar with laughter. Her appearance only reminded Harte of how unique the other girl had been, the one responsible for his aching tongue. The one who had made him lose all sense before she disappeared.

He gave himself a mental shake. He couldn't afford to let his mind wander back to the girl now. Not surrounded by these men—every one of them members of the Order. Every one of them more powerful than Jack himself.

Harte was careful to keep his face pleasant as they all waited for Jack to finish with the girl, who was now sitting squarely on his lap. The one sitting directly across from him was J. P. Morgan, Jr., the heir to Morgan's fortune and his standing in the Order. The younger Morgan wore a knowing expression, as though he understood exactly how uncomfortable Harte felt.

Morgan lifted a neatly rolled cigarette to his mouth and took a long, squinting drag, exhaling the smoke through his nose as he spoke. "Jack's mentioned you before. Says you're quite the man to see perform."

Harte inclined his head as though he hadn't noticed the way Jack's cousin sneered the word "perform." Like he was no better than an organ grinder's monkey. "I'm happy to hear that he's spoken so well of me."

Morgan, still squinting, gave a shrug. "He's mostly mentioned how you're wasting yourself—your talents—on the stage."

Harte let his mouth curve up ever so slightly. "My talents were made for the stage. And the stage has done well enough by me in turn." He gave his left sleeve another small tug, well aware that he was drawing attention to the jeweled cuff link that glinted there.

Vanderbilt leaned forward. "You're quite the enigma, Mr. Darrigan," he said. "What is that, Irish? Or is Darrigan simply your stage name?"

"I'm afraid it's the only name I lay claim to," Harte answered, his voice dangerously even.

"A man of mystery, are you?" Jack's cousin drawled. "I've heard about you. A classic tale—come from nowhere and here you are, the toast of Broadway. Why, even my mother has seen your performance. She swears you gave the most amazing demonstration." He gave a humorless laugh. "Insisted that you must have some sort of real power."

"Your mother is too kind."

"Is she? I've often thought she was rather flighty," Morgan said with an indifferent shrug. "She was nervous, but I told her, of course, that it was impossible. We all know that if you were that sort of filth, you would have already been taken care of, don't we?" The threat was clear. "The Order would have heard about it. So, it must be mere tricks you do, I told her. Illusions. Not true magic at all."

Harte kept his face in that careful, pleasant mask that had been his ticket out of the slums and into the footlights. "I'm sure the Order would have already taken care of any threat if I posed one. I have the utmost respect for the work they do to keep us safe from those who would threaten our way of life. But I assure you, there's nothing simple about my tricks," he said easily, while dread inched along his skin. He was in too deep. There were many variables he hadn't prepared for—first the girl, now this circling around magic.

Damn Jack for throwing me into this.

"No?" the younger Morgan challenged, a smirk creeping at the corners of his mouth.

Harte didn't react to it. "If Jack's spoken of me, then I'm sure he's told you—I've made a careful study of the hermetic arts," Harte said, inclining his head. "Alchemy, astronomy, theurgy. The usual branches of the occult sciences. I don't perform *tricks*." He forced himself not to glance over at Jack for help, keeping his focus steady on Jack's cousin. "I present demonstrations of my *skill* and the knowledge I've acquired through my many years of study."

"Yes. He might have mentioned something like that," Morgan said.

"You didn't believe him." It wasn't a question. The smug certainty in his own superiority was clear as day on Morgan's face. As was the disbelief that anyone not of their own class could have mastered any sort of power. It took a considerable amount of effort on Harte's part not to smile at the irony of it.

"I make my own decisions," Jack's cousin told him, squinting through another deep drag on his cigarette before he snubbed it, violently, on the marble tabletop. "Though when it comes to Irish filth"—he raked his eyes over Harte's pristine, perfectly tailored clothes—"or whatever it is you are, there's rarely anything to decide." He leaned forward, malice glinting in his eyes. "What was that rumor I heard about you? Oh, yes . . . the bastard son of a Chinaman."

The other men at the table shifted. Even if Jack was the wastrel of the family, good breeding and manners went deep.

Luckily, Harte didn't have the problem of good breeding. His mouth curved wickedly, the barbing response already loaded on his tongue, but before he could speak, he felt the familiar brush of magic and the unsettling feeling that someone was watching him. His words were forgotten, and he went on alert.

He was on his feet instantly, searching.

Morgan laughed. "Going somewhere, Darrigan?"

The others chuckled, but Jack was still too busy with the waiter girl to even notice how badly things were progressing at the table.

Harte couldn't find any sign of the girl's green velvet dress or whiskey-colored eyes. *Maybe it was Corey's security,* he thought, which wasn't any better. There had already been too much magic in the air, and magic was something Harte Darrigan couldn't risk being associated with. Not with these men, members of the Order who posed an even greater threat than Corey's security.

Morgan smirked over his glass of champagne. "Feeling out of your depth, are you?"

Jack finally looked up from the bit of silk and muslin on his lap. "You can't be leaving already," he said, sputtering in confusion. "You . . . you haven't even finished your drink." As if that was the point that truly mattered.

Harte ignored Morgan and gave Jack a wry look. "I'm not really thirsty anymore."

"But—"

"Jack, gentlemen, the one thing my many years onstage have taught me is when to make an exit." He gave the other men a nod, allowing his cold gaze to linger on Morgan, to send the message that he wasn't afraid of him. "I'll see you later, Jack."

Truth be told, Morgan's barbs hadn't hurt nearly as much as Harte's swollen tongue.

A moment later, he was pushing through the crowd toward the door, but he couldn't shake the feeling that someone was watching, tracking him, as he moved steadily into the cool freedom of the night beyond.

IN THE DEAD OF NIGHT

He'd barely made it to the end of the block when Harte heard Jack's voice calling him through the din of the crowded sidewalks. He didn't stop at first, just continued barreling down the sidewalk—away from the Haymarket. Away from the whole mess of a night. But Jack was determined.

With a sigh, Harte stopped and turned, giving Jack a chance to catch up. He might as well get this over with. . . .

Jack had the kind of patrician good looks most of his class sported: straight, narrow nose; light eyes; strong, square forehead. He wasn't that much older than Harte himself, but the humiliation in Greece had done a number on him. Away from the glittering lights of the dance hall, he looked worn, run-down. His face was flushed and damp from the exertion caused by his sprint. It made his puffy skin and the shadows beneath his eyes look that much worse.

"What is it, Jack? Coming back for another round? Was there some insult you forgot to get in yourself?"

"You left," Jack said, ignoring Harte's sarcasm and his anger. His bloodshot eyes betrayed his sincere confusion. As though no one had ever walked out on him before.

It was probably the truth. Even if Jack was his family's current black sheep, few would have risked word of an insult getting back to his famous uncle. Harte probably couldn't afford it either, not if he wanted Jack to trust him, but he was too on edge to care. Morgan Jr. and the rest had come too close to the truth, and in that instant he'd seen all his careful plans crumbling between his fingers.

"Look, Jack, I only came tonight because you invited me. I wasn't expecting to be the evening's entertainment. Usually my audience pays for that particular pleasure."

"It's not like that, Darrigan—"

"It was *exactly* like that, Jack."

"I didn't expect them to be there, and then . . ." Jack took a deep breath, as though he was trying to steady himself.

"And then you sat there with your hand down a girl's dress and let your cousin insult me."

Jack had the decency to look the slightest bit uneasy at this charge. "I'm sorry, Darrigan, but—"

"But nothing, Jack. Aren't those the same ones you're constantly complaining about? *They* don't understand your genius. *They* don't understand the dangers we face," Harte mimicked. Then he pinned Jack with a caustic glare. "I thought we understood one another—"

"We do!" Jack protested.

"But tonight you tossed me to the wolves," Harte continued.

He took a breath and stepped back from Jack. It was too easy to call up the old indignation, the bitterness he thought he'd long ago put to rest. It was too easy to still let their words affect him. Which wouldn't do, not in a situation as delicate as this one.

He needed to keep his wits about him and his head cool. He needed to make sure he—and not his emotions—were in control. He'd been working on earning Jack's trust for too long to screw it all up now.

"Look, let's go somewhere and talk," Jack offered. "I'll buy you a drink and make it up to you. We can talk. Without them."

"I don't know . . . ," Harte hedged, making a show of checking his watch. *Let Jack be the eager one,* he told himself, mentally pulling back. You couldn't force a con. The mark had to believe it was his own idea.

Jack was already stepping to the curb. "Let me get us a cab. There's a quiet bar over on Fortieth—"

"It's getting late, and I have an early show tomorrow," Harte said, staying where he was.

Because the last thing he wanted was another smoky barroom. He needed to walk, to clear his head. He needed some space away from Jack Grew and all the feelings the evening had stirred up.

He needed Jack to want it.

"Anyway, I'm more than finished with this evening." Harte pulled his overcoat around him against the brisk winter air.

Jack let his arm fall to his side, and for a moment he looked like he wasn't sure what to do. Then he straightened, his eyes wide and his expression suddenly eager.

"You know," Jack said, "you should come."

"Come where?" Harte asked. He kept his tone flat, so Jack wouldn't guess at how the invitation affected him, how his heart had kicked up in his chest and how it felt suddenly too much even to breathe.

"Come to the gallery opening. As my guest."

I'm close. So very close. "I have the eight o'clock show . . . ," he started.

"Oh, right," Jack said, his shoulders sinking.

"But I'm not on until well after nine," Harte continued. "I'm sure I could swing by for a little while."

"You should," Jack insisted, looking relieved.

"I'll think about it," Harte said, the thrill of this small victory coursing through him. But he forced himself to keep his expression noncommittal, placid.

"I'll send you over an invitation, just in case."

"Sure, Jack. You do that." Harte gave a small salute. "I'll see you around," he said, and without another word, he turned and left Jack Grew behind with the noise of Satan's Circus.

As he walked, the elevated train thundered by overhead, coughing its coal-fired way to its final destination, and the city grew quiet. The crowded sidewalks gave way to streets lined with serene townhomes, but in that silence he felt a chill, and he knew danger of some sort had followed him.

Keeping his gait steady, he turned right, following to where the street opened onto Madison Square. Then he slipped into the quiet of the gardens and waited.

It didn't take long before he saw his stalker pause at the gates of the park. Harte recognized him immediately. Cursing under his breath, he considered his options. Finally, he decided that the direct route would be best.

"Why are you following me, Nibsy?" he asked, stepping out from the shadows.

The lenses of the boy's spectacles flashed in the moonlight. "Harte Darrigan? Is that you?" Nibs called, like he hadn't been following Harte all the time. Like it was a surprise to run into an old friend in an empty park in the dead of night.

"You know damn well it's me. You've been following me for three blocks." He walked toward the boy until they were nearly toe-to-toe. "Were you at the Haymarket, too?" he demanded, wondering if the sense of unease that had driven him to his feet might have been Nibsy and not the girl after all.

"The Haymarket?" The boy sounded confused, but Harte didn't believe the act for a second. People tended to overlook Nibsy Lorcan because he didn't have any discernible affinity, but then, neither did Harte. Nibs kept his secrets close to the vest, but Harte knew that anyone Dolph Saunders trusted as much as he trusted the boy had to have something to him. It should have been easy enough to find out for sure, but Nibs had a way of staying just out of reach—a defense mechanism, Harte supposed. One that seemed to serve him well.

Even now Nibsy took a step back.

"Don't try to tell me you didn't know I was at the Haymarket," Harte said, too tired to deal anything else that night.

Behind his glasses, the boy's eyes were unreadable, but Harte got the sense they were taking everything in.

"Yeah, you got me all right," Nibsy said affably enough. "Bridget told me you were meeting with Jack Grew."

So they were finally coming to it. New York might have been one of the biggest cities in the world, but Harte should have known he couldn't do anything without everyone knowing his business. "Yeah, I met with him, all right. With Vanderbilt and Chandler and a couple of others, too. What business is that of yours? And why were you waiting for me to start with?"

"I needed to talk with you. They won't let me backstage anymore." There was a tone of reproach in his voice.

"It's a new policy," Harte said, skirting the truth. In fact, it was *his* new policy. A few weeks before, Nibsy had started showing up and pestering him about Dolph's proposal again. It got so bad Harte could barely think straight, much less get ready for his next performance.

Besides, he had plans of his own, and he couldn't chance Nibsy running into Jack.

The boy frowned, like he understood this wasn't exactly a lie, but it also wasn't exactly the truth. Which was what worried Harte about the kid—he always seemed to know a little too much when he shouldn't have known anything at all. "Does your meeting with Jack Grew mean you've thought about Dolph's proposition?"

"Not a chance," Harte said, shaking his head.

In truth, Harte had done little else *but* think about Dolph's proposition. It was the reason he'd been getting friendlier with Jack. Harte wasn't about to join the ragtag crew Dolph Saunders was assembling. He'd had enough of working for other people to last him a lifetime. But he'd thought a lot about *why* Dolph was assembling them—and about how he could do the same job, but better, and on his own.

"Dolph's still eager to have you on board," Nibsy said, rubbing his hands a little for warmth. "He needs you to make a go of it."

While Harte could appreciate a bit of theater as well as the next person, he wasn't buying the meek-and-humble routine Nibs was playing for him. "Why's that? Far as I can tell, Dolph isn't hurting any for talent. All I can do is make some rabbits disappear."

Nibsy didn't react, and he didn't call Harte on the lie, which made him wonder how much Dolph had shared with Nibs. "Dolph still thinks you're our way in. With you on board, the job would be a certain bet," Nibsy said, ducking his head to look over the rims of his glasses. "You gotta at least consider it."

"It's been a long day, Nibs. I had two curtains today, and three more tomorrow. The only thing I'm considering is the way my bed's going to feel when I finally sink into it." Harte clapped the boy on the shoulder, squeezing gently. It wasn't the kid's fault that Dolph had put him up to this, but Harte wasn't soft enough to care. "Take care, and stop following me, will you?" he said as he walked past Nibs.

"So what do I tell Dolph?" Nibsy called.

Harte turned, walking backward for a few steps. "Tell him I'm still not interested in the suicide mission he's cooked up." Not when he had plans of his own.

BRIDGET MALONE, I PRESUME

The Haymarket

The first thing Esta noticed when she came to was that she wasn't alone. Her head still ached from the blow, and she was slumped against a damp wall in a room that smelled dank and old, the way basements do.

She kept her breathing steady, her body still as she slowly moved her hand down her leg. Her fingers finally found the edge of her boot, but Dakari's knife was gone.

All at once the air went out of her lungs. Her eyes opened as her chest constricted in a desperate attempt to breathe.

"Ah, so I was right," a rasping voice crowed. "You *are* awake."

Esta's vision struggled to adjust to the sudden brightness, and when it did, she saw that the light in the room wasn't coming from a lamp, but from a person holding a dancing flame in the palm of her hands.

"That's enough, Werner," the woman said, nodding to the boy standing next to her. He glared at Esta, but a moment later she could breathe again.

"You're maybe wondering where you are?" the woman said with a sly, satisfied smile. She was small and surprisingly willowy, considering the rasping tenor of her voice. With her coppery hair and fair skin, she might have once been pretty, but now she only looked worn. The boy was about Esta's own age with a squint-eyed glare and a smirk on his face.

Esta didn't particularly care where she was, because she wasn't going to be there for very long. She focused on the seconds that ticked by, but her head felt wobbly and unclear, and when she tried to slow time, she felt a splitting pain behind her eyes. She couldn't keep the panicked gasp from escaping her throat when time slipped out of her grasp, eluding her.

"That would be the opium," the woman said as Esta tried to pull herself back up against the wall. "We couldn't have you leaving us too soon, could we now? You'll find it impossible to call on your affinity so long as the poppy remains in your blood, so it's best you resign yourself to being our guest for a while longer. Until we decide what your fate will be."

"Please," Esta said, forcing herself to make her voice small. She noticed the sticky sweetness hanging in the air now, the fuzziness in her head.

"You've caused me quite the problem, girl," the woman cut in, her voice barely above a whispering growl. "The man you laid low is Mr. Murphy, and he happens to be one of Mr. Corey's best customers and one of the most powerful men in the city. There's few daft enough to cross him as you did. He'll not rest until he finds the girl who broke his ugly gob, and he'll not be satisfied until he pays someone back in kind. That someone isn't going to be me. He's a right nasty one. The type to enjoy every second of your pain, if you understand what I'm saying?"

Esta made no move, but the woman gave a wan smile nevertheless.

"Ah. You *do* understand, then." The smile fell from the woman's face, and her eyes went cold. "So you'll understand that you don't have much time before Mr. Corey turns you over to him. Unless you give me a good reason not to, of course."

Esta schooled her expression to give nothing away. Not a blink to tell the woman that the idea of being at the large man's mercy was more than repulsive. Not a twitch to give away the panic of not being able to call on her magic.

"You think you're so brave? That you can protect yourself from the likes of him?" the woman scoffed. "Here, let me show you. . . ." The fire in her outstretched hand grew, danced, as she brought the flame up closer to her face and pulled down the high collar of her dress with her other hand. Beneath the lace, her skin was scarred in a gnarled mass.

Esta couldn't stop from wincing.

"I was pretty once, like you. You go on with your determined eyes and stiff spine, but the strongest spine will snap easily with a boot pressing down on it. Murphy has eyes everywhere in this city. Magic or no, you'd not last two days without help or protection."

"You can give me protection from Murphy?"

The woman nodded. "If you can make it worth my while. You've caused a right mess for Mr. Corey, and his messes always become mine. I hate messes, girl, so if you're not worth more than the problem you've caused, I'll hand you over to Mr. Murphy wrapped in lace and tied with a bow of the finest silk. And I won't think twice about whether you ever see daylight again."

Esta started to protest, but the woman raised her hand. There was no sign of burns or scarring from where she had held the fire, and Esta's skin tingled again from the magic that seemed to saturate the air in the room.

"However . . . Murphy isn't one of *us*. And I'd just as soon he go hang than get one bit of pleasure he hasn't rightly paid me for. If you prove to be a smart girl, *perhaps* I know of someone who could protect you . . . so long as you *remain* useful, that is." The woman stepped closer. "Tell me, why did you come to be in my ballroom when you clearly weren't looking for the company of a man?"

"I came to find Bridget Malone."

The woman didn't react, save for a small muscle that ticked near her eye. She studied Esta a little longer, and then she exchanged a glance with Werner, who gave a subtle shrug.

"Bridget Malone, you say?" the woman asked. Her voice, if it was possible, had gone even rougher.

"I was told that she finds places for people with certain . . . abilities," Esta said, never once breaking the stare with the woman. "People like us."

"And what *abilities* do you claim?"

Esta tried to focus again. The cloud of opium was already starting to dissipate, and its power over her was starting to wane. "I'm a thief," she said simply, sticking as close to the truth as was possible.

"A thief?" Even through the rasp of the woman's voice, Esta could hear her doubt. "There's already enough of those in the city to fill all the cells in the Tombs thrice over. Why would anyone have use of another?"

"Because I'm the best of them. I can steal a diamond, an elephant, or anything in between. No one can stop me"—Esta leaned forward as though sharing a secret—"because no one can *see* me."

Werner laughed, but the woman simply watched Esta, searching her face for some signs of the lie.

The woman's mouth made a pinched shape of disbelief. "You can prove this?"

Esta took a breath, closed her eyes, and in the split second it took for Werner and the woman to exchange another, more doubtful glance, Esta had pulled time to a stop, crossed the room, and plucked the brooch from the neckline of the woman's dress. Before the woman's suspicious eyes returned to where Esta had been sitting, she was gone.

When Werner came barreling through the door, the woman wide-eyed behind him, Esta was waiting, leaning against the wall outside the room with a bored look on her face. Using her affinity through the remaining haze of the opium had all but drained her. She couldn't have done anything more to escape if she had wanted to, even if Werner hadn't immediately gone on the attack.

The second Werner saw her, she felt her chest go tight and her throat begin to close, but this time she was ready for the unsettling feeling of being suffocated. She'd never felt magic quite so powerful before, which was worrisome enough. But worse, from the way he was taking orders, Esta understood that he probably wasn't all *that* powerful, not relative to others. Professor Lachlan had tried to warn her, but now she understood—magic *was* different there. Like nothing she'd ever experienced.

But she didn't have time to worry about that fact. If the two knew how little strength she had left, Esta would lose her upper hand, so she pretended a calm confidence she didn't feel. When the woman saw she hadn't escaped—hadn't even tried to get away—she slapped Werner's arm. A heartbeat later, Esta could draw air into her lungs once more.

"A fair trick," the woman said, her face not betraying any hint of surprise or anger or even interest. "But you wouldn't have gotten very far. Not with Mr. Murphy looking for you."

"Who said I was trying to leave?" Esta said, holding up the brooch so the fake stones glinted in the light thrown by the ball of fire in the woman's hand. "I was only proving how useful I could be. Besides, why would I run from the very person I'm looking for? Miss Malone, I presume?"

The woman blanched a little, but managed to hold on to her composure as she reached out and took the brooch Esta was holding. "Please," Esta said. "I need a place to stay. I'm a hard worker, and I will be loyal to any who help me."

"The city doesn't need any more thieves."

"I can make it worth your while." Esta ran her fingers along the edge of her bodice until she found the small pocket sewn into the lining. Relieved that they hadn't found it, as they had her knife, she pulled out the diamond she'd taken in Schwab's mansion. "Here," she said, offering Bridget the stone. "This is all I have."

After a long moment, Bridget took the stone and examined it, then eyed Esta again as she tucked the diamond into her pocket. "Maybe I know somewhere you could go. . . . Where are your people?"

Relief coursed through her, but she tamped it down. It was too soon to celebrate. "Dead. There was a fire. . . ." She let her voice trail off, and she glanced away, sinking the hook into the lie.

Werner shifted uneasily on his feet at the mention of the word. No doubt he'd had his own experiences with the fires that were so were common in this city. She'd learned from Professor Lachlan about the "accidental" blazes that consumed whole buildings filled with magical refugees while the fire brigades—controlled by and dependent on the Order—stayed away.

Bridget's eyes narrowed. "There's no one to come looking for you?"

"No one except your Mr. Murphy," Esta told her.

In the long moment that followed, it took every bit of strength Esta had left not to falter. If Bridget refused to help now, she wasn't sure what she would do. The Professor's plan hinged on Esta exposing herself and Bridget seeing something of interest in Esta's talent, but they hadn't planned on Esta making an enemy of Bridget. If the madam turned her away, or worse, turned her over to Murphy, Esta had already used every ounce of her strength on the desperate bid to prove herself. She had nothing left, not even the diamond. And if they drugged her any more, she'd be beyond helpless.

"How did you know who I was?" Bridget asked.

"I'm good at recognizing a tell," she explained with a shrug. "A good thief knows how to read a mark."

Bridget's features registered her understanding of what Esta's words implied—that *she* had been the mark—but she didn't address the insult.

"You hesitated when I said your name."

Bridget frowned. "I didn't—"

"It wasn't much. And then there was the tiniest tick of a muscle in your cheek. If I hadn't been looking, I wouldn't have seen it at all." Esta conveniently left out the fact that she was always looking, always aware. Professor Lachlan had trained her too well not to be.

Bridget's mouth went tight. Then she spoke to Werner. "Take her to Dolph Saunders. He should be at the Strega this time of night."

At the mention of the name, Esta felt a surge of victory, but she tamped it down. She wouldn't get ahead of herself. Not yet.

"Please . . . ," she said, hesitating when Bridget's eyes narrowed. "Can I have my knife back?"

"What knife?" Bridget asked, her face impassive as flint.

"The one that was in my boot. The one you took."

Bridget's expression never wavered. "After I've saved you from Mr. Corey, after I've offered to help you find protection, you accuse me of stealing from you?"

Esta met Bridget's steady gaze and weighed her options. She needed the knife—the safety and assurance it represented, the link that it was to her own time. But she also needed Bridget Malone to give her an introduction to Dolph Saunders.

Dakari would understand, she told herself.

She'd come back later. There would be time enough to get the knife back.

When she didn't argue any more, Bridget gave her a smug look before addressing Werner again. "If Saunders isn't pleased with her abilities, bring her back here and we'll give her to Mr. Corey." She glanced at Esta, a warning in her expression. "If she tries anything at all, kill her."

A NEW AGE

The Docks

Jack Grew closed his eyes against the throbbing in his head as the carriage rattled onward. Perhaps that last round of drinks had been a mistake. Actually, the entire night had been a mistake, from the beginning to the end . . . though the bit of silk who'd managed to walk away with the contents of his wallet had been worth it, he thought with a small smile. It wasn't like she got away with much anyway. He knew not to bring a heavy wallet to a place like the Haymarket, no matter what the rest of the family currently thought of him.

He'd show them how wrong they were, eventually. It was only a matter of time before his project would be complete, and then his uncle and his cousins and the rest would forget about that unpleasantness in Greece with the girl and recognize his vision. He'd be back in the Order's good graces, and they would have no choice but to give him the respect he deserved.

It wasn't as though he would have *really* married the girl. She'd bespelled him. Tricked him with her power.

Then she'd made off with his grandmother's ring, proving his entire family—including Junior—right. Which, truly, was the one sin he could never forgive her for.

Most days he tried not to think of her—or of the whole mess—but as the carriage rattled on, he couldn't stop the direction of his thoughts. Maybe it was the last round of whiskey, or maybe it was the disaster of the evening, but the memory of his mistakes pulled at him, and he couldn't help but wallow in the past.

He'd gone on his grand tour so naive, so full of expectations. He'd thought he would find great secrets in Europe's hallowed libraries and laboratories to help the work of the Order, but he found a girl instead.

She'd made him believe she was different from the others. For a while he'd been taken in by the sun in her smile and the glimmering promise in her eyes, and he'd started to think that perhaps the Order had misunderstood the threat Mageus posed to the country. But in the end she showed herself to be a miscreant, a criminal like all the others. In the end her betrayal proved that the Order had been right all along. If left unchecked, those with the old magic would take advantage of good people, *normal* people. If left to go free, they would destroy everything in their path.

But, egad, she'd been beautiful. With curves in all the right places and a mouth—

The carriage came to a clattering stop, and Jack grabbed hold to keep from being thrown forward. That last round had *definitely* been a mistake.

"Wait for me," he commanded the driver as he alighted. "I'll be just a minute."

Despite the cold, the air smelled of fish and the heavy metallic tang of oil and machinery. The wind cut harder there, close to the water, so Jack pulled his fur-lined collar up around his neck to ward off the chill as he walked toward his destination, a long, low-slung building nearly indistinguishable from the others. He used his key on the heavy lock and let himself in.

Inside, it wasn't much warmer, but a small stove glowed in the corner where an old man sat hunched over his work, his back to the entrance. Sparks from a welding torch flew up around the man, silhouetting him like a living gargoyle. When the man heard the door slam, he switched off the torch and turned to greet Jack.

"How's it coming?" Jack asked.

The man lifted the heavy welding mask, revealing a face lined by age and scarred by some earlier mishap. "It comes," he said with a shrug.

"How much longer?"

The man considered the question. "A week, maybe more. But you'll need to find a way to stabilize the power it generates before it'll work properly."

Jack frowned. A week wasn't so long, and the Conclave wasn't until the end of the year. He still had time to get it right. Still, with the failures of the night still fresh, impatience scraped at him.

"Let's see how she runs."

The old man frowned. "I haven't connected the receptors. It won't build up a sustained charge—"

"That doesn't matter. I want to see the progress you've made."

Jack walked to the center of the room, where a cloth was draped over a large object. He took the corner and snapped the cloth away, imagining himself in that moment not so long from now when he would make this same movement, revealing his creation, his greatest triumph, to the Order. No one would be laughing at him then.

A large machine gleamed dully in the oil lamp's wavering glow. Wide, orbital arms surrounded its central globe, like a giant gyroscope. Like a gyroscope, it would bring balance.

The body wasn't complete—there were unconnected wires and plugs sprouting from its missing panels—but eventually the machine's inner workings would be covered with sleek, polished steel. A beautiful piece of machinery for a new age. A modern age, free from the threat of the feral and uncontrolled magic of the Mageus.

Jack had been thinking about bringing Harte Darrigan along with him that night to show him the progress he'd made. He had a feeling Darrigan would understand, might even be impressed by what Jack had managed to accomplish in so short a time.

It wasn't enough, though. Jack still hadn't figured out how to contain the energy the machine generated. The Brink could do it, but that was such old, outdated magic. If he could only figure out *how* the Brink did it, Jack could solve his problem, could apply the old methods to his new project.

But the Order kept its secrets close, even from its own members. Until he proved himself, they wouldn't let him into the Mysterium to search for the answers he needed. So he would have to find them for himself.

Jack thought Darrigan might be able to help with that. Considering the amazing feats he'd seen Darrigan do onstage—things that only someone with a deep knowledge and understanding of magic could do—the man must know something that could help Jack solve this last problem.

And Darrigan understood the importance of an audience. Of a little drama. It was what the Ortus Aurea needed—secrecy and small strikes weren't enough. Not anymore. Not with the ever-increasing hordes coming to their shores, and Mageus hidden among them.

What was needed for this new century was a statement of power to prevent the maggots from seeing the city as a haven for their feral magic in the first place. No more simply containing the threat. No more trying to keep them out. It was clear enough that Ellis Island had been a failure. Despite the inspectors, Mageus were still getting in.

No. They had to be eliminated.

He had a feeling that Harte Darrigan would understand that as well, but his cousin had chased him off.

Junior always had been a veritable horse's ass, Jack thought bitterly. So full of his own importance.

"Go on," he told the old man. "Fire it up."

He circled the machine, admiring the metalwork and modernity of it. If it worked—and eventually it *would* work, Jack had no doubt—it would change everything. He would show them all, and then he would be the one to lead the Order into the future.

THE BELLA STREGA

As Werner led her south through the city, the wind whipped like knives tearing at her skirts, but Esta barely felt it. Bridget had told Werner to take her to Dolph Saunders, which meant she was one step closer to her goal.

There weren't many traces of Saunders in the historical records—a journal entry here, a newspaper clipping there. Only whispered rumors had made their way through the years. He was described as a ghost. A madman. A genius. At some point, he'd simply disappeared.

Unlike the other gang bosses, who were only interested in amassing their fellow countrymen and using ties to the old country as a way to recruit, Saunders collected Mageus the way some people collect old coins. But none of the records gave any real answers to how the man managed to bring so many disparate people together under his protection and control—individuals who, by all rights, should have been enemies.

In short, Dolph Saunders had been as powerful as he was mysterious. But whatever he might have been—or might *be*, Esta reminded herself— she needed him. He was the one who'd organized the team to steal the Ortus Aurea's treasures. With Bridget Malone's introduction, Dolph Saunders would be more likely to trust her. But from that point, it would be up to Esta herself to earn a place on that team. From there, she would be working blind.

They continued past theaters with their glittering marquees and restaurants with gilded lettering on their windows. As they walked, she could see the echoes of a future that had not yet arrived—the grids of streets that would remain unchanged through the years, the familiar shapes of buildings that would survive for a century more—but it wasn't a future she could access. She had no way to reach forward through the layers of time and grab hold of the world where she belonged.

As they walked, Werner's posture changed. The comfortable, loping gait he'd had when they'd left the Haymarket went stiff, cautious, and by the time they turned onto the Bowery, the wide street that glowed even more brightly than Broadway, everything about his bearing said he was on guard. Which put Esta on guard as well.

Even in her own time, the Bowery was lined by the shorter buildings characteristic of most of lower Manhattan. Now, elevated train tracks partially obscured them, casting shadows over the people bustling along on the packed sidewalks below. As Werner led her through the crowds, the nearly deafening rumble of a small steam engine shook the heavy metal girders overhead, showering the pedestrians below with soot and filling the air with a cloud of acrid smoke.

They made their way through a crowd gathered around a makeshift table of wooden crates set up beneath the glow of an electric streetlamp. Behind the crates, a boy in a thick scarf and fingerless gloves shuffled cards with the dexterity of a Vegas dealer. Three-card monte, Esta realized, and she couldn't help but smile as she noticed another young boy making his way through the crowd, lifting coins and watches from the spectators as their attention was focused on the sucker losing his money at the table.

Her fingers twitched. It would be so easy to make a living without the countless cameras that watched from every street corner and the wallets filled with plastic cards that could be traced. If she were stuck here for good, maybe it would be okay—

No. She wouldn't let herself even entertain that possibility. She was going to get on Dolph Saunders' team, get the Book *and* Ishtar's Key, and get back to her own city. She wasn't going to be distracted by the promise of a fat wallet. People were depending on her.

Eventually, they reached a corner saloon with an ornate marquee. Brilliant red and white lights spelled out the words BELLA STREGA, and the sign above depicted a woman in black with a waspish waist and dark, cascading hair. Her back was to the street, and she looked over her shoulder, her golden eyes glowing as a smile curved her scarlet lips.

"This is it," Werner said, and Esta thought that he sounded almost nervous about entering.

She followed him through the double doors and practically sighed when the blast of warmth from within hit her frozen face. Cigar smoke hung heavy in the air, and the smell of sweat and old beer was stronger than it had been at the Haymarket.

Along with the stale reek of too many bodies and the cloud of smoke, there was something else about the saloon—a frisson of energy that whispered along her skin and warmed her every bit as much as the coal stove in the corner of the room. It was that same sizzling sensation she'd felt right before Werner had taken the breath from her lungs. Yet another reminder that in this time, magic was different. In her own city, she'd never encountered magic like this, affinities so strong they stirred the very air.

The electric energy was a warning of sorts, but the warmth running across her skin was also a comfort. She had always struggled to feel like she belonged with Professor Lachlan and his team, but as she stepped into Dolph Saunders' lair, Esta felt strangely at home.

Werner pushed Esta ahead of him, toward the back of the saloon, where a man who could only be Dolph held court. He was younger than Esta had expected—he couldn't have been much more than his midtwenties, but his dark hair sported a shock of white that made him seem older at first glance.

Or maybe it was that he carried his authority with an ease that the overdressed boys around him didn't. Dolph was dressed simply, the sleeves of his shirt rolled to expose his strong forearms. One bore the tattoo of a snake that wound around his wrist and crawled up into the arm of his shirt. His hair wasn't slicked back like the other boys, but curled around his lean face, and he wore a patch over one eye that made him look a little like a pirate. Lying across the table in front of him was an ebony cane topped with what looked to be a silver replica of a screaming Medusa.

He wasn't a handsome man. He didn't have the polished charm that Logan cultivated to disarm his marks, but even from across the room Esta could tell Dolph Saunders didn't need something as ordinary as charm to get his way.

"Go on," Werner urged, pushing her forward through the parted crowd.

Esta didn't miss the nervousness in Werner's voice, and she didn't blame him. Though Dolph sat with a slouching indifference, the power he held over the room was obvious from the way everyone seemed oriented toward him. Even those not close to his table tossed furtive glances his way.

Noticing that someone was approaching, Saunders looked up from the conversation he had been having with a light-haired boy sitting next to him. The eye free from the patch was a clear blue, but at their approach, his expression went tight. Her instincts urged her to run, but Esta knew she wouldn't get a second chance, so she stepped forward. Toward the danger he embodied, and toward her only possibility of getting home.

AMBITION AND DESIRE

Dolph Saunders had never liked surprises. He valued the ears and eyes he had around the city, and he paid well for the lips that whispered the secrets many would rather keep silent. So he was less than pleased to see Werner Knopf, Edward Corey's latest lackey, walk into his saloon without so much as a warning.

Dolph glanced at Nibs, who was sitting next to him, but the boy shook his head, an indication that he didn't know the cause for the visit.

Someone was going to pay for this particular surprise. Especially since Werner wasn't alone.

Dolph squinted through the haze of smoke to make out the girl's face. Even with his weakened affinity, he could sense she was powerful. *Another unwelcome surprise.* It was the last thing he needed. Especially now, when he didn't have Leena by his side to neutralize the threat of the girl's magic and when the streets were filled with murmurings about how he had been unable to protect Leena from the Order's power.

There were always murmurings, of course. The new arrivals already carried with them the fears passed down by parents and grandparents who had survived the Disenchantment—the witch hunts and inquisitions that marred Europe's history. In the span of a century, the Mageus had gone from being revered as healers and leaders to being feared by those without affinities. In the span of a century, science and the quest for enlightenment had turned the old magic into a dangerous superstition and the Mageus into pariahs.

Forced to live on the margins of society, they taught their children to hide what they were. Their descendants, desperate for a chance at a different life, believed in the tales told about this city, the promise that magic was protected here. They carried their fears across the seas with them, right alongside their meager parcels, and found themselves trapped.

The girl was new to Dolph, which meant she was new to the city as well, but she didn't seem to be afraid. She didn't vibrate with that same worry and fear of being found out that marked most new arrivals. *Interesting,* he thought, testing the air for some sign of her intentions and finding only desire and ambition. Both admirable qualities—but also dangerous, depending on who wielded them.

He tightened his grip on his cane and, making certain a scowl was firmly in place, he leaned forward to greet Werner and his guest.

"Who's this?" he asked in the boy's native German.

"Bridget found her," Werner replied with a nod to the girl. "Thought you might be interested."

The girl was tall and stood with a straightness that indicated an internal strength he looked for in members of his crew. She had chestnut-brown hair that framed a heart-shaped face and a straight nose that was a bit too long to be called delicate, but that suited her. Her dark brows winged over honey-colored eyes that looked like they knew too much. But those eyes were innocent just the same. A mark against her—innocence didn't do well in his world.

He motioned for Werner to come forward and bent his head so the boy could whisper in his ear about the girl—about how she'd nearly killed Charlie Murphy, a fellow so deep in Tammany's pocket, he'd never find his way out. About how the girl hadn't confessed what her affinity was, but that she'd stolen the brooch from right beneath Bridget Malone's chin and the madam hadn't been able to lift a finger to stop her. Hadn't even seen her take it.

All interesting enough. But again, dangerous considering the fragile state of his own affinity these days.

"Do you know who I am?" he asked, watching every minute flicker of her expression.

The girl was silent before she spoke, but when she did, her voice was clear, deferent but not cowed. "Miss Malone said you were someone who could offer protection."

Once he might have been able to read her as easily as an open book, but even with his weakened affinity, he could taste the lie in her words. She knew exactly who he was but wasn't trying to sway him with overblown praise, as many would have.

"Why would I waste my time doing a thing like that?" he asked, curious about how her voice seemed to suggest fear but not own it. She was either a brilliant actress or someone had taught her—and taught her well.

"I'm a good worker. I'd be loyal to you," she pressed.

"You'd have to be damn near a miracle considering the trouble you'd cause me if I took you on. Charlie Murphy wouldn't be pleased, and the last thing I want right now is Tammany Hall after me."

In truth, Charles Murphy and everyone like him could go sit on his own thumb as far as Dolph was concerned. Those stuffed pigeons at Tammany thought they ran the city. Let them keep thinking it, Dolph had always said to any who worried. The truth would always out. Tammany could chase paper and manufacture votes—he had other plans.

"I can make it worth your while," the girl said, straightening her spine. She was nearly as tall as Werner when she stood at her full height.

"I have more than enough dips right now," he said after weighing his choices. He glanced to Werner. "Send her back to Corey."

"*No,*" the girl said as she twisted violently and freed herself from Werner. "You don't have any like me."

The crowd around him went still and watchful at the commotion as she managed to evade the boy's attempt to grab her again.

Dolph raised a hand for him to wait, and the girl stepped closer to his table.

"I can steal anything," she said. "My marks never see me coming or going. I've never once been caught. *Never.*"

It didn't take any magic to see there was no lie in her words this time.

Again, Dolph tried to sense the flavor of her affinity. Before that night on the bridge, it would have been an easy enough thing to accomplish, but not anymore. The barroom was too full of magic for him to separate the girl's from the others.

"You *need* me," she added, pushing a loose piece of hair out of her eyes.

He huffed out a breath, amused. She must have known that he could take everything she held dear and twist it to breaking, but still she wasn't afraid. It took quite a bit to impress him, but Dolph Saunders thought this girl might have enough backbone to do just that. Maybe if things weren't so precarious.

Nibs cleared his throat.

Dolph frowned at the interruption. He would have made an example of anyone else, but Nibsy was rarely wrong about his impulses. And at the moment Nibs was eyeing the girl thoughtfully.

"You think we should keep her?" Dolph asked.

"What could it hurt to see what she can do?" He glanced over at Dolph. "She might have her uses."

Dolph turned to the girl. "I doubt you're anything special," he said, a bold-faced lie. But best make sure the girl didn't know he was too interested. "Still . . . if Bridget thinks you might be of help—"

Before he could finish speaking, the lights in the barroom surged, glowing so brightly that many of those drinking at the bar and at tables around the room squinted, raising their arms to shield themselves from the glow. The lights pulsed twice, the energy in the room flickering and crackling, and then the electric in the barroom went out completely.

The city was used to the power surges and outages that came with the ever-growing expansion of the electrical grid, but this had been something more. The second the room had plunged into darkness, he felt like what little remaining magic he had was gone.

For a moment he felt the shock of being hollowed out. *Empty.* Like a living death.

LISA MAXWELL

It had lasted less than a minute, but the stark terror he'd experienced when his magic was briefly torn from him left a coldness behind that went clear to the bone. Even after the lamps were lit and the room was aglow, his skin still felt chilled despite the stuffy warmth of the saloon.

A BAD BUSINESS

iola Vaccarelli watched as the lamps around the edges of the saloon were lit, illuminating the apprehensive expressions of the patrons. She understood the nervous glances they traded with one another, because she'd felt it too. The blackout had been something more than the usual inconvenience.

Dolph caught her eye from across the room. He was already making his way through the uneasy crowd to where she stood behind the bar.

Leaning on the bar for support, he spoke in low tones, as though he didn't want anyone else to hear. "You felt that?"

Viola made a pretense of polishing a glass, but gave him a subtle nod as she kept her attention on the room, alert for any sign of attack. "What was it?" she murmured low enough so the patrons at the bar couldn't hear.

Behind her, a man called for another drink, but she ignored him and set a glass in front of Dolph instead.

"No idea."

But she didn't miss the way his hand tightened on the cane. Ever since the night on the bridge, the night they lost Leena, Dolph had been changed. She knew the loss had been a blow, but there had to be something more to have made him so different. Where once he never betrayed his worries, now he was often on edge.

The customer down the bar was whistling now, hooting to get Viola's attention as he thumped his glass on the counter. "Hey! You hear me or what, puttana?" the man called.

Dolph glanced over and began to push himself away from the bar, but Viola tapped his arm and shook her head slightly. She didn't need protection, at least not from some drunken stronzo making a nuisance of himself.

"Scusa," she said, her other hand already finding the familiar cool weight of the knife she had tucked into her skirts. "I'll be right back."

"Try not to kill him too badly," Dolph said, pulling away from her and smiling softly into his glass.

Viola made sure she had the man's attention before she gave him a slow, warm smile. He elbowed the customer sitting next to him, gloating at his success, as she began to approach him. She let him think she was interested, amused even at his antics, and with the smile still on her face, she drew the knife and with a flick of her wrist sent it sailing through the air.

The satisfying *thunk* of it finding a sheath in the cast zinc vibrated down the length of the bar, and she didn't hide her laugh at the look of surprised horror that flashed across the man's face. She took her time closing the distance between them to retrieve her blade, and when she finally made it to the end of the bar, she leaned across to whisper a warning into his ear.

When she pulled back, away from the rank stink of his body and the beer on his breath, she saw that the man's face had all but drained of color. *Va bene.* Good.

"Thank you for not skewering him," Dolph said with a hint of humor when she returned.

Viola made a throaty sound of disapproval under her breath. "You've told me it's a bad business to kill the customers, no?" she said tartly. She had trouble controlling her accent when she was angry, and for a moment she heard her mother in her own voice and felt a fierce pang of longing.

"I appreciate you watching out for my bottom line," Dolph mused. "Perhaps you could also watch out for my property? I'll have to pay to repair what you've done to my bar." He frowned thoughtfully. "I'm not even sure I *can* repair the mark that knife of yours left."

Viola shrugged off his concern. "Leave it as a warning," she said, picking up another glass to distract herself.

"I might," he said after a second.

She could practically feel him watching her, as he often did when he was trying to press her into opening up to him. But she didn't have anything to say. What was done was done. She'd made her choices, and if she had regrets, she'd save them for Father McGean.

"What sort of game was that trick with the lights?" At first the voice seemed to come out of nowhere, but then Jianyu materialized next to Dolph, his elbows resting on the bar as though he'd been there all along.

He probably had been, Viola thought with some irritation. Jianyu's ability to disappear was a skill that came in handy when Dolph needed to know things, but it was less opportune for the rest of them. In Dolph's crew, it was nearly impossible to keep secrets—no matter how personal they might be.

Jianyu had been with them only a little over a year. Maybe Dolph trusted the boy after so short a time, but Viola was still uneasy around him. Especially when he looked as humorless as he did then.

Dolph lowered his voice and slipped into Cantonese, and the two went back and forth for a moment in tense, low tones, effectively keeping Viola from their conversation. As her frustration—and temper—began to grow, she thumped the glass down to get their attention, but they were too engrossed in their argument to notice.

Just as she'd finally had enough and was about to say something, Jianyu's posture changed. "You really think it could have been the Order?" he asked, doubt thick in his voice. "It doesn't seem their style to strike so broadly. Too much risk that it would affect more than our kind."

Viola hated to admit it, but . . . "He's right. The Order usually prefers to strike in secret."

"I don't know what else it could have been," Dolph admitted. "There's been no word on the streets?"

Jianyu shook his head. "Not even a whisper."

"I don't like it," Viola said. "Nothing good happens when the rats all go to ground."

"I agree," Jianyu said, giving Viola an appreciative glance. Then he tilted his head to gesture across the room. "Who's the girl? I saw her come in with Werner. She moves like a cat about to pounce."

Viola couldn't keep herself from smiling at the aptness of the description.

"Bridget sent her." Dolph downed the rest of the ale and passed the glass back to Viola. "Tells me she's a thief."

"You have enough of those already," Viola said, dismissing the idea as easily as Dolph had.

"Bridget doesn't usually waste my time. Nibs thinks she might be of use."

"You will try her?" Jianyu asked.

Dolph squinted across the room to where Werner and the girl stood. "Yes. I think I will," he said. "Profits have been down lately, especially with the last raid. If she can work the Dead Line undetected, she could be an asset."

The girl didn't look like much. She was tall, yes, and she held herself with a calmness that Werner certainly didn't have. But her clothes were too fine, her skin too fresh and soft. It took strength to last in Dolph Saunders' world, and from across the room, Viola wasn't sure the girl had it.

"And if she can't?" Viola asked, almost feeling sorry for her.

"It won't be my loss, now, will it?"

No, it wouldn't be, Viola thought. Dolph was good to his people and did what he could to protect them. Certainly he'd feel regret about her loss, as he did about Spot and Appo . . . and certainly he mourned Leena still. But he valued those who could take care of themselves.

In that way he wasn't that different from the other bosses. In the Bowery it wasn't always a matter of good and evil. Often it was a matter of what you could live with. What—or who—you were willing to sacrifice to survive. It was a lesson she'd learned well enough herself.

Dolph clapped Jianyu on the shoulder. "I need information. If it was the Order, they'll be celebrating. Someone will slip up."

Jianyu finished his drink. "I will look into it myself."

Dolph tilted his head toward Viola, who came closer. "That girl—I want you to keep an eye on her for me tonight, eh? She'll have no second chance here."

TO STEAL THE NIGHT

Esta watched Dolph Saunders make his way back across the sawdust-covered floor of the saloon to where she and Werner waited. He walked unevenly, putting his weight on the cane he held in his left hand, but Esta didn't mistake that for a weakness. Not with the way patrons parted for him without a word as he passed.

And not with the way the two at the bar had followed his every move, like he was the center of their universe. The girl behind the bar didn't look much older than Esta herself, maybe seventeen. Then there was the boy who had appeared, it seemed, out of nowhere. One minute the space next to Dolph had been empty, and then in a blink, the boy had materialized.

He wore his black hair in a long braid down his back in an older style she'd seen in Chinatown when she'd stolen the Dragon's Eye. He was dressed in the style of the day: close-fitting vest and trim pants, but his black shirt was made of silk and had a mandarin collar. Like the girl, he clearly had talents of his own, but even from across the barroom, Esta could tell from his posture that he held a wary respect for Dolph.

"My apologies," Dolph said, taking his seat at the small round table once more and pinning them with his one-eyed stare.

"The lights—" Werner shifted into anxious German, as though to keep Esta from understanding.

"It happens," Dolph said, cutting him off.

But Esta understood it was a lie. The flare of the lights had been something more than an outage. It wasn't that Dolph Saunders had any visible tell—he kept his voice calm, his posture easy and still—but with the unease permeating the barroom, the man's stillness spoke volumes.

He turned to Esta and shifted back into the unaccented English he'd originally spoken in. "I've decided to give you a trial."

She bobbed her head in acknowledgment and thanks, keeping all trace of the victory she was feeling from her expression. She was one step closer to her goal.

"Don't be so pleased with yourself. Not yet, at least," he growled. "It's been a slow night, and I've seen at least fifteen leave already because of that trick of the lights. Nobody else is going to come in this late, especially with the power still out. If you're going to work for me, the thing you need to know before we begin is that I hate to lose and I can't stand waste. Tonight will be both—a loss of profit and a waste of my employees' talents. Rectify that. You've got twenty minutes to turn me a profit for this evening." He leaned forward, a gleam in his eye. "Steal me the night, girl."

Esta couldn't help but smile. *Steal me the night,* like it was an impossible task. Like she hadn't been born to do exactly that.

Her limbs might have still felt drained, and the back of her head still ached from whatever they'd hit her with earlier, but her blood was free of the opium's effects now, so without a word she turned and lost herself in the crowd. Even with the electric lights still out, there was barely room to step between the bleary-eyed men and women who stared morosely into their cups. Easy pickings, really.

But these weren't the sort of marks Esta usually gravitated to. They had a desperation hanging about them, an air of exhaustion and hope and regret all mingled with the warmth of their magic. They probably worked long hours to afford what little relaxation an evening at the Strega could give them. She wouldn't steal from them. Not even for Dolph Saunders.

Besides, she had the sense it wouldn't be enough to bring him a pile of their coins. To earn his respect and a place in his world, it would take more than money.

From behind the bar, the girl watched, tracking her through the barroom with subtle adjustments but never actually looking in Esta's direction. No doubt Dolph had instructed her to keep an eye on her . . . which gave Esta an idea.

It didn't take her twenty minutes, but the opium had drained her more than she'd expected, and it took every bit of her energy to slip through time undetected as she made her way around the saloon, selecting her prizes. It was barely twelve minutes later when she faced Dolph Saunders once again.

"You've got more time," he said, barely glancing up at her. "I told you, I can't abide waste."

In reply, she tossed a fat leather wallet onto the table, the money within spilling out of the unlocked clasp. The eyes of the man standing behind Dolph went wide in recognition, and he reached into his coat, searching for the wallet that was sitting in front of him.

Dolph watched as the man picked up the wallet and counted the bills inside. Then he turned back to Esta, unimpressed. "With more time, you could have brought me twice as much."

"I can only bring you what they're carrying, and in this crowd, that isn't much," she told him easily. "If I take all of it, what will they have left to buy your drinks with?"

Dolph Saunders frowned before glancing up at Werner. "Tell Bridget I can't use her."

Esta ignored him. She pulled out a brightly polished brass disk she'd taken from the guy who'd appeared at the bar and set it on the table. It turned out he wasn't actually invisible. When she slowed time, she could see that he'd simply been manipulating the light and shadows of the room, bending them around him to make it seem like he'd disappeared.

Dolph Saunders stared at the disk. "Impressive. Though you can buy these anywhere over on Mott Street these days."

"I haven't been to Mott Street today. Do they sell these there as well?" She tossed a gleaming silver knife with a thin stiletto blade onto the table before he could finish. It slid across the scarred wooden surface and came to a rest in front of him, the sharp point aimed directly at him. The bare tang of the knife had a series of arrowlike marks like the letter *V* cut into the metal.

Dolph Saunders looked up at Esta then, piercing her with that too-steady gaze of his. "You must not value your life to steal from Viola."

"On the contrary—I value myself too much to do anything less." She leaned forward, propping herself on the table so they were eye to eye. "I can steal you all the coins you want. Even if I'd taken every penny from every pocket here tonight, there would have still been room for you to doubt my value. But I can do more for you than steal a few dollars. Like I said . . ." She pulled out her final coup and held it up so the entire table could see. "I can steal anything. No one can catch me. Not your crew . . ." With that, she gently set the silver gorgon head in front of Dolph. "Not even you."

Dolph Saunders picked up the piece that had, moments before, been securely attached to the top of his cane. His features were unreadable as he examined it and confirmed that, indeed, she'd managed to steal the carved silver face from right under his nose. Right out from his hands, to be exact. Then he looked up at her with that cold, single-eyed stare.

Esta shifted uneasily. For the first time all evening, she thought maybe she had gone too far. Maybe she should have stopped with the barmaid's knife. A strange circle of silence surrounded Dolph Saunders' table, as though everyone who'd remained could sense that something in the air had changed—and not for the better.

But then Dolph huffed out an almost amused breath, and his hard mouth turned up slightly into what might have been a smile. It changed something in his face—not that it made him look less intimidating. A smile on Dolph Saunders was like one on a tiger: surprising, unsettling, and most of all, a reminder that the cat had teeth.

He took his time refitting the knob onto his case, shaking his head again as he examined the completed piece. Then he glanced over at the boy next to him, who gave a barely perceptive nod. "Thank Bridget for me," Dolph said finally. "I'll take the girl on. For now, at least."

LISA MAXWELL

Werner backed away from the table, but any relief she might have felt was quickly erased by the realization that she was now alone with Dolph Saunders and the rough-looking boys standing behind his table. They were all built like boxers, and their tailored vests were cut to emphasize their trim waists and wide shoulders. Each boy wore a common uniform of an outlandishly bright shirt and a derby hat cocked to the left over his slicked-back hair.

Not boys, Esta reminded herself. In this city, even boys no older than fifteen would have been men for years. Each would have earned their swagger by surviving childhood, and then by finding and keeping a place in an organization like the Devil's Own. She'd be an idiot to mistake their youth for innocence. Or to forget how dangerous their world had made them.

"What's your name, girl?" Dolph said, peering up at her.

"Esta. Esta Filosik."

"Filosik? I don't know that name. Where are your people?"

"I don't know," she said, giving him the truth. "I never knew them."

Dolph clenched his jaw and studied her. "If you bring me any trouble—"

"I won't," she interrupted.

He waited a second longer, and the whole barroom seemed to be holding its breath, waiting for his final pronouncement.

Dolph motioned for one of the boys to come forward, a ginger-haired guy who was dressed in a red shirt that clashed with his pale, freckled skin. The boy's tightly fitted vest emphasized his broad, stocky shoulders, and a ridiculous-looking cravat was tied in a complicated knot at his throat. His outfit made him look like he was playing at being a gentleman, but a winding tattoo barely visible at the top edge of his collar contradicted the look. The mark on his neck looked like the top of a circle—a wide, ornate arc that clearly had more to it—but Esta couldn't make out any detail in the dimly lit barroom.

"Mooch here'll show you to your room," Dolph informed her when he was done speaking to the boy. "Tomorrow you start working the Dead Line. Don't make me regret it."

THE DEAD LINE

The next morning Esta was already awake and dressed in the same green velvet she'd worn the day before—the only clothing she had left—when the dull *thump* sounded at the door. She opened it to find a familiar silver knife sunk into the wood and the girl with dark hair—and an even darker expression—waiting in the hall.

The barmaid from the night before stepped forward and pried her knife from the door. She was about a head shorter than Esta and dressed in a simple skirt and plain-fronted blouse instead of the low-cut gown she'd been wearing when Esta had stolen her stiletto. Her eyes were the most startling shade of deep violet, and a mass of wavy hair was pinned into a loose knot at the nape of her neck. Her wide, soft mouth was pulled down into a disapproving frown.

"My name is Viola," she said with a low, throaty voice that still carried the faintest hint of her native Italian. She made a show of cleaning the tip of her blade and didn't bother to look at Esta when she spoke. "I don't like you. Dolph, he tells me not to kill you for taking my knife, so I won't. *This* time." She finally lifted her violet gaze, pointing the razor-sharp tip of the blade at Esta as she spoke. "But don't test me again. Capisce?"

Esta raised her hands to signal her understanding.

Viola slid the knife back into the slit in the side of her skirt before handing her a worn wool cloak and giving a jerk of her head. "Come. We'll get you something to fill your belly. Today you work the Dead Line."

Viola took her downstairs to the Strega's kitchen and introduced her to Tilly Malkov, a girl with mouse-brown hair. Tilly offered Esta a hunk of hard, crusty bread, a cup of burnt coffee swimming with cream, and a welcoming smile that crinkled the corners of her soft green eyes.

Esta took the seat at the large kitchen table that Tilly offered her, but as she picked at her bread, she kept a watchful eye on Viola.

After a few minutes, Tilly surprised Esta by touching her hand. "Don't worry so much," she said. As she spoke, a tingling warmth spread like sunshine on a summer's day over Esta's skin. She gave an amused nod toward Viola. "That one isn't so bad. She's all honey and no sting," she said with a wink.

Esta pulled her hand away, feeling unaccountably better, more relaxed, but also more on edge.

"Don't listen to her. Libitina here stings just fine," Viola told her, spinning the point of her stiletto knife on the tabletop with a menacing look in her eyes.

"You named your knife," Esta said, amused even as Viola glared. "*Of course* you named your knife."

The mouse-haired girl only smiled and shook her head, dismissing them both as she wiped her hands on her apron and went back to work at the stove. Viola continued to scowl as she polished her blade, but Esta didn't miss the way Viola's eyes followed Tilly's every move. Or the way her cheeks flushed anytime Tilly glanced up with a warm smile.

When they were finished eating, Viola led Esta out the back entrance of the saloon, onto Elizabeth Street. The snow from the day before was starting to melt, leaving the streets and sidewalks a murky mess that already smelled of the manure and garbage the banks of snow had covered.

"So . . . ," Esta began, in an attempt to break their awkward silence. She pulled the borrowed cloak around her, glad for its warmth. "You and Tilly . . . ?"

Viola turned on her sharply, her expression fierce.

"Sorry," Esta said, realizing her misstep. "It's just . . . the way you watched her," she tried to explain. "I thought maybe—"

"We're friends," Viola snapped, but her cheeks had gone pink again, and Viola wasn't the type of girl who wore a blush well.

"Of course you are," Esta corrected. "My mistake," she said, feeling a sudden ambivalence. She knew better than to let her own modern sensibilities affect her on a job. It was sloppy of her, dangerous. But behind the censure in Viola's eyes was fear . . . maybe even sadness?

Viola stomped off again without another word on the matter.

It was easy enough to keep up with Viola's shorter strides, but harder to let it go. After a block of walking in silence except for the crunch of the snow beneath their feet, Esta couldn't stand the rigid set of Viola's shoulders anymore. "For what it's worth," she said softly without slowing their pace, "she seems wonderful."

Viola stopped short. "Yes," Viola agreed, tossing a wary look toward Esta. "She is." She waited another two heartbeats, as if daring Esta to push again, before she turned and continued down the bustling sidewalk. But this time her steps were softer and her expression didn't have the same wariness as it had moments before.

Unlike the wide boulevard that was the Bowery, Elizabeth Street was a narrow jumble of redbrick buildings all butted up against one another. The shops were opening for the day, and the shopkeepers had already started rolling carts of merchandise out to the sidewalks. Above their cluttered display windows, fire escapes clung to the sides of the buildings. Long underwear and shirts fluttered from them like invisible people who had decided to stop to lean against the railings and watch the scene below.

"The first rule," Viola said, drawing herself up as though the whole conversation about Tilly had never happened, "is you don't take from our own. You work the cars or the streets north of Houston. You work the Line and the banks, but you don't dip into pockets Dolph protects. The second rule, you don't cross any of the other bosses. Dolph works hard to keep Paul Kelly and Monk Eastman off his people. He don't need you messing that up."

"How will I know who's who?"

Viola gave her an impatient scowl. "You'll figure it out. One way or another."

The two went a couple of blocks farther and then cut over a block to where a horse-drawn streetcar rattled to a stop at a curb nearby. Viola opened the door at the back of the bus-shaped vehicle and directed Esta inside. After Viola placed a couple of coins into a battered metal box at the front of the car, they found seats on the two narrow wooden benches along the length of the smudged windows. With the windows closed against the cold, the car smelled strongly of the tobacco spit that stained the floor and the sharp, metallic reek of motor oil.

Outside, the bright signs of the dance halls and glittering windows of cheap jewelry stores gave way to more sedate shops, each piled with canned goods and household items. Then they turned onto Canal Street, past the legendary prison built to look like an Egyptian tomb.

"Have you been with Dolph long?" Esta asked.

Viola glanced at her out of the corner of her eye. "Long enough," she said, turning her attention back to the street passing outside the window.

"And you like working for him?" Esta tried again.

At first Viola seemed to ignore the question, but then, just when Esta thought she wouldn't answer, she turned. "Look. We're probably not gonna be friends, you and me. I don't need any more friends. I don't need the chitchat the ladies make with each other over the weather or the price of meat. I work for Dolph because I want to work, and he lets me. Do I like it?" she said with a shrug. "I'm not married to some fat idiota, having his babies one after another, am I? I work hard, maybe, but I'm good at what I do. Dolph gives me that much. What else is there to like?"

"Nothing," Esta murmured her understanding. She knew what it was to need to feel useful. If Professor Lachlan hadn't found her, she'd probably be unaware of what she was, what she could do. She couldn't imagine what it would be like to never feel the deep, echoing satisfaction of a job well done. To simply be ordinary—or worse, a freak in her world, where magic was nothing more than a bedtime story. Maybe Professor Lachlan had never been what anyone would call an affectionate father, but he'd given her that much.

About fifteen minutes into the jarring ride, the streetcar slowed next to a curb, and Viola gestured for Esta to get out.

"We're at City Hall," Esta said, recognizing the building.

Viola made a dismissive sound in her throat. "We gonna walk a little farther, and then you go on your own."

"On my own?" Esta blinked, surprised at this pronouncement. She'd assumed Viola had been sent to watch her.

"You told Dolph you're a good thief, no?"

"Yes . . . ," Esta said slowly, not liking where this was going.

"The tricks you did last night don't prove nothing. You want Dolph's protection? Then you earn it by working the Line." Viola pointed down the street they were walking. "It used to be good pickings down on Wall Street with all the bankers. Fat wallets. Lots of gold and jewels. Easy items to fence. But a few years back, Inspector Byrnes drew the Dead Line.

"Byrnes is gone, but the Line's still there. Downtown, they pick up any known pickpocket on sight. Dolph loses a lot of his boys that way. But you're new, and you say you can steal anything?" She shrugged. "So you'll work the Dead Line. Maybe you won't get caught."

"And if I do?"

Viola glanced at her, indifferent. "My advice? You don't get caught. The Tombs isn't a place for a girl, not even a big girl like you," Viola said, cocking a mocking brow toward Esta.

They walked on down Park Row, past the towering double turrets of a castlelike building looming above them, and then on past a lonely-looking cemetery, its tombstones like broken teeth sticking out from the remaining snow. When they rounded the corner, Esta found herself staring up at the brownish-gray exterior of St. Paul's.

"This is as far as I go," Viola said, coming to a stop near the deep covered portico of the chapel. "They know me there, but you keep walk-ing, three, maybe four blocks thataway, and you'll find the bankers. Should be easy to make your quota if you're half as good as you claim. If you don't come back . . ." She shrugged. "You'll find your way, or we won't have to worry about you no more."

AS ABOVE, SO BELOW

Viola was right. South of Fulton Street, the city's financial district was heaven for a thief. Bankers and lawyers with fat wallets and jeweled pins. Women with purses filled with coins. Easy pickings.

And a complete waste of time.

Even without using her affinity, it didn't take her long to get her quota and then some. Less than an hour later, she'd found her way back to a streetcar heading north and was on her way uptown.

She still wore the empty silver cuff under the sleeve of her gown, a reminder of what was at stake, of what she had to do. All night, she'd tossed and turned in the narrow, musty-smelling bed—if you could even call it that—thinking about her missing stone. Planning her next move.

Professor Lachlan had warned her it was too much of a risk to change anything about the heist, but he hadn't known—or hadn't warned her—that Ishtar's Key would basically incinerate. She hadn't planned on being trapped in the past.

She was already working blind when it came to Dolph Saunders. She needed more information, more options in case things didn't go as planned, because *nothing* could stop her from getting Ishtar's Key. Not when the future held Dakari, shot and possibly dying. No one would come looking for him, not until he didn't return and it was too late.

According to the clipping she'd lifted from Professor Lachlan's notebook, Khafre Hall was located on Park Avenue. In her own time, that part of Park Avenue was an elevated road leading into Grand Central, but in 1902, the gleaming white facade of the terminal didn't exist. If the world of lower Manhattan felt eerily familiar earlier that morning, the streets of Midtown looked like a completely different world. The soaring skyscrapers that would one day box in the sky weren't even a dream yet. Instead, the avenue was lined by shorter, ornately decorated buildings— stately homes and large hotels, and just north of Forty-First Street, the enormous edifice that was Khafre Hall.

The Order's headquarters might have been named for one of the great pyramids, but with its four stories of white marble, it looked more like a transplanted villa from the Italian Renaissance. Esta didn't have any doubt she'd found the right place, though. High atop the roof, gold statues of various gods glinted beneath the winter's sun. Above the building's main entrance, the cornice was carved with the words AS ABOVE, SO BELOW, a phrase supposedly coined by Hermes Trismegistus, the mythic combination of the Greek god Hermes and the Egyptian Toth that the Order saw as its precursor. The heavy bronze doors were inscribed with a symbol Esta recognized easily as the Philosopher's Hand—an alchemical recipe depicting the secrets of unlocking occult powers.

Professor Lachlan had taught her all this as part of her training. He'd shown her the different representations of the hand to teach her about the theories of alchemy, to explain how the Order misunderstood and perverted the very notion of magic by trying to divide existence into neat parts in their efforts to control it.

The building was impressive, a declaration of the Order's beliefs and a demonstration of their power in this city. The fact that they never rebuilt after the theft of the artifacts was evidence of how much they'd been weakened. But the building as it was now served as a reminder of all she would have to face. Of all she still had left to lose. Even from her vantage point across the street, it looked impenetrable.

The street was quiet, so she took the clipping from its hidden pocket to look over it again for some clue of what had happened. But when she unfolded the delicate paper, the once-clear type looked blurred, smudged. The individual letters seemed to wriggle and writhe on the page, like they were trying to transform themselves into other letters, to rearrange themselves into other words.

Esta blinked hard and rubbed at her tired eyes, sure that she must be seeing things, but when she looked back, the words remained stubbornly unreadable. It was as though the future that had once been an established fact was no longer clear or determined. The heist was no longer an established fact.

"No," she whispered to herself as she brought the paper closer to her eyes. Like she didn't have perfect eyesight. Like getting closer would do something to stop the words from swirling and shifting on the page.

She hadn't done anything wrong . . . had she?

"You!" The voice came from so close that she barely had time to turn before the man from the night before had ahold of her wrist. His face was blackened and bruised from her brutal attempt to escape, but now a hideously gleeful expression lit his features. "I thought that was you."

She tried to jerk away, using her erratic motions as a cover for the way she crumpled the clipping and slipped it into her sleeve. "Let me go," she demanded, struggling against him. "I don't want to hurt you again." And the last thing she wanted was to draw attention from anyone inside Khafre Hall.

Charlie Murphy only laughed and started tugging her across the street. "You won't have the chance to hurt me again, not when I'm through with you." He laughed again, and his grip on her wrist tightened as he wrenched her arm painfully, pulling her close enough that she could smell the sourness of his breath.

"Let me go," she said, refusing to plead.

"I know what you are. I recognized what you did at the Haymarket," he said with an almost unholy anticipation lighting his face. "I'd planned to hunt for you. I was looking forward to seeing the fear in your eyes when we found you."

"So sorry to disappoint," she snarled, grabbing the arm he held her wrist with. Calling on every one of the techniques Dakari had taught her, she twisted violently. The move caught him by surprise, as she'd intended, and he released her with a yelp of pain.

But it only slowed him for a moment. The look of anticipation he'd worn moments ago was now transformed to seething hate. She needed to get away, but before she could pull time to a slow, Murphy's eyes went wide. He went completely rigid before collapsing hard and motionless to the ground.

The way his body had jerked and then fallen had jarred her enough that she'd lost her hold on time, and before she could regain it, her arms were pinned to her sides and she was surrounded by an earthy, spicy scent that reminded her of patchouli. A soft, disembodied voice whispered in her ear to be still, and Esta realized that maybe Dolph hadn't let her go off alone after all.

THE CURRENCY OF SECRETS

Dolph had been right to be suspicious of the new girl. What business could she possibly have here at Khafre Hall?

With her arms wrapped around her, pinning her in place, Jianyu could practically hear her thinking. Her whole body had gone tense and ready to fight, and he was not so stupid as to underestimate her. He'd seen the way she'd dispensed of Murphy, and he didn't doubt she had something equally unpleasant in mind for him. She was no innocent, fresh off the boat and adrift in a dangerous city. She was too well trained.

"Unless you want Dolph to know of this, be still," he whispered.

The girl hesitated, but a moment later the fight went out of her, enough that he could guide her down the street, away from the watching eyes of Khafre Hall. The moment they were around the corner, he let go of the light and revealed himself.

He didn't release her arm, though.

"You followed me?" she asked, eyeing him.

"Did you expect you wouldn't be watched? Dolph Saunders doesn't trust easily, and for good reason, it appears. Why did you come here?"

"I was going for a walk," she said flatly. "It's a beautiful day."

"So you took a stroll in front of Khafre Hall?" he asked, amused.

Her mouth went tight, but she didn't answer. Yes, she was well trained indeed to keep so composed when she'd clearly been caught red-handed. She had to know that lies would be pointless now.

"Why aren't you still working? The sun is barely at midday."

"I'm done," she said.

It didn't seem to be a lie, but she hadn't been downtown long enough to be finished. Especially without magic. He'd followed her, concealing himself carefully, and he hadn't so much as sensed a whisper of her affinity. "Your quota was thirty-five dollars. That's more than most men make in a month," he said.

"I can show you my purse if you don't believe me. But you'll have to let me go so I can get to it." She glanced up at him, a sly look in her eyes. "It's under my skirts."

"It doesn't explain why you're here, at the Order's hall," he said, not taking the bait.

Her expression was steady. "I wanted to see it for myself."

"Why?" he pressed, not yet sensing a lie.

"Don't you want to know your enemy?" she asked.

"The Order, you see them as your enemy?"

"You don't?" She threw the question back at him.

But Jianyu didn't answer. He didn't owe her his story. "I'm going to release you, and then we are going to return to the Bella Strega."

"You'll tell Dolph about what happened, won't you?" she asked, frowning.

"Not if you come quietly." When surprise bunched her expression, he explained. "I find it to be more beneficial at this moment to have you in my debt."

"I'm not sure I want to be in your debt."

He inclined his head. "An astute observation. Feel free to tell Dolph yourself, then, about how you wandered off from your assigned post and were almost caught by a member of the Order outside Khafre Hall."

From the look on her face, he knew it would never happen.

"Of course, you could try to fight me, or you could attempt to run off. In that case, I will tell Dolph everything. You will not be in my debt, but you will also never be safe in this city again. Not with Dolph Saunders and his people looking for you."

She frowned. "I don't like being threatened."

"No one does," he told her. "Though if you truly mean us no harm, my words pose no threat."

Her expression was still shuttered and angry, but also intelligent. He could tell the moment she understood she had very little choice. "Fine," she said sourly. "I'm Esta, by the way. You should probably know my name if you plan on blackmailing me."

He let go of her arm. "I am Jianyu Lee. And I already knew your name."

Esta frowned, looking down at her wrist as though she expected to find some mark. "Great. Glad we got that cleared up," she muttered. Glancing up at him, she made a small flourish with her hand. "Well, what are we waiting for? Lead the way."

When they arrived back at the Strega, Dolph Saunders was sitting in his usual place in the back of a full barroom. Jianyu knew the crowd wasn't there to drink, though.

He sensed the girl's curiosity as she watched the men and women approach Dolph's table, one by one.

It wasn't an unfamiliar scene in the poorest neighborhoods. All of the gang bosses traded in favors and kept their people in line through their debts. Jianyu's uncle, at least in name, often held court in a similar way. On Mott Street, Tom Lee collected bribe money to keep the police away from fan-tan dealers and to provide protection from the Hip Sing highbinders. It was only a small part of the life of Chinatown, but it was one Jianyu knew too well. And one he hated.

He'd come to this country, to this city, because Lee promised him a better future than he'd had in his own country, but he'd arrived to find that Lee had smuggled him into the country not to help him but to use him. With his affinity for light, he could make himself impossible to see, which meant he could strike without warning. But he hadn't left his home, his mother, and everything else behind to be a mercenary for a common criminal like Tom Lee.

Jianyu still didn't know how much he approved of Dolph Saunders' methods, but it was clear that he was different from Tom Lee. The people filling the Strega weren't like those his uncle exploited. They came hat in hand, each with the same stoop to their shoulders that made them look as though they were perpetually carrying some invisible burden. Each would speak with Dolph for a few moments, usually some plea to find a son or for help with their rent or for relief from some other burden.

Debts came due, certainly, but at least Jianyu was never asked to collect on them.

After a minute Dolph looked up and saw them standing at the back of the room. He said something to Nibs, who got up and started making his way through the crowded barroom.

Nibs nodded a silent greeting to Jianyu before turning his attention to the girl.

"You're done already?" he asked, doubtful.

The girl maneuvered her hand through a concealed slit in her skirts and pulled out a small purse. Nibs opened the parcel and thumbed through its contents before lifting his gaze to Dolph and giving him a slight nod.

"I'll take her from here," Nibs told Jianyu.

He bristled at the dismissal but didn't argue. Let them believe him to be obedient. It made it that much easier to know where each of Dolph's crew stood, to know whom to trust. And to file away their secrets for when he might need them.

FOUNDATION WORK

The boy who had dismissed Jianyu was young, with light hair and thick, round spectacles perched on the tip of his thin nose. "They call me Nibs," he said, extending his hand. "Nibsy Lorcan."

Esta eyed him before finally taking it. His ink-stained fingers were firm, but his weren't the rough hands of a fighter, and that fact put her somewhat at ease.

He smiled then, a boyish grin that seemed out of place in the bar-room. "They're all still talking about you. The way you stole the top from Dolph's cane. Everyone's surprised Viola didn't try to skewer you after that stunt you pulled with her knife. No one is allowed to touch her knives—not unless it's the sharp end first, if you know what I mean."

"Delightful," Esta said, feeling suddenly uneasy with so much attention.

The boy peered at her. "I'm not gonna ask you how you managed it. That's your business. For now, at least. But I'll warn you, if Dolph decides you aren't worth the trouble, there won't be anything that anybody can do for you."

"Understood," she said, wondering where Jianyu had gone. She was still on edge after confronting Murphy and then being bested by Jianyu, and she didn't like the idea that he could use her little visit to Khafre Hall against her at any time. "I only want to earn my place here. If there's anything else I can do, any way to be helpful to Dolph—"

"I'll let you know," Nibs said, cutting off the conversation with a gentle smile.

Taking his cue, she changed the subject. "What's happening here?" she said with a jerk of her head.

"It's the weekly gathering," Nibs told her. "People with debts due come to pay them, or to ask for more time. Others come requesting favors."

"Looks lucrative," she mused.

"Oh, Dolph doesn't charge," Nibs said. When she looked at him, surprised, he clarified: "He trades in secrets." The boy shrugged. "Which I guess is lucrative in its own right."

"I bet." She glanced at him. "What secret does he know about you?"

Nibs didn't even blink. "Who says it isn't the other way around?"

She laughed, amused by his unexpected bravado.

The doors to the bar banged open then, a loud clattering burst that had everyone inside looking toward the three figures silhouetted by the light of the afternoon. The boy let out a soft whistle.

"Dolph Saunders!" the middle figure bellowed. "I want the girl."

The barroom went eerily silent as the three men lumbered into the barroom of the Strega. Esta recognized the one on the left as Werner, and at the sight of him, she shifted uneasily, turning away from the center of the room and tipping her head down, to hide her profile.

"Who is that?" she whispered.

The boy's face didn't betray any emotion. "That would be Edward Corey, the owner of the Haymarket. He seems to know who you are. . . ."

Esta's stomach twisted.

Dolph Saunders took his time looking over one last contract, signing his name, and blowing on the ink to dry it. He didn't bother to look up when he finally did answer; he simply picked up the next bunch of papers. "What are you doing here, Corey?" he said, irritation coloring his words. "This isn't your side of town."

"You heard me, Saunders. I'm here for the girl. I know Bridget sent her to you."

The entire room seemed to hold its breath as Dolph considered Corey's statement. "I'm not sure what girl you're referring to. Unlike you, I don't run that sort of business."

"Are you telling me the girl isn't here?" Corey said, taking a few more menacing steps forward. "Or are you telling me that you're protecting her?"

Dolph did look up then. "Anyone here know the girl he's looking for?" he said flatly.

Esta started to move slowly, getting ready to pull time around her and make her escape, but Nibsy's hand snaked out and held her in place. She was stuck. She couldn't do anything without drawing attention to herself, and she couldn't slip through time without giving away what she could actually do to Nibs.

"Give it a moment," Nibs whispered, barely moving his mouth.

A loud scraping noise tore through the silence of the barroom as Dolph Saunders stood, his chair tumbling behind him. "I think you were mistaken, Corey. There's no girl here for you."

"Don't play with me, Saunders. Charlie Murphy wants the girl, and if he doesn't get her, he's going to come after me. I'm not about to let that happen. I'll send him straight to your doorstep. You know he's got friends you can only imagine. They'd pull your license, close this shithole down, and destroy everything you've built for yourself—your entire life—at the snap of my fingers."

"Now, there you've made a mistake," Dolph said softly.

"No mistake. If they find out what you are, they'll take everything you have."

"That would only matter if there was anything I cared about losing," Dolph told him. "But you . . . You have quite a lot to lose, don't you, Corey? You like to play the big man with the boys over at Tammany, don't you?" Dolph shook his head. "I know you're also trying to get yourself in with the Order. You're playing too many sides at once, and if any of them find out what *you* are . . ."

Corey sputtered for a second. "You don't know—"

"I know *everything* about you, Corey," Dolph said, his voice like sandpaper. "I know about the little rendezvous you had with the woman on Broome Street, though I'm guessing her husband doesn't. I know what you had for lunch and what you're thinking about having for dinner. I know who your family is—*what* your family is—so I know you might be weak enough to pass, but I wonder what your friends in the Order would think if they knew the truth?" Dolph paused for a moment, letting the words hang in the air.

"Are you threatening me?"

"Of course not. We're all friends here. We're all in this together . . . unless you turn on us first. But if you don't want everyone else in this city to know as well, you'll get the hell out of my saloon and take yourself back uptown where you belong. You'll deal with Murphy and get him to forget there was ever any girl to find."

Esta began to relax a little as she saw Corey hesitating. His narrow face was becoming an alarming shade of red. "You . . . You . . ." But his words foundered.

"Yes. That's right. Now you're understanding." He glanced at Werner. "I think it's best if you don't show your face here again, don't you?"

Werner nodded weakly, his expression grim as Dolph picked up his chair and sat at the table again, dismissing them all without another word.

Dolph didn't look up again, but four of his larger boys stepped forward, their thick arms crossed over broad chests and a gleam in their eyes that anyone could see was them itching for a good brawl. Corey seemed to get the message, and with a jerk of his head, he left, followed by Werner and the other man.

Esta let out a relieved breath, and the room started cautiously to come back to life.

"Let's go," Nibs whispered to Esta, never letting go of her wrist.

"Go where?"

"Somewhere else," he said. He handed the purse off and tugged her along. "Anywhere else. Trust me. He's going to be in a rotten mood after all that."

They slipped out into the brisk afternoon air. It would be light for a while, but already the Bowery was coming to life for the evening.

"Will Corey really keep Murphy away?"

Nibs shrugged. "He has a good enough reason to. If Murphy found out that Corey was lying to him and the rest of the Order, he'd lose everything. But people don't always act in their own best interest." Nibs peered at her a few seconds longer. "You know, maybe there is something you could do for me—and for Dolph. It would go a long way toward thanking him for protecting you."

"Sure. Anything."

"I'd like you to come see a show with me."

Esta studied him, confused at the odd request. Then, realizing what he was asking, what he intended, her frustration grew. "Look, you seem nice enough," she said as gently as she could, "but I'm not interested."

The boy smiled softly, as though he were amused. "I didn't think you would be. Still, I'd like you to come with me." His tone was sincere enough that she almost believed him.

"I'm only here to work."

"Humor me," he said, tucking his hands into his pockets as he rocked back on his heels. "Consider it part of the job."

Esta narrowed her eyes at him. His position with Dolph made it nearly impossible for her to say no, and he seemed to know it. "Just a show?"

He chuckled. "Okay, fine. There's someone I'd like you to meet." An odd look crossed his face. "But I'm serious about it being part of the job. Dolph's been trying to get this particular guy on the crew for months now, but so far he hasn't been moved by any of my appeals. Maybe you'll have more luck."

"I don't know why I would," she countered

"I got a feeling about you," Nibs said. "Darrigan just might go for a pretty face."

CLASSIC MISDIRECTION

Wallack's Theatre

"T ough crowd tonight," Evelyn said from behind Harte's shoulder as he watched Julius Tannen's monologue fall flat.

He didn't bother to look back at her. He was too busy counting the empty seats in the house. Shorty was right. Things weren't looking good.

At first, the audiences had poured in to see his act. The entire city had been talking about the miracles he'd accomplished on that stage. But the city was only so big. It didn't matter how amazing the effects he presented were—after a while, everyone had seen them. He needed something new.

Better, he needed to get out.

"Any second now they're going to start throwing fruit," he muttered, disgusted.

"I bet you thought you'd escaped from all that when you moved uptown." A smile curved in Evelyn's voice, but there wasn't any warmth. "Just goes to show, even the polish of the upper crust only goes skin deep." She moved closer and lowered her voice. "We missed you last night, after the show."

Harte doubted that very much. Twenty minutes in, they all would have been too numbed by the Nitewein to care about anything but the next pour.

"Still won't tell me who you ran off to see?" she purred, resting her hands on his shoulders and looking up at him. Her eyes were soft, the pupils large and unfocused.

Frowning down at her, Harte wondered suddenly what had made her start drinking so early in the day. But then he realized he didn't really care. It wasn't his place to care. He knew where caring got you.

Harte shrugged off her hands. "No one important."

He didn't need anyone asking questions about his meeting with Jack Grew. It was bad enough that Nibsy Lorcan was following him again. And cornering him like that in the park? It didn't bode well. If Dolph Saunders had an idea of what he was up to . . .

But there couldn't be any way for Dolph to know. Harte had been too careful. Or so he hoped.

He tilted his head, stretching his neck as he tried to loosen himself up. The city had felt almost claustrophobic lately, and the events of the night before hadn't helped things. And not being able to have a proper meal since the girl had assaulted him . . . well, that had only made things worse.

The act onstage was getting the signal from the stage manager to wrap things up, so Harte took one final look at himself in the small mirror on the wall and fixed a smudge in the kohl beneath his right eye as the orchestra trilled the notes that cued his entrance.

Beyond the glare of the footlights, the sparse crowd rustled discontentedly in their seats as he took the stage. The faces in the audience were frowning and clearly impatient to see something worth the price of their fifty-cent ticket. He hadn't planned anything new, but it was too late to do anything about that now.

"Ladies and gentlemen," he called, letting his voice boom over the theater as he settled into the persona he'd perfected for the stage. "I have traveled far and wide to learn the occult arts, the hermetical sciences. Today I bring you evidence that we mere humans might converse with the divine. And that the divine," he said, flourishing his hand to ignite the flare palmed there, "might converse with us in turn."

The ball of fire burst from his palm, hovered for a second in the air, and then vanished. It was a simple enough trick, but it did its job. An interested murmuring rustled through the house as a stagehand rolled out a table filled with props.

"Do not be alarmed," he said, taking up a pair of steel hoops large enough to fit over his head. "This is not the magic of old, wild and untamed, capable of seduction and destruction. There is no danger here," he called, manipulating the rings so that they locked together, came apart. "For my powers come not from the accident of birth, but from careful scientific study and practiced skill. Because I have devoted myself to the mastery of the occult sciences, the powers I demonstrate have no command over me." With a flourish, the hoops seemed to vanish. "Instead, I bend them to my will," he finished, plucking a hoop out of thin air, making it materialize before the audience's very eyes.

The house was silent now, all eyes watching and waiting for what he would do next. Rich or poor, every audience was the same. Some might dismiss tales of the old magic as nothing more than legend. Some might fear its existence still. Most had been taught to hate the people with affinities for it. But like the Order, they all desperately wanted magic to be real. They wanted to believe that something was out there bigger than they were—as long as that something could be controlled by the right sort of people.

He wasn't sorry for using their fears and their hopes, their prejudices and their sense of righteousness against them. For distracting them from the truth. He was simply surviving in a world that hated what he was.

Once the audience was on his side, he felt himself relax into his act. He stripped off his jacket and rolled up his shirtsleeves to show nothing was hidden beneath them before he ran through a series of his usual, seemingly impossible card manipulations and sleight-of-hand tricks. All the while, he drew the audience in with tales of his travels. He told them how he had been a guest in a maharaja's court as he swallowed a dozen single needles and thread, and insisted it was the court's sorcerer who'd taught him to bring the needles back up, threaded neatly at even intervals along the silken string. He'd studied the mysteries of science and alchemy under the most learned men in Europe, and discovered many secrets of the universe in the shadow of the great pyramids.

All lies, of course. He'd never stepped foot off the island of Manhattan, had never even dreamed it was possible until Dolph Saunders had put the idea into his head.

"Ladies and gentlemen," Harte said, drawing the moment out dramatically before he launched into his final effect. "Now I will demonstrate my sovereignty over the forces of life and death. In this, my most daring demonstration, I will require a volunteer. Someone with the strength of will to withstand the lure of the Otherworld and the courage to face what lies beyond the veil of our understanding."

He stepped downstage so that he could see beyond the glare of the footlights, searching for a mark. Usually, he liked to find a man for this effect, preferably a large one who was clearly doubtful or scowling. Someone the audience would believe to be uncertain, skeptical. But as he screened the crowd, he found someone else in the audience—the girl from the Haymarket.

At first he thought she'd come for him. His gut went tight and his whole body felt warm, and for a moment he couldn't move. He could only stare at her, like she was some strange apparition he'd imagined into being.

Then he saw she was sitting next to Nibsy Lorcan, and every last bit of his anticipation went cold.

It couldn't be a coincidence that they were both in the theater, that they had both accosted him the night before. But any of Dolph's people should have known how stupid it was to use magic in the Haymarket. Had the whole thing been some sort of setup? Another way for Dolph to entangle him?

He'd see about that.

Harte made his way down the short flight of steps to the audience, pretending to still be searching for a suitable volunteer. By the time he'd made it to their row, the girl had found something interesting to examine in the stitching of her gloves. Her jaw was tight, and her cheeks were flushed.

Good, Harte thought. *Let her be nervous*. His tongue still throbbed, but damn if the pain didn't also remind him of how it had felt to have her mouth against his. How for a moment—when she had seemed willing to return the kiss—he'd felt a kind of dizzying freedom that part of him itched to have again.

Which just went to show how dangerous she was.

"Miss?" he said, offering her his ungloved hand. "If you would be so kind?"

She glanced up, fear warring with the violence in those strange tawny eyes. "Oh, I'm never kind." She waved him off.

He offered his hand again, but even as she started to refuse, Nibsy was already pushing her to her feet.

"She'd love to," he told Harte. There was a spark of something like anticipation in the boy's eyes.

Seeing Nibsy excited should have put him on guard, but Harte couldn't bring himself to care.

"Don't make a fuss," he murmured when she tried to pull away. Harte was already firmly tucking her arm under his. "You'll only look like a fool." He tightened his arm over hers, pinning her in place at his side.

"I suppose you would know best about that"—she gave him a smile that was all teeth—"seeing how you've made an art of it." Her expression was murderous, but for some insane reason that only made him more curious about her.

Because of his success, girls had been only too happy to smile and fawn on him, but none of them really wanted the person beneath the name. They wanted the polished magician, the showman who could wine and dine them and fulfill their dreams of being onstage themselves. This girl didn't want any of that. She didn't want him at all, at least not that she would admit.

He liked that about her.

Maybe his mother had been right after all—there was clearly something wrong with him.

"Why are you here?" he whispered, focusing on what was important as he led her down the aisle to the stage.

"I was told there'd be entertainment," she said, not caring who heard.

Then she leaned in, as though to tell him a secret, but spoke loudly enough for the front rows to hear. "I think my escort might have overpromised."

Harte swallowed his amusement and schooled his features as the audience tittered. "I see," he said, handing her up the first of the steps to the stage. He followed close behind, and when he got to the top step, he leaned forward and whispered in her ear, "And last night, is that the kind of . . . *entertainment* you prefer?"

She whipped around, outrage sparking in those honey-colored eyes of hers, but he only gave her a wink before addressing the audience.

"Ladies and gentlemen, this lovely creature has been so kind as to grace us with her beauty and courage this fine evening. What is your name, miss?"

The girl scowled at him silently until he cocked an expectant brow. "Esta," she said, apparently realizing that the fastest way off the stage was to cooperate.

"Dear Esta—named for the stars—has graciously volunteered to assist me in one of the most perilous demonstrations of my connection to the powers of the Otherworld." He ignored the girl's snort and motioned to a stagehand, who rolled out a large wooden crate that had been painted to look like an ornate wardrobe.

"If you would examine this wardrobe for any inconsistencies, any false backs . . ." He gestured to the crate. When Esta didn't immediately move, he urged her again. "Please, do remove your gloves and give it a thorough examination." He held out his hands, as though to take her gloves.

The girl gave him another tart look, but she removed her gloves and handed them over to him. The leather was smooth as a petal, and he wondered again where she'd come from and who she was to have such finely made gloves when she was clearly taking orders from Nibsy.

She began inspecting the box, her pert mouth still scowling, and Harte had the sudden, unwelcome memory of the night before, of how her lips had gone soft and almost welcoming for—

"She's a ringer!" a drunken voice called out from the audience, a welcome interruption from the direction his thoughts had taken.

"No, I'm not," the girl called. Then, before he could stop her, she shouted, "You should come up here, too, and see for yourself." She batted her eyes at Harte. "He can come, can't he? You don't have anything to hide . . . do you?"

The audience tittered with laughter.

"Well?" she asked, all mock innocence.

She had him in a corner. *Fine. He'd deal with it, and then he'd deal with her.* He pasted on his most charming smile, as though he were in on the joke, and turned back to the audience. "Of course not."

The heckler turned out to be a large man whose coat was pulled tight across his stomach. While he checked over the cabinet, a nervous and excited energy ran through the audience. But Harte Darrigan didn't make mistakes. Not anymore, and not on *his* stage, where he felt most at home and most in control. No girl was going to change that, no matter how much the sight of her full mouth twisting in amusement reminded him of the night before and how her lips had felt against his. He pressed his still-sore tongue against the sharp point of one of his teeth, to remind himself of what had happened the last time he lost his head over her.

When they both were done, he held out his bare hand to help her into the box, bracing himself for the warmth of her fingers. "If you're satisfied?"

"Oh, I don't know. . . ." There was a vicious gleam in her eyes. "I'm not sure that you have the skills to satisfy," she said loud enough for the audience to hear.

The audience rustled again with more laughter, and someone in the back whistled.

He leaned very close, until he could feel the warmth of her and detect the light, sweet scent from her hair. "No one's ever complained before," he said, offering his bare hand to her again. "Unless you're afraid?"

To the audience, her momentary reluctance probably appeared to be more of her toying with him, but Harte was close enough to see the reason she hesitated before taking his hand. He saw in her golden eyes the inner battle the girl was waging with herself between the choice to meet his challenge or to admit she was nervous. And he saw the moment her pride won.

She gave the audience another dazzling smile, goading them on as she made him wait a moment longer. When she finally slid her long, slender fingers into the palm of his hand, the shock of her warmth was almost enough to distract him from his relief. If he'd had his wits about him, maybe he would have found a way to take better advantage of that moment. But at first he could only look at their two hands joined in the glare of the spotlights—hers soft and surprisingly small against his.

"Well?" she asked, glancing again at the audience she now held in the palm of her hand. "You did promise . . . satisfaction, did you not?"

The heckler, who was still onstage with them, let out a loud, braying laugh, and the audience rustled again, but this time, he fed on their amusement, used it for what came next.

He lifted her hand, presenting her to his public. "The lady will now put herself at my mercy. At the mercy of the powers of the universe around us . . . powers that I control," he said dramatically, as he led her toward the open cabinet. "On my command, she will disappear from this world and travel to the Otherworld beyond until I call her back."

He looked at the girl then, and her tawny eyes were still laughing at him. But when he squeezed her hand gently, pushing his own power through himself, through the fine softness of her skin, those eyes went wide.

She looked down at their joined hands and whispered a single word. It was the kind of curse that most well-bred ladies had never even heard, much less used.

"Maybe later," he whispered as he squeezed her hand again and sent another pulse of energy through his fingertips. He helped her up into the cabinet, relishing the way her brow furrowed in confusion. "Enjoy your trip," he whispered, so the audience couldn't hear.

Harte had to work to keep his face fixed in the serious mask he'd perfected for the stage as he closed the door in her face and latched it securely. He'd enjoyed sparring with her . . . too much. But he didn't have time for her, not on his stage and not in his life. He took the corner of the cabinet and pushed, rotating it like a top. It moved faster and faster, spinning of its own volition, until it was floating inches and then feet off the stage. The audience went silent watching.

Lifting his hands in a dramatic gesture, he made the revolving cabinet stop. Then, all at once, the sides flapped down, so all that remained was a steel-framed box, empty and open. The audience could clearly see the curtain behind it.

A few people in the audience gave some halfhearted applause, but most of the faces remained bored. Unimpressed.

"Perhaps you think this is a matter of mirrors or optical tricks?" He pulled a small, snub-nosed pistol from his jacket, and the audience grew attentive, suddenly interested in what would come next.

"Perhaps you could help me again, sir?" He gestured to his heckler to come forward, then handed him the pistol and a single bullet.

"If you would do the honors of loading this gun?" He turned to his audience. "To guarantee that this is no trick of mirrors, that the girl has well and truly disappeared, I will fire the bullet into that target," he said, gesturing to a large padded mat behind the empty frame of the cabinet.

Harte found Nibsy in the audience and met the boy's eyes. Nibsy's expression was impassive, apparently unconcerned with the girl's safety.

When the man was done with the pistol, Harte took it from him, leveled his arm, and took aim. A drumroll began, low and ominous.

"No!" a female voice called out from the audience.

Harte didn't react. His finger tightened, and the bullet exploded out of the gun, through the empty box, and into the padded target behind.

Scattered applause grew, but the audience was still quiet, waiting. Just the way he liked them. It was never enough to make the volunteer disappear. The real trick was bringing her back.

"Never fear," he said, letting his voice carry over the crowd. "Though the fair Esta is no longer in our world, I will summon her to return.

Behold—" With another wave of his hand, the walls of the cabinet began to rise, like a flower closing, and the cabinet began spinning again, more slowly now as it sank back down to the stage floor.

He approached it and gave it one more spin, making sure the front door was facing the audience, and then opened it with a triumphant flourish.

The audience went completely silent, and then after a moment, laughter began to erupt.

Harte turned to see the cabinet, empty. The girl wasn't there.

He cursed under his breath and tried not to look as frantic as he felt. He turned back to the audience. "Ladies and gentlemen, if you allow me to—"

"Are you looking for me?" a now-familiar voice called.

His skin felt suddenly hot. He could hear his own heartbeat in his ears, as his entire career flashed before his eyes. The audience shuffled, turning and craning their necks to see the source of the voice.

The girl stood and waved. "I'm over here," she called from one of the center rows of the theater.

The people around her startled. She might as well have been a ghost the way she'd appeared in their midst. Their mouths hung open as she excused herself, climbing past two people who sat gaping as she moved toward the center aisle.

At first the audience was too shocked to do anything more than stare, and a deafening silence filled the cavernous house. Even Harte couldn't do much more than stare. She'd managed to seat herself in the middle of a row without anyone noticing her. As he gaped, dumbfounded at how she'd outmaneuvered him again, the applause started slowly and then grew until the audience began coming to their feet, whistling and calling for more.

The girl was already half gone before he came to his senses and realized he needed to go after her. She blew him a kiss and gave a wave from the back of the theater before ducking through the doors to the lobby. Harte found Nibs sitting in the middle of the standing ovation. He gave Harte a smirking salute, then got up and started pushing his way through the frenzied crowd, following the girl.

MASTER OF THE
OTHERWORLD

E sta let her feet carry her out of the theater—and far, far away from Harte Darrigan. She barely noticed that night had already fallen over the city; the icy chill in the air didn't even touch her. She couldn't feel anything but the shock of finding herself no longer inside the cabinet onstage but out in the audience.

Pushing her way through the crowd gathered on the sidewalk outside the box office, she didn't bother to apologize or slow her steps, not even when she careened into a large man helping a woman out of their carriage. She had to get away.

She had to figure out what the hell had just happened.

She remembered getting into the cabinet, remembered feeling the sizzling heat of his magic against her palm and knowing he'd done something to her. She remembered the wink he'd given her—the one that promised trouble—before he locked her into the wardrobe. But after that . . .

Nothing.

Nothing at all until she found herself watching Harte Darrigan from the audience again. Not until the audience's laughter at seeing the cabinet empty shook her from her stupor.

She didn't know how she'd come to find herself in the middle of the theater—much less in the middle of the row—but she could guess. From his clear agitation when he realized he was alone on an empty stage, Esta understood that she was still supposed to have been inside that cabinet. She must have decided to leave, to use her own magic and get herself into the audience without any of them realizing. But she couldn't remember actually doing it.

From the moment Nibsy had said Harte Darrigan's name, Esta knew she was about to meet the person she'd been sent to stop—the Magician. The moment he'd walked onstage, she'd also recognized him immediately as the boy from the Haymarket. At first she'd been uneasy, but after watching him for a few minutes, her worry turned to relief. With his overblown drama and tacky stage magic, she couldn't believe that this was the Magician. Stopping him would be easy, she thought.

But sitting in the audience, shocked and without any understanding of how she'd gotten there, she realized the Magician was more than he appeared to be. That he would be a formidable opponent.

Luckily, it had taken her only a second to gather her wits and retake control of the situation. The surprise at seeing her in the middle of the audience had transformed his entire face. He'd looked so disarmed that she almost felt guilty for the laughter her little disappearing act caused. *Almost.*

But then the look on his face changed from surprise to something else, and she knew she had to get out of there—fast.

"Esta!"

She barely heard the voice calling her name as she darted through the crowd, faster now as she tried to outpace her panic. The Magician must have erased her memory or manipulated her in some other way. It was magic, clearly, and not the half-baked stage magic that made up the rest of his tricks. But what was his affinity, and how far did it reach? Could he still affect her now—still control her?

The thought made Esta shudder for reasons that had nothing to do with the cold. Professor Lachlan was depending on her to stop the Magician, but he already had the upper hand. And now he had her on the run.

Esta pulled up short, coming to a dead stop that forced the people behind her to dodge around her. *No.* She wasn't going to let him chase her off. That wasn't going to happen again.

She turned back to find the street sign of the intersection she'd crossed, but lurking above her, as though she'd conjured him in her thoughts, was the Magician.

Larger than life, Harte Darrigan looked down with stormy gray eyes from the huge billboard that took up most of the theater wall behind her.

"Esta! Wait!" Nibs finally caught up to her. He was panting, but his face was glowing with excitement as he caught her arm. "That was excellent. I couldn't have planned it better myself. How'd you manage it?"

"I don't know," she murmured, pulling away from him. She was quickly growing aware of the cold now, of how it cut through the velvet of her dress, and she rubbed her arms, trying to ward off the chill.

Nibs handed her the cloak she'd left behind. "You don't know?" he asked, surprised.

She shook her head as she pulled the cloak around her, but it did nothing to dispel the cold. "I can't remember how I got out of that box or how I ended up sitting in the theater."

"Interesting." Nibs glanced over his spectacles at her.

"You could have warned me about what he could do," she said, turning on him.

He didn't so much as flinch at the heat in her words. "I thought it would be better for you to go in without expectations. Anyway, you played it brilliantly. You threw him off, which is something I've never managed," he said, admiration clear in his voice. "Dolph'll be pleased."

She couldn't quite feel buoyed by that news. Not at that moment.

"I wanted to see what you could do. And you weren't ever in any *real* danger. I was only trying to get his attention." His expression was smug behind the thick lenses. "And you certainly did that. Dolph was right to keep you," he said.

She glared at him. "What's that supposed to mean?"

"Just what I said. He made a good choice in not giving you back to Corey. You're a damn good thief, but there's more to you than that, isn't there?" he asked, squinting through his lenses at her.

"There's only one way to find out," she challenged, making sure to meet his eyes. Daring him to accept it. "Give me something to do other than stealing purses."

He studied her a long, tense moment, and she could practically hear the calculations he was making in that mind of his. "Maybe we will," he said.

They walked in silence for a while before they found a streetcar heading in the right direction, but all the time, she swore she could feel the eyes of the Magician following her home.

OLD FRIENDS

Harte took his bow quickly, barely hearing the applause and not bothering with his usual flourishes. His whole body jangled from the surge of adrenaline he'd felt at seeing the girl—*Esta*, she'd said her name was—materialize across the room. His mind was already racing with the possibilities. He had to find her. He *had* to know how she did it.

He pushed past Shorty, who was shouting at him to get back onstage and finish his act. He just needed to duck into his dressing room to grab his overcoat and keys, but when he pushed open the door, he found that the room was already occupied.

"John," Harte said, covering his surprise at finding Paul Kelly's second-in-command sitting in the chair near his dressing table. John Torrio was about nineteen, not much older than Harte. Torrio had the same swarthy skin and hard-nosed looks, but not the polish or the style of his boss, and Harte's *ex*-boss, the leader of the Five Point Gang.

Pat Riley, better known in certain circles as Razor, was examining a set of handcuffs that were dangling from the mirror. Harte had been dodging Kelly and his boys for months now—ever since Dolph had told him about the Book—so having these two appear unannounced and unexpected could only mean their boss was done being patient.

He reached beyond the depths of his unease and pulled up what he hoped was an affable, confident smile. "Gentlemen, what do I owe this pleasure?"

"Kelly sent us," Torrio said, straightening the sharp lapels of his suit as he spoke. "But I'm sure you know that, seeing as how you've been avoiding us. The boss needs your services again."

"I'm not in the game anymore," Harte said, keeping a wary eye on Riley. "Kelly knows that. The last time was supposed to be the last time. We had an agreement."

Riley dropped the cuffs so they clattered onto the table and turned to look squarely at Harte. "The agreement's changed."

It always does, Harte thought, fighting the urge to scream in frustration.

John Torrio slouched comfortably in Harte's dressing chair, his eyes projecting the lazy confidence of someone who had Paul Kelly's full authority behind him. "You know Kelly's got eyes everywhere, Darrigan. You telling me you thought you could be rubbing elbows with J. P. Morgan's people and nobody wouldn't notice?"

"You're here because I had a drink with Jack Grew?" Harte asked.

"And Morgan's son."

"I don't know Morgan's son. And he doesn't want to know me," Harte said, eyeing his coat over Torrio's shoulder. He shouldn't have bothered to come back for it. He could have caught up with the girl *and* managed to miss these two.

Though, now that he stopped to think, maybe he should let her go. She was involved with Nibsy somehow, which meant she had to be tangled up with Dolph Saunders as well. The last thing Harte needed was that particular complication, especially with Kelly's men sitting in his dressing room.

Still, that trick of materializing across the theater in a fraction of the time it would have taken anyone else to do it—the crowd had gone wild. If he could replicate it, he wouldn't have to worry about ticket sales for a long time. Even if she was wrapped up with Nibsy Lorcan, Harte wanted to know how she'd done it. But first he had to get rid of the two men standing in his way.

"But you *do* know Jack?" Razor insisted.

Torrio nodded. "That's enough for the boss."

"Jack's only an admirer of my work," Harte said easily, which was true enough. "He thought I could teach him how to pull coins out of his ear. Make him as rich as his uncle."

Torrio snorted, half-amused. "I bet he did. But like I said, your new friendship interests Mr. Kelly. Greatly."

Harte made a show of unrolling the sleeves back down his arms, all the while keeping part of his awareness on the two men. "I meet lots of people," he told them. "I wasn't aware I had to check with Kelly every time I had a drink with someone."

Razor Riley growled in answer. "Watch yourself, Darrigan. Kelly told us to talk to you. He didn't say we had to be nice."

Harte ignored Razor and kept his focus on Torrio. "What interest does Kelly have in Jack Grew, anyway?"

"You know the boss," Torrio said with a shrug. "He's always interested in growing his connections. Jack Grew's pretty high up in the world."

Harte couldn't hide his surprise. "Jack's a nonstarter," he said truthfully. "From what I hear, he was this close to being shackled to some fisherman's daughter in Greece, because all his brains are in the wrong head. The boy wouldn't be able to tell his ass from his armpit without Daddy to help him, and the whole family knows it. Kelly wouldn't be able to get within ten feet of him before Morgan's people got wind of it."

"Such little faith you have," Torrio drawled, picking at his nails before he lifted his eyes to meet Harte's. "You really think Mr. Kelly don't know what he's doing?"

"Kelly wants you to work on Grew," Razor clarified.

"Work on him?" Harte repeated, feeling a cold twist of understanding in his gut.

"You know what he wants," Torrio said, taking his hat from Harte's dressing table.

It was one thing to use his affinity on shady politicians from Tammany or on the boys in the neighborhood, but tangling with the Order of Ortus Aurea? It was too risky, or Harte would have already done it. With magic, he could have wrapped Jack around his finger a lot easier. But he knew that if the Order got wind of it, they'd end him. Or worse.

"I don't have any sway over Jack Grew," Harte hedged.

"That ain't the way I hear it. The way I hear it, you got the *touch* with difficult people." Torrio's mouth twisted into something that might have been a smirk. "Kelly wants an introduction."

"I can't understand why."

"Not that it's any of your business, but the word around town is that the Order's having an important get-together soon. Word is that anyone of any importance in the city will be there. Kelly don't want to be stuck in the slums forever, Darrigan. He wants an invitation to that gathering. He wants an invitation to the Order. And he's confident you can make that happen. . . . After all, you already have an in with Jack."

"Jack Grew and his like, they're from a different world than us," Harte said with a shrug. "They could barely stand to have me at their table, and—"

"I'm sure you'll figure something out," Torrio interrupted. He gave Harte's cheek a not-so-gentle pat.

"If I don't want to figure something out?" Harte asked.

"You know Kelly has ways of persuading. It would be a shame if anyone found out about any of your little secrets, now, wouldn't it? Never know what might happen to you."

There were any number of secrets Paul Kelly knew about Harte Darrigan, any number of things that could ruin him if his old boss decided to expose him.

"I see," Harte said slowly.

"I thought you might," Torrio said as Razor Riley sat stone-faced behind him.

"I need time to think about it. Figure out the best way in."

"Mr. Kelly thought you might say that. He has the utmost faith that you'll make the right choice. Me? I ain't so sure. I think you might need a push in the right direction." Torrio shrugged. "I'm more than happy to give you that push."

"Well, this has been most enlightening, boys." Harte held out his hand, a last-ditch attempt to take control of the situation. "Give Kelly my regards, won't you?"

Torrio looked at the outstretched hand but didn't offer his own. "You put on a good show, Darrigan, but your time's running out to make good." He gave a jerk of his head before leading the way out of the dressing room. Razor gave Harte a look that said he wouldn't mind if Harte screwed up, and then he followed Torrio, shutting the door behind him.

Harte threw the lock on the door before he sank into the chair near his dressing table. It was still warm from Torrio's body, which only served to remind him how much trouble he was in. Paul Kelly, a member of the Order? He couldn't fathom it. But if it came to pass . . . Harte couldn't help but shudder.

He still remembered the first time he'd ever met Paul Kelly, about five, maybe six years ago. Back then Dolph Saunders had taken him under his wing, and he'd felt like the world was his. So when he found out his mother was back in the city—someone had seen her in one of Paul Kelly's cathouses—he didn't ask Dolph for help. He went to see for himself.

He'd gone to curse her for leaving him, but once he'd realized what she'd become, he understood what his actions had done. He couldn't leave her there. It had been easy enough to get her out. But of course Paul Kelly heard about it and came after him.

Back then Kelly was beginning to make a name for himself. Mostly, his gang was made up of rough-looking Italian boys who didn't need the evil eye to give someone a bad day, and they had Harte before Dolph even found out about it. But Kelly saw something valuable in Harte's abilities, so he gave Harte a choice that day, which was more than he gave most: work for the Five Pointers, or end his short life in the Hudson. Harte picked the Five Pointers. Despite everything he'd been through, he'd still been too naive to know the Hudson might have been a better bet. He was wearing the Five Pointer's brand before Dolph could do anything to help him.

A few years after that, when he'd collected enough of Kelly's secrets, he'd negotiated an exit from the gang. He'd renamed himself, made a whole new life, and started working theaters and dime museums in the

Bowery, learning his craft from some of the old guys. He thought he'd made it out, but it wasn't even six months later when Kelly called on him for a "favor." *For an old friend.* But one more led to another and another.

He'd tried not to think too much about the way his favors for Kelly often lined up with his lucky breaks in the theater business. He told himself that it was his skill more than Kelly's pressure that had gotten him the first gig north of Houston or his first appearance in a Broadway house. But Torrio and Razor's appearance only underscored the truth—Dolph Saunders had been right about Kelly having him on a leash. The only way to get away from Kelly's influence was to get out of the godforsaken trap of a city.

And the only way to do that was to get the Book before anyone else did.

Harte picked up the handcuffs Razor Riley had moved. They were the first cuffs he'd ever cracked, back when he was a stupid kid from Mott Street who'd gotten picked up for lifting a half-rotten orange from a peddler's cart. Breaking those cuffs and getting out of the Black Maria wagon bound for the boys' mission had been his first taste of what it might feel like to choose his own destiny. He'd kept them as a reminder of how far he'd come, and of how far he still had left to go.

Sure, Dolph Saunders and Paul Kelly were both breathing down his neck, but he had something neither of them had and both of them wanted—a willing contact in the Ortus Aurea. It would still be tricky, convincing Jack to trust him enough to get him into Khafre Hall. It would be damn risky going against an organization that snuffed out Mageus for sport. But those cuffs were a reminder that he'd been in tough spots before.

He hung the cuffs back on their hook where he'd be able to see them. His entire life had been one big escape act. Getting out of that prison of a city wouldn't be any different.

CHANGING FEATHERS

Esta spent the next few days working the Dead Line without complaint—and staying far away from Harte Darrigan. The letters and words in the news clipping she kept tucked against her skin had not stopped shifting. The future, the heist that needed to happen, was still undetermined, a fact that made her nervous, anxious. If the heist didn't happen, she'd never get back.

On Wednesday, she worked on Wall Street, fleecing unsuspecting bankers in the sleeting rain. With the rotten weather, it took longer than the day before to meet her quota, especially since she was relying on her skill rather than her magic whenever possible. She understood that in *this* city, magic was as much a liability as a tool, a mark for an unknown enemy to track her or find her.

Despite the rain, it was still early when she made it back to the warmth of Tilly's kitchen, exhausted and hungry. The kitchen wasn't empty. At the end of the long, heavy table, Dolph sat huddled with Viola, Jianyu, and Nibs. They didn't pay any attention to her arrival, but when Tilly heard the door open, she turned from what she was doing at the sink. Seeing it was Esta, she wiped her hands on the apron covering her dress and grabbed a covered plate to bring over to her.

"You're back early," Tilly said. She set the plate on the end of the counter and took the cloth off the top to reveal sliced hard cheese, salami, and some grapes that had already been picked over.

Leaning a hip against the counter, Esta selected one of the remaining grapes. "The streets are a mess," she said. "I got my quota, so I came back. I didn't feel like melting today."

Tilly gave her a quizzical look. "Melting?"

"Nothing," Esta said, realizing her slip.

"Another new dress?" Tilly asked, teasing.

Esta shrugged as she popped a grape into her mouth. "Change your feathers often enough, and the mark won't recognize the bird." The words came naturally, without thought, but the moment they were out, the grape suddenly tasted bitter. They were Professor Lachlan's words, lessons she'd been taught until they were a part of her. And she was failing him.

That close to the stove's warmth, she unwrapped herself from the damp cloak she'd been wearing. She nodded to the table where Dolph sat with Viola, Jianyu, and Nibs, their heads all bent close together and their voices low. "What's going on there?"

Sliding a cup of milk toward Esta, Tilly gave her a wry look. "Big plans, like always."

Dolph thumped the table with his fist, and Viola said something vicious in Italian as she gestured wildly with her hands.

"They don't seem to be going too well."

"They're not, from what I can tell," Tilly said, turning back to the sinkful of dishes.

Esta picked up a towel and took one of the wet plates from where Tilly had set them on the counter. Wiping at the plate, she kept an ear toward the group at the table. "What are they trying to do?" she said, keeping her voice low.

Tilly glanced over at her out of the corner of her eye. "Something that will probably get one of them killed," she murmured. She shook her head, obviously disgusted with the whole idea.

"It's not possible," Viola snapped. "You want that we walk into a crowded room, take everything right from under their noses, and get away without being caught. All while cleaning out everyone in the room *at the same time*? Sei pazzo!"

"We've been over this. Jianyu can slip in undetected," Dolph started.

"And then what?" Nibs asked gently. "He's no thief, Dolph."

"He steals secrets well enough," Dolph insisted.

"Secrets don't have *weight*," Viola said, punctuating her words with her hands. "This is different. You want him to take everything? To rob a room filled with members of the Order *while* we take the exhibit? It's too much for one person."

"Maybe we don't need to take all of it?" Jianyu offered. "Taking a prized piece or two should be more than enough."

"No!" Dolph thumped again. "It's not. They can't know what we're after. If we take everything, they're less likely to know why they were robbed."

"Then what do you suggest we do?" Viola asked.

"We'll send you," Dolph said.

"Bah! Be serious. I'm no thief, and you don't want them dead, do you?"

Esta took a sip from the cup of milk, using the excuse of the movement to glance over at the tense group around the table, but she practically choked when she found Nibs watching her.

"What about her?" Nibs said as she was turning away.

"What?" Dolph snapped.

"Esta, the new girl. She's lasted nearly a week downtown, hasn't she? You know she's talented—you couldn't even stop her." He shrugged. "Why not have her fleece the crowd? Jianyu can focus on the art."

Dolph turned to look at her with his icy stare. He studied her a second, his features tense. "No," he said after a moment, and turned back to the table.

"She does have light fingers," Jianyu pressed, his eyes sliding over to her. He gave her an unreadable look, a reminder of what he had over her.

"No," Dolph said again, as though that was the end of that.

"I agree," Viola said, glaring at her. "Not the girl."

For some reason it was Viola's dismissal that rankled. "Why not 'the girl'?" Esta asked. She took a step toward them, never letting her gaze drop from Viola's. "You need something taken, and it's what I do. I managed to take that knife right out of your pocket, didn't I?"

"You haven't managed it since," Viola snapped, her eyes narrowing. "Haven't bothered to try."

"Enough," Dolph said before Viola could come back at her.

Esta looked to Dolph. "You know I'm more than capable."

"But I don't know if I can trust you."

"Only one way to find out," Esta challenged.

Dolph didn't speak at first, simply stared at her, his cold blue eye serious.

"You're all worse than a couple of tomcats fighting over an alley," Tilly said, bringing a plate of food to the table. "Esta's fine, Dolph. I have a good feeling about her, and if you were honest with yourself, you'd know you trust her."

"You don't know that," he said, glancing at Tilly.

"I know she'd already be gone if you didn't." She gave him a stern look. "Use her. Maybe you'll be less likely to get somebody killed that way."

"Tilly's right," Nibs said. "We can use the girl."

"The girl has a name," Esta muttered.

"Fine," Dolph said, taking one of the biscuits Tilly had brought over. "Take a seat," he said to Esta. "But know this—if you even think to cross us—"

"You'll be dead before you lift a finger," Viola finished.

Jianyu was silent, not adding his own warning, but his eyes were steady, watchful.

Luckily, she wasn't planning to cross them. Not yet, at least.

THE CORE OF MAGIC

It was long after the Strega had closed its doors for the night when Dolph finally made his way back to his lonely apartment. Once, it had been filled with warmth and life, but now the silence served as penance. He settled himself at the table by the fire to look over the floor plans for the Metropolitan and the notes he'd collected about the exhibition so far, as well as Jianyu's latest report.

Sometime later, a sharp knock at the door stirred him from his solitude. He glanced up at the clock and saw that he'd worked well past midnight, far too late for someone to disturb him if it wasn't important. "Come," he barked, stepping in front of the table to block the view of the paperwork.

Viola entered, and Dolph relaxed a measure, taking his chair again as he motioned for Viola to close the door behind her. Her unease permeated the air around them.

"What is it?" he asked, gesturing to the empty chair across from him.

Viola shook her head. "I won't stay long." But she didn't immediately speak.

"It's been a long day, so if you have something to say, you'd best get to it."

Her eyes found the sheets of papers and notes on the table, and then she glanced up at him. "You really think it's wise to include the girl in this?" she said finally.

"That seems to be the current consensus," Dolph said, sinking back into his own chair.

Viola scowled. "I don't trust her."

"You don't trust anyone, Vi. Except maybe Tilly, and even then . . ."

He gave a tired shrug. What was there to say about that, if Viola wouldn't say it herself?

Not that he blamed Viola for being so wary. She'd trusted her family, hadn't she? Raised as the dutiful daughter, she'd done everything they'd asked of her—became her brother's weapon when he began making enemies that came with the reputation he was building in the neighborhood. But when they'd heard whispers that she was getting too close to one of the teachers at the night classes she attended, they'd made the woman—and any hint of an affair—disappear and tried to sell Viola off to the highest bidder. For her own good, of course.

As young as she had been and with the family she came from, she'd risked her life leaving their house, and she'd risked everything else in trading her loyalty to him for protection. Not that she had trusted him enough to tell him everything that had happened. But he'd found out on his own. He always did.

Still, he'd never forget the day Viola arrived at the Strega, her lip split and crusted over, the skin around her left eye as purple as the iris. She'd walked through the saloon doors with her chin up, her shoulders back, and had promised him that she would do anything he asked of her if he would keep her family from dragging her back. Because if they tried, she would kill them rather than live under their control, and she didn't know if she could live with that.

Viola had kept her promise to him for more than three years now, and he'd come to depend on her. Come to almost enjoy her flashes of temper and to respect her intractable will. But he didn't have the patience for any of it that night.

Viola was silent at first as she took the seat opposite. Then, after a thoughtful moment, she leaned forward and spoke in low, halting tones. "We could wait awhile, you know. There's no reason to rush. Or we could do as Jianyu suggested and only take the art. It would be enough to embarrass Morgan without risking everyone to a green girl we still don't know."

Any other time, Viola's point would have been well taken. Usually, he'd spend months watching and waiting before he'd even consider taking someone new into his confidence. But this time . . .

"We can't wait." He'd been searching for answers for too long now, and he was still missing an important piece of the puzzle. He pushed a sheet of paper that held a list of names.

"What's this?"

"More have gone missing."

Viola studied the list, her eyes squinting and her mouth moving soundlessly as she tried to make out the names. "People always go miss—" She stopped short and looked up at him in surprise. "Krzysztof Zeranski?"

Dolph nodded. The city had a tendency to swallow the weak, but Mageus with stronger affinities, like Krzysztof, were usually better at avoiding that fate. Lately, though, it seemed that some of the most talented—and most powerful—were disappearing again, exactly as they had last year. "He helped with a fire on Hester Street last week. It's possible he was seen."

Viola handed him back the list. "What does this have to do with the job at the Metropolitan?"

"The Order is up to something. Look at that list, Viola. Krzysztof has a talent for calling to water. Eidelman grows nearly impossible blooms at his flower shop over near Washington Square, and anyone knows you talk to Frieda Weber if you want the sun to shine on your wedding day. They all could be confused for elementals."

Viola shook her head. "But they're not. Water, air, earth—they all are part of one another. To call to one is to call on the very core of magic itself."

"I know that and you know that. Hell, every Mageus was born with that knowledge deep in their bones, but the Order and their like—people who've never felt the call to connect with the world around them—fall back on the myth that you can separate the parts of magic to make it more manageable. Look at the Brink itself—as though you can separate the affinity from the Mageus without damaging both? It's impossible. No Mageus can fully recover from what it does to them, and every time one of our rank is laid low by it, magic as a whole is weakened.

"Maybe I'm wrong about this. Maybe I'm seeing patterns that aren't there, but I don't think so. This happened before, when we lost Leena. These names suggest that it's starting again. I can't ignore that fact, just as I can't forget that every day we wait is a day closer to the Conclave. They're planning something—something bigger than we've seen before—and we're running out of time to figure out what it is. We need the Ars Arcana."

"This is about the Book again?" she asked, clearly irritated.

"It is," he said.

"You really think a simple book is so important?"

"Leena never would have sacrificed herself for a *simple* book, Viola. Not unless it was *exactly* that important. I trusted her in life, and I'll trust her in this. I'm convinced the Order has the Ars Arcana, and I'm convinced we need it to beat them."

Viola's violet eyes were still unsure. "If we were truly brave, we could take on the Order without worrying about some stupid book. What chance could they stand against us? Conigli, all of us, for not fighting them."

Dolph shook his head. "Maybe once that would have been true, but now? Magic is dying, and it has been for some time. Away from the old countries, every generation forgets a little more. You've seen it yourself, haven't you? How each generation is a little weaker than the one before it. Maybe one hundred—even fifty—years ago, we might have stood a chance, but I wouldn't risk a stand now. No one with any sense would."

"So we wait until we're ready. We build our power," she argued. "We could take our time, chip away at the Order's power until they're weak enough to defeat."

"You don't understand. . . ." He leaned forward a bit. "What I'm trying to do is about more than simply bringing down the Order. If I'm right about the Ars Arcana, it contains the very secrets of magic itself."

"We *have* the secrets of magic." She tapped her chest. "It flows in our very blood."

"True, but we've forgotten. We could be *so* much more. The Order wouldn't be able to stop *any* Mageus from fulfilling their destiny ever again. We could make this whole country a haven for our kind." When she continued frowning, he pressed on. "This has become bigger than me, bigger than what I lost when the Order took Leena from me."

"What does any of this have to do with the museum? The Book isn't there."

"The Morgan exhibit has pieces I need to examine," he said, sliding the exhibition program toward her. Jianyu had managed to lift one from the printer where it was being made, so Dolph knew exactly what Morgan had. He knew exactly what he needed.

She glanced up at him, a question in her eyes.

"Getting into Khafre Hall won't be enough—the Order will have the Mysterium protected by more than a locked door. I'm expecting something like what they kept Leena in before they killed her—something that would hurt any Mageus who tried to come close. We'll need to break through that protection," he said, taking the program back from her and pointing to one entry in particular. "I think this might work."

She studied the entry doubtfully. "Morgan wouldn't put anything so dangerous—so important—on display," she challenged.

"He might if he didn't realize what he had," Dolph argued.

"You can't know that for sure."

No, of course he didn't know for sure. But it wasn't as though he could simply walk into the museum and examine the piece himself without raising suspicions. "I know enough, and Nibs is optimistic."

Viola studied him with narrowed eyes. "No . . . There's something more. Something you're not telling us."

"If I'm not telling you, then it's not your business to know," Dolph said, his impatience seeping into his words.

But Viola didn't seem to heed the warning in his voice. "You used to trust me, you know."

He let out an exasperated sigh. "I *still* trust you, Vi."

"You keep secrets from us." She shook her head. "You've always kept secrets from us, I suppose, but now I think there's something more. If you aren't careful, you're going to get us all killed."

"Are you saying you want out?" he asked tightly.

She studied him with eyes as sharp as the knives she had hidden in her skirts. The clock *tick-tick-ticked* out the seconds as they passed, each moment feeling like one closer to everything unraveling.

Leena would have known what to say to soothe Viola. She would have told him if this whole gambit was a mistake. But would he have listened?

"Are you saying I have a choice in the matter now?" Viola asked, her eyes never leaving his.

"You've always had a choice," he said, keeping his voice level, his expression placid. "But when you pledged your loyalty and took my mark, you understood the consequences of making it."

Her expression didn't so much as flicker. "I don't need your threats, Dolph. Mark or no mark, I keep my word."

"I know that, Viola," he told her. "If you don't want in on the Metropolitan job, I don't want you there. Too much is at stake for anyone not to be all in." He paused, lowered his voice. "We could use your help on it, though."

"Fine," she said after another long moment. "But if the girl crosses us—"

"I don't think she will."

"Will you give her your mark before?" she asked.

He should. Anyone he let close enough to do a job like this should have been made to take his mark, but with his affinity hollowed out and weak, the marks were pointless. He wasn't sure what would happen— what he would reveal—by marking the girl without his magic intact.

Viola frowned at his hesitation. "You're too soft on her."

"I'm not."

"You admire her," she insisted.

"She's a talented thief, but—"

"I can see why," Viola continued, ignoring him. "She's stubborn and too bold. She reminds me a bit of Leena in that way. But you're letting your sympathy cloud your judgment. I worry you trust her for the wrong reasons."

"I worry you dislike her for the wrong reasons," Dolph said softly.

"What are the right reasons, Dolph?"

But when he went to answer, he found that he didn't know anymore.

THE METROPOLITAN

Central Park East

Esta checked her reflection in the glass covering an eighteenth-century watercolor. The disdainful eyes of the wigged man in the portrait stared back at her, and she had the sudden, uneasy sense that he could see right through her. She only hoped no one else could.

Ignoring his disapproving gaze, she craned her neck from right to left to make sure that every stray hair was still tucked up into the silk tarboosh, the fezlike hat that all the servers were wearing that night. It was lucky, she supposed, that they were wearing them. She was nearly as tall as most men, and it was easy enough to wrap her chest to hide her curves, but without the hat, it would have been harder to hide her hair and pass as one of the male servers. Otherwise, she didn't doubt Viola would have made an argument for cutting it.

The silken pants and long tuniclike coats—all part of the exhibition's general theme—were a bonus too. To finally be out of the long skirts she'd been wearing made her feel freer than she had in weeks. Not that the serving uniforms or any of the decorations were even remotely authentic. With the shine of the silk and beaded details that glittered as she moved, the outfit looked more like something from a Vegas show.

To her own eyes, she still looked too feminine. There was no disguising the soft skin on her face or her thick, dark lashes, but she knew enough about people by now to know that they only ever saw what they expected. If they even looked at the help at all.

"You—boy," a voice shouted from the end of the hall. "Get away from there!"

Esta startled at the voice, and turned to find a large, broad-shouldered man in a dark suit coming her way. One of the museum's guards. She stepped away from the portrait and lowered her eyes.

"Don't you have somewhere to be?"

"On my way now, sir," she said, coughing out the words in a tone lower than her usual voice. She kept her head down and tried to put some swagger in her step as she moved past him.

Steady, she told herself. *Not much farther now . . .*

But as she passed, she felt tendrils of energy reach out and brush against her. Her skin tingled with awareness, and she nearly stumbled from the surprise of it.

He's using magic.

There shouldn't have been any other Mageus in the museum—Morgan was part of the Order, and the exhibition would be filled with its members—but the flicker of magic came again as she continued to walk away.

She kept her eyes down and moved as fast as she could without looking suspicious, but she didn't relax until she turned out of that gallery, into the quiet emptiness of a wide hall filled with statuary.

When she was well out of earshot, she cursed to herself and broke into a jog. She rounded the corner and took the steps in a far stairway two at a time. At the bottom, she turned into a larger sculpture gallery and kept her pace up as she rushed through it.

"Leaving so soon?" A shadow stepped out from behind a large urn.

Esta stopped dead, her heart in her throat, and turned to find Nibs. "What are you doing in here?" He was supposed to be outside, waiting to orchestrate their getaway.

"I could ask you the same," he said with a frown. "You should be upstairs with the other servers. I vouched for you."

"I wasn't trying to leave," she said. "I was coming to find you."

He gave her a doubtful look.

"We have a problem with the guards—they're Mageus."

His brows bunched over his round glasses as he studied her. "You're sure?" he asked, suspicious.

"Of course I'm sure. I know magic when I feel it, and the guy who saw me upstairs? He was using it." She glanced over her shoulder to make sure he hadn't followed. "I think he might have been checking me somehow."

Nibs frowned. He didn't seem half as concerned as Esta thought he should be. "If he was checking for your affinity, he must not be strong enough to find it unless you use it."

"How can you possibly know that?"

"You're still standing here."

The fact that he was right didn't make her feel any better. "I thought Morgan was a member of the Order."

"He's in the Inner Circle, their highest council."

"Then don't you think Mageus are the *last* people who should be here tonight?"

"You're here," Nibs pointed out. "I'm here."

"Yeah, to take the art. Not to guard it."

Nibs considered that. "It could be another team." His brow furrowed again, and he stared off in that half-vacant way he did when he was thinking. "But that doesn't feel right."

"They're working for Morgan?"

"Or the museum. But seeing as how Morgan's on the main board of directors here, it amounts to the same thing."

"That doesn't make sense," she told him. "The Order hates us."

"True, but it wouldn't be the first time they used us against each other. There are plenty in this city desperate enough to do nearly anything, including working for the Order." He glanced at her. "Look at the Haymarket. Corey might not be in the Order yet, but he's trying to get in. He might not be all that powerful, but he's a Mageus, same as the guards he employs. Even if he keeps his own identity a secret, his people all know who he rubs elbows with, but they think they're protected because they work for him. They're willing to rat out other Mageus, even though the unlucky ones get handed over to the Order."

Esta realized then how much danger she'd really been in that night. "That's horrible."

"Maybe, but you can't really blame them. Corey pays, and he pays well. Bad enough that the Order forces us to live in the worst parts of the city and uses their influence with the public to keep us in our place, but that's not enough for them. No, they still have one weakness—they can't sense magic like we can. But if they turn us against each other, it solves the problem."

"We didn't plan for this," Esta said. "We have to call it off and get out of here. *Now*. We can come back when we've figured out a different way in—"

But Nibs wasn't listening. He glanced down the hall toward where the guests were beginning to arrive, his eyes soft and unfocused. Then, all at once, he seemed to come to some decision. "No."

"No?" She gaped at him.

"Jianyu's already inside the gallery."

Esta went very still. "It's already locked?"

Nibs nodded. "And the room is half-full of Morgan's guests."

"We won't be able to warn him," she said, as the realization of how tight a spot they were in sank heavy in her stomach. "The second the doors open, he's done."

It had seemed simple enough when they'd laid it all out earlier. Without motion sensors or cameras, it should have been an easy job of evading a few guards. Morgan was set to inspect the gallery and his exhibition before the show. Concealed, Jianyu would slip in with him and wait until they'd secured the room. There were no windows, no other doors—no way in or out except through the locked and guarded entrance to the next gallery where the reception would happen.

At eight o'clock, Morgan would give a speech, and then the doors to his exhibition would be opened to his guests. By then Jianyu would have cleaned out the room and hidden himself along with the loot. The guests—all the leaders of the city and newspapermen reporting on the event—would be the first to see that Morgan's so-called great exhibition was nothing more than some empty frames and glass cases. All that would be left was for Jianyu to sneak out in the confusion. Easy.

All the while, Esta would be using the distraction of the robbery to clean out the rest of the guests—jewels, cash, anything that would embarrass Morgan further.

"We have to get him out of there," she told Nibs.

Except that now Jianyu was locked in a room, blocked by a crowd that contained Mageus playing for the enemy, watching for any sign of magic. When the doors opened, the walls would be bare and the guards would find Jianyu, who would be using his affinity to conceal himself. Once they found him, everything could be traced back to Dolph and the rest of his people.

"Even if you could get him out, you can't call off this job," Nibs said. "Dolph wants this done, and he wants it done tonight."

There has to be a way. "So we'll have to do it without magic, which means we'll need a distraction," she said, thinking through the plan and imagining what the Professor would have done, how he'd taught her to use what was available. "The best we can hope for is to throw them off, to point them away from Jianyu and away from Dolph. And we'll need backup if everything goes wrong."

"What are you thinking?" Nibs said, curious now. Interested.

"I think we need Viola," she told him, hoping that the half-baked idea she was formulating on the fly would work. And hoping that Viola wouldn't kill her for what she was about to ask her to do.

CLEVER THIEF

Harte made his way through an empty gallery toward the sound of voices ahead. He'd been to the museum before, countless mornings on the free-entry days, when he stared at paintings that promised a world beyond the narrow strip of land he was trapped on. Usually, on those days, the rooms would be filled with the chattering of women more interested in discussing the fashions of the other visitors than looking at the art. So that night, the silence felt like a gift. It transformed the whole place into his own private gallery, allowing him to imagine—just for a moment—that he'd attained the life he'd dreamed for himself.

He stopped in front of a landscape, a dramatic vista of glimmering rivers and sky-capped mountains in the distance. Places like that existed. Places that were clean and open, free from the stink of the city with its coal-laden air and trash-filled gutters. He had to believe that someday he would see them for himself. He took a moment more to let the image fortify him, and then he continued on toward his destination.

Eventually, the voices grew louder, and he came to the large, airy gallery that held a series of medieval altarpieces. It was currently serving as a space for less spiritual concerns—the cocktail party for J. P. Morgan's many guests. Servers in brightly colored tunics carried trays of champagne to Morgan's guests, who glittered in their jewels and silk.

Harte handed his invitation to a doorman, who gave it only a cursory glance before handing him a program and nodding for him to continue. But as Harte passed through the entryway, he felt the warning warmth that signaled magic in the air. It crawled across his skin, tousling his hair as it inspected him.

The guards are Mageus. It was an unexpected and unsettling development, to say the least, but Harte forced himself to keep walking into the crowded room as though he hadn't felt anything. People without affinities could rarely feel magic the way Mageus could, so Harte didn't allow himself to so much as pause. Instead, he pulled everything he was inward, locking down his own power with a speed that made his skin go cold.

The guards weren't the only challenge he faced in that room. The gallery was filled with a veritable who's who of New York society—bankers from Wall Street and politicians from Tammany, and many of the millionaires who'd built their houses along Madison or Fifth. A few well-known reporters lurked by the far wall, making notes with stubby pencils in their palm-size tablets as they watched the crowd with sharp, perceptive eyes. Harte recognized Sam Watson, the *Sun* reporter who'd done a feature on his act the previous summer. The story had helped ticket sales, but Harte hated how it had made him feel like an insect on display.

He also hated that at least a small measure of his success was owed to the same man who'd made it his mission to write so regularly—and viciously—about the dangerous Mageus that might be lurking among the newly arrived immigrants. Seeing Watson that night wasn't all that surprising, but the last thing Harte needed was for Watson to start dropping hints about his pedigree—or lack of one—in front of Jack.

Before Harte could turn away, Watson spotted him and began making his way across the room. "Harte Darrigan," he called, extending his hand with a slick grin. "I'm surprised to see *you* here."

"Oh?" he said, shaking Watson's hand. It would have been easy enough to get rid of the reporter, but with the guards, Harte was forced to deal with him.

"Doesn't seem like your usual crowd." Watson nodded toward the full room. "Or maybe you're here as the floor show?" he suggested with a less-than-friendly smirk.

"I think you're mistaking me for one of the chorus girls you like so much," Harte said breezily, but he clutched his hands behind his back to keep himself from punching the ass. "Evelyn sends her regards, by the way."

"Really?" Watson said a little too eagerly, but when he realized Harte was only toying with him, his expression went dark.

"How're things in the newspaper business?" Harte asked before Watson could needle him any more.

While Watson was prattling on about his latest editorial, something drew Harte's attention to the far side of the gallery. One of the servers stumbled, nearly running into a man in tails in an attempt not to drop a tray of empty glasses. The man reached out to steady the boy, and when he did, the server's hand dipped quickly into the man's pocket.

He watched with interest as the server used the confusion as a distraction, nimbly slipping whatever he'd taken into his tunic.

No, not his . . . *hers.*

Harte almost laughed out loud. With the shapeless tunic and her dark hair tucked beneath her cap, the girl blended in with the rest of the staff well enough. No one—him included, until that moment—was paying any real attention to the people bearing trays of drinks and canapés. But he was paying attention now.

"Would you excuse me?" Harte asked Watson. He didn't wait for a reply.

He was almost halfway to her when he heard his name over the din of the crowded room. "Darrigan!" Jack's voice called again, unmistakable this time.

Harte turned to find Jack pushing his way through the crowd and lifted his hand in greeting. If he went for the girl now, Jack would probably follow him, so he gave Jack a short nod and gestured toward a server carrying a tray of champagne. After retrieving a glass for himself and a second for Jack, he made his way back through the crush of the room.

"Good man," Jack said, accepting the drink.

"Thanks for having me." Harte lifted the glass in a silent toast as he scanned the room, looking for the girl. "This is quite the event."

Jack downed the champagne, set the empty goblet on a passing server's tray, and picked up another one. "Same as always, but my uncle seems pleased. Might even be happy enough to get him off my back for a while."

"Best of luck with that," Harte said, barely sipping at the drink as he looked again for some sign of the girl. He didn't see her, which didn't make him feel any better, but he ignored his nerves and pulled on the mask he always wore for Jack. "Have you had a chance to look at the exhibit yet?"

"I have." Jack's eyes lit. "There's at least one piece that looked interesting—one of the Babylonian seals he collects."

"A seal?" Harte asked, trying to picture it.

"A small cylindrical piece about so big." Jack held up his thumb and forefinger two inches apart. "It makes an imprint when rolled across wet clay or rubbed with ink. They were often used as signatures, but my uncle tends to be more interested in the ones used as amulets. Most are made from ceramic or stone, but I believe the one I was examining was carved from unpolished ruby . . . astounding, really, considering the size of it. But my uncle interrupted me before I could find out for sure." He scowled. "Now it's under glass for the foreseeable future."

Before Harte could ask anything else, a drumroll sounded through the room, ending with a sudden *crack.* A shout of *"Aiiiieeee!"* went up, and the crowd turned, almost as one, to see what was happening.

"I believe that's the entertainment. It'll probably be the only redeeming thing about this bore of an evening," he murmured. "Shall we?"

"After you," Harte said affably, following Jack through the press of bodies to a space where the crowd had moved aside to allow the performers room.

A procession was coming through the grand arched entrance of the gallery. First came two men in the same sort of billowing pants the servers wore, but their outfits were more extravagant, with heavy embroidery and intricate details on their vests and shoes. They carried wide, flat drums on their hips and were followed by another musician plucking a driving tune made up of minor chords and melodies on a pear-shaped guitar.

A figure wrapped in gauzy silken veils appeared in the doorway, and then she was spinning, dropping the veils as she undulated across the floor, until she was in the center of the room. The curves of her stomach and chest were exposed in flashes of skin and then hidden again by the gossamer fabric she whipped around her, and her fingers tapped tiny cymbals to the rhythm of the drums as her hips twisted and snaked.

"Egad," Jack said with a laugh as he elbowed Harte hard enough to nearly spill the champagne Harte was holding. "It's a damn good thing the old man left me in charge of the entertainment, isn't it?" He tossed back the last of his champagne, licking his lips as he watched the girl dance.

Harte couldn't blame him. He was also finding it difficult to take his eyes off the dancing girl. Her costume seemed to hide as much as it revealed, teasing the audience as her hips moved in an almost indecent rhythm. She was the embodiment of a mystery, especially with the bottom of her face covered by a veil that fluttered beneath her strange violet eyes—

Viola?

Harte looked more closely, awareness prickling. It *was* Viola. First the girl, and now this? It had Dolph Saunders written all over it, and Harte didn't want to be anywhere close when whatever they were planning happened.

But how was he supposed to leave so early without making Jack suspicious?

In the center of the room, Viola was still dancing. Harte was going to start backing away, using Jack's interest in the performance to his advantage, but when the music changed, she dropped her finger cymbals and, in a dramatic motion, reached behind her back and withdrew a brace of thin, silver knives that glistened in the brilliant electric light of the gallery.

Harte stopped short, watching warily as Viola danced with the knives splayed between her fingers. He'd heard about what Viola could do with a knife, the way she could hit any target from any distance. Whoever her target was that night didn't stand a chance, but then again, neither did she. The second she used her affinity, she'd be found out.

Without warning, the drum snapped out a rim shot, and Viola let a knife fly. *Swiiip*, it sailed through the air and took a cap off a server's head, pinning it to the wall behind. The room erupted into wild applause, and Jack elbowed him, absolutely delighted at the show.

But there had been no spike of energy, no telltale warmth to give away her magic. *Maybe her skill with the knives is simply that—a skill,* he thought, when none of the guards moved to stop her.

As she spun, all eyes in the room were on her, waiting for her next move with the kind of nervous excitement Harte had seen before dogfights or before bare-knuckle matches. It was the desire to see violence done to someone else, to be close to the blade of danger without ever being cut.

It wasn't anything Harte himself was interested in anymore. He'd had too much violence and danger in his life already. The only thing that interested him now was what the girl was doing. He saw her then, the only one moving across the room instead of watching the entertainment, inching her way toward the door to the gallery beyond.

So that's her game, he thought with sudden uneasiness.

In the middle of the floor, Viola was still dancing, now weaving through the room, pulling one of the dour-looking guards into the dance with her gossamer scarf. The other guards laughed, slapping each other as they watched her draw their friend into the center of the room. Away from the door he was supposed to be guarding.

Misdirection, Harte understood. It was the heart of any illusion, and Viola's was particularly effective.

Swiiip. Another knife sailed through the air, pinning the sleeve of another guard to the wall. More laughter erupted as he tried to free himself.

Harte began to move toward the closed gallery, to where the girl was standing with her back to the door, her hands behind her. Again, there was no betraying energy, no sign that she was using any affinity.

Clever thief. Talented, too, if she could pick that lock without looking *and* without magic. Luckily, she was too busy concentrating on her task to notice him approaching her, but she went completely still when he sidled up next to her.

"Fancy meeting you here," he said, dipping his head low so that no one else would hear. He was ready this time for the effect she had on him, the talent she had for distracting him when he should most be paying attention.

Her eyes widened, but that was the only indication of her surprise. "Go away," she told him, her hands still working behind her.

He had to admire the backbone in her. "You know, you can't use magic in here—they have Mageus watching for it."

"I'm aware," she said, glancing at him.

He frowned. "If you're doing what I think you're doing, you'll never get out of here without it."

"It's sweet of you to think I need saving, but I'll be fine. If you'd be a dear and leave me alone, that is."

"Save *you*?" he said, widening his eyes dramatically. "Is that what you think I'm doing?" He inched closer. "I'm only interested in saving myself. You do what I think you're about to do, and I might get caught in the crossfire."

"Then maybe you should get out of the way."

He moved closer, lowering his voice so only she could hear. "Maybe those men in the dark suits would be interested in meeting you. I'm sure they'd have a few questions about why you're dressed like that."

"I'd be happy to give them some answers," she said too sweetly, batting her eyes at him innocently. "I'm sure they'd love to hear all about a certain magician who has more magic than they realize up his sleeves."

"You wouldn't," he said, almost amused in spite of himself.

"I might," she said, but her eyes were laughing at him. "I've decided I kind of hate you, you know."

He found himself smiling. "I assure you, sweetheart, the feeling is mutual."

"Well, then . . . Since we seem to understand each other now, you might want to move."

The smile fell from his face. "Mo—"

The word was only halfway out when he felt the breath of air as a silver knife flashed between them. It was enough to make him step back.

Then the lights went out.

A CHANGE IN PLANS

Her heart was still pounding from the surprise of having Harte Darrigan materialize out of nowhere. She'd been so busy focusing on the feel of the lock, letting the vibrations from the pick guide her, that she hadn't even seen him until it was too late.

Thank god for Viola. Or thank god Viola had only distracted him, when Esta was pretty sure Dolph's assassin would have been just as happy to skewer them both. She'd definitely wanted to earlier, when Esta had explained her plan for Viola to create a distraction by replacing the troupe's dancer. She had a feeling Viola didn't forgive easily.

Not that she had time to worry about that. The second the lights went out, Esta slipped into the next gallery, leaving behind the gasping, buzzing crowd in the antechamber.

"Jianyu?" she whispered. "Are you here?"

"Where else would I be?" His voice came out of the darkness. "What is happening? This was not the plan."

"Plan's changed," she said, sparking a small flame and lighting the nub of a candle she'd carried in her sleeve. Then she lifted her tunic and removed the clothing she'd hidden there. "They have Mageus for guards. If you use your affinity, you'll never get out. Here—" She tossed him the gauzy pants and scarf. "Loosen your hair and put these on. And be quick about it."

Jianyu rubbed the silky fabric between his fingers. "These are for a woman."

"Yeah. Get moving." She took the bundle of objects Jianyu had collected and began fastening them beneath her clothes. She wrapped a rolled canvas around her upper thigh and tucked a couple of small carved cylinders into the fabric binding her breasts.

Jianyu wasn't changing. He simply glared at her. "You want me to dress as a *woman?*"

"That's the basic idea," she said, sliding a smaller canvas around her other ankle, fastening it in place with the garter for her socks.

"No," Jianyu said, dropping the sapphire silk into a pile at his feet.

Esta turned on him. "We have *maybe* two minutes left before the lights come back on. That means we have less than two minutes to get you out of here before we can't. In about ninety seconds, I'll be on the other side of that door and on my way to the carriage out back, and you'll be on your own. You can either get over your fragile masculine pride and put on the damn skirt or deal with the Order yourself."

After a moment of stony silence, he began unbraiding his hair, glaring at her all the while. He looked like he wanted to kill someone, and Esta knew he probably could, but he didn't argue as he made quick work of the rest, covering his head and face with the gauzy scarf. It didn't do much to hide his masculinity. If anyone bothered to really look, they would know he was a man dressed in women's clothing.

Not that they had any other choice at that point. She'd just have to hope that people would only see what they expected to, or that they wouldn't bother looking at all.

"Very pretty," she taunted as she slipped the last item into her waist-band. "Ready?"

Jianyu glared at her.

"Maybe relax your shoulders a bit?" she suggested. "If you want to get out of here, you need to at least *try.*"

"I *am* trying," he snapped, pulling himself up even taller and broader than before.

We are so screwed.

"Okay, well, try harder," she said, adjusting the scarf over his face to cover his scowl. "When you get out there, you need to pretend like you've been there the whole time. Follow Viola's lead." She snuffed the candle with her fingertips.

On the other side of the door, the crowd had grown frantic, which was convenient because their noise covered the sound of the latch as they entered the outer room. She made sure the lock caught, so it would look like the gallery had never been breached.

"Go," she whispered, pushing Jianyu into the crowd as the lights came back on.

There was a moment of shocked silence, before the crowd's voices rose again, louder than they'd been before. Men barked for someone to explain what had happened, and women gasped, grabbing at their jewels to make sure they were all in place.

"If you could give me your attention—" A voice came from somewhere on the other side of the room, low and male and full of its own importance, but it took a few more tries before the crowd would quiet enough to listen to the man speaking.

Nearby, Harte Darrigan blinked at the brightness, squinting as his eyes adjusted to the sudden return of the light. Esta feigned confusion like everyone else as she sidled away from his reach. In the far corner, J. P. Morgan had found something to stand on and was telling the crowd to stay calm, that it had simply been a problem with the power, but it had been solved and there was no reason to worry. The evening would go on as planned.

Not quite as planned, Esta thought as she lifted a tray from a nearby cart and made her way through the crowd. Afraid to jostle the items beneath her clothing, she walked cautiously.

In the center of the room, Morgan was commanding the musicians to begin playing again, and they immediately launched into another driving tune that was all drums and cymbals. Esta cringed as she saw that Jianyu was standing stiffly, his arms crossed over his chest, instead of making an effort to blend in. But no one seemed to notice. A few more minutes— another pass around the room for Viola and the boys, a careful exit for herself—and they'd all be safe.

Esta kept her pace steady as she moved ever closer to the arched entrance of the gallery, accepting empty glasses from people who seemed willing enough to forget the momentary darkness now that the lights were back on. From across the room, Viola caught her gaze and gave a subtle nod before she led the troupe—including Jianyu—beneath the arched entry, out into the museum. Their music faded as they moved away, until it stopped altogether.

They were out.

Now it was up to her to get their haul—and herself—out safely as well. Because if she was caught, there would be no one left to help her.

She was already halfway to the entry, only a few yards more to freedom, when Morgan began his speech about the collection. His voice boomed through the room as he declared his deep affection for the Ottoman Empire, for their great discoveries and mystical art.

Almost there, Esta thought, closing the final few feet between her and the exit. *A little farther—*

Then someone snagged her arm, and she startled, nearly dropping the tray of glasses. She looked over her shoulder to find Harte Darrigan's stormy eyes boring into hers. With the tray of stemware balanced precariously in her other hand, she couldn't shake him off. If his hand moved a few inches up her arm, he'd definitely feel the roll of stolen parchment she'd wrapped there, and especially after that little stunt she'd pulled on his stage, she didn't know what he would do.

"Let me go," she whispered furiously.

He studied her a moment longer with eyes that seemed far older than his years. Then he took the glass he was holding and placed it on her tray. "You missed one," he said. He still didn't release her arm.

She was trapped.

Panic seized the breath in her chest, made her feel as though every heartbeat was a step toward her inevitable end. Morgan's voice was still droning on, but he sounded very far away—like she was listening to him through a long tunnel. It felt like she was stuck in the spaces between seconds, unable to go back and make another choice. Unable to do anything to change what was about to happen without putting herself—and everyone else—in more danger.

But the sudden eruption of applause brought her back to herself. The room snapped into focus, and the panic that had strangled her receded to a dull ache. Her mind raced.

They were about to open the doors to the other gallery. In a moment they would see that the collection was gone. Once that happened, the museum would be locked down. She'd be trapped, strapped from head to toe with pieces of priceless art. She had to get out before that happened.

But he didn't release her. "Don't you want to see the exhibition?" he asked, his voice steady.

He knows. And now he was toying with her.

She glared at him and tried to tug away again, but it was too late. The *click* of the lock echoed through the room and the gallery doors opened with everyone watching, waiting to see Morgan's jewel of a collection.

A gasp rang out in the crowd as the gallery doors stood open, exposing the ransacked room, the missing collection.

The Magician glanced over as the news of the theft filtered through the crowd, and then he looked back at Esta. His eyes were curious and, if she wasn't mistaken, more than a little appreciative.

She could *not* be caught. Not now, before she had saved the Book and retrieved her stone. And not there, in a room filled with members of the Order.

With a quick motion, she flipped her tray toward him.

Instinctively, his whole body sprang into action. He released her and lunged for the tray to catch it before the glasses fell. But though he'd let her go, the racket of the glasses crashing to the floor caused the people around him to turn. Already another server was coming to help.

The mouth of the room was only a few feet away, but dark-suited men were moving to block any exit. She'd never make it, unless . . .

Esta knew it was a risk, but she couldn't be trapped. She had to get the art out. She had to get *herself* out. There wasn't a choice. So she pulled time around her and ran for it.

She didn't bother to see whether the guards sensed her magic as she slipped past them and into the hall. She didn't stop for anything, just ran as fast as her feet would carry her, down the winding staircase and back through the statue gallery to the service entrance. Barreling past another guard, who was frozen in midrun toward the gallery, she made it out of the museum, into the quiet night, but she didn't release her hold on time. She moved effortlessly through the silent, still world. The bare fingers of the park's trees, so much smaller than in her own time, were dark shadows against the star-filled sky as she passed the knifelike point of Cleopatra's Needle. They waved her on as she made her way down the lane to where the carriage was waiting.

The others would be gone, she knew. If everything had gone to plan. She didn't release time until she reached the dark body of the carriage. The horses nickered when she knocked, using the rhythm of beats she'd been taught. To her relief, the door opened.

But that relief changed to caution when she saw that Dolph sat concealed in the shadows, waiting. "You have the items?" he asked as she took the seat opposite him.

She gave a nod, and he rapped on the roof twice with his silver-topped cane to signal the driver. With a lurch, the carriage started off, rattling down the cobbled road.

The small, dark space felt too close, too confined with Dolph's long legs taking up most of the room between them. She pulled her legs as far from his as she could and tried to shake off her nerves. He'd taken a risk in allowing her to help them, and everything had gone wrong.

"Well?" His voice was low, expectant.

She began unfastening the items, taking them from their hiding places beneath her clothes. Dolph took them from her, one at a time, but his expression lit at the sight of a small, carved stone cylinder. He tucked it away in the inner pocket of his coat, like it was something more important than the rest.

After a few long moments of silence punctuated only by the rattling of the wheels and the strained squeak of the seat beneath her, Dolph spoke. "Nibs told me what happened tonight."

"He did?" Her mouth went dry.

"You took quite a risk, going through with things," Dolph said. "You could have gotten yourself out and left Jianyu to his own fate."

She relaxed a little. He wasn't talking about her use of magic. "That's true," she admitted. "I could have."

"You thought about it," he challenged, his expression unreadable in the dappled shadows of the coach.

"No, actually. Once I knew Jianyu was trapped, it never crossed my mind."

"I find that difficult to believe," Dolph said.

Esta leaned forward until her face was lit by the flickering light coming through the small window. She wanted him to see the truth of her words, the sincerity of her intention. Dolph Saunders needed to trust her if she was ever going to get into Khafre Hall. She needed to be on that crew if she was ever going to get close enough to stop the Magician and get her hands on the Book . . . or her stone. Her only way back was through Dolph.

"I never considered getting myself out," she told him. "You trusted me with this, and I was not going to betray that trust. My only thought was to find a way to get *everyone* out safely. I did my job, like I promised I would."

He considered that for a moment, but his expression didn't change. Instead, he leaned back in his seat lazily, his fingertips drumming against the silver Medusa that topped his cane. "Your job was to fleece the crowd," he said, his lean face grim in the shadows of the coach.

"Who said I didn't?" She pulled out a necklace studded with enormous diamonds and emeralds. The stones glimmered as they dangled from her fingertip. "Mrs. Morgan sent this along with her compliments."

Dolph's finger stopped moving. "Did she?"

Esta did let her mouth curve then. "Well, maybe she would have, if she had known it was gone."

As Dolph took the necklace from her, his expression grudgingly appreciative, Esta didn't feel any sense of victory. Dolph might be pleased, but she couldn't help worrying about what it meant that the Magician had seen her. Harte Darrigan would know Dolph was behind the robbery, and she didn't know what he might do with that knowledge.

And she couldn't help but worry that her use of magic to escape might come back to haunt her. To haunt them all.

A DAMN GOOD TRICK

I t had been a damn good trick, making all that art disappear in a matter of the two minutes or so the lights had gone out, and with none of them using their affinities. But the girl had left a mess in her wake, the least of which was the mixture of leftover champagne Harte was covered in and the crystal goblets shattered on the floor around him.

She seemed to have a way of quite literally disappearing every time they met. It was something to do with her affinity, he knew. He should have been annoyed by her habit of leaving him empty-handed and looking like an idiot, but that, too, was a damn fine trick, and he couldn't stop himself from admiring her for it. Even if this time she'd left him in a precarious place.

There had been no way around talking to the squat police captain. He stood, dripping and smelling like a cheap clip joint, as he relayed a version of what he'd seen.

He could have handed the girl and Dolph and the rest of them over, which would have certainly improved his standing with Jack, but that would've come with certain risks. Considering that the girl knew enough about him to make her dangerous, he hadn't been sure that telling the police everything was the best idea.

Better not to be caught in his own net. Better to have something up his sleeve against Dolph Saunders—and the girl—just in case.

If he'd been smarter, he would have left the minute he saw the girl. He had known something was about to happen, and he should have left instead of trying to find out what she was up to. Now he'd missed his curtain, which wouldn't go over well, considering the talk Shorty had given him the other day. He'd have to do damage control when he got back.

"The papers are going to have a field day with this," Jack said dully as he came up next to Harte. "The whole family is going to blame me, you know. So much for getting them off my back."

"It's damn unfair," Harte agreed, pretending more sympathy than he actually felt. "How much did they get away with?"

"Nearly everything of any real value." Jack glanced across the room to where J. P. Morgan and his son were still in tense discussions with the police chief. "At least three canvases were cut from their frames. Even if they're returned, they'll be irreparably damaged. And all the seals are gone, including the one I told you about." Then he noticed Darrigan's shirtfront and jacket were a mess—stained and damp. "What the hell happened to you?"

Harte made a show of examining his damp lapels. "Accident with one of the servers."

"Accident, you say?" Jack frowned, looking over the ruined jacket. "Which one was it? I'll look into it, make sure they're taken care of for you."

"Oh, don't bother," Harte said, waving it off. The last thing he wanted was for Morgan—or anyone else—to look too closely at him. Especially not when they were investigating a crime. "It happened when the lights went out. I don't think it could have been helped."

"Damn mess," Jack muttered. He glanced over at Harte, lowering his voice so no one would hear. "The head of security told my uncle there were definitely Mageus involved."

"Oh?" Harte said, trying to mask his surprise with bored indifference. "They know that for sure, do they?"

Jack glanced back at his uncle again and then pulled Harte away, steering him toward a quiet part of the room. "It's something new the director was trying. Employing people with, shall we say, *special* qualities. My uncle—and the Order—approved of it, if you can believe that. They didn't bother telling me, or I would have told them it was a mistake. As though they'd ever willingly give up one of their own."

"Thick as thieves," Harte agreed, eyeing the guards, who were still watching the room.

He reminded himself that the guards' affinities couldn't be *that* strong—they would have caught the girl, otherwise. Still, it wouldn't do to linger. It wasn't worth the chance. "Well," he said, clapping Jack sympathetically on the shoulder, "I've already missed my curtain, and I need to get back to explain things."

"I *am* sorry about that," Jack said with a frown.

Darrigan pasted an easy smile on his face. "I'm sure when the story hits the papers tomorrow, I'll be able to talk my way out of it," he said.

Jack snagged his arm. "You don't know how they did it, do you?"

Harte froze. "Excuse me?"

"How did they get everything out of that locked room? I watched them secure it earlier myself. No one was in there, and no one could *get* in there, not with this gallery filled with people. The lights weren't out for more than a minute or two." Jack hesitated, eyeing Harte. "It was a little like one of your tricks."

Cold unease trickled down Harte's spine. "I don't do tricks," he said carefully.

"You know what I mean . . . onstage?"

"Those are *effects*, Jack. Demonstrations of skill. Whatever magic might have been involved tonight isn't any I'm familiar with, and I'm a victim here as much as anyone—someone managed to take my watch in the confusion." He held up the empty chain to display the missing pocket watch.

"I know that." Jack rubbed his hand over his mouth. He looked tired and hungover, and it wasn't even past midnight. He looked *vulnerable*. "I'm sorry for dragging you into all of this."

"You know," Harte said carefully, taking advantage of the moment. "Maybe you're right. Maybe I *could* help you with this."

Jack looked up. "You could?"

"Of course, Jack. That's what friends do. They help each other. I don't know anything about the old magic, of course . . . but you're right. I know how to make things disappear better than anyone. Maybe I could figure out how they did it. I'm not making any promises, but I'd be more than willing to look into the matter."

A desperate hope lit Jack's eyes. "I'd appreciate it, Darrigan. I really would."

"And if we happened to figure it out, your uncle would appreciate it too, wouldn't he?"

"I'm sure he would."

"He'd have no reason to keep you out of the Inner Circle, would he?" Jack shook his head.

"And once you're one of them . . . you could put in a good word for your friend, couldn't you?"

"Of course," Jack said, understanding. He gave Harte a knowing smile. "It's what friends do."

Harte nodded. "Let me think about it and see what I can come up with," he told Jack. "I'll let you know."

"Thank you," Jack said, grasping his hand to shake it.

"But let's not tell anyone yet, okay? I wouldn't want to get their hopes up." *Or their suspicions,* Harte thought as he took the risk to send a small pulse of his power against Jack's hand.

When he released Harte's hand, Jack stared at him for a moment, a little dazed. "I'll talk to you soon, then," he said, before he turned away, heading toward the ransacked gallery.

Harte watched him go, the mixture of the pull of his affinity and adrenaline singing in his veins. He was closer than he'd ever been to hooking Jack and gaining the entry to the Order that he needed if he wanted to get the Book. If he wanted to get out of the city. But he had to be careful and take his time. There was no room for a single misstep. The girl knew too much. Dolph was too powerful. And if Harte wasn't careful, he and all his dreams could end up as shattered and pointless as the shards of crystal still littering the floor.

HIDDEN DEPTHS

Bella Strega

S itting cross-legged on her small cot of a bed, Esta chewed at her lip as she read Professor Lachlan's news clipping again. Once they'd returned to the Strega the night before, Dolph had thanked her again and left her to herself. But Esta hadn't been able to sleep much, not after she checked the clipping. She kept checking it throughout the night, hoping that something would be different. Yes, the letters had stopped wavering and the words had finally resolved themselves into clear sentences, but that hadn't improved things.

The story had changed.

No fire. No destruction of Khafre Hall. Instead, the article was a bland piece about a party the Order had thrown to thank their newest member, Harte Darrigan, for apprehending the mastermind behind the Metropolitan Museum robbery, a saloon keeper named Dolph Saunders. Some items were still missing, but the article said that because Saunders died on his way to the prison on Blackwell Island, authorities didn't have high hopes for recovering them. Especially since Saunders' crew had scattered, abandoning his saloon and other holdings, which were being confiscated by the city.

Of course he'd died, Esta thought as her stomach twisted. To get to the island, they would have taken him out of Manhattan . . . right through the Brink. Dolph wouldn't have stood a chance. None of them would have.

Somehow the future had changed. Most likely, her being there had changed it. The Magician's treachery was even worse now, and she didn't know what other implications that might have. She had to fix it, but she had no idea how.

A knock sounded at the door, startling her. "Coming," she called as she tucked the clipping back into its protective wax sleeve with shaking fingers and then slid the small packet down the front of her corset.

When she opened the door, Jianyu was waiting on the other side.

"Can I help you?"

His expression was unreadable. "Dolph wants to see you."

Her chest went tight. "What for?" she asked, glad that her voice didn't sound as shaky as she felt. She thought he'd been pleased with her when they arrived back in the Bowery late the night before, but with her unsettling discovery of the changes in the news clipping, she wasn't taking anything lightly.

"It was not my place to ask," Jianyu said evenly. "He's waiting in his apartment downstairs."

"Okay," she told him, smoothing her rumpled skirt. "Give me a minute?"

Jianyu nodded, but just as he turned to leave, he seemed to change his mind. "You dressed me as a woman."

"I did," Esta admitted, feeling more uneasy with every moment that passed beneath Jianyu's watchful gaze.

"It was insulting."

Esta frowned. "Only if you think women are somehow less than men."

"Are they not?" Jianyu asked, sincerely surprised and confused.

Frustration spiked. This was a different time, she reminded herself, and yet . . . "A woman saved you, so you tell me."

Jianyu seemed to consider this. "It is true that things would have been difficult for me without your help."

Esta snorted. "More like impossible."

"Then I suppose I am in your debt."

"Or we could just call things even," Esta said.

Jianyu studied her for a moment, and then he gave the barest nod and left without another word.

Esta watched him go, wondering what exactly had just happened between them. She wasn't sure, but she thought maybe she'd found another ally. That fact made her feel somewhat better as she made her way down to the door of Dolph Saunders' apartment. She hesitated for a moment, calming herself and gathering her wits about her, before she knocked.

"Come," a familiar voice called from inside.

The door was unlocked, so she eased her way into his rooms and was greeted with a welcome breath of warmth. A coal stove burned in the corner, and near it, Dolph sat at a small desk, making notes in his ledger. He didn't bother to look up when she came in, but the sight of him so soon after she'd read about his death shook her. If she didn't fix things, she was looking at a dead man.

"Jianyu said you wanted to see me?"

He must not have noticed the way her voice broke, because he never took his concentration from his ledger as he gestured for her to come in. "Give me a second," he said.

"Of course," she told him, finally taking a look around his home.

Dolph was a man of few words. He never dressed in anything but black or dark grays, which gave the impression that he was perennially waiting for a funeral to begin. With all his glowering, she didn't expect his apartment to feel so comfortable.

A faded floral carpet covered most of the bare floorboards, and the room had a softness that her own didn't have. The furnishings were worn and well used, but the delicate spindles of the straight-backed chairs against the wall and the graceful camelback arch of the small divan were the selections of someone with an eye for decorating. In all, it had a distinctly feminine feel, which was only underscored by the wispy lace panels over the windows on the back wall of the front parlor.

Above a small shelf lined with books hung a painting that Esta recognized. It was one of the larger oil paintings they'd liberated from Morgan's collection the night before. In it, a young man reclined beneath an apple tree, a dog at his feet and a wide book open in his hands as he pondered a fallen apple. Dolph had, apparently, wasted no time in making it his own.

The news clipping had mentioned the painting as part of the evidence they had against him, so seeing it hanging on his wall was another reminder of his new fate. She wanted to tell him to get rid of it, to get rid of all the evidence he might have, but she wouldn't be able to explain herself. She needed him to continue to trust her if she was going to fix things, so instead she gestured to the newly framed canvas.

"Is that supposed to be Isaac Newton?" she asked as she studied the scene. With the apple resting on the ground by his feet, it could have been depicting him discovering gravity, but it was a strange painting, otherwise. A crescent moon hung opposite a bright sun, and the book the figure held in his hands bore odd symbols that looked like a series of interlocking circles and parallelograms, with a star in the center. It wasn't any math or science she'd ever seen.

Across the room, Dolph's pencil stilled and he looked up, his pale eye taking her measure for a long moment. "It is."

"But this looks so . . . mystical. I thought he was a scientist."

Dolph's brow furrowed. "There never was much of a line between science and magic, especially not that far back. Early sciences—alchemy or theurgy, for instance—were just ways for those without affinities to try to do what Mageus could do. Newton wasn't any different, but Newton's the least interesting thing about that piece."

Then Dolph turned back to his ledger, making it clear he wasn't interested in further conversation on the topic.

Esta was about to ask him what the most interesting thing was, when she heard Professor Lachlan's voice in her head—*Patience, girl.* How many times had he reminded her to take her time, to avoid whatever impulse drove her forward until she thought the situation through and considered all the possible outcomes?

Too many times. And there was even more at risk now.

So she bit back the question and occupied herself instead by looking over the books in his small collection—Voltaire, Rousseau, and Kierkegaard, all in their original languages. She wasn't surprised, somehow.

Eventually, Dolph finished whatever he was doing in the ledger and closed it. "Tell me what you know of Harte Darrigan," he said finally.

"The Magician?" she asked, suddenly wary. *He can't know*, she reminded herself. "Not much," she hedged. "Nibs took me to see his show the other night."

"I'm aware. He told me that Darrigan was quite taken with you."

Esta frowned. "I don't know that I'd use those words, exactly."

"Really?" Dolph leaned back in the chair a little, crossing his arms over his chest and giving her the full weight of his stare. "What words would you use?"

Pain in my ass, thought Esta, trying not to let her nervousness show. *A pain in yours, too, if I don't stop him*. Not that she could tell him what she knew, how things might have changed. Dolph had no reason to believe her, and without her stone, she had no way to prove it.

"I don't know." She shrugged. "He seems talented enough, but I was onstage with him for less than five minutes."

"You talked with him again at the museum."

Her stomach twisted again. "I didn't plan that—"

"I never said you did," Dolph murmured. "But as I said, he seems taken with you."

"I'm not interested in him, if that's what you're worried about."

"And if I want you to be interested?" Dolph asked.

"I'm still not interested," Esta told him, firm.

He didn't say anything else at first as she stood there, growing increasingly uncomfortable.

"Was there something you needed from me?" she asked, breaking the silence when she couldn't stand it anymore. "I still have my quota to bring in today, and it's pointless to steal wallets if the money's already been spent."

"You won't need to worry about that today," he told her.

"Why?" she asked, her throat tight. "Did I do something wrong?"

He lifted himself from the chair without answering and took his time about rinsing his teacup and saucer in the long enameled sink in the attached kitchen. Esta shifted, trying not to let her impatience get the best of her as he set the cup aside to dry and crossed the room to fetch his coat. He'd already stepped past her and opened the door before he spoke again.

"Walk with me," he said, a command if ever there was one.

Curious and more than a little worried about her position with him, she didn't argue. They walked in a wordless, companionable silence through the dimly lit hallway, down the narrow stairs, and out onto Elizabeth Street.

"Am I allowed to ask where we're going?" she said once they'd gone more than a block without Dolph saying anything.

He glanced at her. "If I said no, would that stop you?"

"Probably not," she admitted.

"And if I don't want to tell you?"

"I'd probably be curious enough to follow you anyway."

"Fair enough," Dolph said. "We're going to be making some calls today."

"On who?" she asked.

He gave her an unreadable look and didn't answer as he continued on.

Two blocks later, they arrived at a building that looked like all the other tenements in the neighborhood: same worn redbrick walls, same cluttered fire escapes, same small children playing out on the walk, watched over by a tired-looking woman with a scarf wrapped around her head for warmth. Inside, it smelled of coal smoke and garlic, of onions cooked days before and too many bodies. The halls were narrow, like the ones above the Strega, and the walls were stained with the residue of the lamps burning softly in the windowless space.

On the fourth floor, Dolph knocked at a door and was let into an apartment by an older woman wearing a shapeless dress and an apron.

Inside the apartment, the air was filled with a sharp chemical scent. The furniture had been pushed up against the walls, and five children—none older than ten or eleven—sat in the center of the floor around a pile of silk flowers. They barely looked up at the visitors, quickly turning their small faces back to the task before them as they glued the tiny silk petals onto wire stems one by one.

"How are you, Golde?" When the woman gave an inarticulate shrug, Dolph went on. "I came to see about your husband," Dolph said, switching into German.

The woman shook her head. "He won't see anyone."

Dolph seemed to accept this and didn't press. "How is he?"

The woman twisted her hands in her apron as she sat at the table and began gluing her own flowers. "The doctors say he'll heal."

"His position?"

She shrugged, a small movement that broadcast her fear and worry without a single word. "Filled, I suppose. He'll find another. We'll get by."

Esta crouched down to watch the children at work as Dolph talked to the woman about the state of their affairs—the rent that needed to be paid, the groceries she could barely afford. The little ones looked at Esta with the same tired, cautious eyes as their mother, but the youngest held up one of the silk flowers as an offering, her fingers red and raw from her work.

Esta took the delicate bloom carefully and pretended to give it a sniff. The girl smiled softly. Suddenly Esta felt the warm pulse of magic, and the flower petals began to move, fluttering open and closed.

The girl grinned, proud of the demonstration, and Esta pulled a coin from her pocket and presented it to the child, whose eyes widened. "Go on," she whispered, but the child didn't seem to understand, so Esta placed the coin in the small hand and closed it.

"Where's your oldest, Josef?" Dolph asked, nodding to where Esta knelt with the children.

"Out," the woman said, her tone bleak. "Sometimes he collects coal for us during the day. Keeps us in warmth at least."

"And the other times?"

"With his father sick, he runs with a group of boys from the street." The woman shrugged, defeated. "I don't like them, but what can I do? He's nearly fourteen. I'm lucky he hasn't left altogether."

"Send him to me when he gets home. I have some work I can give him." When the woman frowned, Dolph spoke again to reassure her. "Nothing dangerous. I need someone to make small deliveries. He's welcome to collect your coal while he's out."

"My husband won't want any of your bargains," the woman said warily.

"No bargain required, and I won't ask your son for his oath, if that's what worries you. He's too young to be making those decisions, but he needs to be kept busy. Kelly or Eastman won't be so understanding if he gets mixed up with them. The boy can keep the position even once your husband's well, so long as he spends his nights at home with you."

The woman didn't argue the point any further, simply nodded her head and turned back to the flower she was piecing together.

Dolph glanced at Esta. "We've other stops to make."

At the next building, they visited a girl who couldn't have been any older than Esta herself. The baby on her hip fussed and a toddler played at her feet as Dolph accepted her cup of coffee and sat to talk with her.

"Dzień dobry, Marta. I came because I heard about Krzysztof.... There's been no sign of him? No news?" he asked in Polish.

The girl shook her head as she stood to stomp out the paper doll the toddler had just set on fire with nothing but his will and his affinity. "Nie," she said sharply, cracking the child across the hand, which caused him to begin wailing and set the baby off as well.

Dolph bent down to look at the little boy and placed his finger against his lip. The little boy seemed startled at the sudden attention and went quiet, his small lip still quivering as he tried to catch his breath. Taking a handkerchief from his pocket, Dolph wiped the snot that was running from the boy's nose, then ruffled his hair and offered him a wax-wrapped piece of caramel before turning back to the boy's mother.

The little boy remained silent, watching Dolph talk to his mother as he jawed at the candy. In the course of their conversation, Dolph promised the woman that someone would deliver laundry to be done from the Strega. They settled on a generous price, and he assured her he'd look into her husband's whereabouts himself.

The whole time Dolph spoke to the boy's mother, Esta couldn't help but picture him shackled in a prison boat, heading toward the Brink.

She'd been six when Professor Lachlan first explained the Brink to her. Until then, she hadn't understood they were trapped in the city. He'd taken her to the Brooklyn Bridge and told her about the Order. The farther they had walked along the bridge, the colder the summer day felt. Even before they came to the soaring arches of the towers, Esta had become so scared that she'd cried. Tourists eyed them both suspiciously as Professor Lachlan had picked her up and carried her back to where they'd started. If it had been terrifying to simply be close to the Brink, she couldn't imagine the horror of crossing.

Dolph didn't deserve that. *No one* did.

The morning wore on, with Esta pretending not to listen to the discussions Dolph had with one family after another. Each apartment was more cramped than the last, each family more desperate. Most of them had children who were wild to be outdoors but who clearly had affinities they couldn't control yet. And without control, the children had to be kept hidden.

By the time it was past noon, the sun had burned away the hazy clouds and the air was teasing them with the promise of spring.

"You hungry?" Dolph asked.

"I could eat," she told him as her stomach growled in response. She still didn't understand what his purpose had been in taking her with him, showing her all he had.

She followed him back through the neighborhood. Despite relying on his cane, Dolph walked at a quick pace through the crowded streets. He had a way of moving that made his limp seem more like a strut. A confidence that fooled you into thinking there was nothing wrong with his leg.

When they came to Houston Street, Esta was surprised to see she recognized their destination. In her own time, Schimmel's Bakery was on the other side of Houston, but when she stepped up into the tiny storefront, the smell of bread and onions wrapped around her and squeezed her with nostalgia. All at once, she was a small girl again, remembering the times Dakari had taken her out for a snack after their training session, an apology and reward all at once. And they'd often gone to Schimmel's for a knish.

She let the memory of her other life wash over her for a moment. Dakari's kind, crooked smile. Mari's tart comebacks to every one of her complaints. Even Logan's condescension. And Professor Lachlan . . . trusting her to get this job done, one way or another.

They were all unreachable to her. With the changes in the news clipping still tucked against her skin, she wasn't sure if she'd ever be able to reach them again.

In all her trips, all the jobs she had done, she had never felt so untethered from her own history, which she could only hope still lay somewhere, unreachable, in the future. Esta never wallowed, but she allowed herself a moment to miss it—the indoor plumbing and the speed of cars and the streets that weren't filled with shit. And the people she cared about.

"What will you have?" Dolph asked, eyeing her as though he understood her mind had been elsewhere. But he didn't call her on it and he didn't press, and she found herself unspeakably grateful for that.

They took their order to go, shifting the warm, heavy pastries between their fingers to keep from being burned as they walked and ate.

It tasted the same, Esta thought. A hundred years, and the way the starchy filling of the knish melted in her mouth, dense and warm with just enough salt, took her right back to being ten years old. To the fall days when she would sit with Dakari on a bus bench, trying to eat the whole thing before it went cold as he reviewed the day's lesson, her progress and her mistakes.

She'd been nearly eleven before she could finish a whole one on her own, but now, with her hunger gnawing at her, one didn't seem nearly enough.

"Exactly how many languages *do* you know?" Dolph asked.

The knish suddenly tasted like ash in her mouth. Esta swallowed the bite she'd just taken, choking it down as her stomach flipped nervously, and then regarded him as blankly as she could manage. "I'm not sure what you mean."

Dolph gave her an impatient look. "I watched you today as we made the calls. You were listening."

"I wasn't—"

But he shot her a look that made her swallow her protest. "How many?" he pressed.

"Several," she admitted finally. It had been a major part of her training, and luckily she picked them up quickly.

Dolph took another mouthful of his knish. "You didn't think that relevant information to mention before?"

She shrugged, choosing her words carefully. "Not everyone appreciates the skill. Like you said, I *was* listening today. A lot of people see that as more of a liability than an advantage."

He nodded. "Lucky for you, I'm not one of them."

She blinked up at him, relieved. "You're not?"

He shook his head. "But don't think you can hide things from me without it costing you my trust."

"I won't make that mistake again," she assured him, ducking her head and hoping he couldn't read the lie in her words.

"See that you don't."

After that, they walked in silence for a while before she felt brave enough to ask the one question that had been bothering her all morning. "Why did you bring me along today?"

"In part, I wanted to see how you would react to the people I protect. There are too many who believe we should keep to our own, and they're not willing to cross new lines. A lot of people never talk to anyone who isn't from the village they grew up in. A lot of people are only interested in protecting their own. That's what the Order wants. They don't want Mageus to realize we have more in common than we have differences, because keeping us divided means their own power stays secure.

"But I also wanted you to see with your own eyes what I'm trying to do and what's at stake if we fail." He popped the last of his knish into his mouth and finished it before he continued. "Golde's daughter took a liking to you." He gestured to the flower Esta still had tucked into her hair.

"She was sweet," Esta said, feeling suddenly defensive.

"She is. But what life does she have to look forward to? She'll live out her days in those rooms, or other rooms like them, without any chance for something more. All because she can make a silken flower bloom. If she's lucky, the Order will never touch her directly, never let her building burn down around her or cart off her father or husband for crimes they didn't commit. She probably won't be lucky. Few are. Marta wasn't so lucky. Her husband disappeared a little over a week ago. She has no other family here. If I didn't step in, what would become of her and her children without him?"

"And that's it?" she asked, still trying to figure out what made this man tick. If everyone had a weakness, everyone also had an angle. She didn't believe that Dolph Saunders was any different. "You just help them, with no expectation of reward? No conditions?"

He considered her question for a moment before he spoke, and when he finally did, his words were measured. "I'm no saint, Esta. I'm a businessman with multiple properties, with employees who depend on me, with people in this neighborhood whose respect I've earned. I'd like to continue being that man. I've always been ambitious, maybe too ambitious for the life I was born into. If the Order falls, that's good for me, for my businesses. For my future prospects in this city. If I'm the one to bring the Order down, people will be grateful and I will reap the benefits. There's no doubt of that, and I'd be lying not to admit it.

"But I also know what it means to starve. I've slept on the streets and I learned how to escape from those who would hunt me. I know the strength of will it takes to fight back from the bottom, and I know that not everyone has that strength. So, yes, I have my own interests, but I'm not completely without a heart, whatever the rumors about me say."

Esta studied him for some sign of the lie in his words. Professor Lachlan had taught her everything he could, had trained her to bring down the Order that pressed them into narrow lives. But he'd never concerned himself with the world beyond their small crew. To free themselves was enough. But here was Dolph Saunders, a man who had every reason to be out for himself, for the power he could grab, telling her something different. "And you trust them? You trust all the people you help not to give you up to the Order?"

"What choice do I have?" he asked wryly. "No one can survive on their own. Not even me.

"Do you have any other questions?" he asked, but in his tone was a clear indication that he was done answering them.

She shook her head. She already had too much to think about.

"You handled yourself well last night. Jianyu probably owes you his life."

"I did my job."

"So humble?" Dolph's mouth curved slightly. "I think you have depths you're still hiding from me, Esta Filosik. I'm not sure I like that about you."

She frowned, worried by the sureness in his voice. "I would never do anything to hurt you or anyone you protect." It was a lie, but she managed to choke it out with admirable ease. She'd been trained well, after all.

Yet all her training couldn't stop the twist of guilt she felt now that she knew Dolph and the rest. There was no way to do what Professor Lachlan had asked her without hurting them all in the end. And if she hurt Dolph, she was hurting every person he helped in turn.

"But how far would you go for them?"

Esta didn't answer at first. She understood he was appraising every move she made, every word she spoke. Agreeing too readily would mark her as a fool, or worse. When she finally answered, she spoke only the truth: "If it was to stop the Order? I'd risk everything."

"So would I," he told her. He hesitated briefly before he spoke again. "I have plans for the Order," he explained. "Perhaps you could help me with those plans. Nibs seems to think you might be able to."

Licking her lips, Esta considered her next words carefully. "I . . . I'm not sure if Nibs is right, but I'd be willing to do whatever I can."

"I'm glad to hear that," he said, though his expression didn't soften. "Then I have a job for you. We can call it a test to see how serious you are and how much I can depend upon you. My plans depend on someone joining us. Someone who has been quite reluctant to do so."

"Harte Darrigan," she said, putting the pieces together.

"He saw you at the museum, and he knows you work for me. That makes him a liability."

"I'll make sure he's not," she promised. She'd put to rights whatever she'd done and put Harte Darrigan back in his place.

Dolph chuckled. "If I wanted him dead, I'd send Viola," he joked. "My plan *depends* upon Darrigan's help. I want you to get him for me."

SPARKS OF POWER

The Docks

The old fool was never going to finish with his tinkering. Jack paced the dirt floor of the warehouse as the sound of metal on metal and the blast of the welding torch grated at his raw nerves. Ever since the robbery at the museum, he'd paid the old man double to work around the clock to finish the machine. It should have been done by now.

Finally, the old man backed away from the machine and gave it one more look. "That should do it."

"Have you made the adjustments I sent you?" Jack asked, holding up the roughly cut diamond. There would be hell to pay when his father found out how much he'd spent on the stone, but if this worked, it wouldn't matter. If this worked, they would thank him. He'd be a goddamn hero.

He didn't know why he hadn't thought of it before, but something had clicked when he'd learned that his aunt had lost a family heirloom at the museum—a priceless necklace filled with rare emeralds and diamonds. They were singular, irreplaceable . . . and they had given him an idea.

Of course he couldn't simply generate power with a machine, no matter how complex and modern it might be. He needed an object for the power to be focused into.

Didn't the Order depend on their artifacts to keep the protections secure in the Mysterium? He'd never seen them himself, but he'd heard about them—five gemstones that one of the most powerful alchemists to have ever lived had collected from five ancient civilizations steeped in magic. That alchemist had found a way to imbue the artifacts with power through complex rituals, power that the Order could draw on still. True, only the Inner Circle understood the secrets of the artifacts, but Jack was no idiot. He'd spent the last year learning everything he could—everything his uncle and the others would permit him to. If those stones could hold magical power, why couldn't this one?

It had cost him everything he had—and some that wasn't actually his to give—to convince the antiquities dealer to part with the stone. But he needed something more than a simple jewel. This diamond had been found in the tomb of Hatshepsut, the same pharaoh who had erected the very obelisk that now stood in Central Park. There was a symmetry to it that buoyed Jack's confidence. It could work.

"I've made the changes," the old man said with a less-than-hopeful look as he took the stone and examined it. "But I don't see how a bit of rock will be enough to defuse the power buildup this thing generates."

"It's not your job to see. Just follow instructions," Jack ground out. "You *have* followed my instructions, haven't you?"

The old man nodded.

"Then there shouldn't be any problem," Jack snapped. "Get this installed in the central globe, and then start her up. Let's see if you're going to disappoint me again."

The old man gave a worried nod and then went back to the wiring. A few minutes later, he connected the power and a buzzing roar began from somewhere deep within the heart of the machine. Then the large, orbital arms began to rotate, slowly at first and then faster, until the center globe began to glow.

"It won't hold," the old man said, shielding himself behind a large metal toolbox as he started to pull on the wires.

But Jack was confident, or if not confident, desperate enough to give it a chance. "No! We'll wait. See what she can do."

Egad, it's a thing of beauty. Sleek and modern, powerful in its promise. The arms spun, crossing each other in a blur of motion, like erratic rings of Saturn. Bolts of energy—of magic—leaped between the twin poles of the sphere. A perfectly contained universe. Only this was a cosmos *he* would control.

Let the Order laugh about his other failures. They would eat their words in the end. With this machine, he would do what they had only ever dreamed of doing. He would put a stop to the ever-encroaching threat of the Mageus. He would end them, once and for all. And when they were gone, when the city was clean and free from their corruption, the Order would recognize his brilliance, would reward him as they moved into the future, returning the city—the entire country—to the promise it had once held.

"Mr. Jack," the old man shouted.

"I said to wait!" he yelled, barely able to hear himself over the noise the machine made. His eyes were wide and his hair whipped at his face, lifted by the wind the machine created in the center of the room. It felt as though he were standing on the edge of a precipice between the past and the future, and the violent charges of energy that licked at his skin only made him want to move closer to the edge.

His machinist pulled himself farther behind the metal box, but Jack stood in the open, daring fate to contradict him again. If the blasted thing exploded, let it take him with it. That would be easier than admitting he'd failed again. Or having to explain to his father where the money in his trust fund had gone.

But the machine didn't explode. It picked up steam, the bolts of energy dancing around the central globe, chilling the air that whipped around them. Sparks of life, of power.

"It's holding!" he said, unable to contain the laugh as the wonder and a dangerous hope grew in his chest. "It's working!"

The old man peered out from behind the toolbox, his eyes wide.

Jack laughed again, relief and excitement mixing in a heady cocktail that had his blood humming. *It worked.* "This is only the beginning," he said, more to himself than to the man who had built the machine.

It would be *his* beginning. No one else's.

He walked to the controls and made a few adjustments, levering the machine until its power was focused exactly where he wanted it. He pointed that power toward the part of the city that was no better than a rat's nest, considering the vermin that hid themselves there. He would take back his city.

Jack smiled. *Balance, indeed.*

"Send word if anything changes," Jack called, fitting his hat on his head as he made his way out into the cold. His machine worked. He'd been right about the diamond. Everything would work out. He needed a drink to celebrate.

A DIFFERENT KIND
OF DANGER

Wallack's Theatre

After the week he'd had, Harte needed a good night. He'd managed to talk his way out of missing the performance when he got caught up at the Metropolitan—the front-page spread in the *Sun* had helped with that. But because it had mentioned him by name, Paul Kelly's boys had been back. Kelly hadn't been happy to see that Harte had been making progress with Jack and not cutting him in on the action.

Harte thought he'd managed to convince Torrio and Razor that he needed a little more time, but then he'd spent the rest of the week waiting for the other shoe to drop. And avoiding Jack, because he still had no idea how he was going to explain the museum robbery without putting himself at risk.

It didn't help much that the audience had been cold so far, barely impressed with his sleight of hand and only somewhat amused as he made the impossible seem possible. But they hadn't turned on him yet. The almost full house had everything to do with what was about to happen—they were waiting with growing impatience for the debut of his newest, most death-defying escape.

The man he'd selected from the audience to secure his handcuffs and chains had already returned to his seat with the smug assurance that there was no way Harte could get out. He made a show of wriggling and writhing to demonstrate how secure they were, because it never hurt to add a bit of drama. When two stagehands lowered him into the clear tank of tepid water, bound in chains and wearing nothing more than a pair of bathing shorts, the audience went gratifyingly silent as he sank to the bottom.

The screen hadn't yet been lowered in front of the tank when the theater lights surged, pulsing like a heartbeat for a moment, and then went completely dark.

Even under the water, he could hear the frantic murmuring of the crowd, and he felt an answering panic. He knew it was impossible, but he swore the flare of the lights before they went out had pulled at his affinity, had made him feel a hollow ache that darkened the edges of his vision and caused his head to swirl.

But when he gasped, the mouthful of water he took in reminded him of where he was and what was at stake. He forced himself to let go of his panic and to focus on taking advantage of the unexpected drama of the situation.

Working quickly, he slipped the metal pin from its hiding place under a false fingertip, and contorting himself as he'd practiced hundreds of times before, he wedged it into the locks on the cuffs. By the time the stagehands lit the kerosene lanterns at the foot of the stage a few minutes later, Harte was already out of the tank, dripping wet and holding the heavy chains in his outstretched hands.

The crowd went wild. Even in the dim light, he could see the amazement on their faces as wonder replaced fear. He'd not only escaped the water—this time, he'd also defeated the utter darkness that had alarmed even the most cynical men in the audience.

He gave the house his most dazzling smile and took his bow, letting the rumble of the crowd's approval roll over him. But their thunderous applause did nothing to alleviate the unease that clung to him, as cold and uncomfortable as his wet drawers. He gave his audience one last grateful salute before he ceded the stage to Evelyn and her so-called sisters.

As the first of the three girls sashayed into the spotlights, the crowd erupted again, this time in hoots and whistles. Apparently, a pair of legs was all it took for the audience to forget their amazement. The realization dulled the usual shot of adrenaline he got from being onstage, leaving him feeling jittery and nervous, aching to flex his affinity again.

Harte handed the unlocked chains to one of the stagehands and pulled a robe around himself as he navigated the maze of ropes and pulleys backstage and made his way back to his dressing room.

He wasn't surprised, somehow, to see the girl waiting for him. He'd been expecting something like this for days now, ever since he'd almost ruined her chance to escape at the museum. Still, her appearance, a burst of color and fire in his drab little dressing room, made him pause.

"I'm guessing Dolph sent you," he said, closing the door behind him.

She was dressed in a deep-plum-colored skirt and a creamy blouse that draped over her curves without hiding them. Her dark hair was pulled back from her face and gathered loosely at the nape of her neck. Delicately carved jade combs accented the burnished-chestnut curls. Dressed as she was, she could have passed for one of the ladies on Park Avenue, but the wicked spark in her eyes was at odds with the polish of her clothes.

It wasn't that long ago that John Torrio had been sitting in that same place, and Harte had the sudden thought that he wasn't sure which of the chair's occupants might be more of a threat to his own well-being.

"Back to assault me again?" He tucked his hands into the pockets of the robe and wished like hell she hadn't come.

Most of all, he wished there wasn't a part of him that was glad to see her again, safe and whole. And in his dressing room.

"Unfortunately," she said, leaning toward him almost conspiratorially, "I'm under strict orders not to. This time, at least."

"How disappointing that must be for you," he drawled, relaxing a little into her humor.

"You have no idea." She sighed dramatically and leaned back in his dressing chair. Shadows thrown by the lamp flickered across her face, and he had the distinct feeling she was laughing at him, despite the serious expression on her face. "I did want to thank you, though," she said, and he could tell that the words cost her.

Amused despite himself, he crossed the room to where his clothes were waiting for him on the radiator. "For?"

"For not telling anyone what you saw the other night," she said.

He glanced back at her. "Who says I haven't?"

She frowned, her dark brows pulling together. "Morgan looked pretty upset in that picture on the front page. I doubt I'd be here if he had any idea who was involved."

"He was," Harte admitted. "Very upset. I wouldn't thank me just yet, though."

"No?" She tilted her head slightly, an almost imperceptible shift, but enough to tell him she was worried.

Good. Let her worry. She kept him on his toes every time they met, so it was only fair he got to do the same. Never mind how much he was growing to like their games.

"You never know when I might happen to remember something." He gave her a meaningful look. "Something that the police might find interesting."

"Are you trying to blackmail me?" she asked.

"Not trying, no. Not yet, at least." He smiled pleasantly, because he had the sense it would irritate her even more. "But give me time, and I might find something I want from you."

She let out a derisive laugh. "In your dreams."

He winked. "Every night, sweetheart."

"Look, as much fun as this has been, I'm only here because Dolph needs a favor from you."

"I'm well aware of what Dolph wants from me. I'm also pretty sure I've already made my answer clear about that particular topic."

"I'm supposed to change your mind," she said, fluttering her thick lashes in his direction.

Understanding the ruse for what it was, he laughed. "Seeing as there isn't any shortage of beautiful women in my business, even a figure as fine as yours probably won't be enough to turn my head." He gave her a wry look as he stripped off his robe and hung it over the dressing screen. "No offense, of course," he said as an afterthought.

"None taken."

If he'd been hoping to make her uncomfortable, it didn't work. She didn't seem the least bit concerned now that he was standing in little more than a pair of sodden shorts. Or that she was in a mostly darkened room alone with him. She didn't even look away. If anything, she seemed to be enjoying herself. Her expression was one he recognized too well—the anticipation of the game. Which only served to irritate him more.

"Considering I have information that could make Dolph's life much more uncomfortable, it seems like I'm the one who should be asking for favors," he said.

"What sort of favor would you like?" she asked, her gaze unwavering.

He'd just stood on a stage in front of three hundred people, but he felt suddenly, inexplicably bare. Like she'd turned his own state of undress against him.

"I'd have to put some thought into it," he said.

"Be careful you don't hurt yourself," she said, her eyes wide in mock concern.

He shook his head at her cheek and stepped behind the dressing screen to shuck off his wet shorts and pull on dry ones. And to give himself some space so he could think.

It was unnerving, the way she looked at him so directly, without a blush to her cheeks or any sign of discomfort at all. But he also admired her for it . . . not that he had any plans to let her best him again.

"There's got to be something you want," she said. "Something Dolph can do for you to change your mind."

"Dolph Saunders doesn't have anything I want," he said truthfully as he pulled on his warm pants. From the other side of the screen, he heard the sound of metal on metal, and he looked to see what she was doing.

"There's no key for those," he warned when he saw her playing with the handcuffs that hung from his dressing table.

"Really? Then I suppose I should be extra careful." With a flick, she locked one of the iron cuffs around her wrist. "Oops." She brought her gloved hands to her mouth, which only drew attention to how pink her lips were. How soft they looked. How they'd felt against his.

He remembered those lips. . . . He also remembered the teeth behind them. Some things weren't worth the trouble.

"Guess I'm stuck." Her eyes never left his. "I'll just have to hang around here for a while . . . until you see things my way."

"Like I said, I'm not interested in whatever Dolph wants from me." Which wasn't the complete truth. He was more interested than ever in getting himself out of town, especially with Paul Kelly's boys breathing down his neck. It just wasn't enough to make him interested in getting caught in Dolph Saunders' web. Whatever Dolph had planned, it would be dangerous and reckless, like it always was. Now that Dolph didn't have Leena to ground him, it would probably be even more so. "I've never really had a taste for suicide."

"Your act indicates otherwise," she drawled, the handcuff still dangling from her wrist like a bracelet. "You were dying out there."

"Funny." He gave her a dark look.

"It's a bit stale, don't you think?" She stepped toward him slowly, a challenge if ever there was one. "Houdini already has the market on escape acts. You need something"—she waved her hand vaguely, letting the cuff swing loose on her wrist—"you know, to spice things up. I'd be happy to give you some pointers, if you'd like."

If she hadn't been so bad at seduction, he would have been more irritated about the Houdini comment. She would have been better to come at him straight, not that he'd be telling her that anytime soon.

"*You're* going to give me pointers?" He wanted to laugh, but then she leaned close, and the scent of her strangled his senses and made his throat go tight.

"Don't you remember?" she whispered in his ear. "The crowd loved us."

"Did they?" He turned his head so their faces were barely a breath apart, and he sensed that she had to steady herself.

Interesting. She didn't want him to touch her, but she also didn't want him to know she was avoiding it. He could use that.

"Well, they loved *me*," she said, her pink lips twitching in amusement. "They were simply tolerating you."

He could feel the warmth radiating from her, and she smelled like sunshine. Like fresh laundry and soap. That close, her eyes looked even more like dark honey, but they also held a challenge, and he never could refuse a dare. He leaned closer still, enjoying the way she tensed as she stopped herself from backing away. Enjoying turning her game back on her.

"Tolerating me, you say?" He stopped short of touching his lips to her neck.

"Mm-hmm," she murmured, suddenly sounding awfully breathless.

"What if what I want is you?" he asked.

"I'd say you couldn't have me."

"No?" And then he latched the other handcuff around her wrist.

Her eyes widened, and she backed away from him, but to his surprise, she didn't panic or curse him for seeing through her ruse, as he'd expected. She didn't look thrown at all, just examined her locked wrists and did the one thing he didn't expect: She *laughed.* Delight sparked in those glittering eyes of hers.

"You said there's no key?" She didn't seem the least bit worried.

"I lost it years ago," he told her with a shrug. He turned away from her to take his shirt from the radiator and slip his arms into its warmth, satisfied with the spot he'd managed to maneuver her into. Until he remembered the lock she'd picked at the museum.

But by the time he turned back around, her wrists were already free, and she was dangling the unlocked handcuffs from her fingertip.

YOU CAN'T CON A CON

I 'm afraid it's going to be harder than that to get rid of me," Esta said, enjoying the look on Harte Darrigan's face at how quickly she'd managed to escape.

It was a pretty enough face, she supposed. He had rough, brooding good looks at odds with the refined act he put on, both of which were only improved by the smudges of kohl beneath his eyes. But she knew from her experience with Logan that charm and good looks often only went skin deep. Darrigan was too good of a performer to reveal whatever was beneath that charm of his, and she was too smart to be taken in by the charm itself—or whatever was beneath, come to think of it.

Still, she had to admit, she'd enjoyed the view when he'd taken off the robe to expose the wet shorts he was wearing. Who wouldn't? They'd clung to his well-muscled thighs, which only complemented his flat stomach and broad, defined shoulders. He had an angry-looking, angular welt on his right shoulder, like a brand or a scar, which was at odds with the uptown act he put on. An injury from some past life, she suspected. Otherwise, his body was damn near perfect—definitely the result of a lot of hard work.

She couldn't help but admire that, and not only because he was nice to look at. It meant he knew what it was to work at something, to master it. He knew what it meant to not *only* depend on magic.

It was a lesson she'd learned as a girl. When Professor Lachlan first taught her how to dip into a pocket for a fat purse, he never let her use her affinity. Only once she could lift a wallet without tipping off the mark did he show her how magic could amplify and augment her already developed skills.

Admiration or not, she wouldn't let herself be distracted. Not by the magician's corded arms or by his teasing smile, which was probably another mask. According to the news clipping, the Khafre Hall job *wasn't* a fact anymore. She had to get Harte Darrigan on board, to make sure he was part of the team *and* to make sure he wasn't the one who gave up Dolph. She didn't have time to swoon over some boy, no matter how pretty he was.

He took the cuffs from her, frowning as he examined them.

"I didn't break them, if that's what you're wondering," she said when his brows drew together in a puzzled expression. She held up the hairpin she'd used. It was the only useful thing about the elaborate style that one of Dolph's people had done for her earlier that day.

Esta had tried to tell them that Harte Darrigan wasn't going to be impressed by a new outfit or hair, but they'd insisted. *Seduce him,* they'd said, but a con only works if the mark wants what you're selling.

The handcuff trick *did* seem to impress him, though. For a moment at least.

But a second later, he shrugged indifferently and pulled his armor back into place as he hung the cuffs from the hook where she'd found them. "An easy enough trick to manage with some practice, I suppose. It's not a secret that I keep those here."

"Try another pair," she challenged. "There's not a lock that's ever stopped me before."

"After that trick at the museum, I don't doubt it. But I know how to pick a lock too, sweetheart."

"Bet you I'm faster."

As he studied her, she could see the internal struggle. A part of him, she knew, itched to test her, to show her that *he* was better. But the other part eventually won out. "Like I said, I'm not interested in your games, and I'm still not interested in whatever Dolph Saunders has planned."

"Maybe you should be." She took another step toward him. "How long do you think this gig is going to last for you?" she asked.

"As long as I want it to." He gave her a smug look and then set to fastening the buttons on his shirt.

"The same tired tricks can only work for so long."

"They're not tricks," he corrected. "They're *effects*. And I can always come up with new ones."

"Same tired audience, though. Eventually they're going to want something new. *Someone* new."

"You have no idea what you're talking about," he said, but his expression wasn't so sure.

"But if the Brink came down," she continued, ignoring his outburst, "you could get out of this town."

"Who says I want to?"

She couldn't help but laugh at that. The yearning in his expression was so stark, it was unmistakable. "If you could leave New York, you could have a new town whenever you wanted one. A new audience every night. The whole world would be open to you."

A strange expression crossed his face for the briefest of moments, transforming it. But then he seemed to collect himself, and his usual mask of pleasant indifference snapped back into place. "Who says I need Dolph Saunders to get out of this town?" He finished straightening his collar in the mirror before taking a black silk tie from the hook nearby.

She didn't like this newfound confidence of his. "He can offer you protection," Esta said, grasping for some other angle to disarm him. She reached for the information she'd been armed with. "You *and* your mother."

Harte went very still. "I don't take threats lightly."

"It wasn't meant to be a threat," Esta told him, confused at his reaction.

"Considering that very few know I even *have* a mother, I'm not sure how I could take it as anything else." He was still tense.

"Everybody has a mother," Esta said with a halfhearted laugh, trying to appear more relaxed than she felt. Something had changed when she mentioned his mother. Apparently, Dolph and Nibs had given her just enough information to hang herself. Any ground she might have gained had slipped away, taking more with it.

Harte was silent for another long, uncomfortable moment, studying her as though he was looking for some hint at what her game was. In that moment, he looked every bit the Magician she'd expected to encounter. Cold. Ruthless. And completely capable of double-crossing anyone.

After a moment, he spoke. "I'll consider Dolph's proposal if you tell me something."

"What's that?" she asked, wary.

"What, exactly, does Dolph have on you?" He took a step toward her, his head cocked to the side in a question.

"Nothing," she lied. He was too close and the room felt suddenly too small. She lifted her chin. "I'm useful to him."

"Is that all you are?" Harte asked, studying her more intently. "Useful? It seems so . . . *pedestrian*."

She couldn't stop the image of Charlie Murphy, red-faced in the street, from flashing through her mind. And she couldn't help but think of Dolph, sailing to the prison on Blackwell Island, helpless against the Brink.

"Ah, so he *does* have something on you," he said, satisfied. "I figured as much."

"You figure wrong," she said, but the game had already changed. She'd managed to hold her own at first, maybe even caught him off guard with the handcuffs, but now he was on the offensive.

Harte Darrigan shook his head. "No, I don't think so. Dolph has never been one for charity cases," he told her. "Whatever help or promises he's made you, he'll take it out of you in kind. That's how all the bosses downtown work, and he's no different. Once you're in, it's impossible to get away."

"You don't know what you're talking about," she said, lifting her chin. Hadn't she seen with her own eyes what Dolph was doing, how he was helping the weakest among them?

He ignored her protests. "Tell me, do you already wear his mark?"

"His mark?" she asked before she could stop herself.

She cursed inwardly when Darrigan smiled, because she knew she'd just revealed that there were other things about Dolph Saunders she didn't understand, things that Harte Darrigan knew about, which gave him an edge she couldn't afford.

"I'm sure you've seen the tattoo he gives those in his crew. It's always been the price of admission for his protection." He turned from her then and took a vest from a hook on the wall. "It's not one I'm willing to pay." His storm-cloud eyes were steady on her, determined. "Ever."

She hadn't been around long, but she had noticed the tattoos that some of those around the Strega wore. She just hadn't understood what they were. "He may be willing to negotiate that point," she told him, a bluff if there ever was one.

He tossed a disbelieving look in her direction as he buttoned the vest. "I can't imagine he would. No mark, no way to control me."

Just then, his dressing room door opened, and Esta turned to see a woman with aggressively red hair peek her painted face in. "Harte, dear," she started to coo, but when she saw Esta, her eyes narrowed. "Oh. So sorry," the woman said, not at all sounding like she was. "I didn't realize you were entertaining."

"I wasn't," Harte told the woman, who stepped into the room without being invited. "She was just—"

"Having the most delightful chat with a dear old friend," Esta interrupted, using the woman's unexpected appearance to her advantage and taking back control. She infused her words with the notes of an Eastern European accent as she offered her hand to the woman. "It's so lovely to meet one of his *leetle* theater friends," she said with a smile that was all smug condescension. "I am Esta von Filosik, of course."

The woman's eyes went cold. "You say you're a friend of his?"

"No—" Harte started to say, but not before Esta spoke over him.

"Of course!" she lied easily. "We met ages ago, in Rastenburg, when he studied under my father. We were but children then, but we became"—she paused dramatically and slid a warm look to Harte—"quite *close*. Did we not, *darling*?"

"So this is what you've been running off to?" The woman's mouth went tight.

To Esta's immense satisfaction, Harte Darrigan—for once—seemed at a loss for words.

"He left to continue his studies, but now we are reunited," Esta told the woman, sidling up to Harte and slipping her arm through his in a proprietary way. He started to pull away, but she held him tight. "And you are?"

"Evelyn DeMure," the woman said, making an obvious show of looking Esta over from head to toe.

As she did so, Esta felt the warm energy of Evelyn's magic wrap around her, and she had the sudden feeling of being drawn to her, the sudden desire to release Harte. She couldn't seem to stop her arms from falling away. . . .

"Evelyn," Harte warned.

A moment later, the warmth faded, but Esta had already released her hold on his arm.

"Is there something you needed?" Frustration simmered in his voice.

Evelyn gave Esta a smile that was mostly teeth before she turned to Harte. "A letter was delivered for you just now," she said, holding out a crumpled envelope. "Next time get someone else to take your messages, would you? I'm not your errand boy."

"No one could confuse you for a boy, Evelyn," he said with a grin obviously meant to charm, but the woman didn't soften. His smile faltered as he took the letter from her outstretched hand. He tore the edge of the envelope, but even once he pulled out the folded sheet of paper, Evelyn didn't seem in any hurry to leave.

"I thought you weren't allowing visitors backstage anymore?" she said, glancing again at Esta with a look as sharp as one of Viola's knives.

Harte didn't seem to hear her. He was too busy reading the note, his brows furrowing over narrowed eyes. Then, all at once, he balled the paper in his closed fist, and when he looked up, the fury in his eyes had Esta wanting to take a step back.

"Usually I wouldn't," he said, looking at her with a stony, unreadable expression. "But for an *old friend*, I had to make an exception."

Everything in her went on alert. Esta had no idea what was in that note, but something had changed in him. All playfulness was gone. She didn't know what this new game was, and she had a feeling that she shouldn't stick around to find out.

"I was actually about to leave," she told Evelyn. "It was lovely to see you again, Harte. Do think about my proposition?"

He stared at her, his mouth tight. "Perhaps we could discuss it in more detail?" he said flatly. "Soon."

It was a victory, but she couldn't help feeling like there was something else happening that she didn't understand and wasn't in control of.

"Tomorrow, perhaps?" she asked, hopeful and wary all at once. "We could continue our discussion?"

His gray eyes bored into her. "I'm not sure about tomorrow—I've got some things to clear up. It might take a few days," he told her. His voice carried a curious note of determination.

"I'll look forward to it," she told him, trying not to show her unease. Then she pasted on a smile. "Until then? It was lovely to meet you," she told Evelyn, before turning to take her leave.

Just as she was opening the door, he grabbed her wrist and tugged her back toward him.

"That isn't any way for old friends to part, now, is it?" he asked softly, almost playfully, but the look on his face didn't match his tone.

He was already pulling her toward him. "As you said, we were once so very . . . *close*."

She had to force herself not to pull away. Esta needed Evelyn, who was still watching with ice in her eyes, to believe that she was who she claimed to be. Within the hour, the entire theater would know about the curious visitor in Harte Darrigan's dressing room. You couldn't *buy* gossip as effective as that. He'd be stuck with her.

But before she could find a way out of his grasp, she was in his arms. All at once she was back in the Haymarket. His eyes held no warmth or seduction, but her stomach flipped just the same at the intensity she saw there.

He gave her a moment to pull away, to refuse him and what she knew was about to happen. But pulling away would mean destroying the cover she was trying to establish. Instead, she looked up at him, met the challenge head-on. Dared him to go through with it.

It's an act, she told herself, when amusement sparked behind those gray eyes of his, when they softened just a little. Professor Lachlan had warned her about the Magician. *Don't be taken in by him. Get the Book before he does and stop the—*

Then his lips were on hers and she felt the warm energy of his affinity wrap around her, sink into her skin, violating the boundaries between them in a way she didn't have time to prepare herself for and couldn't protect herself from. His energy was hot, electric, and there was something about it that pulled her in even as she knew that it was a trap.

Despite the heat of his magic, the kiss itself held no passion or warmth. It was over before it had barely begun, but something had happened. He'd gained something more than her embarrassment.

"Until later, then, sweetheart?" he murmured as he released her. His expression was impassive, even as his eyes glittered with victory.

"I'll look forward to it," she said, and was glad to hear that her voice trembled only the tiniest bit. It wasn't fear but fury that jangled through her—fury at him for laying a hand on her, fury at herself for not being ready. Then she let herself out of the dressing room and pulled time around her so that she could get out of the theater without anyone seeing her shake.

THE MESSAGE

Harte stared at the open door, trying to figure out what he'd just heard and seen. The wild thoughts and images twisting through the girl's mind didn't make any sense at all.

"Well," Evelyn drawled, her rouged lips pursed. "That was instructional."

"Yeah," he said, more to himself than her. "It was." And yet he couldn't help but think he knew even less now than before.

"You two are old friends?" She gave an indelicate snort. "And I'm the Virgin Mary."

Her words shook him from his thoughts, and he finally realized Evelyn was still watching him. Her bright hair and painted face looked tired and garish in the dim light of his dressing room lamp. It wasn't only the shadows that it cast over her face that made her seem older, a worn-out shell of who she might have once been. It was that he was looking at her now compared to the girl—to *Esta*—and seeing their intrinsic difference.

The kiss had left him with more questions than answers, and it had shaken him in a way he couldn't think too closely about.

From the way she ran out of there, he had a feeling that it had shaken her, too. Rightly so, he supposed. After all, when he took her off guard and pushed past her defenses, he'd sensed that while the girl might have come with a message from Dolph, she'd also come for herself.

"So the note . . . Was it important, or what?" Evelyn asked, nodding toward it.

"Just something I have to take care of," he told her. He tucked the crumpled paper into his pocket and grabbed his jacket. "I have somewhere I need to be."

He left Evelyn in his dressing room and headed out with the sinking feeling that he might already be too late.

The paper had been monogrammed with the familiar symbol of the Five Point Gang—a cross with an extra arm that mirrored the legendary intersection of Orange Street, Cross Street, and Anthony Street, which was now the turf of Paul Kelly. It was the same symbol they'd branded into the skin on his shoulder when he'd made the choice to take Kelly's offer. Seeing it would have been enough to set him on edge, but the address written in a strong, slanting hand—Kelly's own—was only a block from the apartment he'd rented for his mother last May.

He knew at once the note was a warning about how much Paul Kelly could still control Harte's future. Certain it would be pointless to go to his mother's apartment, he went off in search of the address in the message instead.

The toffs who went slumming south of Houston might have thought that Chinatown was where the opium dens in the city were, but in reality, joints were hidden all over town. Knowing his mother, it wasn't a surprise that the address on the paper led to one of the worst he'd ever seen.

When he found her on a low platform in a dingy basement on Broome Street, he was already too late. She was barely conscious, her head supported awkwardly by a small wooden stool and her hand loosely clutching the long pipe. Scattered on the floor nearby were three shells, their curved bowls containing the dark evidence of her latest binge.

He had his suspicions about how she'd obtained so much of the sickly sweet drug, but he didn't really want to know. It was bad enough that he had to see her like this. And to realize he still cared enough to be disappointed.

Still, even as her cracked lips moved in some silent conversation within her drug-induced dream, she was alive and mostly safe. Whatever she'd done to him—what he'd driven her to do—pieces of the woman he'd once known remained beneath the years of disappointment and madness. Part of her would always be the fairylike creature who had spun tales of a distant land for the small boy he'd once been.

It was his own fault she'd chosen to leave him. His own fault for driving her away.

Her hair was gray now, and he couldn't stop himself from cringing as he pushed the greasy strands away from her face. "Ma," he said gently, trying to rouse her. "Come on. It's time to go."

She opened her drowsy eyes. Her light irises were glassy, her pupils large and vacant-looking from the effects of the drug, but she smiled at him before her eyes drifted shut again.

"No, Ma," he told her through gritted teeth. "You have to wake up. We have to go." He had to get her out of there. He needed to get her somewhere safe before Kelly or his men found her again. Or before she ran up an even bigger bill he would end up paying.

A soft moan gurgled from her throat in response, but her face remained slack, her breath shallow. Then she opened her eyes again, and for a moment they focused on him. "No," she whispered. "Please, no . . ."

"I'm not going to hurt you, Ma," he said, pulling his hand back from her.

"Leave me alone," she told him, her voice ragged with fear and disgust. "Unnatural boy. *You* made him go. You took him from me."

"I know," he said tightly, because it was easier to agree than to argue. "It's all my fault." Which was the only truth that mattered anymore.

He'd only been a boy. He hadn't known what he was capable of or how to control what he could do. When she found out he'd made his father, a drunk who'd rather use his hands to beat them than to make a living, leave, his mother had turned on him. She'd risked everything to try crossing the Brink to find his father.

She didn't get through it, though. Even her desperation to find the man she loved wasn't enough to push her past the terrible boundary. But she'd tried. She'd touched its power, and it had certainly changed her. There were days Harte wondered if death wouldn't have been a kinder fate. When he found her again, years later, she wasn't the woman she'd once been. Instead, she spent her days chasing anything that would take away the ache of the emptiness the Brink and his lout of a father had left behind.

Maybe Harte should have hated her for abandoning him. Maybe there was a small part of him that did. But in the end, he reserved his true hatred for the father who had deserted them long before he'd actually left.

And for *himself*. For driving her away.

She raised her hands slowly and gazed at them with unfocused eyes, as if noticing them for the first time. "These used to work miracles. The women used to come to me even when I was a girl," she said, her voice still carrying the soft notes of his childhood. Then her expression turned sour. "But you took it from me."

His jaw tensed. "You can blame me later. Right now we need to get you home."

She looked up at him, her pale green eyes lost in her own memories. "Little Molly O'Doherty can make you pretty enough to win any man, they'd say. I can't anymore, and it hurts—" Her voice broke, and she closed her eyes again. "It aches so terribly, and I wanted it to stop, if only for a little while. I needed—"

"You don't have to explain it to me," he told her, his throat tight with regret and shame for what she'd become. What *he'd* pushed her to. "Can you get up?"

He didn't want to have to touch her again. The rank sweat—or worse—was overpowering enough from where he was. It reminded him too much of what her leaving had cost him—of nights spent in trash heaps trying to get warm, the stink of unwashed bodies that had hunted him because they could.

Because no one had been there to stop them.

Because deep down, he had known he deserved it all.

He cursed when his mother wouldn't move, and wondered if maybe he could pay the man at the door to keep her until the drug wore off. He could collect her then—or maybe send someone else for her.

He needed to go. He'd moderated his breathing, but he was still starting to feel the haze of the poppy's smoke wrap around him, leaching out the frantic energy that the girl and Kelly's note had left him with, and he hated it. Hated the way it dulled who and what he was. Hated the way that part of him wanted to stay for a while and allow the quiet emptiness to fill him up. Just for a little while . . .

"I'm going now, Ma," he said, shaking off the temptation. "I'll be back in the morning, when you're feeling better."

Standing to leave, he looked at her one last time, hating her and loving her just the same. She was yet another thing tying him to the city, his duty to her like a straitjacket holding him against his will. A locked box he couldn't find a way out of.

He was barely out the door when he heard frantic shouts and realized that a crowd had gathered down the block. The smell of wood smoke and something else, something harsher and more chemical, hung in the air, and he saw that buildings nearby were on fire. On either end of the block, the blaze raged toward the center—toward the building where his mother was.

It couldn't have been an accident, two buildings burning like that. Two buildings bookending the room where his mother lay half unconscious. Not with the note he had still crumpled in his pocket.

The note, it seemed, wasn't the only message Paul Kelly had sent him.

Cursing the whole way, he ran back down the short flight of steps into the basement den, shouting for the sleepy-eyed guard to rouse the others. He grabbed his mother, his stomach turning and his throat tightening as the stink of her unwashed hair and clothes assaulted him. The smoke-filled night would be a reprieve compared to what she smelled of, but he pushed through his revulsion and got her out of the building, through the crowd, and into the waiting taxi at the curb. He gave the driver her address, and tried to keep her upright as the carriage rattled to a start across the uneven pavers.

When he leaned out the window, away from the smell of her, he saw Paul Kelly's men watching him from the shadows.

THE CENTER WON'T HOLD

Bella Strega

Usually, the noise of the crowded barroom was enough to settle Dolph's nerves on even the most frustrating of days. He always sat against the back wall, in part because he only had to watch one direction for an attack, and in part because he could watch the events of the night without being involved in them. From his usual table, he could observe everything he'd built, test the mood of the Bowery, and plan for all he still wanted to accomplish without anyone bothering him.

Though the room was already nearly filled with people drinking and laughing, Dolph found himself restless. There had been reports of a fire down on Broome Street. He'd sent some of his people to help stop the flames and get the innocent out, but there was only so much they could do without alerting suspicion. People would be hurt, and he was impotent to do anything about it.

Tilly had gone out on some errand, or he would have been in her kitchen, allowing her easy way to soothe him. He needed some of her soup, its heady, golden broth laden with matzo balls, or some of her fresh bread that tasted like life itself.

He needed the *Book*. But to get the Book, he needed Harte Darrigan's help.

The girl wasn't his last chance to hook Harte Darrigan—he *knew* that—but she was close to it. And she'd been gone a long time.

It rankled, still not knowing what she was capable of. A thief for certain. Most likely trustworthy, based on her performance at the museum. But she was still hiding something from him, and since he didn't know how her affinity worked, he couldn't predict how she might move against him. And he couldn't ask, not without revealing his own lost affinity. His crew expected him to already know.

Not that long ago, he wouldn't have worried at all. Leena, with her calm strength, would have been able to neutralize the girl if she attacked with her magic. And before the Brink, he would have been ready, would have known the flavor of that magic from the moment they'd met.

Before the Brink, he would have been able to do so much more. With a shake of her hand, he could have used her affinity for himself for a time, without harming her, just as he could with any Mageus. Once, his talent had made him seem limitless. Now he had to settle for pretending, for running a long con on those who trusted him.

He wasn't so green as to think that the game could last forever. Someone would eventually realize his weakness . . . and take advantage of it. The only question was who—and when the betrayal would come.

As though spurred on by his dark thoughts, a commotion erupted from the front of the building. He went on alert, ready for the danger, as the double doors of the barroom sailed open, clanging against the wall from the force. The crowd turned almost as one to see who had arrived. And then murmuring began, sweeping through the saloon like the fires that often tore through the Bowery's most dilapidated tenements. Like the one earlier that night had.

Dolph was nearly halfway across the room when he saw it wasn't any danger at all, but Jianyu, standing in the open doorway. The look of distress on the boy's face had Dolph's neck prickling in alarm, but he moved faster when he saw who Jianyu carried.

"We're closed," Dolph shouted. "Viola! Shut it down. Mooch, Sean— get everyone out of here."

His crew was well trained. They didn't ask questions or hesitate, but snapped into motion like a well-oiled machine. His employees were already gently guiding the other patrons toward the exit, but everyone was craning their necks to see what had caused the confusion.

"He's killing her!" someone shouted, and Dolph felt the anger and fear of the crowd turn, almost as a single unit, toward Jianyu. Their once-unsettled murmurs grew into an angry, noisy jumble of languages. Energy spiked throughout the room as each person drew their affinity around them—whether for protection or to attack, Dolph didn't know. A moment later, the first slur tore through the room, its guttural sound as vicious and ugly as the hatred behind the word, and the tenor of the crowd changed, transforming into something more dangerous.

Dolph raised his cane and brought its silver cap down with a vicious crack against the last-call bell with an earsplitting clang. "I said we're closed! Out! All of you!" He took a step forward, swinging his cane in front of him and not caring who it hit, as he helped to herd the crowd out into the night.

"Push those out of the way," Dolph called, pointing to a pair of shorter, square tables that lined the wall as he latched the door. "Put her over there on the floor, where she won't hurt herself."

WHAT HAPPENED ON
FULTON STREET

Jianyu carried Tilly, writhing and moaning in his arms, toward the spot that had been cleared for them. Around him, Dolph's people drew closer. He could feel their wariness, their distrust.

Before he could settle her, Viola pushed her way to the front, wiping her hands on her apron.

"Che cos'è?" she started to say, but the words died on her tongue when she saw who he had, and she went dangerously still. "What did you do to her?" Viola growled.

Jianyu felt her magic before she had even drawn her knives. Hot, angry, it assaulted him like a blast from a furnace, and the pain that gripped his entire body had him gasping for breath. His blood felt like fire, his lungs like dried cement. He struggled to stay upright, to keep from dropping Tilly, whose writhing made her difficult to hold.

"Viola! Enough," Dolph barked, catching him by the elbow before he toppled over. "Unless you want him to drop her, leave him be. Someone get Nibs in here. Now!"

Viola's eyes were sharp and bright, but a moment later, the heat receded from his blood, and Jianyu drew in a deep, heaving breath. Suddenly aware of the grip Dolph had on his arm, he pulled away and took the final few steps on his own to settle Tilly on the floor.

"Hold her legs for me, Vi," Dolph directed, as he took hold of Tilly's upper arms to keep her from scratching at her face and neck. Already the skin there was red with raised welts from her own nails.

She was still thrashing about as she moaned in agony, but her color had all but drained on the long walk back—she looked deathly pale.

"What happened?" Dolph demanded, his expression cold.

Jianyu went on alert at the suspicion in Dolph's voice. He'd been stupid to let his guard down, to believe that he could make a life for himself away from his own people. To believe that he could be accepted outside the streets of Chinatown, when he was barely accepted within their boundaries.

Of course he'd heard the same slurs hurled at him before, and at others on the streets of the city. He should have been used to it, but the surprise at hearing it *here*, in the place he thought of now as his home? To be accused of killing the girl he was trying to save? It shouldn't have been any more than he expected. But then Viola turned on him as well. And now Dolph was looking at him with ice in his pale eyes.

He expected at any moment to feel the burn of the tattoo on his back, but to his surprise—and relief—it never came. Which meant Dolph must trust him still. The knowledge was enough to unclog his throat and allow the words to break free. But he wasn't sure it was enough to heal the rift he felt in the room.

"I cannot say for sure. . . ."

"Try," Dolph commanded, his temper flaring. "What was she doing near the Brink?"

"She wasn't at the Brink," Jianyu told him. "This happened on Fulton Street."

SOMETHING NEW

By the time Esta made it back to the Bowery, the shock of whatever Harte Darrigan had done when he kissed her had mostly faded, but she didn't feel any better about her situation. On the streetcar ride downtown, she couldn't help herself from checking the clipping. It still hadn't changed back. Whatever success she'd had with Harte Darrigan, it hadn't been enough. She wasn't sure what *would* be enough.

She carried that worry with her back to the Bowery, and the moment she stepped into the Strega, it swelled. Something was very, *very* wrong. It was late, well into the time when the bar should have been packed with throngs of Mageus drinking away their sorrows and stress, but the saloon was nearly empty.

"We're closed!" one of the bowler-hat boys grunted, standing to block her way. His name was Sam or Sean—something with an *S*—but she was new enough that he didn't recognize her.

Luckily, before she had to really argue her point, Nibs came and waved her in.

"What's going on?" she asked, taking in the small crowd at the back of the room. The energy in the air was hot, erratic. Even from across the barroom, she sensed that everyone was on the edge of using whatever magic they had, and their fear snaked through the space like a living thing.

"Dolph shut us down about an hour ago," Nibs said, his expression more uncertain than she'd ever seen him. "It's Tilly."

When Nibs finally pushed them through the gathered crowd, she saw Dolph talking in low tones to Jianyu, while Viola held Tilly's legs to the ground to keep her from thrashing about. The mouse-haired girl was writhing like she was on fire. Her eyes were wide, staring at the ceiling, and her throat and face were red from where it looked like she'd raked her own nails down her skin.

"What happened to her?" Esta asked, watching as Tilly grimaced, moaning and trying desperately to get free.

"We don't know," Nibs told her.

"Bring me some Nitewein," Dolph told Jianyu. "Double the poppy."

Jianyu looked grim as he nodded. He pushed his way past the group and returned a few minutes later with a bottle of inky liquid. Dolph told a few others to help Viola hold Tilly, and then, kneeling over her, he coaxed the liquor down her throat himself.

Tilly took one halting sip at a time, choking on the liquid at first and then gulping it desperately. Little by little the writhing stopped, and Tilly's arms went limp at her sides, her eyes glassy and vacant.

Dolph waited to make sure Tilly was calm before pulling himself stiffly to his feet. His skin was flushed, and a sheen of perspiration glistened on his upper lip as he ran a hand through his wavy hair.

"Take her upstairs," Dolph told a pair of the bowler-hatted boys, one of whom scooped the girl up into his arms. "Go on and be with her," he said to Viola as he handed her the bottle of Nitewein. "Let me know if there's any change."

Nibs spoke to Esta in a hushed tone, as if he didn't want anyone else to hear. "Dolph thought it was the Brink, but Jianyu said it happened down on Fulton Street, near the Dead Line."

"What was she doing on Fulton Street?" Esta asked.

"Trying to help someone," Dolph said, approaching them. "Golde's son, Josef. You remember her?" he asked Esta. "We visited their home just the other day. He was with a group of boys. They were playing some game, daring each other to go farther downtown, when something went wrong. One came back here for help. Everyone else was out dealing with a fire over on Broome Street, so Tilly went. Found Jianyu on the way."

"I felt the cold energy in the air, warning us away," Jianyu told them. "But she insisted on helping the child. She'd barely reached for him when she went straight as a rod and fell backward." He closed his eyes for a moment, as if remembering what he'd seen. "Then she began shaking and moaning, as though being flayed by a thousand whips. She could not hear me when I called to her, so I pulled her back, away from the boy's fallen body. I brought her back here."

"What about the boy?" Nibs asked.

"I could not carry both, and I could not risk being struck down if I wanted to get her back safely. She was still breathing, and I thought maybe . . ."

"You did fine," Dolph told him, clapping Jianyu on the shoulder. "You could have left her—plenty would have. I'm grateful you brought her back, and I'm grateful you came back to us as well."

Jianyu's cheeks flushed, but he didn't look as though he agreed. From his wary, unsure expression, it was clear he thought he had failed in some way.

Dolph didn't seem to notice.

"We'll need to send someone down to check and see if the boy's still there," Dolph said to Nibs. "If he is, I don't want anyone getting close enough to end up like Tilly. Jianyu said it felt like the Brink, so until we know more, that's how we'll treat it. Be sure to take someone who won't be at risk with you."

"What about his mother, Golde?" Nibs asked.

"I'll go tell her myself."

Nibs frowned. "You don't think it could be the entire Dead Line?" he asked Jianyu.

"I don't know," Jianyu said.

"We better hope it's not," Dolph said. "It would cut the city in half. Still, something as big as this . . . Someone has to know something." Dolph glanced at Jianyu. "I need information. Someone will have talked."

Jianyu gave a serious nod. "I'll go myself," he said.

"Do that," Dolph murmured.

After Jianyu bowed slightly and headed out into the night, Dolph turned his attention to Nibs. "After you take care of the boy, people will need to be warned. We'll need to be vigilant, at least until we figure out what's causing this."

"I'm on it," Nibs said, and hurried off in the direction of the Bowery, taking a group of the bowler-hat boys with him.

Dolph waited until they were gone before he looked to Esta. "Well?" he asked, dispensing with any pleasantries.

She knew what he was asking. "I think he'll talk," she told him, wishing that alone was enough to fix the future. To save Dolph from that fate. "He said he had something to take care of, but he should send word to you soon."

"What else?" he asked, eyeing her as though he knew there was more.

She hesitated. "He won't take your mark." When Dolph was silent, she continued. "I told him it was negotiable."

Dolph's expression creased. "That wasn't for you to say."

"I didn't have much choice if I wanted to keep him interested. Maybe if you'd warned me, or if I even knew what the mark was, I could have come up with something else." She leveled a frustrated glare in his direction, ignoring the danger he posed. "He's willing to talk now. From what I understand, that's more than anyone else has managed to get from him."

Dolph glared back at her, but he didn't argue any further. After a long, tense moment, he turned to glance back at the door where they'd taken Tilly up to the apartments above. It stood empty and silent.

"How bad is it?" Esta asked. But Dolph didn't have to answer for her to know the truth. She could see it in his anguished expression, in the tightness of his posture.

"For Tilly, it's as bad as it can be," he said. "For the rest of us? It's something new, and that rarely bodes well for our kind."

THE WEIGHT OF NIGHT

Dolph waited until the Strega was completely clear before he locked the doors and ventured out to discover what he could. Pulling his cloak around him and the brim of his cap low over his face, he headed south, toward Fulton Street and the notorious Dead Line. When the lights of the Bowery grew dim and the streets grew darker still, he switched the patch over his eye, so that he could navigate the night without falling into a coal cellar or some other trap laid for unsuspecting marks.

Rats rustled in the gutters as he passed, and the wind cut through his heavy cloak, but the cold March winds barely touched him. How could they, when everyone already said ice ran in his veins?

Let them say it, he thought bitterly. Ice or no, his ways had saved enough that he wouldn't apologize for them. He'd carved out a life for himself, hadn't he? He'd battled against all odds to achieve what he had. His own family had seen him as a liability, had tossed him out when he couldn't work anymore at the factory that had mangled him as a child. To them, he was another mouth they couldn't feed, so they had sent him away to save the others.

He couldn't blame them, really. Desperation and fear could make anyone do nearly anything, and sometimes a single sacrifice was necessary to save many.

Back then, Dolph had been so angry, full of vinegar and bile. He'd been too stubborn to accept death or the boys' workhouse as his life, lame foot or not. And he'd been too smart to follow anyone else. While the other urchins begged for bread or stole coins from fat pockets, the secrets Dolph stole helped to make him who he was. Those secrets would either save him—or kill him—in the end.

Let the others fight over ragged strips of land they could never own. He knew the truth—there was a whole land made for him and his kind. Or there would be soon, if he had anything to do with it. Once the Brink came down, the Mageus could be free to do whatever they would. Once the old magic was restored, no one would be able to stop them. Without the Order of Ortus Aurea holding them back, they could remake the whole country as a land for magic. Those without it could learn for themselves what it was to live narrow, hen-scratched lives.

They were close now, closer than he'd ever been. Soon he would have Darrigan, and then he would have Jack Grew, and then the Order would be in his sights. But first he needed to deal with this new danger that had risen up in their midst.

He walked on, not bothered by any of the shadowy figures who huddled in doorways, their cigarettes flickering like fireflies in the bitter night air. Before he was within a block of Fulton Street, Dolph could already sense something wasn't right. There was a cold energy sizzling in the air like a live current, a warning to any with magic to stay away.

He pushed on, closer still, until he could force himself to go no farther. At the corner of Fulton and Nassau, he turned east and followed the icy energy along the length of Fulton. It felt almost as though he were walking along the perimeter of a high-voltage fence that was invisible to the eye. *Like the Dead Line has come to life.*

Dolph continued to walk, feeling his way along the Line as it ran down Fulton. As he walked, he fought the strangest urge to reach out and run his fingers through the energy beyond the sidewalk's edge, to stir its power.

Maybe it was some new trap. Or maybe it was because he'd been touched already by the Brink, that its power was now a part of him.

Magic was like that. Whether natural, like that of the Mageus, or corrupted, like the power the Order was able to wield, like called to like. Magic, whatever its form, could tempt the weak with its promise of power. Which was part of what the Sundren were afraid of—that magic was a drug, like the opium that trapped so many. Those without an affinity for it feared that magic was a compulsion. Those who had touched power knew it wasn't a completely unfounded fear.

In the old countries, there were stories of magic—and Mageus—run rampant. Plagues and deaths blamed on the same people who had once been asked to heal and guide. But that was before the Disenchantment, before the Ortus Aurea and other Sundren like them began hunting his kind and penning them in, destroying even the memory of a world permeated by the old magic as they took power for themselves.

The Order believed themselves to be men of reason. They called themselves enlightened, but in the end they were merely human, wanting what they didn't have and taking what wasn't theirs because they could.

This new danger was definitely man-made. Unnatural. The power it radiated felt broken, as though a part of the world had become unmoored from itself. Whatever had happened to the Dead Line, like the Brink, it had been designed to control. To punish.

He had no idea how this new threat worked. He wasn't sure if it was simply a line or if its power had engulfed the entire southern end of Manhattan, and he wasn't sure if it was like the Brink—which would allow entry into the city but not escape—or if it would destroy any who crossed in either direction.

But if this new line *was* the Brink, if it marked a constriction of their territory, who was to say it wouldn't move again? If it continued to creep north, they would have nowhere to go.

Across the street, Jianyu materialized out of the night and began to walk toward him.

"What news did you find?"

Jianyu shook his head. "No one's talking. Khafre Hall is dark. If this is the Order's doing, they are very quiet."

"It couldn't be anything *but* the Order's doing," Dolph argued. "Things are changing, and I can't say they're changing for the better." He glanced over to Jianyu, read the stiffness in the boy's spine, the closed expression on his face. "About earlier . . . I'm sorry for what Viola did."

Jianyu's expression didn't change. "She was afraid. People do all manner of things when fear drives their hearts."

"Still. You're one of us, and I don't want you to ever doubt that. The people in the bar, the things they said earlier? They don't speak for me, and they won't be allowed to darken my doorway again."

Jianyu inclined his head, but he didn't respond, and Dolph couldn't tell if he believed the sincerity of his apology or not.

Dolph couldn't blame him. After all Jianyu had been through, after all the city and the country had done to his people, why would he trust anyone, much less Dolph, who made it his business to remain as mysterious and unknowable as he could?

"You'll keep looking?" Dolph asked. "For Tilly?" he added, knowing that whatever Jianyu might think of him, he would do what he could for the girl.

"Of course," he said, and with another small bow, he disappeared into the night.

The weight of the night on his shoulders, Dolph turned back toward the Bowery, back toward Golde's apartment and the empty place at her table. Back to his streets, his own home, and all the people he was no longer sure he could protect.

A ROOM FILLED WITH FEAR

As the sky started to lighten outside Viola's window, Esta rubbed her eyes and stretched out the kinks in her back. She had finally convinced Viola to give Tilly more Nitewein a few hours before dawn. The first person who had offered her kindness in this city was now slumped on her side in the bed, her thin shift damp with sweat, her eyes glassy and unfocused. She looked three feet from death's doorstep, but at least she wasn't screaming anymore.

Esta dipped the rag back into the bucket of murky water and placed it against Tilly's feverish forehead once again. At the feel of the cool cloth, Tilly moaned.

Viola paused until Tilly settled again, but then continued to pace in the corner of the small room.

"You can sit down anytime now," Esta told her. So much for the cold, fearless assassin—Viola had been wearing a hole in the floor for most of the night.

"I still don't like it. Tilly, she never had the Nitewein. She would have hated to be like this," Viola said, her voice trembling as she gestured vaguely toward the girl in the bed.

"She wasn't exactly having the time of her life with all the screaming and moaning," Esta muttered. If she thought Viola would accept sympathy, Esta would have offered it. Instead, she gave Viola something to strike back at, a distraction from her worry.

"What did you say?" Viola demanded.

"Nothing. Never mind." Esta dipped the rag and placed it against Tilly's feverish brow again. Neither of them spoke for a long while, but Viola's fear filled the room as she resumed her pacing.

"Does she know how you feel?" Esta asked softly, not looking at Viola.

Viola's footsteps went still and a long, uncomfortable moment passed during which Esta wondered if she'd gone too far. But then . . .

"No," Viola said, her voice barely a breath but containing more heartbreak than a single word should be able to hold.

Esta met Viola's eyes. "You never told her?"

Viola let out a ragged breath and looked at the bed where Tilly lay. She shook her head. "It doesn't matter. Her friendship is enough."

Esta took the cloth and dipped it back into the water, not knowing what to say, what comfort to offer. She didn't know if Tilly had known or understood how Viola felt, but from the warm smiles she'd seen the two share, Esta couldn't help but think that maybe she did. And Esta knew Tilly cared for Viola, even if it wasn't in quite the same way. Still, she wasn't sure whether saying anything would help Viola or make things worse, so she kept her thoughts to herself.

But she stayed.

The morning passed slowly into afternoon, the streets outside the window growing noisy with the business of the day, but nothing inside the room had changed. Tilly had not improved . . . if anything, she seemed to be more pale and her cries more desperate every time the Nitewein began to wear off.

Tilly's cries had Viola strung tight as a garrote wire, and when Viola's temper snapped each time they had to give Tilly more Nitewein, Esta's was the only exposed throat in the room. Which would have been an easier burden to shoulder if Esta wasn't aware of just how deadly Viola could be. By the afternoon, Esta's shoulders were tight and her eyes felt like someone had thrown sand into them from the lack of sleep. She couldn't remember the last time she'd eaten, and as much as she wanted to help Tilly, she wished someone—anyone—would come and relieve her.

As if in answer, the door to the room opened, its uneven hinges creaking, and Dolph Saunders limped into the room. His hair was a riot of waves around his face, and his eyes were ringed with dark circles.

When she saw him, Viola stepped forward, putting herself between Dolph and Tilly.

"Stand down, Vi. I'm not here for that," Dolph told her, sounding tired and drawn. "And despite your impressive skills, you know well enough that you couldn't stop me if I were."

Viola's jaw clenched, but she didn't argue.

Dolph turned to Esta. "Have you slept any?" he asked, his voice gruff.

"About as much as you did, from the looks of it," Esta told him.

"You've been here all day?" He seemed surprised.

"Most of the night, too. It's not like I could sleep with the noise she was making." She nodded toward Tilly.

"Noise?" Dolph asked, looking at Viola.

"Mostly it was the screaming that kept me up," Esta told him. She shrugged, willing away her own exhaustion. "I thought I might as well help since I wasn't getting any sleep."

"She should have been sedated." Dolph glared at Viola.

Viola crossed her arms. "She is now, if that makes you happy."

"Immensely," he drawled. Then he turned back to Esta. "How is she faring?"

"I don't have any idea. She's quiet now, though."

Viola stepped forward. "She'll come through. Don't you worry none."

With an impatient glare, Dolph turned to Viola. "I'll worry when I'm ready to, and not a second before." Then his tired expression seemed to soften as he leaned into his cane. "We'll give her a bit more time. Keep her sedated this time," he told Viola sternly.

"She'd hate this," Viola said softly, her worried eyes locked on the pale girl in the bed.

"Hate it or not, it's necessary. Keeping her calm is the most we can do for her now. Her affinity is still there, but it's been broken somehow. It'll be up to her to decide whether she's strong enough to go on without it."

"Of course she'll be strong enough," Viola told Dolph, her jaw set determinedly. "She always was."

"I don't disagree, but surviving this will require a different sort of strength than she's had to draw on before. Time will tell." Dolph turned to Esta. "Come with me." He didn't wait for her to follow.

Just before Esta made it to the door, Viola grabbed her wrist.

The girl's strange violet eyes bored into her. "Thank you. For what you did for her," she said, her voice breaking. "And for me."

"It was nothing," Esta told her, an easy enough truth.

But Viola only squeezed her wrist more tightly. "No one else came," she said simply, before she let Esta go.

Esta slipped out of the room and found Nibs and Dolph waiting for her in the hall.

"Should I make the arrangements?" Nibs was asking.

Dolph shook his head. "Not yet. There's a small chance she could still pull through. We'll give her some time."

Nibs frowned. "She's a talented healer."

"I'm well aware of that," Dolph said as he led the way down to the staircase at the end of the narrow hall. "But Tilly's always been stronger than most. And her magic isn't completely gone. She's been loyal to me, so we'll give her—and Viola—time before I decide."

"Decide what?" Esta couldn't help asking.

"I won't let her suffer," Dolph said shortly. "And I can't allow her to become a liability."

A dark understanding rose in Esta. "So you'll—"

"I'll do what needs to be done to protect those who depend upon me," he growled, pulling himself to his full height as though daring Esta to cross him. When she didn't, he spoke again. "Darrigan sent me a note today, as you said he would. He'll meet with me in two days' time. With both Viola and Tilly otherwise occupied, I'd like you to be around—in case I need your help with him."

Esta nodded. "Anything else?"

"Yes," Dolph said, looking her over. "Go get some sleep. You look like something dragged from the gutter."

A HOMECOMING OF SORTS

Wallack's Theatre

Harte looked at the bottle of Nitewein someone had left on his dressing room table and considered his options. Going to Dolph Saunders for protection would be bad enough as a last resort. It was worse to be forced into it.

He picked up the bottle and tipped it side to side, watching the dark, viscous liquid coat the sides of the green glass. Removing the stopper, he took a sniff. Flowers and something sweet cut through with the bite of cheap wine. It smelled like an opium den and a saloon all mixed together, revolting and beguiling just the same.

How bad could it be if it made him forget what he had to do?

After pouring himself a glass, he sat staring at his reflection. He had his mother's chin, and his hair waved like hers, but he saw too much of his father looking back at him for his liking.

His nerves were jangling as he slowly lifted the glass.

The smell hit him, sweet and floral and sickening, and all at once a memory rose from that time after he'd rescued his mother from Paul Kelly's brothel. She never could stay sober for long, and every time she went missing, he'd have to hunt through smoke-filled basements to find her and keep her from any more trouble. He would try not to look as he pulled her clothes around her and dragged her back home, but she'd only hate him in the morning anyway. For seeing her like that. And for taking her away from the only thing she'd let herself love other than his father.

Unnatural boy.

He put the glass down and resealed the bottle. In the mirror, his reflection stared back at him, doubtful. After he was done cataloging his faults and putting away his regrets, he reached for his pocket watch before he remembered it had been stolen.

Not that he really cared if he was late.

Harte hated everything about the world below Houston—its rotten, trash-lined streets, the tumbled rows of tenements teeming with desperation and despair. Even the air, which was permeated by the stench coming from the outhouses behind them. So he hated what he was about to do even more.

He didn't have to go in, he thought, as he came to The Devil's Own Boxing Club. He should have stayed away months ago—maybe none of this would have ever happened. Nothing was stopping him from turning around and going right back to where he belonged, to his uptown theater and his clean, airy set of rooms. To his porcelain tub and a bath of boiling-hot water. To the life he'd built out of nothing. A life that *could* still be enough.

But the fire said otherwise.

He'd managed to get his mother sober enough to leave her at a new address, but how long would it be before Kelly and his boys found her again? And they *would* find her, because Harte had no intention of letting Paul Kelly anywhere near Jack. He couldn't imagine what Kelly wanted with the Order of the Ortus Aurea, but if he ever managed to get their power behind him, it wouldn't mean anything good for his kind, and especially not for Harte himself.

Much as he hated admitting it, Dolph Saunders was the only way he saw to get around that possibility. After all, Dolph had a reputation for protecting outcasts from the wrath of the other gang bosses downtown, including Kelly's own sister, Viola. Let them fight each other while Harte made his move. If Dolph was right about what the Book contained, he'd be out of the city and safely on the other side of the Brink before any of them realized what had happened. They would be stuck inside, unable to reach him, and he'd be free.

He ignored the twinge of guilt he felt when he thought of the other Mageus who would still be trapped. *But they're already trapped.* If anything, he told himself, their lives might be better if the Order didn't have their Book.

When he gave the kid on the other side of the door his name, he was let through to a long, familiar hallway to the back of the building. The closer he got to the end of it, the stronger the scent of sweat and blood and the more vivid the memories.

He'd spent the year after his mother had abandoned him—and before he was forced into Paul Kelly's gang—hanging around The Devil's Own. Back then, Dolph had still been a lanky teenager. He'd seemed larger than life to twelve-year-old Harte. Even with his limp, Dolph had commanded the respect of anyone who knew him in the Bowery, and of anyone who dared cross him. It was the kind of respect Harte himself craved, and Dolph had become something of an older brother, the mentor and protector his own father had never been. The boxing club had become a safe space for him—or at least it had been safer than the streets where he'd spent too many nights. He'd learned to fight there, to protect himself in ways that had nothing to do with magic. And he'd spent more nights than he could count eating at Dolph and Leena's table in their rooms above the Bella Strega.

After he'd gotten caught up in Kelly's gang, he'd stayed away from them both. It had been more than three years since Harte had even talked to Leena, but the ache of her loss hit him then, suddenly and far too late. She'd been only a handful of years older than him, but she'd mothered him in ways his own mother had never been able to. Still, even after he'd heard she lost a baby, Harte hadn't risked crossing Kelly—or Dolph—to visit her. But now that he was back, surrounded by memories he thought he'd put aside, he was overwhelmed by the thought of her being gone. Leena had been too stubborn and determined to do anything she didn't want to do, but Dolph should have never put her in a position to be harmed by the Order.

Leena had meant everything to Dolph, so Harte didn't have any illusions about how disposable *he* would be. And he didn't feel all that much remorse for what he planned to do in the end. The Book would be his, and Dolph Saunders could go hang for all he cared.

When he reached the main practice room, he found Dolph in the same place he'd seen him so many times before—perched on a low stool, his chin resting against his silver-tipped cane as he watched two of his boxers pummel each other in the ring above him. They were both bare-chested, their skin already slick with sweat and their chests heaving with exertion. They couldn't have been more than fifteen or sixteen, but already, each sported the tattoo that marked them as Dolph's—a double ouroboros that featured a skeletal snake intertwined with a living one.

Life and death, Dolph had once told him, back when they'd still been friends. Survival was about balance. The threat of death could inspire you to carve out a life worth having.

Once, Harte had been eager to take Dolph's mark, but Dolph had said that, at twelve, he was too young to make that decision. He'd considered it again when he'd wanted to get out of Kelly's gang. Dolph could have easily given him the secrets he needed to buy his freedom.

He'd thought that trading one mark for another was something he could live with, and he'd come to the boxing club to do just that. But because he'd been early that day, Harte had seen what happened to those who crossed Dolph Saunders. He understood then what the mark was capable of, what *Dolph* was capable of.

He would never forget it—the way the man who was years older than Dolph had cowered and begged for another chance. The cold look in Dolph's eyes as he rejected the pathetic appeals. Dolph had motioned for two of his boys to hold the man still, and then he'd simply touched him with the head of his cane. The second the silver Medusa touched the tattoo, the mark came to life. The two snakes began moving, and the man's skin rippled as the ink turned the color of blood.

And then it did become blood. The man screamed like a banshee until the two boys dropped him, and he fell unconscious to the floor. By then, the air in the room had gone cold and energy crackled, but Dolph had barely seemed to notice. He'd given a curt nod, and the two boys had dragged the man away—unconscious or dead, Harte couldn't tell.

Harte had turned around and left that day, and he had vowed to never take another's brand again. He would do everything on his own, trust no one but himself. Even if it meant never *truly* getting away from Kelly's reach.

Except now he might have a way. Stealing the Ars Arcana from the Order—from Dolph—might be a crazy, impossible death wish of a way, but Harte was about desperate enough to take it.

"You're late," Dolph said with his usual brusqueness. He didn't bother to turn around. "I don't like to be kept waiting."

"Last I checked, I'm not one of your lackeys."

"Not yet," Dolph said, finally glancing over his shoulder to pin Harte with his blue-eyed stare.

"Don't get ahead of yourself, old man."

Dolph didn't react to the nickname the way he usually did. Instead, he let out a tired breath and gave Harte an unreadable look. "I'm glad you've come."

Suspicious, Harte crossed the room to where Dolph was sitting. "I'm only here because that skirt of yours conned me into it." It wasn't the truth, of course, but it was better if Dolph thought he still had the upper hand.

One of the boys nailed the other with a right hook that sent blood splattering. A few drops landed on Harte's polished black boots, and it took everything he had not to wipe it away in disgust.

"That's enough for today," Dolph told the two bloodied boys. "You're losing your touch if you were taken in by a pretty face, Darrigan."

"What can I say? She was persuasive. But she's not your usual type," Harte said as he watched the boys leave. "Though she does remind me a little of Leena, too much of a hellcat to fall in line easily . . . So maybe she is your type after all. My mistake."

"Don't," Dolph growled.

"Where'd you find her?" Harte pushed, ignoring the tension that had risen between them at his mention of Leena. He knew it was a low blow, one she'd have taken him to task for, but he would use whatever advantage he could. And he'd hold Dolph accountable for what he'd done to her.

"You're not here because of her." Dolph eyed him. "You think I don't know that Kelly's men have been breathing down your neck lately?"

Harte went still.

"Oh, come off it," Dolph said. "I have eyes in every part of this city. I heard about the fire the other day, and I know that Razor Riley helped to set it."

Harte held up his hands. "You know what? I was wrong. Turns out I can't do this," he said, taking a step backward, preparing to leave. "I'd say it was good to see you again, Dolph, but you don't deserve the effort it would take to lie." He turned and let his feet take him toward the door, but he hadn't finished crossing the room when Dolph spoke.

"You know I can protect you from Paul Kelly. Your mother, too. I would have done it years ago if you weren't so damn stubborn and proud."

Harte stopped where he was, but he hated Dolph that much more for knowing the one thing that would keep him listening. "I'm still not willing to pay the price for your help. I'm not taking your mark," he said. He kept his eyes focused in front of him.

"I haven't offered it," Dolph said, his voice tight.

"You did once." He turned back to look at Dolph and let his old friend see that he wouldn't be swayed. "I came that day, you know. I saw what you did to that man—what *your mark* did to him." It had taken him two years more to gather enough of Kelly's secrets to negotiate his exit from the gang, but he'd solved his own problems then. He'd do it again if he had to.

"I didn't realize . . ."

"Did Leena know?" Harte asked. "Did she have any idea what you were playing at?" Back then Harte had left because he was afraid, but now he knew enough to understand that what Dolph's mark had done stank of ritual magic.

Dolph's jaw went tight. "That's none of your—"

"Leena never would have been okay with it."

"She didn't know how dangerous things were," Dolph snapped, "or how precarious our position was." He took a breath as though trying to calm himself. "Leena was too good for this world," Dolph said softly.

"Your Leena?" Harte laughed. "Maybe she *was* a saint—she must have been, to put up with you—but she was also tough as nails and smarter than anyone. I bet she was livid when she found out you were dabbling in ritual magic. I would have bought tickets to watch that fight."

From the flush in Dolph's cheeks, Harte knew he was right. "She understood."

"I bet she did," Harte mocked, shaking his head.

"Do you really think I'm the first Mageus to try strengthening my power?" Dolph asked.

"Of course not." Stories of Mageus trying to make themselves stronger by using ceremonies or ritual objects were as old as magic itself. They were the source of legends about witches and shamans, magical creatures the Sundren feared.

No, Dolph wasn't the first to try to claim more than he was born with, and he wouldn't be the last.

"Weren't *you* the one who taught me the cost of what the Order was doing, the way they damaged magic itself each time they manipulated the elements and claimed power that wasn't theirs?"

Dolph scowled at him. "You weren't around then. You don't know what it was like—I didn't know who I could trust or who I could depend on. So, yes, I did what I had to do to protect mine. How else was I supposed to fight against the Order?"

"I don't know." Harte shook his head. Dolph couldn't even see how many lines he'd crossed to get what he wanted. "But you weren't supposed to *become* them."

"I'm *nothing* like the Order," Dolph snapped.

"No?" Harte pressed. "The Order thinks what they're doing is right, that they're only protecting what's theirs—their land, their people, their country. That's how everyone else sees it too. The whole city believes them, believes Mageus are something to be feared and lets the Order have their way. Your mark could destroy a person—*did* destroy a person. How is that *any* different from what the Order does? How will you be any different if you get this book you're after?"

The muscle in Dolph's jaw jumped, and his whole body radiated tension. "Considering how cozy you've been getting with Jack Grew, I can't imagine you really care."

"You're right. I don't." The Order, the Bowery, the city itself. It was all the same to Harte. Each one was holding him down, holding him back. He'd throw them off one by one, until he was free, or he'd die trying.

Dolph glared at him. "Did you come because you're finally willing to join us, or only to remind me of my failures?"

They'd finally come to it. He wasn't sure he could do it until the words were already out: "You want my help," Harte told Dolph. "I'm willing to give it in exchange for protection. I want Kelly off my back—for good—and I want my mother safe. But you'll have to take my word for a guarantee. I won't be branded by you. Not for anything."

It was a gamble. If Dolph rejected his offer, he'd have to deal with Kelly on his own. If Dolph demanded that Harte take his mark, he'd be as shackled to Dolph as he'd been to Paul Kelly, and Harte wouldn't—couldn't—let that happen.

A long minute passed, the two of them standing in stony silence, waiting to see who would break first.

"Fine," Dolph said. His hand was gripping his cane so tightly his knuckles were white. "I'll take your word. But if you go back on it, I'll destroy the life you've built for yourself one piece at a time. I'll make sure the entire city knows what you truly are. If the Order doesn't finish you off, Viola will."

"Fine with me," Harte said. If everything went to plan, he wouldn't be in the city to care. And if things went as badly as they could go, he'd gladly take a quick death at Viola's hand over whatever Paul Kelly or the Order would dish out. "I have to say, I'm a little surprised you agreed."

"Things have changed," Dolph said. "We can't afford to wait for the Order's next move."

He told Harte about what had happened to Tilly, about how she'd had her magic stripped from her. How at that very moment, she was fighting for her life.

"You think the Brink has moved?" Harte asked, chilled by the idea.

"I don't know, but this latest attack makes me more sure than ever—we have to take the Order down. To do that, I need the Book. To get the Book, we need a way into Khafre Hall as well as a way *out* that doesn't involve getting everyone killed."

Harte gave a hollow laugh. "Is that all?"

"Probably not, but it's the minimum. If you don't have Jack Grew on the hook already, you will. It's only a matter of time. I've heard about him: brash, quick-tempered, and has something to prove. He's the perfect mark."

"That's the problem. *Everyone's* heard about him, and he knows it. He's skittish," Harte said. "Unpredictable. His family knows it, and they watch him pretty closely. I'm not one of them, no matter how well I shine up. If they warn him off, he'll listen, because he has too much to lose with them right now." He gave Dolph a knowing look. "Especially after that mess at the Metropolitan."

"So make him think he can't lose." Dolph gave him an impatient glare.

"I've been trying, but it's not so easy. He wants me to find out what happened at the museum." He paused, never blinking, as he sent the clear message that he knew Dolph had been behind the robbery. "I'm assuming you don't want him to discover the truth."

"So give him something better."

"What are you proposing?"

"Use the girl," Dolph said. "She can help you hook him. She's already established her cover, hasn't she?"

"The long-lost-lover angle," Harte said, realizing exactly how deep her game had been the day before. She'd penned him more ways than one.

"The daughter of one of your illustrious teachers. I bet she would have secrets Jack Grew would love to learn," Dolph said with a satisfied smile. "Secrets that could make him a huge success in the Order. *That's* what he really wants."

He hated the fact that Dolph was right.

"I already told her, I work alone," Harte said.

"Not anymore. And not if you want my protection," Dolph told him. "You won't take my mark, but you *will* agree to work with Esta. Otherwise, you're welcome to take your chances with Kelly and his boys. Your mother, too. I won't make this offer twice."

Harte's jaw was so tight his temple ached. "It's not much of a choice when you put it like that."

Dolph shrugged. "There's always a choice. The question is which one you're willing to live with."

"You or Kelly," Harte said, his voice as threatening as his mood. "Why do I feel like I'm only getting to pick my poison?"

"It's still a choice," Dolph drawled.

Harte shook his head. "You always were a bastard."

"Takes one to know one." There was the hint of amusement in Dolph's expression.

"Fine. We'll do it your way. But when this is over, you don't bother me again. You don't contact me or try to find me. If we're all not already dead, you don't even know me. Period."

The amusement faded from Dolph's face. "Agreed. But if I get any hint of you going against me or mine, I won't hesitate to end you. My mark or no, I will strip you of everything you hold dear."

"You should have gone on the stage," Harte said dryly. "You've developed quite the flair for the dramatic. If that's all?"

"That's all." Dolph nodded. Then he softened his voice. "It really is good to see you again."

"I can't say the feeling is mutual," Harte said, but he couldn't stop his mouth from curving up. "Keep my mother out of Paul Kelly's grasp, and you won't have anything to worry about on my end. I'll get what you need." Harte extended his hand to shake on the deal they'd made.

Dolph shook his head. "I wasn't born yesterday, Dare. I have a few things to take care of, but I'll be sending Esta to you in a couple of days."

"What do you mean?" Harte asked. His hand dropped to his side.

"She'll be staying with you and keeping an eye on things while the two of you work together."

"She can't stay with me." He shook his head. "I don't want her there."

Dolph laughed. "I won't call you on that lie, but you're going to have to take her."

"You know it'll ruin her," Harte argued, unexpected anger curling in his stomach at the thought. "Her reputation won't recover."

"That won't matter if the Order kills us first." Dolph pulled himself to his feet. "You worry about keeping your end of our agreement. She'll let me know of any unwanted developments."

Harte could only stand there, his frustration rising as he watched Dolph limp off in the same direction the two boys had gone, dismissing him without so much as a good-bye. The reek of the sour, coppery dried blood wrapped around his throat, choking him. He wasn't sure if he'd managed to negotiate a good deal or simply tied a noose around his own neck.

"That's it?" he called out. "You're going to send me the girl, and I'm supposed to figure out the rest? I take on all the risk, and you sit, safe in your castle."

"I've already given you everything you need." Dolph turned to look at him over his shoulder. "But—"

"Yeah?" he snapped, his frustration mounting.

"The girl's currently under my protection," Dolph said softly, "so if you actually *do* ruin her, you'll answer to me."

PART

III

RUINED

The Docks

The machine was in ruins. Metal fragments were lodged in the wood of the walls and in the chest of the old man. The hulking globe in the center looked like it had melted.

Jack nudged the body with his toe. *Dammit.*

All of his work had been for nothing. Months of work. Months of waiting. Wasted.

"Get this cleaned up," he told the boy who'd brought him the news. He tossed him a coin. "Then put out word that I need a machinist. Now."

"And the old man?" the boy asked, eyeing the body warily.

"Dump him in the river."

Jack didn't stay to make sure the work was done. The warehouse, even with all its square footage, felt claustrophobic. Like the walls were pressing in on him, squeezing him until there wasn't a drop of blood left for him to give. He'd risked everything, gambled everything, and he had been *so* close. *Dammit.*

He kicked over a barrel and sent a pair of rats skittering away.

There was still something he was missing. Some key to making the machine work. There had to be, because he wouldn't let himself believe that *they* were more powerful.

Reason and logic would prevail.

He would prevail.

The machine should have been perfectly functional. The problem would have been easy enough to figure out if the High Princept would just let him consult the Ars Arcana. Certainly, the Order's most important artifact, their most sacred text, would have the answers he needed. But there were parts of Khafre Hall only the Inner Circle had access to, and the Mysterium, with all its secrets, was one of them. So unless something changed, he was on his own.

Tugging at the collar of his shirt, Jack stomped back out to the carriage. When his father found out what had happened to the money in his trust fund . . . when his uncle and the rest of the Inner Circle found out . . .

Jesus. They'd never let him in. Worse, he'd never be able to set foot in society again.

Dammit.

He needed more information. He needed the Order to trust him enough to let him into the Mysterium, because he knew the answer was there. Solving the Metropolitan robbery would go a long way toward getting into their good graces, but Harte Darrigan had been avoiding him the last few days. He was trying to be patient, trying to give the magician a chance to work on the problem, but at this rate, the machine would never be done in time for the Conclave.

He needed to figured out what he was missing, and fast, or he'd be ruined.

But most of all, he needed a drink.

DREAMS FROM WAKING

Bella Strega

Something had happened. It had come suddenly and absolutely, as a wave might overtake a small boat out to sea, leaving Viola struggling to stay afloat. For three days she'd watched her friend suffer, writhing and moaning despite the laudanum in the wine. For three days she had paced the floor in Tilly's room or sat on the edge of her narrow bed, holding her hand and whispering everything she'd wanted to say for so long.

Night and day she'd stayed. Tilly couldn't hear her, but night and day Viola continued whispering, using her mother tongue, because the words felt right in that language. Her meaning felt somehow more suited for the soft melodic rhythm of the country that had made her.

But her words and prayers had not been enough.

Neither had her power.

She was an assassin, but only because that was what the world had made her into. Because her brother had needed a black hand of death to smite his enemies, and his life was the one her family valued. His success was all that had mattered to them. She might have been made an assassin, but her affinity had never been intended for death. And nothing they did, nothing anyone could do, had changed that.

But it wasn't enough. *She* wasn't enough.

Even now she could sense Tilly's blood, the beating of her fragile heart, the energy that was the very signal of life within a body. Even now she pushed everything she was, every ounce of power she had, into her friend. She had been doing it for days, but no matter what she did, the broken part wouldn't heal.

Because Viola could only command flesh, and what was broken in Tilly was something more.

Around dawn, something had changed. The wave had come over them, cold as the lonely sea she had once crossed, and the fight had gone out of her friend. That spark of energy that signaled a life began to waver, and for the first time since Viola had seen Tilly writhing in Jianyu's arms, she truly worried that Tilly might not pull through.

Since then, Tilly's skin had gone even more ashen, and now she lay still, her chest rising and falling in uneven, ragged breaths that rattled in her throat. Viola had heard that sound before, but now she could not— would not—allow herself to believe its message.

She barely noticed when Esta went to find Dolph, or when he arrived. Even when the room began to fill with the people from his crew who had loved Tilly, who had depended on her calm, steady presence in the Strega's kitchen, Viola was scarcely aware of them, she whose every day was filled with the rushing thrum of rivers of blood, the beating drumbeats of a world filled with hearts.

The crowd in the room might as well have been made of stone that morning for all she noticed them as she fought against the truth lying in Tilly's bed. As she willfully ignored the way her friend's hands had turned cool, the way her fingertips and nails had lost all color.

Dolph stepped forward from his vigil at the foot of the bed. "You know what needs to be done, Vi. You know it's time to let her go."

Viola shook her head, pressing her lips together. "She'll be better tomorrow. I know she will."

Dolph rested his hand on Viola's shoulder. "I understand," he said softly. "I know exactly what it's like to watch someone you care for slide away from you. To watch your own heart cease to beat."

Viola swallowed down the hard stone she felt in her throat and turned to him. "She is not dying."

"Her magic's gone," Dolph told her. "It has been for days. Now she's going too. It's time we let her. It's time *you* let her."

"She will not die," Viola repeated, her voice barely a whisper. "She will fight. She will be better. I just need to give her more time."

"You know that's not true," Dolph said gently. "Yes, she did fight. You've helped her, and she fought hard, but what's happened is too much. It would have been too much for any of us. Think of what it would be like, what it would mean to lose your power. Can you imagine not being able to reach a part of yourself? To feel it stripped away?" His voice broke, and he paused for a moment to compose himself. "To live without it."

Viola grimaced. "No," she whispered. All at once she realized what he must have felt watching Leena die. No wonder he had seemed so changed after.

"Tilly's fought hard enough. Allow her the rest she's earned."

Anger spiked through her, drowning the pain with a sense of righteous fury. She would not be commanded. She would *not* be the instrument of death. Not this time. She would use her affinity to keep Tilly's heart beating and in doing so atone for all those other hearts she'd stopped. And no one would stop her. Not Dolph Saunders. Not even with the threat of his mark.

Dolph staggered a bit, his lean face twisting with pain as she let her power fill the room, as she found all the parts of him that made him a living man and started to pull them apart one by one. Slowly, so he could feel what she felt. She was so focused, she didn't notice the way the others rustled in fear, backed away.

"You know I'm right," Dolph gasped, gripping his cane as he tried to stay upright. "Do this last thing for her."

Viola shook her head, her vision blurry with tears as her power crackled through the room.

"Free her," Dolph said, barely able to stand. The veins in his cheeks had turned dark, like tiny rivers floating to the surface of his skin. "Kill me if you must, but let her go," he rasped.

Yes. She would kill him for even suggesting it. She'd killed before, and for lesser reasons. But despite what people believed, she did not often kill like this. Years ago, she had learned to throw knives, to carve out a life with the sharp tip of a blade, because she knew her god damned her for using her gift to take lives, as her brother wanted, rather than to save them, as she could. But she would use everything she was now. She would risk the fires of hell and everything that came with them for Tilly. For herself.

Dolph staggered to his knees as she pushed her affinity toward him, felt the pulse, the light . . . and the broken pieces that even she couldn't heal.

She realized then what he'd been carrying since that night they lost Leena. The secret he'd been hiding from them all.

The fight went out of her. She released her affinity, let go of her hold on Dolph, and crumpled against Tilly's barely moving chest, unable to stop the sob that tore from her throat. She stayed there, emptying herself of pain and grief, for who knew how long.

Until she had nothing left.

Until she finally felt the warm, steady hand on her shoulder.

She shrugged Dolph off and wiped the wetness from her cheeks.

"It's time," Dolph said. "Allow her to go in peace."

Viola turned to the crowded room, her eyes burning from the tears she'd shed. Who were these people? Not the family she'd been raised by, when blood was supposed to be thicker than anything. No, that family had turned from her. They'd wanted her to be what she could never be, and she had chosen again. She saw now in that motley group that she had chosen well. And so had Tilly.

"She wouldn't want them here for this," she told Dolph. "She wouldn't want them to see." Because it would be hard for them to watch, and Tilly would have hated their suffering. And because Viola knew somehow that Tilly wouldn't want them to understand what she could actually do.

Tilly had seen through the mask she wore, had never believed her to be the coldhearted assassin the rest saw. One person knowing her truth had been enough. It had to be, because Viola's role was her shield. It allowed her to survive in a world that would rather see her dead. Tilly had understood that as well, and she had given Viola friendship, even when she could not give more.

Dolph nodded, and one by one the silent crowd in the room began to depart. A few were brave enough to come forward and touch Viola gently on the back or the shoulder before they went. Then the new girl, Esta, came forward to take her turn as well.

Esta touched her shoulder gently, like a bird landing on a branch. "I think she must have known how you felt for her," she whispered.

Viola shook her head, wondering as she had before how this strange girl could see her so clearly. "She would have despised me," Viola whispered.

"I don't think she would have. Tilly understood people." Esta gave her shoulder a gentle squeeze. "She loved you. Anyone could see that, even if it wasn't in the way you hoped."

Viola looked up, wanting to believe those words, and found Esta's eyes glassy with tears but free from lies. Free, too, from the judgment she expected there. "I still don't know that I like you," she said. "But Tilly did. And you're right. She *did* understand people. Better than I ever could. You'll stay?"

"Yes," she whispered to Viola. "Of course."

Viola's throat was too tight to do more than nod her thanks, and then she turned her attention back to Tilly. She was afraid to look away, afraid that the moment she blinked or stopped watching, she'd miss Tilly's last breath. Or that she would cause it.

A suffocating silence blanketed the room, broken only by Tilly's rasping, uneven breath.

"Viola . . . ," Dolph whispered gently. "It's time."

Viola ignored him and took Tilly's hand in hers, rubbing her thumb over the pallid skin as her whole body trembled with the effort not to let her grief spill out and drown her. She lifted the limp hand to her cheek, closing her eyes and imagining for a moment that she was strong enough to save her friend. That this was all a horrible dream.

But Viola knew dreams from waking. She knew the thick scent in the air and the rasping sound in Tilly's throat, and she'd never looked away from death before. She wouldn't look away now.

Viola opened her eyes and took a long, deep breath as she placed Tilly's hand gently across the girl's own stomach. Then she whispered one last thing into her ear.

Tilly blinked, turning her eyes ever so slightly to look up at Viola. For a moment her gaze was focused, as though she had come back to herself long enough to see who it was who stood above her—just long enough to say good-bye.

Tears blurring her vision, Viola pulled her hand away, and with it, she pulled away her affinity, that fragile thread holding Tilly to this world.

Life and death, two sides to the same coin. Her family saw her as a killer, and so she had become one. Everyone else believed her to be a killer, because they forgot that death is simply the other side of life. But Viola never forgot. She couldn't. She'd tried to save her friend, and she'd failed.

Tilly's chest heaved in a final, ragged breath. And then her body sank motionless back to the bed, her empty green eyes staring sightlessly above.

THE TREE OF KNOWLEDGE

Esta felt the room go cold, the magic draining from the space like air sucked from a vacuum. Viola reached over, her always-steady hands shaking, and gently traced her fingertips over Tilly's face, closing the girl's eyes. Then she stared, mute and tearless, at the girl's still body.

As Esta watched, she remembered suddenly what Logan had looked like, pale and unconscious in the narrow bed after the mess at Schwab's mansion. How was it possible that she hadn't thought about him for days now? Had life in this city been so all-consuming that she'd lost sight of why she was there? Then she thought of the clipping, still tucked safely against her skin—if the heist didn't happen, if she changed too much just by being here, what would happen to all the people she'd left behind?

"Come," Dolph whispered, nodding toward the door. "We'll give her the space she needs to grieve."

In the hall, he gave a silent jerk of his head to indicate that she should follow him. When they reached his rooms a floor below, he opened the door and ushered her through it. He gestured for her to take a seat in one of the chairs near the bookcases, and then he poured himself a drink.

Esta was almost grateful to see that he seemed as shaken as she felt with what they'd witnessed. After downing the first glass of whiskey, Dolph poured himself another and then sat in the armchair across from her. He didn't speak at first. Instead, he swirled the liquid in the chipped cup he held in his broad, calloused hands before taking another long swallow. Finally, he looked up at her.

"Thank you for staying," he said, his voice no more than a whisper. His jaw was tight, and in his eyes she could see the pain of losing Tilly, and if she wasn't mistaken, maybe the pain of something more.

"It was nothing," she told him, still unsteady from the rush of Viola's magic.

"No, that's not exactly true." His eyes were shadowed with the evidence of sleepless nights and worry. "Most aren't willing to bear witness to pain that can't be remedied. Most find it easier to simply turn away. On behalf of Viola—and Tilly—I thank you for not doing that."

They sat there for a long while, an impromptu wake. Dolph took a drink every so often from his glass of whiskey, while Esta waited for him to speak or to dismiss her so she could escape the heavy silence.

He set his drink aside. "Harte Darrigan visited me yesterday. We've come to an understanding. I have you to thank for that."

"Good," Esta said. "I'm glad I could help."

"I'm sending you to him."

"What?" She sat up straighter.

"You'll need to pack your things."

"Wait. . . . You *gave* me to him?" she asked, incredulous.

"Of course not," Dolph said. "I want a pair of eyes I trust on Darrigan at all times. What you did at the museum for Jianyu and the rest of the crew, what you did today for Viola . . . You're one of us now. I'm trusting you can keep him on task."

Esta felt the instinctive need to argue. She didn't want to leave the Strega, didn't want to go stay with Harte Darrigan. But she stopped herself. This was what she'd been hoping for all along, wasn't it? Dolph was handing her the perfect situation—a chance to get close to the Magician. A chance to stop him before he ruined all their futures. She wouldn't waste it. "What do you need from him?"

"Darrigan hasn't always been the polished magician he is now. Once, he wasn't any different from any of the boys in the Bowery. But he's managed to carve out a new life for himself, and that new life comes with some very powerful friends."

"He knows people in the Order?"

Dolph nodded. "Specifically, he's become friends with a fellow named Jack Grew, who happens to be J. P. Morgan's nephew. I don't need to explain to you how important a contact like that is, not with what's happened to Tilly. I need information, and Darrigan is our best chance to get it. His connections are our best opportunity to get a crew into Khafre Hall."

She feigned surprised. "You're not planning to rob them?"

Dolph nodded.

"That's a bigger risk than the Metropolitan," she said, pretending to be more concerned than she actually was.

"It is, but if we do it right, the rewards are bigger too. I want to end their reign over this city, over our kind." Dolph leaned over to take a book from the shelf. "I want to make this land safe for magic."

He opened the volume—a ledger or journal of some sort. Its pages were filled with the same strong, even hand. He took a small envelope from between the pages and pulled out a worn scrap of fabric, which he handed to Esta.

She looked closely at the faded and smeared letters. "That's *blood*."

Dolph nodded. "Someone died getting that message to me. A woman named Leena Rahal, a woman I trusted with my life."

"What does it say?" She frowned, playing dumb to lead him on. She didn't need him to know that she knew Latin as well as any of her other languages. "Something about a book?"

"Have you ever heard of the Ars Arcana?"

Esta shook her head, keeping her eyes on the bloodied words so the lie wouldn't show.

Dolph flipped through the pages of the journal, and finding the place he wanted, he held it out to her. On the page was an image that she recognized easily enough from her many lessons with Professor Lachlan—the Tree of Knowledge. This image was different from others she'd seen, though. Usually, the tree's wide branches held symbols representing the ancient mysteries, alchemical notations that were attempts to explain the interworkings of heaven and earth. In this version, though, the tree was aflame, and at the source of those flames was a book. Like the bush Moses found, like the fish in the center of the Philosopher's Hand, the book wasn't being destroyed by the fire.

"There are stories passed down through time of a book that holds the secrets of the old magic—the Ars Arcana, or the Book of Mysteries. Some believe it contains the very beginnings of magic. Others believe its pages hold the history of Mageus, but legend has it that whoever possesses the Book also can wield the power it contains. Of course, like the Golden Fleece or the philosopher's stone, the Book is supposed to be nothing more than a story—a myth," Dolph told her. "But I believe the Ars Arcana is real, and I believe the Ortus Aurea has it."

"Because of this?" she asked, holding up the scrap.

"In part, but the more I've looked into it, the more sure I've become. That image isn't a simple picture. It's a complex arrangement of symbols—the book aflame, the moon and stars circling. It should look familiar to you." He gestured toward the painting hanging over his shelves, the one she'd helped to steal.

"Newton is holding the same book, with the same symbols on its pages," she realized, looking between the two.

"The circular symbol there is called the Sigil of Ameth, the Seal of Truth. The Order believes an initiated magician could use it to unlock power over all creatures below the heavens—and some above as well. The Ars Arcana is supposed to contain the one true sigil. I don't think it's any coincidence that J. P. Morgan, one of the highest-ranking members of the Order, owned that painting. I think Morgan couldn't help himself from bragging about his knowledge. The Order has the Ars Arcana. I *know* it."

"You want to steal the Book," she said, letting her excitement show.

"We could use the knowledge it contains to destroy the Brink. Without the Brink and the Book, the Order would be finished. More than that, I believe we could let magic—old magic, *true* magic—grow free again. *Libero libro.* The Book will free us."

"Does Harte know all of this?"

"He knows what I'm after," Dolph admitted, "and he knows the Book could bring down the Brink."

Which is why he took it, Esta realized. *He wanted it for himself.*

But then . . . why had he disappeared? Why had *the Book* disappeared? It didn't make any sense. There had to be something more to what happened, and she would have to be smart—and more patient than she'd ever been—to figure it out. Or risk disrupting the future even more.

"Why are you telling me all of this now?" Esta asked.

"Because I need you to understand the importance of what we are undertaking. It will be difficult to do what I'm planning. Khafre Hall is a fortress. Without someone on the inside, the job will be impossible. Jack Grew's our way in, and Harte Darrigan is our way to him. So you'll go to Darrigan and you'll make sure he gets Jack on the hook."

Before she could ask anything else, they were interrupted by a sharp knock at the door.

"Come," Dolph said, his eyes never leaving Esta's.

Nibs opened the door. "There's news."

"Well, get in here and tell me about it," Dolph barked.

With a nod, he stepped into the room and closed the door softly behind himself. "Whatever happened to the Dead Line," Nibs said, "it's done. Gone."

Dolph's brows drew together. "What do you mean, gone?"

"The crew you had patrolling over on Fulton said that it just disappeared. One minute it was there, and the next, there was a flare of energy and they couldn't sense it anymore."

"When was this?"

"A couple hours ago," Nibs said. "I went down to check for myself before I came to you. I wanted to make sure. But it's gone, all right."

"That was right about when Tilly got worse," Esta realized.

"It was," Dolph said, his expression stony. He finished his drink before he spoke again. "Gather your things and get yourself to Darrigan's. I want Grew on the hook, and I want it to happen before anyone else has to die."

EVEN KITTENS HAVE CLAWS

Harte's Apartment

Knowing how Dolph Saunders worked, Harte had half expected the girl to be waiting for him when he got back to the theater. Actually, he'd planned on it. He'd spent the long walk back from The Devil's Own thinking of all the things he wanted to say to her—the rules he'd establish to put her in her place and keep her there. When she didn't appear, he couldn't help feeling almost disappointed. And when she *still* hadn't made an appearance by the end of the night's second show, he could only wonder what Dolph was up to and whether he'd keep the bargain they'd made.

Even prepared as he was, the last thing he expected to find when he let himself into his apartment late the next night was the girl, curled up like an overgrown kitten on the narrow couch in his front parlor. She was fast asleep, her head resting on her arm and her breathing soft and even. At first he simply stood there staring. In sleep, her features looked different—softer, somehow.

Not that he was fooled into thinking she was harmless—even kittens had claws, after all. And he'd had enough experience with this one to know hers were sharper than most.

He wondered how long she'd been there. She looked uncomfortable with her neck tipped to the side at such an awkward angle. Her dress was a shade of blue that reminded him of the spring sky, but the hem was marred with the grime of the winter streets. He cringed at the sight of her damp boots up on the clean chintz upholstery. They would leave a mark if she stayed that way.

With a sigh, he went over to the sofa. "Esta," he whispered. "Come on. Wake up." She didn't seem to hear him, so he reached down to shake her arm gently. "I said wake—"

The next thing he knew, he was flat on his back on the carpet, staring up at the ceiling. He had no idea how she'd managed to move so quickly out of a dead sleep, but it had taken less than a second for her to sweep his legs out from under him with her ankle and twist his arms around to pin him to the floor. Her eyes were wide and furious, but they weren't really lucid until she blinked away the sleepiness in them and saw him beneath her.

"Oh," she said, confusion flashing across her otherwise intense expression.

"Off?" he choked, barely able to breathe.

"Sorry," she murmured, her voice still rough and drowsy as she shifted off him. "But you shouldn't grab me like that," she said sourly, as though her nearly breaking his neck had somehow been *his* fault.

"You shouldn't break into people's homes if you don't want to be grabbed." He lifted himself to his feet and went to turn on another light. "And I *didn't* grab you. I was trying to wake you. Your boots are ruining the furniture."

She blinked, her face wrinkling in confusion as she looked at her feet. "They're clean," she argued, but she reached down and began unbuttoning them anyway. When she'd pulled off both boots, she left them in a heap on the floor and didn't bother to cover her slender ankles.

"How did you even get in here?" he demanded, trying to gather his wits. There was something he was supposed to be telling her right now, something he was supposed to say. "I was expecting you at the theater yesterday not in my very locked, very secure apartment. Not in the middle of the night."

"No *so* very secure," she argued. "And it's barely past midnight. I didn't mean to fall asleep," she said, fighting off a soft yawn.

Her hair was a mess, half tumbled down from sleep, but Harte focused on what was important . . . if he could just remember what that was.

She gave in to the yawn. All the action did was call attention to her mouth, which made him remember other things that weren't exactly helpful at that moment.

He'd made a mistake. A tactical error. This was never going to work if he couldn't focus long enough to take control.

"So, am I going to be taking the couch, or are you going to be a gentleman and give me your bed?" she asked, batting her eyes innocently.

"The only way you're getting into my bed is if I'm in there with you," he told her.

"Not likely," she drawled.

"Then I guess you're taking the couch," he told her. "Best you learn now, I'm no gentleman."

"Figured as much," she said, pulling herself up and tossing him a pillow as she walked toward the back of the apartment.

"Where are you going?" he asked.

"I need to use the facilities," she told him. But she walked right past the open bathroom and into his bedroom, and before what she was doing completely registered, she'd shut his bedroom door and clicked the latch in place, leaving him holding the pillow.

It took a second for him to process what had just happened, but once he did, he stormed across the apartment and pounded on the door. "Open this door, Esta."

"No, thanks," she called from within. "I'm good here."

"I mean it. I'll bust it down if I have to."

There was a rustling sound from within that he refused to think about too closely. It couldn't be the sound of petticoats falling to the floor or her gown being unlaced. He would *not* allow himself to imagine her disrobing on the other side of the door. And even if she were, he would not let himself care.

"Feel free. It's your apartment," she said, and he could practically hear the shrug in her voice.

He ran his hands through his hair in exasperation. "What are you doing in there?"

"What do you think I'm doing?" she called.

He had a sudden vision of what she would look like in his bed, her dark hair spilled out across his pillow, but he locked that image down and threw away the key. "I think you're trying to take my bed," he said, inwardly groaning at his bad luck.

"I don't think I'm trying at this point." Her voice came from closer to the door now.

His bed was going to smell like her if she slept there, and then he'd never be able to sleep soundly again. He pounded again and then eyed the door. He could probably break it down. "I want my bed, Esta."

The door cracked open and her face appeared. Her shoulders were bare except for the lacy straps of her chemise, and she'd taken her hair down so it fell around her shoulders in loose waves. "Think of this as me helping you better yourself," she said, as she tossed a small object at him.

He grabbed for it out of instinct, giving her the time she needed to slam the door in his face and click the lock in place once more.

"Better myself?" He looked down at the object he was holding—the pocket watch he'd lost at the Metropolitan exhibition. "What's that supposed to mean?"

"Just what I said, Darrigan," she called through the closed door. "By the time I'm through with you, you'll be a real live gentleman."

The next morning when he woke, his neck was stiff from sleeping on the couch. He pulled himself up and ran a hand over his face, trying to rub away his grogginess and to will away the dreams of dark, silken hair and lacy chemises that left him feeling restless and unhinged. He was still in his clothes, since Esta had locked him out of his own room, but now, across the apartment, the door to his bedroom stood open.

Approaching the door warily, he saw that his bed was rumpled and unmade. The blankets were thrown back, and in the center of the bed, the mattress sagged where someone had slept, but the girl wasn't there. She wasn't in his tiny closet of a kitchen, either. As he pulled on a fresh shirt, he had the brief, impossible hope that maybe the night before had all been part of the same awful dream. Then he heard the off-key singing coming from his bathroom.

He knocked on the bathroom door. "Esta?"

The singing went suddenly silent. "You didn't tell me you had a bathtub," she called.

"I didn't invite you to use it, either," he said, trying not to think of her soaking in the white porcelain tub. It didn't matter if it was his sanctuary—the mark of how different *this* life was from his old one. He didn't need the image of her tawny limbs, or any other part of her, naked in the warm water. In *his* warm water.

He heard the sounds of sloshing, and a moment later the door opened. Esta was standing with one of his large towels wrapped around her. Her shoulders were bare again, and wisps of her hair that had fallen from where she'd piled it on her head were stuck to her damp skin. Water was still dripping down her neck and her legs, leaving puddles on his tiled floor.

For a moment he couldn't think, much less speak.

"You have a *bathtub*," she said again, and she made the word sound like something miraculous. Her face was scrubbed clean, pink from the heat of the water, and she was smiling at him as though he'd just saved her life. "I'm never leaving."

Then she shut the door in his face. *Again.*

His hands clenched into fists at his sides, and for a minute he had to focus on breathing. He had to remind himself that this would be worth it in the end. It would all be worth it when he walked out of the city a free man and left all of this behind him.

He turned without a word, grabbed an orange from the bowl on his kitchen counter, threw on his hat and coat from the stand by the door, and left, slamming the door behind him. He'd go to the theater. People there might eat knives, dance with bears, and shimmy across the stage half-naked, but at least they didn't make him feel insane.

THE SCENT OF BETRAYAL

Paul Kelly's

There was something about the warming weather that drove the desperate a little wild. With spring came more boats, and with those boats, more immigrants hoping to carve out their own piece of the rotten fruit that was the city. And as spring teased the promise of summer, tempers began to flare. Always with something to prove, the new crop of boys would try their luck with knives or guns as they worked to claim meager pieces of territory. Street corners. Back alleys. Nothing worth dying over, but they did just the same.

With his cane and uneven gait, it was nearly impossible for Dolph to go unnoticed by those who might not know any better. It would have been easier to use the cover of night to do what needed to be done, but some business required the stark light of day—to send a message that he didn't fear anyone in the city. Not the Order of Ortus Aurea, whose constant presence kept his kind crawling in the gutters. Not the men at Tammany, who'd clawed themselves to the top of the city only to forget they'd been born in the slums. And not Paul Kelly, who seemed to be planning a move to establish himself as a true rival.

Kelly fashioned himself as a nob, and if it weren't for that crooked nose of his, evidence of his days as a boxer, he probably could have blended in at the Opera. He sure spent enough to dress the part. But at heart, Kelly—whatever his adopted moniker might suggest—was a paisan. The fancy clothes, the well-heeled style, it was all a cover so he could pretend he was different from every other dago fresh off the boat, crawling through the muck of the city to make something of themselves.

When Dolph entered, Kelly's men came to attention, their hands reaching for the guns they kept beneath their coats, but Kelly waved them off. "Dolph Saunders. Quel est votre plaisir?" he asked, slipping into perfect French.

So, he doesn't want his boys to hear us, Dolph understood. "Il est temps de rappeler vos hommes." *It's time to call off your men.*

Kelly's wide mouth turned down. "I'm not sure I can. My boys have been having a good time of it," he said, nodding to John Torrio, who sat at the table across the room.

"They went too far setting that fire," Dolph growled. "Six people died in those blazes, four of them children."

Kelly gave a careless shrug. "You said you wanted pressure on Darrigan."

"On Darrigan, yes," Dolph said. "But killing innocents wasn't the deal."

"There aren't any innocents in this town," Kelly told him. He pulled a silver case from his inside jacket pocket and took his time selecting one of the thin, perfectly rolled cigarettes inside.

He had style, Dolph admitted, feeling tired and older than his own twenty-six years. Kelly was only a couple years younger than Dolph, but he had something that felt new. Kelly had a different style, one that drew the boys who filled the barroom around them. One that could be dangerous if it ever found a wider audience.

Dolph took the seat across from Kelly without waiting for an invitation. "That may be, but I have Darrigan now. Our deal's done."

Kelly took two long drags on the cigarette and let the smoke curl out of his wide nostrils. "You know, I got to thinking. . . . Why would Dolph Saunders need Harte Darrigan? And why would Harte Darrigan be sniffing around with Jack Grew, especially when Jack's a member of the Order? I thought to myself, those two things can't be coincidences." He squinted a little as he took another drag. "So I asked myself, what do they know that I don't?"

"I don't know what you're talking about," Dolph said easily. "Harte was mine first, that's all. I wanted him back."

"That's a nice story." Kelly smiled around the cigarette. "But I don't buy it. You're no stranger to taking what isn't yours. Speaking of which, how is my dear sister these days?"

Dolph allowed himself a cold smile. "She sends her love. It comes with a blade and a handful of curses I couldn't repeat in mixed company. Might offend the delicate sensibilities of your boys there."

"Sounds like Viola." He gave Dolph a challenging look. "She'll betray you eventually, you know, and return to me. I'm family, and she knows the importance of family. Il sangue non é acqua."

"I'm not sure *she* knows the truth of that."

"She will," he said, and the threat was clear.

"She's under my protection."

"For now," Kelly said smoothly, and then shifted onto a new topic. "I've been hearing things around town about this big shindig the boys in the Order have planned—this Conclave at the end of the year. Word is, anyone who's anyone will be there."

"Only if you're a member of the Order," Dolph said.

Kelly's expression never changed. "So maybe I'll become a member."

Dolph let out a surprised laugh before he realized Kelly was serious.

Kelly leaned forward, his expression determined. "I'm not like you, Saunders. I aim to be someone someday."

"You're already someone," Dolph argued. "You control half the blocks south of Houston right now. You didn't need the Order for that."

"No, I didn't need them, but it wouldn't hurt to have that kind of power on my side, now, would it?" He smiled, a leering sort of grin that had all of Dolph's instincts on alert.

"It's a pipe dream, Kelly. The Order only takes their own kind. You might have power and you might even have enough money, but it will never be the *right* kind of money to get in with the blue bloods uptown."

Kelly took another long drag on the cigarette and eyed Dolph like he was weighing the pros and cons of giving anything away. Then he stubbed it out in the crystal bowl sitting on the table next to him, twisting the slender butt between his meaty fingers. "Maybe you're right. But like I said, I was curious, so I started asking around. And I started listening. And what I hear is that you're after some book the Order has."

Dolph felt suddenly paralyzed. *Someone had talked.* Someone he'd trusted had said too much, given too much away. There was a weak link in his organization, maybe even a rat.

"So I said to myself, Dolph Saunders and I, we are smart men, well read and erudite and all that. But there's no book worth risking the wrath of the mayor's precious little boys' club unless it's some powerful book."

"If those rumors were true, I'd deserve whatever I got for my stupidity," Dolph said, leaning back in his chair and making a show of his amusement.

Kelly smiled like he could see right through him. "Playing dumb doesn't suit you, Rudolpho."

Dolph remained silent. He didn't let his expression so much as flicker. "I don't know what you're talking about."

"So that's how it's to be?" Kelly shrugged as he lit another cigarette. "Fine. This isn't a tea party. You want me to call my boys off Darrigan, I'm going to need something more from you, something Darrigan can't give me. You and I both know he can do an awful lot. And this book . . . From the sound of things, *it* can do an awful lot too. Maybe more than even you can."

"A deal's a deal, Kelly." Dolph stood to take his leave. "I already gave you what you needed on the mayor, and Darrigan's playing nice now."

Paul Kelly laughed, the smoke from the cigarette spilling from his nose, like he was some sort of demonic beast. "I'm not your dog, Saunders. I won't be brought to heel. As far as I'm concerned, Darrigan's still mine. You want him outright, it's gonna cost you."

Even as Kelly spoke those words, Dolph was already planning how to deal with this new development. His grip tightened on his cane. "Name your price."

"I want the Strega."

Dolph laughed. "I'll see you in hell first."

"Your words, not mine," Kelly said easily.

"You're going to regret the day you crossed me," he said, standing.

Paul Kelly gave him a smile that was all teeth. "I doubt that, Saunders. I doubt that *very*, very much."

Dolph didn't say anything as he turned to go. If he were honest with himself, he would have admitted that he'd sensed betrayal growing thicker in the air for weeks now—the uneasy energy of a lie being told, the heady anticipation that marked the casting of rigged dice.

But Dolph hadn't been honest on the day he was born, and he certainly wasn't any better now. Not when he'd lost so much. And not when everything depended on keeping those losses a secret.

TEMPTATION COMES
IN MANY FORMS

Wallack's Theatre

The bottle of Nitewein was still sitting on Harte's dressing room table. He swore he could hear it calling to him ever since the girl had taken up residence in his small apartment.

It was bad enough that she'd blown through his neat, orderly life with her very presence—the off-key singing that carried through the bathroom door as she soaked in his porcelain tub, the silk stockings draped over the parlor furniture. The smell of the floral soap she used that didn't seem to match the hard-nosed stance she took on absolutely everything, but suited her just the same. It had permeated the air in his apartment, and he had the feeling that the scent of it would remain even after she was gone.

And she *would* be gone. As soon as the job was over, she'd leave. Just like everyone left. Just like he would leave as soon as he could.

Well, good riddance, then.

He wanted her gone.

He wanted his life back.

He wanted a way out of this mess he'd found himself wrapped up in. He picked up the bottle of Nitewein and rolled the liquid around inside it.

Evelyn appeared in his open door. "You look horrible," she said.

"Thanks." She wasn't wrong. He had deep circles under his eyes from not sleeping. But how was he supposed to sleep on that lumpy couch that barely held him, especially when he knew *she* was less than ten feet away? Maybe it really had been too long since he'd been with a girl. That had to be all it was.

He eyed Evelyn.

She seemed to read his mind. "What?" she said with a sly smile.

"Nothing," he told her, dismissing the idea. It would be a mistake far worse than a glass of Nitewein.

But Evelyn seemed to have read his thoughts and was already sauntering across the room. He felt the caress of her magic. He should have stopped her—*really, he should*—but the warmth that rubbed against him soothed something inside him. That part of him that had started pacing and prowling the first day the girl opened his bathroom door dressed in nothing but a towel. *A towel, for god's sake.* Like any man in his right mind could have resisted that.

Harte *had* resisted, though. It had taken a good long walk and two stiff drinks before the show that day, but he hadn't gone back to his apartment, not until he knew Esta was asleep. And he'd resist Evelyn, too. Because nothing good could come from leading on a siren.

"Did you need something?" he asked, studying himself in the mirror. He took the pot of kohl and the small brush and started to dab it under his eyes, but his hands were shaking and he smudged it. Harte cursed under his breath.

"Let me," Evelyn said, taking the brush from his fingertips. She settled herself on his lap, and before he could stop her, she was brushing at the smudged kohl with her fingertip. At each gentle *tap, tap, tap*, tiny sparks of warmth began to relax him.

This close, he realized her eyes were the most amazing shade of blue. Like the open seas. Like freedom and possibility.

Her red mouth pulled up as she took the brush and gently applied the kohl to the edges of his eyes. As she worked, he felt more relaxed than he had in days. In *weeks*. The soft weight of her on his lap felt like an anchor in a stormy port.

When she was done, she gave his left eye one last smudge with the pad of her thumb, and he couldn't have stopped himself if he wanted to. A moment later, their mouths tangled. She tasted like wine, he thought vaguely as he pulled her closer, desperate for more of her. And more, as their mouths mashed in a fit of heat and impatient fury.

It was like he was drowning and she was air. And he couldn't get enough of it, of her. He barely heard the door open. He was only faintly conscious of someone entering the room.

"Well, this is a pretty picture," a voice said somewhere on the edges of his consciousness, but he ignored it and dived deeper into Evelyn's kiss.

It wasn't until Evelyn was ripped from his lap and he sat gasping for air that he comprehended it was Esta who'd come in. She had Evelyn by the hair and was dragging her out of the room, and all Harte could seem to do was sit and stare mutely.

"Bitch," she said, tossing Evelyn out of the room. "You come near him again, and it'll be your last time."

"You and what army is going to stop me?" Evelyn sneered.

"I'll leave that to Dolph Saunders."

"Dolph Saunders?" Evelyn looked suddenly uneasy.

"We understand each other, then," Esta said, laying on her false accent thick.

"I understand fine," Evelyn sneered. "You're going to regret this."

Esta didn't bother to respond, simply slammed the door in Evelyn's face. Then she turned to Harte, her golden eyes on fire. "You have something on your face," she said, taking the glass of water on his dressing table and, without any warning, tossing it directly in his face.

He sputtered in surprise. "What—?"

"Oh, save it. You're lucky I came when I did." She crossed her arms. "I can't believe you fell for her."

"I don't answer to you," he snapped, feeling more uneasy than angry. But inside, he was a ball of panic and fury. *What the hell just happened?*

"After that little display, maybe you should. Lord knows you can't take care of yourself." She shook her head. "There's enough magic in the air here to suffocate a person."

"Magic?" he asked, stunned. His mind still hadn't caught up to what was happening . . . what *had* happened.

Esta stared at him like she was waiting for him to put the pieces together.

Then he felt it—Evelyn's affinity was still snaking through the room like opium smoke, curling about him. Still calling to him. *Shit.* Right when he most needed to keep his wits about him, he was losing his damn mind instead.

Turning back to the mirror, he saw for the first time the mess he was—the dark streaks running beneath his eyes from the water, the red ringing his mouth like one of Barnum's clowns. No wonder Esta looked like she wanted to kill him. He wanted to kill himself when he thought about how stupid he'd been to let Evelyn touch him.

"You're welcome," she said.

"What are you doing here, anyway?" he asked, taking out his frustration on her.

"You've been avoiding me," she said, a furrow between her eyes. "You never came back to your apartment last night."

"You were already asleep." Harte tried wiping the red from his mouth.

"You weren't there this morning," she pressed.

"I left early."

"Like I said, you're avoiding me. You promised Dolph you'd help get Jack," she pressed. "You made a deal."

But he'd had enough of women for one day. "Dolph can go hang."

"You don't get it, do you?" she snapped. "People are disappearing. Tilly is *dead*." Her voice broke at the admission.

"Dead?" He hadn't realized. "I knew she was hurt, but—"

"She's gone." Esta's shoulders sagged, and it seemed like all the fire in her had faded.

"When?"

"A couple of days ago—before Dolph sent me."

"I'm sorry," he said softly.

"Are you really?" she asked, her voice flat, cold. He didn't have an answer for that. "This thing we're doing? It's bigger than Dolph—bigger than either of us. I don't care what you think about me or how angry you are that you're stuck with me. This isn't exactly a picnic for me, either, you know. But you need to pull yourself together and get over it. We need to get to work before you lose Jack Grew completely." She softened her voice. "Or before anyone else has to die."

Her words hit him like a slap, but he shoved away the pang of guilt he felt when he saw the sadness in her eyes. She wasn't some innocent in this, whatever she might pretend. She was there because Dolph Saunders had penned him into a corner, but he knew that wasn't the only reason.

"That's a nice speech. But tell me something, Esta. Why are you really here?"

Her eyes went suddenly wary. "I don't know what you mean. Dolph sent me to watch you. Why else would I be here?"

"You tell me. Who's the old man?" he asked, taking a step toward her.

"What?" The color drained from her face. "I don't know what you're talking about." She turned to go, but he grabbed her wrist.

He remembered the images he'd seen when he kissed her the last time she was in his dressing room. "I know about the old man with the crutch, in the room lined with books."

"How could you possibly know that?" she whispered, not bothering to deny it. Her golden eyes were wide with disbelief.

"I know you're not *only* here because of Dolph," he pressed, ignoring her question. "You're here for yourself—because the old man told you to find the Magician."

"Please," she said, trying to get away from him. "You're hurting me."

He saw then how tightly he was grasping her wrist and released her immediately. "I'm sorry," he said, shaken by the sight of the red mark he'd left on her delicate skin. He took a step back from her as she rubbed her wrist, hating himself for how easily his temper had spiked. How easily he'd become his father's son.

When he turned back, her eyes were steady on him, calculating. "You were in my head." She took a step toward him, closing the distance he'd put between them. "Is that what you do? Climb into people's heads and violate their most private thoughts? Do you have any idea how *wrong* that is?"

He ignored the familiar wave of shame. "You cornered me in my dressing room and lied to Evelyn about who you were. So, yeah . . . I took a look. I needed to protect myself. I needed to see exactly what your game was."

"When you kissed me," she realized, raising her fingers to her lips. "Then you should have your answers already." She lifted her chin, her eyes filled with disgust. And if he wasn't mistaken, with fear.

"It doesn't work like that," he snapped, hating his own limitations. And hating that what he'd done—what he *was*—had made her afraid. . . . Just as it had his mother.

She huffed out a laugh. "You really expect me to believe that?" she asked, but her voice shook, at odds with her show of confidence.

"It's the truth. I only get impressions unless I focus pretty intently, and if you remember, I was a little too distracted to really focus." He tucked his hands into his pockets. "I saw the old man, the library, and I heard him say 'Find the Magician.' That's it. That's all I know." He didn't look away, wouldn't back down from this. "Who *is* he, Esta? I need to know why you came for me. I need to know why you're *really* here."

Her mouth went tight, and for a moment he thought she would continue to lie to him. Finally, she spoke. "He's my father." Her eyes were steady, even as her voice shook. "Or, rather, he's as close to a father as I ever had. He raised me. Trained me to pick locks and lift wallets. He made me who I am."

He studied her, searching for a sign of the lie, but all he found was a sharp pain in her expression that he recognized too well. "Where is he now?"

"He's dead," she told him, her voice hitching. "Gone."

Even through the haze Evelyn had left behind, he felt like a veritable ass. "I'm sorry. I didn't know."

"Yeah, well . . ." Her mouth went tight. "Some affinity you have, isn't it?"

Harte ignored the insult. "If he's dead, why did you still come to find the Magician?"

Esta licked her lips. "Because he told me to. He could see things. He had an affinity for knowing about things that would happen."

"And why did you need to find me?"

She took a breath, still wrestling with herself, but then she met his eyes. "He said that you were going to disappear with the Book that Dolph's after. And if you do that, the Book will never be recovered. You're going to destroy any chance we *ever* have of defeating the Order."

"And you believed him?" Harte said, suddenly cold.

"He'd never led me wrong before," she said. And that much, at least, sounded like the honest truth.

"For what it's worth, I don't have any plans to destroy the Book."

"For what it's worth, I wouldn't let you." She shook her head and let herself out.

The room felt strangely empty once Esta was gone, as though she'd taken something vital with her. He looked at his reflection again, the smudges under his eyes, the stain of red that left his lips looking bloodied.

Who knew how far Evelyn would have taken things if Esta hadn't interrupted? He owed her for that, even if she'd only done it because Dolph needed him. But he didn't know how he'd ever pay her back with anything but betrayal.

THE GLASS CASKET

Harte was still avoiding her. He always came back to the apartment late, long after she was asleep, and he would be gone before she awoke every morning. After she'd given everything away in his dressing room, maybe that was safer. She'd been cornered, and she'd acted on instinct. Too bad her instincts tended to get her in trouble. *Like what happened with Logan.*

But with every day that passed, the news clipping remained stubborn in its insistence that Dolph Saunders was going to die.

Enough was enough. She had a job to do—she needed that book and she needed Ishtar's Key. And Dolph was sure they couldn't do anything without Harte, which meant she needed him, too. He couldn't avoid her forever.

After breakfast, she set off for the theater to confront him, but it wasn't Harte she found when she arrived. The first person she ran into was the red-haired harpy.

"You're back," Evelyn said, sounding like she meant, *Go away.*

"Of course. I'll be around quite a lot from now on," Esta said in her falsely accented voice as she headed toward Harte's dressing room.

"He isn't there," the woman called, a mocking note in her voice. "He's down below."

Straightening her spine, Esta gave Evelyn a cold smile before she turned and made her way through the maze of the backstage hallways and then down a staircase to a damp-smelling room beneath the theater. She thought she heard water and wondered if the theater wasn't built over one of the hidden rivers in the city. Just ahead, there was a light, and as she moved toward it, she heard a familiar voice letting out a string of curses.

"Harte?" she called, navigating through the cluttered storage area until she came to where he was working.

The Magician had pulled a vanishing act, because the boy before her could have been any factory worker, any laborer in the city. He was dressed in worn brown pants held up only by a pair of suspenders. They sagged low on his narrow hips, and his shoulders and arms were bare beneath his sleeveless shirt, which was damp with sweat. He looked more unbuttoned and human than she'd ever seen him.

Then he flipped the visor up on the welding mask and ruined the effect.

"Get in," he said, pointing to the table where the strange, coffinlike tank he'd been working on was sitting. His eyes were a little wild.

She took a step back.

"I mean it. Get in. I need to see if this will fit you."

"Why?" she asked suspiciously. "Looking for new and inventive ways to dispose of my body?"

"The thought did cross my mind once or twice," he said dryly.

She bit back a laugh. "Nice of you to spring for a glass coffin. Wood is so 1899."

He glared at her, scratching his chin. "It's not a coffin. It's a—wait. Maybe you're right."

"I usually am."

However hard his eyes were, Esta sensed that he was too excited to really be mad. "We *could* go with the defying-death angle. The Glass Casket has a nice ring to it, don't you think?"

Esta eyed him. "What do you mean, *we*?"

"You and me. If I'm stuck with you, I'm going to make use of the situation."

"I thought you'd decided on avoiding me," she said, crossing her arms.

"Didn't you say we had to get to work?" he said, frowning at her. "I've been getting things ready."

She narrowed her eyes at him, not trusting the excitement in his expression. "Ready for what?"

"We're going to run the lost heir on Jack."

"Am I supposed to know what that means?"

He frowned. "It's a con game. If it works, Jack's going to believe that we have something he'd do anything to get. *You're* going to be the lost heir."

"What, exactly, am I the heir *of*?" she asked, walking over to run the tips of her gloved fingers against the smooth glass.

"You, sweetheart, just happen to be the long-lost illegitimate daughter of Baron Franz von Filosik, who was rumored to have found the secret to the transmutation of basic elements before his untimely death."

"Is that an actual person?"

"Of course it is." He paused. "Wasn't that all part of Dolph's plan? I figured that's why you introduced yourself to Evelyn with that name."

She glanced up from the glass box, trying to hide her surprise. After all, she'd been improvising about who she was that day in the dressing room. She'd given her own name, not one Dolph had invented. Not that Harte needed to know that.

"Of course it was the plan," she said, trying to stay in control of the situation. "Who was he, this Baron von Filosik? What did he do?"

"Dolph didn't explain it?"

"He just gave me the name," she lied.

Harte gave her a knowing look. "Yeah, that sounds exactly like something he'd do."

Esta relaxed a little with his acceptance of her story, but she couldn't help but wonder if the Professor had known somehow that the name he'd picked after he found her in the park would come in handy one day.

"Well?" she pressed. "If this con is going to work, I should know my own fictional father."

"You will, but for now all you need to know is that the transmutation of the elements is basically the Holy Grail for most alchemists. The good baron died in a fire some years back, along with all his secrets. Or so people thought." He waggled his eyebrows at her. "But now his secret daughter has returned to continue her father's work. And she's lonely and afraid and could use a protector."

She rolled her eyes at him. "And *that's* supposed to be me?" she asked, doubtful.

"If you can pull it off? Yes," he told her. "As far as Jack Grew's concerned, you've recently shown up in town in need of help from an old friend—that would be me. We just have to make him believe that it would be better if *he* were the one you relied on. After all, you'd be very grateful to such a person, wouldn't you? You might even be willing to share your father's secrets with that person."

"So we make Jack believe that I have my fake father's secret files?"

"And we make him think you're vulnerable enough to give them up with the right *encouragement*. In this case, an introduction at Khafre Hall."

"You really think that will work?"

"It's what we have."

"Which is *such* a ringing endorsement."

"Look, Jack's been interested in my act for months now, but he's like the rest of them—he believes that his family's money and status makes us fundamentally different. That's what will catch him—he won't be able to accept that you would choose me over him if you had the option."

"He's going to rescue me from you," she realized, appreciating the simplicity of trapping Jack with his own greed and narrow-mindedness.

"That's the basic idea. He'll have to prove himself to you somehow, and that's what will trap him."

"But what does this death trap have to do with me being the daughter of some dead baron?"

"You have to earn your keep somehow," he told her, the corner of his mouth kicking up wryly. "So you're helping me with my demonstrations."

"I don't know," she hedged, eyeing the box. "That doesn't really seem necessary."

"It's all part of the con." He ran a hand over the glass case. "That disappearing thing you did was a great effect. We're going to build on it to hook Jack into believing that you have secrets that could help him with some experiments he's been doing."

"What kind of experiments?"

"No idea," Harte admitted. "I haven't been able to get him to tell me yet. Like I said, he still doesn't completely trust me. He's been using me for information, but he's still keeping me at arm's length." He glanced back in the direction of the stairwell, as though checking to make sure no one else could hear. "So how did you do it?" he whispered. "The disappearing thing. I'm going to need to know what I'm working with."

"I'd be happy to." She leaned in. "Right after you tell me what you're really planning to do with the Book. Because I don't believe for a second you really plan to hand it over to Dolph."

He pulled back, his eyes wary. "Or we can work around it."

She gave him a shrug. "If you insist."

They stared at each other for a moment, neither wanting to be the first to flinch. Neither wanting to be the one who gave up any ground. To Esta's relief, his excitement to show her the glass casket won out.

"Okay, then . . . Come take a look at what I've done here. I want you to see how it works." He closed the hinged lid and then opened it, to show her how smoothly it moved. When he depressed a hidden lever at the end of the case, the glass lid slid silently free of the frame, like a car window rolling down. "I've been working on this for a while, but I finally figured it out." Then he grinned.

Esta's stomach did an unexpected—and definitely unwanted—flip. When his mouth turned up like that, into a real smile instead of the one he pasted onto that smug face of his onstage, he looked almost boyish. Almost like someone she'd like to know . . . if she wasn't who she was and he wasn't who he was. If he hadn't just all but admitted he was making his own plans.

But they *were* who they were, and she couldn't let herself forget that *he* was the one she was supposed to stop. If he betrayed the team, it would mean more than the loss of the Book. But now, it might also mean the death of Dolph Saunders. What would happen to his crew—to all the people who depended on him—if he were gone? What chance would any of them have against the viciousness of the city and the Order that controlled it without Dolph to lead them and to protect them?

"You made this?" she asked, stepping around so that the glass box was between them.

"Yeah. I've been working on the idea for a while. I was going to do it myself, but with your . . . whatever it is you do, I think it'll be better." He slid the glass back into place and closed the lid. "Most people do this effect behind a screen or with a box, where no one can see what the girl is doing. But with you, we can do something new." He ran his hand over the glass coffin. "The girl—that'll be you—will disappear right before the audience's eyes. No mirrors or screens, no capes or hiding. *Poof.* You'll be gone." He eyed her. "Assuming, of course, you can manage it."

"I can manage it," she said, "but don't you think it's a little risky to have me disappear like that? It'll raise suspicions about how I did it. Maybe about what I am."

"No, it won't," he said, his gray eyes dancing. "That's the beautiful thing about it. No one will believe you *actually* disappeared, because no one will expect you to have real magic. They expect that everything I do onstage is a trick, an illusion. Half the audience will be telling the other half that they knew how it was done."

Even though she knew he was still up to something, *this* version of Harte Darrigan was disarming. His face was smudged and his hair was standing up in a riot of loose waves. His clothes were rumpled, and although he was attempting to play things cool, he was practically vibrating with anticipation. It was all a hundred times more compelling than anything she'd seen him do onstage. It seemed so authentic. This Harte Darrigan seemed so *real.*

All part of his game, she reminded herself. For all she knew, it was just another con.

"Are you going to get in, or what?"

Esta hesitated. "You aren't going to trap me in there?"

"I'm not promising anything," he joked, but when she gave him a doubtful look, he let out an impatient huff. "You saw how the mechanism works, didn't you?" Then he held out his hand, a challenge in his eyes.

Frowning, Esta took his hand and allowed him to help her step up onto the table and into the glass box. It was a tight fit with the bulk of her skirts.

"Good," he said, looking her over. "Now lie down, would you? I need to make sure it's not too long or too short."

She barely had enough room for her hands to be at her sides.

"There's a small lever by your right toe. It'll take some practice to find—"

She hit the lever, and he had to jump to catch the glass top from sliding too quickly. "You were saying?"

He scowled at her. "And *now* we close it."

"But—"

Before she could protest, he was already pulling the top down and locking it with a bronze padlock. Fog from her breath started to build on the glass, inches from her nose. Suddenly, the air felt too warm, too close.

"There aren't any air holes," he shouted, his voice muffled by the glass. "You'll have to work fast."

No air holes? She was going to kill him.

Her foot fumbled for the latch but missed the first time.

If he doesn't finish me off first, that is.

"We'll have a cue or something," he was shouting, motioning to the lever near her foot. "Some sort of hand motion or signal to . . ."

She pulled time around her, slowed the seconds, and depressed the latch. The glass released, and she slid it away from her face, taking a moment to breathe in the cool, musty air of the basement and allowing the prickle of panic to recede from her skin before she climbed out. Composing herself, she wiped her sweaty palms on her skirts and then slid the glass back into place before examining Harte. Nearly frozen mid-word, his eyes gleamed.

He loves this.

Whatever else he pretended, whatever he'd done or was going to do, she could see that he wasn't pretending his excitement for this new trick—effect. *Whatever.* The point was that he loved it as much as she loved the rush from lifting a fat wallet or hearing the tumblers of a lock click into place.

She felt that strange lurch in her stomach, one that she didn't like at all, so she released time and watched Harte sputter midsentence.

"...let you know—*oh.*" His face split into a surprised smile. His stormy eyes lit, unguarded and unaware that he was showing her something new about himself. "Yes! That's it exactly." Then he seemed to realize he'd revealed too much. "You'll have to wait for my cue, of course," he said, back to his usual arrogance. "You don't want to come out too soon and ruin everything. We'll have to—"

"You locked me in an airtight box," she said flatly, interrupting him.

His brow furrowed. "That's kind of the point. If there's no sense of danger, the audience won't care."

"You. Locked. Me. In. An. *Airtight.* Box," she said again, enunciating each word through her clenched teeth.

"Maybe we should add something more," he said, not paying any attention to her outrage.

"You could have warned me before you locked me in. You *should* have warned me."

He ran a hand through his already mussed hair. "You got out," he said, looking at her as though he didn't understand her point.

"You could have killed me!"

"I didn't—" he started to say, but when she stepped toward him, he put his hands up defensively. "Okay, you're right. I'm sorry. I should have warned you."

"Dolph isn't going like it if I end up dead."

"You're probably right about that, too." He ducked his head and unlatched the bronze padlock. "But other than the almost dying, what do you think?"

She shrugged, reluctant to give him any credit at all. "It'll be okay."

"Okay?" He laughed. "No. This will be like nothing anyone has *ever* seen. If this doesn't convince Jack that you have something he wants, nothing will. This has to work."

"It will," she said, looking over the glass coffin again. "We'll make it work. Together."

"We just might," he said, his expression changing. "Here's to bringing down the Order." He held out his hand, his eyes serious. Esta considered all the reasons she shouldn't let him touch her, but in the end she placed her gloved hand in his. He squeezed gently, but the warmth she felt thrum through her had nothing to do with the peculiar energy left behind by magic.

The atmosphere between them grew thick, charged. She pulled her hand away.

"Esta . . . ," he started, but hesitated as though he didn't quite know what he wanted to say.

Before he could figure it out, a voice called from close by. "Harte?" Evelyn said, stepping into the light thrown by his work lamp.

The moment broken, he took a step back from Esta, looking suddenly embarrassed. Or guilty. "Yeah?" He wiped the hand that had just shaken hers on his pants.

"Shorty wanted me to let you know you're on in twenty."

"He sent you down here?" he asked, a frown tugging at his mouth.

Evelyn put her hands on her hips. "Is that a problem?"

"No. Sorry. Thanks for letting me know. I'll be up in a minute."

"I'll see you upstairs," she said sweetly, before giving Esta a pointed glance and then slinking back from wherever she'd come.

Esta watched her go, wondering how long Evelyn had been standing in the shadows. And how much she'd heard. But if Harte was concerned, he didn't show it.

"Look, I've got to get ready for the show, but stick around, would you?"

She glanced up at him, surprised. He'd never invited her to stay and watch his show, or to wait for him after.

"So we can practice again," he finished, tugging at one of his suspenders. "I'm thinking once we work on the timing, I can get ahold of Jack. It shouldn't take us that long to get it right."

"Oh, right," she said, feeling suddenly stupid. *Of course.* "Dolph would want us to get this going. We've taken long enough."

"So you'll wait?"

"Yeah," she said, pasting on an encouraging smile. "Absolutely."

After he'd disappeared up the steps, she let the smile fall from her face and ran her hands along the smooth glass of the box. It was a good idea, a good effect, she had to admit. It *might* even be enough to convince Jack Grew that she had something he wanted, but they couldn't take any chances. The trick needed to be better than good—it needed to be spectacular.

IMPROVISING

arte had never seen Esta so on edge. After he'd explained how they would run the lost heir on Jack, they'd settled into a steady—if not quite comfortable—rhythm as they prepared for the Friday-night performance. Everything he'd thrown at her—and it had been plenty—she'd given back to him in turn, and with a smirk on her face that told him she was enjoying herself. But standing in the wings, her apple-green silk gown glinting in the lights from the stage, she was going to chew a hole in her lip while she watched the act before him.

"You'll be fine," he said, resting his hands on her bare shoulders. He felt her stiffen, but she didn't pull away, even when he rubbed his thumb gently over the pink scar on her arm. She wouldn't tell him what it was from, but the angry pucker of skin had drawn his attention and his concern.

"Don't," she whispered, turning her head back to look at him with a frown. Her honey-colored eyes were serious, and if he wasn't mistaken, scared.

"I wasn't," he told her. "I wouldn't."

She snorted her disbelief at his words, but she didn't pull away, and he realized that he liked the way her skin felt under his fingertips. Soft, when there had been so little softness in his life for so long. He knew enough not to depend on it, though, because it couldn't last. Not with so much standing between them. He had to get out of the city, and for that he had to remember that she was just another thing standing in his way.

He dropped his hands from her shoulders.

"Do you think he's out there?" she asked, peering past the stage into the theater.

"Second box to the right," he told her. "There's no need to be nervous. This is going to work."

"I'm not nervous," she said, tilting her head to the side. "Just ready."

"You'll come on when I give the cue, just as we rehearsed."

"I know. I know," she said. "You've gone over this a hundred times. *Two* hundred times." But her voice didn't have the usual bite.

"Don't forget to—" The organ trilled his introduction, and it was too late for any more instructions. "*Just* like we practiced. You'll be fine."

She nodded, but there was something in her eyes that worried him. "Esta—"

"What are you waiting for?" Shorty hissed. "That was your cue!"

Unable to wait any longer, he gave her what he hoped was a stern but encouraging look, and took the stage.

Word that he was debuting a new effect had gotten out, and the seats were nearly full. The audience went gratifyingly silent when he stepped into the spotlight, and when he lifted his arms to salute the crowd, a rumble of applause rolled over him, settling his nerves and steeling his resolve. He worked through his usual bits, and the audience seemed willing enough to watch, because they knew something bigger, better was coming.

"Ladies and gentlemen." The words came as easily as the prayers his mother had taught him when he was a boy, but this time, much more was riding on his performance than a good night onstage. "I have a special treat for you this evening. A new demonstration and a new beauty for you to feast your eyes upon." He held out his hand, as they'd practiced, and Esta glided onto the stage.

If she'd been nervous before, there was no sign of it now. She walked like a debutante, like she'd been born to tread the boards. But then maybe she had. After watching Esta the past few days, he'd come to understand that she was one of the best grifters he'd ever seen. Maybe even better than him.

"May I present to you Miss Esta von Filosik of Rastenburg. I studied under her father, the foremost expert on the transmutation of the elements. He made great breakthroughs in the hermetic sciences before his untimely death, and now Miss Filosik has come to these shores to share her father's secrets with all of you. Tonight she will demonstrate her mastery over the powers of the Otherworld by cheating death"—he paused dramatically, letting the crowd's anticipation grow—"in the Glass Casket."

Excited murmurs rustled through the crowd. As the assistant rolled the box onto the stage, he chanced a glance in the direction of Jack's box and was relieved to see him leaning forward against the railing of the balcony, watching with clear interest.

"If you would?" he said, offering Esta his hand, as they'd practiced.

She hesitated, though, and didn't take it as she was supposed to.

"My dear," he said, offering his hand again.

"Oh, I don't know." She shook her head and took a step back.

He offered his hand again and forced the smile to stay put on his face. *This can't be happening. Not again. Not now.* "Come, my dear. It's perfectly safe."

A slow smile curved her lips, and he had the sudden feeling that he wasn't going to like what happened next.

"Oh, I bet you say that to all the girls," Esta told the audience in her throaty accented voice as she crossed the stage, ignoring his outstretched hand and turning all his careful planning on its head.

He could practically feel the audience's confusion and their amusement. Hushed whispers rustled through the room as they waited to see what the girl would do next, and whether he would be able to regain control.

Harte Darrigan had survived his mother leaving him, a childhood in the streets he'd rather forget, and working for a boss who thought it was easier to kill people than to talk things over. He'd made a life from keeping his cool in sticky situations, but none of that had managed to prepare him for being in the spotlight—*his* spotlight—with Jack Grew in the audience and himself completely at her mercy.

He was afraid to look in Jack's direction, afraid to see what his reaction would be. This whole con depended on Jack feeling like Harte was real competition, feeling like he had something to prove and someone to beat.

She could ruin everything.

He'd let himself believe that he'd taken control of the situation, but he'd been as easily conned as any mark, taken in by a pair of honeyed eyes and pink lips and the soft, clean scent of flowers. He had known she was up to something. Worse, he'd let himself forget that anyone working for Dolph Saunders had to be a snake. And he had the sinking feeling he'd just been bitten.

Then something shifted in the audience. The murmuring died a bit, as though they wanted to see what would happen next.

He hadn't lost them yet. He could still save this.

"Please, if you would simply step into the casket, we can continue our demonstration." He held out his hand. *"As we planned,"* he said through clenched teeth.

She let out a dramatic sigh, raising her hand to the curve of her chest—a move he had no doubt was intentional. "Oh, all right, *darling*," she said with a wink to the audience. "But there *are* easier ways to get rid of me."

Someone in the audience chuckled.

"My father always said a handsome face would be the death of me," Esta said dramatically. Then she shrugged. "I hate when he's right." Finally, she took his hand and climbed the steps to sit in the glass box.

"What are you doing?" he whispered, as he made a show of helping her arrange her skirts.

"I'm improvising," she told him through her smile.

Improvising? He'd show her improvising.

Her eyes went wide when she understood what he was about to do, but she didn't have time to stop him before he closed the lid.

It was wrong of him, maybe even a little cruel. He knew she hated to be in there. Through all their practicing, he'd gathered that there was something about being in that small, confined, airless space that made her jittery like nothing else could. They'd worked it out so he closed the lid at the last possible second.

That was before she went off script. He couldn't afford any more of her *improvising*, so he shut the lid tight, latched on the padlock, and tossed the key into the audience with a flourish. Esta made a good show of it, frantically pounding at the glass to get out. At least, he thought with a twinge of guilt, he hoped it was only a show.

He gave the signal for the stagehands to bring out the second part of the trick—a contraption that suspended an iron weight over the glass box by a piece of rope.

"Fire. The most volatile of all the elements," he told the audience as he set off a flare in his hand and used it to light a candle beneath the rope. "If I am not able to call upon my mastery of the Otherworld's powers, the flame will burn through this rope and the weight will fall, crushing the casket . . . and Miss Filosik with it."

The theater was on the edge of their seats, watching the girl struggle against the glass box, watching the candle eat away at the fragile rope. Waiting with violent glee to see whether she'd live or die.

He picked up his scarlet cape and twirled it over his head. *One . . .*

Over the casket where the girl writhed and slapped at the glass. *Two . . .*

He closed his eyes and sent up a quick prayer to the god he'd long given up on that he hadn't overplayed his hand. Then he twirled the cape in front of him, obscuring the audience's view for less than a second, as the candle ate through the final bit of rope.

Just as the weight fell, shattering the glass.

Three.

A MISSTEP

She took a moment to enjoy Harte's dazed look of relief before she gave the shocked audience her most dazzling smile.

"I guess Papa was wrong," she said, and the audience went wild.

She took her time raising one arm, like he'd taught her, to take her bow. The thrill of the crowd's rolling applause sank into her, warming something deep within her.

In that moment, she understood Harte a little better.

He was staring at her, and for once, he was speechless. Not that she blamed him. She hadn't exactly warned him about the costume change she'd orchestrated. She'd paid the theater's seamstress, Cela, to create the scrap of a costume she was now wearing, because she'd been watching in the wings for days now, and all that watching had taught her something—it wasn't only wonder and awe that sold an act. A little skin didn't hurt either.

Evelyn and her sisters, if that was what they really were, had about as much talent as a trio of alley cats in heat, but they knew when to show a little leg and to give a little tease. And they got the audience's attention every single night.

Harte's face was turning an alarming shade of red as she made one last curtsy and took herself off, stage left. She was barely out of the footlights when he came charging behind her. He ripped the robe from the stagehand's grasp and wrapped it around her.

"What the hell was that?" he asked. "And what are you wearing?"

"Do you like it?" She opened the robe to give him a better look.

In her own time, the outfit—a corseted top with off-the-shoulder sleeves and a pair of bloomers that came to midthigh—would have been laughably modest. The entire thing was made from a gorgeous midnight-blue silk and was studded with crystals that glittered in the dim light of the wings like a field of stars. Old-fashioned as it might be, she loved it. Not only was it beautifully made, but after the long skirts and layers of fabric she'd been wearing for weeks now, she felt lighter. More like herself.

Harte opened his mouth, but all that came out was a choked sound. He tied the robe back around her again.

She decided to take it as a compliment.

He was still sputtering in anger when Evelyn came up to them and wiped at Harte's cheek with her fingertip. "You got something on your face, there." Then she laughed at him and walked off.

He reached up, still wordless, and rubbed where she'd touched. His brows furrowed as he saw the red stain on his fingertips, and when he looked in the small mirror on the wall, he turned an even deeper shade of red.

"You kissed me?"

Esta shrugged. "I thought it would be a nice touch."

She hadn't planned it, but when she had pulled the seconds around her and made time go slow, it seemed too easy to simply get herself out of the box and slip the green gown off. He'd been so bossy all afternoon, she couldn't resist playing with him a little—giving him back some of what he'd given her—so she'd left the bright red imprint of her lips on his cheek before she let go of her hold on time.

To the audience, it all happened at once—the amazing escape, her metamorphosis into the new outfit, and the mark on his cheek. For them, she'd gone from seconds-away-from-death to victory in a blink.

"You should have cleared it with me," he said, rubbing at the red spot and making it worse as he smeared it.

"Funny. I've thought that every time you've kissed *me*. Besides, it worked, didn't it?"

"It doesn't matter if it worked," he told her, turning to her with an expression so angry, she took a step back.

Esta pulled the robe tighter around herself and headed toward Harte's dressing room. She didn't bother to check if he was following her. She didn't need to—she could practically feel him breathing down her neck.

She tossed off the robe as she walked into the room. Before she had time to turn around, he'd slammed the door, closing them into the small space alone and away from the prying eyes of the other performers. She turned, her arms crossed, and propped herself against his dressing table, refusing to be intimidated. "What is your problem? Tonight went well. Better than well. They loved it."

"This is *my* act," he said, stalking toward her. "It's *my* call what happens out there. You don't get to change it without my say-so."

She'd known he'd be a little annoyed, maybe even upset by her not telling him, but she truly hadn't predicted that her little addition to the act would make him so *furious*. Their almost-easy partnership for the last few days had made her forget her position, and she'd miscalculated, forgotten how different things were between men and women in this time. Harte might have acted more enlightened than most, but he was still a product of his time. Of course he'd take any adjustment to his act personally. She should have realized.

Not that she was going to apologize. The risk had worked, and he was going to have to deal with it. She turned her back to him so that she could use the mirror to take off her stage makeup.

His face appeared in the mirror behind her, looming over her shoulder. "I thought after this week—"

"Darrigan!" Shorty poked his head through the door before she could finish. "Good job, kid. That was a helluva trick you two did out there," he said as he came into the room, a cigar clamped between his teeth. He gave Harte a rough thump on the back that seemed to shut him up and then handed him a slip of paper. "Message for you," he said with another thump on the shoulder before backing out and closing the door behind him.

"What is it?" Esta tried to peer at the message while Harte used his shoulder and his height to keep its contents away from her.

"It's from Jack," Harte said. "He wants to have dinner with us tomorrow night."

She tried not to gloat—*really* she did—but she couldn't help smiling. "You're welcome."

"Don't," he growled, his expression hard. "This didn't happen because of what you did out there. It happened *in spite* of it." He waved the paper at her. "You could have ruined everything."

"But . . ." Her smile faltered.

"Did you even consider that your little improvisation might not have worked? We hadn't rehearsed it. I've been working for months to get Jack to believe that I am what I say I am. We had *one* chance for Jack to see you for the first time. *One.* Any misstep could have ruined all of that."

"I'm sorry," she said, suddenly struck by how impulsive she'd been. How thoughtless.

"You're lucky I don't call this whole thing off," he told her. "I could tell Jack everything I know about you and the Met. I could wash my hands of Dolph Saunders and this whole mess of his."

"No!" She stepped toward him and grabbed his arm. "Please, don't."

"Why shouldn't I?" he said. "Why shouldn't I wash my hands of the lot of you?"

Shame burned her cheeks, and she might as well have been standing in Professor Lachlan's office, listening to him tell her the exact same thing. "Because it's not their fault," she said softly. "Don't punish them for what I did."

He studied her, and she could barely breathe while she waited for his answer. "This is the Order we're talking about, Esta. If they find out what we are—if *Jack* finds out what I am—it's not going to end well. I won't let your carelessness take me down with you. If we're going to do this, I have to be able to trust you to do what you say you're going to do. Otherwise, I'm done. I'm out for good. Damn Dolph and the lot of you."

"You don't have to worry," she promised. "It won't happen again." She forced herself to meet his eyes, hoping that he didn't see the lie there.

"You're sure?"

"Yes," she insisted, praying he would believe her. "You can trust me." *At least until the very end.*

A NEW PARTNERSHIP

The Haymarket

Ever since he'd confronted her after their performance, Harte had noticed that Esta was more subdued. Not cowed, by any means, but watchful, like she was waiting for something. But as the hack pulled up to their destination, she looked downright nervous.

"I'm not going in there," Esta said, when she realized where the carriage had stopped. "You should have warned me. I never would have come."

"I thought you'd appreciate the surprise," he said, confused by her reaction. "After all, this *is* where we first met."

"You don't understand," she said, trying again to tug away from him. "People in there . . ." She hesitated as though searching for the right word. "They might recognize me. It could ruin everything."

Ignoring the stiffness in her posture, he held her out at arm's length and took a moment to look her over. She was wearing the dress he'd picked from the ones she'd bought—or taken. He never knew for sure with her. It was a golden color with beads that caught the light no matter how she moved. Strings of more beads were all that covered her shoulders, and the neckline dipped dramatically to showcase the gentle slope of her chest and the garnet collar that sat around her throat. She looked like a living flame.

She'd argued that something more inconspicuous would be better. In the end, though, she'd agreed with him that Jack needed to be impressed by her and had worn the dress. But seeing it in his apartment was different from seeing the gown in the moonlight. And knowing that he'd picked it for her, that she'd willingly worn it for him, was another thing altogether.

And he didn't want to think too much about how that made him feel.

"They won't recognize you," he said, giving her a smoldering look meant to tease as much as to assure her. "No one would—not looking like that."

The compliment had the effect he'd intended, and she snorted, crossing her arms over her chest. "I know a line when I hear one, Darrigan."

He met her gaze before he spoke. "Then you should know that wasn't a line."

She gave him her usual scowl, but her shoulders relaxed a little and she looked more like herself.

He took her hand and tucked it through his arm. "Are you ready?"

"I don't think—"

"This will work. Just stay close, and you'll be fine." He started to lead her toward the Haymarket, but when they were almost to the door, he stopped, remembering something. "If anything should happen tonight—"

"You just told me everything would be fine."

"It will be," he assured her. "Whatever you do, though, no magic once we're inside. Corey's security is trained to detect it, and they won't hesitate to act if they sense you using it. You're lucky you got out without them catching you last time."

Esta stopped in her tracks and looked up at him. Her mouth was slightly open, and she was looking at him as though she'd never seen him before.

"You were trying to help me," she said. "That night when we first met. You had a reason for manhandling me, didn't you?"

"I have no idea what you're talking about," he told her, and before she could press him about it any more, he led them toward the dance hall's entrance.

Inside, the band was playing a ballad—Harte recognized the melody as one of the songs Evelyn belted out onstage each night. He led Esta through the crush of people and around the main floor of the ballroom. "I want a table upstairs, where we can see the whole floor. I don't want to miss Jack when he comes in."

Fastening an aura of ease and charm around him like armor, Harte made his way through the room slowly, knowing exactly how uncomfortable she was with being paraded around and introduced to various people they encountered. She smiled and said all the right things, but every time he stopped to chat with someone, her posture grew more rigid and her smile more strained. He'd been around her long enough now that he was starting to learn the subtle shifts in her mood. Esta might always act as though nothing touched her, but tonight her eyes were giving her away. She was still on edge.

Eventually he found them an empty table at the balcony railing with a clear view of the first floor. Below, the Haymarket was alive with color. Women in brightly colored gowns swirled around the dance floor, while pink-faced men leaned against the central bar, laughing too loud as they held their tumblers of whiskey. Across the table from him, Esta was quiet, watching the room with guarded eyes.

After a few minutes of silence, she spoke, startling him from his thoughts. "You love all of this, don't you?"

"What?" He took his eyes from the door to look at her.

She was sitting with her elbows propped on the table, her chin against her folded hands, a question in her eyes. "The attention. The way so many people know who you are and want to talk with you. You pretend to be indifferent, but underneath you're like a cat with cream."

He shrugged off his discomfort at how clearly she'd seen through him. "I'm not going to complain," he said. "There are a lot worse ways to spend an evening." *Like starving in a gutter. Or trying to stay clean when the whole world is determined to make you filthy.*

"What were you thinking about just now?" she asked, sitting up a little straighter, her eyes focused completely on him now. "Your whole expression just . . . closed up."

She was too perceptive by half. "Nothing," he told her, feigning ignorance about her concern.

It was clear she didn't believe him. She was still staring at him as though he'd give up all his secrets if she were patient enough. But that couldn't happen. He called over a server and ordered a bottle of champagne, avoiding her eyes and her expectations as the waiter poured two glasses.

"To our new partnership," he said with his practiced, pleasant smile as he raised a glass to toast her.

She only watched him with those serious eyes of hers, and didn't bother to lift her glass or take a drink. "It's an impressive mask you wear," she said. "Even knowing it's there, I can barely see a crack."

He placed his glass on the table, untouched as well. "I'm not sure what you mean," he said stiffly. "I am exactly what I appear to be."

"That's probably more true than you know." Still not taking the champagne, she turned to watch the room below.

After a few minutes, he missed her attention and wanted her to turn back, if only to spark at him again. That, at least, was more amusing than this sullen silence. But Esta's attention was on the floor below. She drummed her fingertips softly against the base of her champagne flute as if waiting for something to happen.

Or maybe she was waiting for *someone*, he thought with a sudden unsettling jolt of unwelcome jealousy.

It all served to remind him that they weren't *really* there together by choice. She wasn't really his or even on his side. They were sitting on opposite sides of the board, playing each other in hopes of gaining the same prize. But he had so much more at stake, and if push came to shove, he wouldn't let her be the victor.

He stood and held his hand out to her. "Dance with me," he said, not allowing himself to think about the motivation behind his impulse.

She looked up at him, her eyes betraying her surprise. But she didn't make any move to accept his invitation.

Now that he was standing, he felt like an idiot. "I think our mark arrived," he lied, when he started to fear that she would refuse him and he'd be forced to sit down, humiliated.

"Oh?" Still, she didn't reach for his hand.

His neck felt hot. The people at the table next to them laughed at something—probably him—and he had to fight the urge to tug at his collar and adjust the cuff links at his wrists. "We should make sure Jack sees us," he pressed.

"Of course," she murmured, but there was no pleasure or anticipation in her eyes as she *finally* took his hand and allowed him to lead her down to the dance floor.

Harte recognized his mistake almost immediately. He'd never been one for waltzing, usually preferring instead to work the edges of the room or the men near the bar. So he'd forgotten how it felt to take a girl by the waist, to hold her smaller hand in his and pull her close as he spun her around the room. He'd forgotten the way his head could spin as the music wrapped the couples in its hypnotizing rhythm, the way the entire world could narrow to one pair of golden eyes.

He felt drunk, suddenly, even though he hadn't touched the champagne either. Off-balance. Inexplicably swept away by the song, by the moment, and against all his better judgment, by *her*.

One glance at her face showed that she didn't feel the same. She moved gracefully, allowing him to lead her across the floor, but she wasn't really *with* him. Her concentration was on the room around them, not on the small, private world they were creating within the span of their arms and the rhythm of their steps. The realization was like water on a fire, and by the time the song wound down to its close, Harte had sobered. Convenient, because as Esta made her final curtsy to him, he caught sight of Jack Grew over the top of her head.

He offered his arm to escort her off the floor, and when she accepted it, he bent his head toward hers. "Are you ready?"

She gave a small nod as she met his eyes. He wasn't sure what he saw there now—determination? Resignation? It worried him that he couldn't read her, didn't know what she was thinking. Not without using his affinity, and doing that would mean losing the one ally—however tenous that might be—that he had. But the time for delaying was over. They had work to do.

TO SINK THE HOOK

The orchestra at the Haymarket had just finished a cloyingly sentimental waltz that had grated against Jack's already-raw nerves. He was at the end of his rope. He'd put everything he had left—and a lot that wasn't his to take—into rebuilding his machine. The new machinists had been working day and night to restore the hunk of metal and wire, and it was nearly ready to try again. But trying it again was pointless unless he could figure out how to stop the blasted thing from exploding.

He was running out of time—his father's ship would leave from London in another week. When he arrived in New York, his men of business would tell him about the emptied accounts, and Jack would be on a one-way train to Cleveland, or some other godforsaken uncivilized place in the wilds of the Midwest. He wouldn't be around for the Conclave, much less to make his triumphant return to the Order's good graces.

But at least the Haymarket stocked passable scotch.

He raised the glass to his lips, anxious for the numbing burn and the taste of smoke and fire, but when he tilted it back, he found it empty. He peered down, wondering when he'd finished the drink. Then he lifted the empty glass to signal the barmaid to bring him another while he waited for Darrigan and his doxy to show up.

The thought of them arriving buoyed him a bit. The demonstration they'd done the night before had been remarkable. Impossible. He could use a little of the impossible on his side right now.

Over the racket of the crowd, he heard his name and lifted his head to find Harte Darrigan walking toward him. On his arm was the girl from the night before. Tall and lean, she could have been an Amazon in another life, but in this one she was a vision in a gown spun from gold. If the dress wasn't enough to convince him that she was different from the usual theater types, the jewels at her neck would have been. No chorus girl had jewels like that.

"Thanks for the invitation tonight," Darrigan said as he closed the distance between them, offering Jack his hand as he approached with the girl.

"I'm glad you could make it," Jack said, taking Darrigan's hand. *Damn if it isn't good to see him again,* he thought suddenly. *Everything is going to be fine.*

Darrigan made a small flourish with his hand as he brought the girl forward. "May I present Miss Esta von Filosik." Harte smiled warmly at the girl. "Esta, this is a good friend of mine. A *very* important man in our city, Mr. Jack Grew."

Jack couldn't help but preen a bit under the praise. "Miss Filosik," he said, with a slight nod of his head. This close, he saw that his original impression had been right. Her face was free from any paint and her clothes were so well fitted that they must have been custom-made.

"You must call me Esta," she told him, offering her hand. She spoke with a foreign lilt to her voice, but it wasn't the gutteral sound that filled the saloons of lower Manhattan. Instead, it had the refinement of someone well bred and educated. "Any friend of Harte's is one of mine."

"Esta it is, then." He took her hand and bowed low over it, lifting his eyes to take in the shapely bodice of her gown, the creamy expanse of her chest.

She gave him a slow smile, peering up at him through her lashes, but then her eyes went wide. Her mouth opened in a soft *oh.*

Well, well, he thought with anticipation as the girl stared at him as though she appreciated what she saw. . . .

"We arrived a bit early and were taking a turn around the floor. There's a table waiting upstairs," Harte told him. "If that's all right with you?"

Jack released the girl's hand. "That sounds fine."

"Wonderful." The girl gave him a slow, encouraging smile. "I believe the champagne should still be cold."

"Champagne, you say?" He looked down at his empty glass, feeling that much better about the days ahead. "That sounds as perfect as you look, my dear."

DÉJÀ VU

E sta cringed inwardly at Jack's obvious come-on. A hundred years, and men never figured out that lines like that didn't work.

As Harte led her back to their table, it took effort to keep her features relaxed. She was still unsettled from the premonition she'd had when Jack had looked up as he bowed over her gloved hand. She'd been overwhelmed by the memory of those same eyes in a darkened hallway, when he was pointing a gun at her before he turned it on Logan.

If Harte hadn't started talking again, she would probably still be frozen. But she reminded herself that there was no way Jack could know her or remember her: She'd first met him in 1926, some twenty-four years from now. She would be fine. She'd get through this.

Ten minutes later, though, she regretted having him at their table. Harte was a different person around him, condescending and dismissive of everyone, including her. It was a part of their plan, she told herself. He was only giving Jack an opening, using her—the mistreated mistress—as bait. But it was still an ordeal to sit through.

He was even worse than Logan, Esta thought as she listened to the two men bluster at each other. Logan had a sort of natural charm he used to disarm his victims, but Harte's was something more. Whatever charm he came by naturally had been cultivated and honed with the precision of an artist. It was so overwhelming that his mark had no choice but to be taken in by it.

She did know better, and she'd almost been taken in by it, she admitted, thinking of the warm fluttering in her belly as they'd danced. The moment he'd taken her in his arms, she'd felt trapped and protected all at once, and she hated herself for almost liking the feeling. Hated that she'd had to focus on something—*anything*—else during the dance, because he was looking at her with an intensity that made her cheeks warm.

The whole ordeal had made her feel things she didn't want to examine too closely. Unnerved. Unbalanced. And maybe most dangerous of all, *unsure*.

All part of his game, she reminded herself—a game she *had* to win.

As she kept half of her attention on the conversation at their table and the other half on the ballroom, she couldn't help but think that Dakari's knife might still be somewhere in that building. It grated at her, the knowledge that she was a thief who couldn't even steal back something that belonged to her. And it worried her, going back to her own time without that bit of proof about what once had been. After the way the clipping had changed, who knew what future she'd be going back to?

Jack was nearly through the first bottle of champagne when a flash of coppery hair caught her eye. Down on the floor, Bridget Malone was making her way along the edge of the room.

Esta was on her feet before she realized what she was doing.

"Sweetheart?" Harte asked, a warning threaded through the endearment.

She didn't care about his warnings, though. He had Jack well enough in hand. She *had* to try. "Would you gentlemen excuse me?"

"Where are you going?" Harte asked through his clenched teeth.

She could still make out Bridget's fiery hair moving through the crowd. "Just to powder my nose, *darling*," she said with a shy smile. "It will only take a moment. . . . If one of you could direct me?"

"Back behind the bar," Grew told her as he reached for the bottle again. His face had turned blotchy and red from the warmth of the room and the amount of wine he'd consumed.

She could tell Harte wanted to protest, but she promised to return quickly before he could, and then made her way through the crowd.

At first she went in the direction Grew had pointed, but when she was out of view, she cut beneath the overhang of the balcony and headed in the direction Bridget Malone had taken.

When she reached the corner of the room, she found that Bridget had vanished. There wasn't a door or hallway for the madam to have gone through, but the woman was gone. Confusion settled over Esta as she searched for some answer to Bridget's disappearance.

She found it a moment later when a portion of the wall slid open and one of the waiter girls emerged carrying a tray of clean barware. Before the panel slid shut, Esta picked up her pace and slipped through the opening into the dark silence of an empty hallway.

At the end of the passageway, Esta could just make out the glow of the flame Bridget held in her hand. From the smell of roasting meat that filled the air, the passage was also connected to the kitchens, but Esta wondered where else it might lead and whether it was connected to the lower floors. The room Bridget had kept her in before was below, in the cellar of the building.

The light wavered, and then the woman turned a corner and the passageway fell into shadow. Beams of light filtered through small holes in the wall, and Esta went to one and peered through to find a private dining room. From the looks of it, the passage was lined with more openings, probably so the management could keep tabs on their patrons without their knowledge.

She peered through the next set of openings and found another room, this one filled with men smoking cigars and talking in voices amplified by alcohol and a sense of their own invincibility. Among them was the man who had assaulted her weeks ago, Charlie Murphy. His nose was still crooked, but the bruises on his face had healed. Not that it improved his looks any. She watched them, trying to follow the flow of their conversation. They were discussing some event—a gala to celebrate the spring equinox, from what she could understand. That was when it hit her— they were all members of the Order.

"It didn't last long enough," a bald man was arguing as he pounded on the surface of the table, causing the stemware to shake.

"Nearly a year," another said.

"In the past it was more like a decade. The stones are dying."

The stones?

"They aren't dying," the bald man insisted. "But I agree there's something fundamentally wrong. I can't believe it's the artifacts themselves, though. Maybe there was a problem with the ritual?"

"I'd like to see you tell the Inner Circle that." Murphy laughed. "More likely it's a problem with the maggots we've been able to find. My father used to say the Irish were bad, but these newest arrivals? Dirty and uneducated, and don't even get me started about the Jews and Catholics."

"You're probably right. What power could possibly be derived from rabble like that? I'll tell you what needs to happen—"

A waiter entered carrying trays of food, and the men seemed to take it as a signal to change the topic. Dolph had talked about people going missing. She wondered if this was connected to it in some way.

The end of the hallway beckoned as the server made a show of carving the roast. In his presence, the men turned their conversation to mundane topics. Sports and stocks and the damnable traffic that was growing every day. Anything but magic.

Esta was growing impatient. Too much time had passed already. If she was going to get Dakari's knife, she had to go now. If only she could use her affinity . . . If she could slow time, she could be done in a blink. But she couldn't chance that. She had to make a choice. Did she go for the knife or stay and see what more she could discover? Dakari or Dolph's crew? Her own past or her new present? There wasn't time for both.

She had one job—to get the Book and to get home. Nothing was more important than that, not even Dakari. But the men on the other side of the wall were talking like there was a problem, like the Order had a weakness. Which was a fact that could only help them. Dolph and Professor Lachlan—all the Mageus.

Dakari would understand.

She peered through the openings and listened again, but before she could catch the thread of their conversation, she heard a familiar voice.

"What are *you* doing here?" Bridget Malone was suddenly there, next to her in the darkness, and looking none too happy to see her.

A TRAP IN A TRAP

Harte glanced over the dance floor below, looking for some sign of Esta's return. She'd been gone too long. Had she run into trouble? Or was she up to something?

"So tell me, Darrigan, how did you *really* meet the lovely Miss Filosik?" Jack tipped what was left of the bottle into his glass. The champagne fizzed and foamed over the edge of the bowl, dampening the white cloth on the table. "Are you and she . . . ?" He waggled his eyebrows suggestively.

"We've been friends since we were children," Harte said, leaving his answer open enough for Jack to make his own assumptions.

"Really?" Jack smirked.

"Yes. Believe it or not, the story I told onstage was true. I know Esta from my travels abroad. Her father was one of my first teachers. Perhaps you've heard of him . . . Baron von Filosik?"

Jack's face bunched, and Harte could practically see his alcohol-soaked mind trying to place where he'd heard that name. It took a moment, but then Jack's bleary eyes widened a fraction. "Not the Baron *Franz* von Filosik?"

"The same," Harte said easily, relieved that Jack had finally made the first step toward entering his little game.

"*You* knew the baron?" Jack asked.

He pretended he didn't notice Jack's surprise. "I was lucky enough to have lived with the baron when I was just beginning my quest for knowledge about the mysteries of the elemental states. He saw some talent in me and admired my drive to understand the secrets of the occult arts. It was he who directed me to the Far East and provided me with the introductions I needed to finish my studies. This was all before his untimely death, of course."

Jack frowned, puzzled. "I didn't know he had any family."

"Few did. Franz never married Esta's mother. It's maybe the only thing that saved her when his estate burned to the ground. I'm sure you've heard about that, the great tragedy it was. All of his breakthroughs were lost. His vast knowledge, gone."

"It probably set us back fifty years, maybe more," Jack agreed.

Harte leaned forward, his voice low. "Except, I don't think everything was destroyed."

Jack's brows went up, and even though his eyes were barely focusing, Harte saw interest in them. He could practically feel Jack's willingness to be convinced, to believe. It wouldn't take much more to push him the rest of the way.

"Esta has a trunk she keeps under lock and key. Won't tell me what's in it, won't let me see what it contains." Harte glanced to the left and right, making sure it looked like he was worried about being overheard. He lowered his voice. "I think it might be some of her father's papers."

"You don't say?"

Harte nodded. "You know what he was working on when he died, don't you?"

Jack looked momentarily thrown off. "Oh, yes. Wasn't it the . . . ?" He hesitated. "The, um . . ." He snapped his fingers, as though the words were on the tip of his tongue.

"The transmutation of basic elements," Harte supplied helpfully.

"Of course," Jack agreed. Then he blinked through his alcoholic haze like someone just surfacing from sleep. "You're not saying he created the philosopher's stone?"

"Rumor had it that the good baron was *very* close to a breakthrough." Harte leaned forward. "In his last letters to me, he hinted that he'd been successful at isolating quintessence—"

"Aether?" Jack whispered, excitement clear despite the glassiness of his eyes.

Harte nodded. "But he died before he could answer any of my questions or tell me anything more."

"Right," Jack agreed. "Terrible tragedy."

"It was." Harte hesitated, like he wasn't sure if he should share a secret. "More so if, as Esta believes, his death wasn't the accident it appeared to be."

Jack blinked. "She believes it was foul play?"

Harted leaned closer. "She believes someone found out what the baron was doing, how close he was to unlocking the secrets of divine power. Imagine what might be possible with that information. You could make the elements bend to your will."

"Yes." Jack licked his lips. "Imagine that. . . . But who would want to stop him from such a great discovery?"

"When I studied with him, the baron had suspicions he was being watched. He confided in me once that he worried there were those in the local village—Mageus—who didn't want him to succeed. He'd made arrangements so his work wouldn't be lost in case anything happened. If that trunk of hers contains what I think it might, it would be a discovery of amazing importance, Jack."

"You think she could be convinced to share it with us?" Jack asked, his expression unabashedly hungry.

"That's my problem." Harte frowned. "We're old friends—more than friends, really," he said, imbuing his voice with a lecherous note, "but she hasn't let me see what's inside. I think she's still testing me to see if I can help her. She's tired of living on the edges of society. She's the daughter of a baron, and while her father was alive she lived like one. But with his death, she lost her income and any standing in her town. So she's come to this country, like so many come, to start again. She wants her old life back, to live like the daughter of a baron is entitled to live, and whatever's in that trunk, she believes it's enough to gain her entrance to the highest society." Again he glanced around and then lowered his voice. "She's been implying she wants to get the attention of the Order. Of course, I thought of you. With your help, with your connections, she might be willing to share her father's work with us."

"She might not have anything, though," Jack said, frowning. "She could be leading you on. It's in a female's nature to be manipulative and deceitful."

"It could be that she's lying," Harte acknowledged, "but she was the one who designed the effect you saw last night. It's quite extraordinary what she's able to do."

"Designed it *herself*?"

"As much as it pains me to admit it, she still won't tell me how she accomplished it. I think she's been teasing me, withholding that information to get what she wants."

"Well, we can't let her get away with that, can we?" Jack said with a roguish grin.

"You have an idea?"

"Maybe with the right enticements, I could soften her up, find out if she's being honest about what she has."

"You'd do that for me?" Harte said, pushing down an unexpected jolt of jealousy.

"Of course. We're friends, aren't we, Darrigan?" Jack took another long drink. "And it's not as though it would be a chore to breach her defenses."

Harte's hands clenched into fists beneath the table, but he kept his expression the picture of eager appreciation. "I'd be awful grateful. I'd hate to be made a fool of, but if she does have her father's secrets, she could be very useful to me."

"To both of us. Miss Filosik and her secrets don't stand a chance," Jack said, raising his glass.

"Not a chance at all," Harte agreed pleasantly as he watched Jack finish off the last of the champagne. He couldn't have scripted the evening any better himself. Jack had fallen for the bait just as they'd planned for him to, but Harte couldn't shake the feeling that he'd made a misstep somehow. He just wasn't sure what it was, or how it might come back to bite him later.

Still, successes should be celebrated, so he pasted on his most charming smile and was about to call for another bottle when a shadow fell over his table. Harte looked up to find Paul Kelly standing over him.

"Hello, Darrigan," Kelly said genially. He was dressed impeccably, as usual, in a crisp suit, but his eyes held a warning. "Fancy meeting you here."

A moment of silence passed, where Harte was too shocked by Kelly's appearance to utter a word. It was as if he'd awoken to discover all those months of freedom had been nothing but a dream. He was thirteen years old again, looking at his certain death.

"Aren't you going to introduce us?" Kelly asked expectantly, shaking Harte from his stupor.

Jack glanced at Kelly and then looked to Harte. "Do you know this gentleman?" he asked, and Harte could see the confusion in Jack's bleary gaze as he took in Kelly's well-cut clothes and his long-ago broken nose.

He was stuck. Kelly was making enough of a name for himself that Jack might recognize it, and if he did, it might destroy all the work Harte had done to make himself seem respectable. But if he refused, Kelly was sure to make a scene.

"This is an old acquaintance of mine, Jack. Paul Kelly, Jack Grew. Jack, allow me to introduce you to Mr. Kelly."

Jack, who thankfully showed no sign of recognizing the name, shook Kelly's hand, and then to Harte's horror, he asked Kelly to join them. "We were just celebrating a mutually beneficial opportunity we stumbled upon," he told them.

"Were you?" Kelly asked, taking the seat Esta had left open. He eyed the waiting glass of champagne. "I'm a bit of a businessman myself," Kelly told him.

Jack sputtered a bit, making some excuses and trying not to reveal what they'd been talking about as Paul Kelly sat on the other side of the table with his usual cold-eyed stare.

Harte felt as though he couldn't breathe. He'd risked everything— including his mother's life—to keep Kelly away from Jack, and now they were sitting at a table together. He needed to get out of there, he thought as he glanced again to the floor below, hoping for some sign of Esta's return.

"You have somewhere to be?" Kelly said as he took a slim cigarette from a silver case.

"No," he lied. "Nowhere at all."

Before Kelly could call him on his lie, a whistle sounded from the floor below. Harte turned in time to see a squad of helmeted police-men making their way into the ballroom, the beginning of a raid on the prostitutes that strolled the floor and the illegal gambling that often took place in the back rooms.

"Well, gentlemen," said Kelly, who didn't seem the least bit surprised at the raid. "I think it's time we make our exit."

THE MISSING KNIFE

Bridget's face was shadowed, but Esta could still make out the remains of a purplish bruise across the side of Bridget's cheek.

"I came for my knife," Esta said, realizing as the words tumbled from her mouth how absolutely stupid they sounded.

"What knife?" Bridget asked, looking both harried and confused at the same time.

"The one you took from my boot," Esta insisted.

"I didn't take anything," Bridget said, glancing beyond Esta, toward the entrance of the passageway. "You're mad if you think I did, and you're mad for coming back here after I went to the trouble to get you away."

"There was a knife," Esta said as ice settled into her veins. There had to be. *Because if there was no knife, there might be no Dakari.* But Bridget didn't seem to be lying.

"I'm not a thief . . . unlike some," Bridget snapped. "You need to get out of here. Do you have any idea what will happen to you if Corey sees you here?"

She took hold of Esta's wrist and tugged her toward the ballroom. But when she eased the panel open to enter the barroom again, the room on the other side had erupted into a riot. Women screamed and men tumbled over each other to avoid the clubs that the police were using on the heads of anyone who struggled to get away. "We have to go," Bridget said. "Come on. If they see us without escorts, they'll assume we're working girls. It's the whole point of the raid. They'll arrest us for sure."

But Esta had an escort. She looked up toward the balcony, but with the mess of people tearing at one another to get away, she couldn't tell if Harte was still there.

"Where are you going?" Bridget shouted as Esta pulled away and began shoving her way through the crowd, pushing against the flow of people. She was so intent on searching for Harte that she didn't notice the policeman behind her until she heard the shrill scream of his whistle. And she didn't notice the baton he held until it came down on her head.

THE WATER'S EDGE

The ballroom was in chaos. As soon as the whistle sounded, Harte felt paralyzed by the memories crashing into him. He was eleven again, cornered in the alley where he'd made his bed that night, unable to escape.

"Darrigan!" Jack was pulling at him, saying something.

But the sound of the whistles and shouts drowned out everything but the memory of being dragged from his sleep and into a Black Maria packed so tightly with filthy men and women that he couldn't move. Couldn't get away from the stink of them. Couldn't get away from their hands. Grabbing at him, pulling at him . . .

He couldn't breathe.

Jack's voice came to him from somewhere far off. "This way, Darrigan."

Harte let himself be led, panicked confusion keeping him from processing what was happening until they stepped out into an alley that reeked of rotten meat and piss, the smells of his childhood. It took everything he had not to retch.

When the cool night air hit his face, he gasped, sucking the air into his lungs. He was barely aware of Jack shaking Paul Kelly's hand, thanking him for the help getting out of the hall.

"Good seeing you again, Darrigan," Kelly said with a rough slap on his back, before he hailed a cab and disappeared into the night.

As he came back to himself, Harte had the sudden—and delayed—realization that he was no longer inside the Haymarket.

"What are we doing out here, Jack?"

"We're not getting swept up in the raid, that's what," Jack said. His hair was sticking up at an odd angle and the shoulder of his jacket was torn, but he looked pleased with himself. Almost exhilarated from their escape. "Damn nice of Kelly to help us out of that mess."

"We can't leave without Esta," Harte said, starting to go back.

Jack caught him by the arm. "Are you insane? The girl will be fine. All those jewels? They'll let her go. Hell, they'll probably escort her home. Come on. I can't be caught up in this, and I can't imagine you'd want to spend a night in the Tombs either."

He pulled his arm away from Jack, but Harte didn't move. He couldn't be taken to the Tombs, he thought as the wave of panic crested over him again. *Not again.*

"Are you coming or not?" Jack asked, tugging at him.

Harte looked back at the rear door of the Haymarket. "But Esta—"

"She'll be fine."

He turned on Jack. "You can't know that."

Jack gave him a shrug. "You're right. I can't. Think of it this way: If she gets caught up in the mess, at least she won't be keeping the baron's journals from us anymore." He elbowed Harte as he laughed at his own joke.

Harte's fingers closed into a fist and it took everything he had not to drive it into Jack's pretty white teeth. But to do that would destroy the con and any chance of ever getting the Book.

"Come on," Jack insisted. "There's something I want to show you."

He couldn't leave Esta, but he also couldn't let Jack get away. Not when he was so damn close.

"Well?" Jack asked, impatient.

She was probably already outside, halfway back to their apartment— *his* apartment, he corrected. She'd be fine, he told himself. If the tables were turned, she would probably do the same. She'd *improvise*, wouldn't she? She was good at that.

"Fine," he told Jack, looking back at the door one last time. "Let's go."

They walked a block west, avoiding the noise coming from Sixth Avenue, where some of the Haymarket's customers and waiter girls had tried to avoid the police but ran right into them instead. If Esta had gone that way—

If she went that way, she can get out of it. Whatever magic it was that allowed her to move like lightning, disappearing and reappearing in barely a blink, she'd be fine. He needed to stay with Jack. They were too close to let him off the hook now.

The cab they found smelled like someone had been sick in it earlier, but Jack didn't give any indication that he noticed. Instead, he slouched back in his seat with his eyes half-closed as the carriage started off.

After a while, though, it became clear that Jack wasn't taking them toward the mansions on Fifth Avenue, as Harte had expected. When he saw the spires of Trinity Church, a landmark well below the safety of Canal Street, he started to worry.

"Where are we going?" Harte asked as the carriage rattled on.

Jack opened his eyes enough to squint at him. "You'll see," he said with a self-satisfied smile. Then he closed his eyes again and, a few seconds later, let out a soft snore.

As they rode, Jack dozed drunkenly while Harte considered his options. But the carriage never stopped as it followed a route that cut deeper and deeper into the poorly lit neighborhood streets, each progressively darker and quieter than the last.

When they approached the eastern edge of the island, Jack snorted and came awake with a jerk. When he saw where they were, he looked excited, anxious, and suddenly more sober than he had all night. But as they followed the shoreline, the closer they came to the towering span of the bridge, and the more uneasy Harte became.

He couldn't cross that bridge, but he also couldn't stop the carriage without risking all the work he'd done to get Jack this comfortable. More important, Harte couldn't let Jack realize the *real* reason he couldn't cross the bridge.

Every block they passed brought the bridge closer still. Harte glanced at Jack's wrist, noticing the sliver of exposed skin between his cuff and his gloves. He'd wait until they turned toward the bridge, just to be sure. Until the danger of the Brink was worth the risk—

But then Jack rapped on the driver's window, and the carriage came to a shuddering stop. "We're here," he said, excitement and anticipation shining in his eyes despite the effects of the champagne.

Harte took a breath, relieved that the carriage had finally stopped, but he didn't let his guard down.

The docks that bordered the river in that part of town were a forest of ships' masts and a maze of warehouses crouched close to the ground. Harte wasn't familiar with the area. The river's edge was the domain of the longshoremen and the river rats who raided the cargo. Most people were smart enough to stay away from the docks, where the roughnecks often looked away if a body was dumped into the river. And most Mageus would have never chanced coming that close to the Brink that silently circled the island somewhere just offshore. Even now, even with the water still some distance away, Harte could swear that he felt the chill of it.

Jack gave the driver orders to wait and then led them through the uneven grid of buildings bathed in moonlight, swinging his arms at his sides and whistling the occasional off-key tune like they were walking through Central Park and not one of the dodgiest parts of the city. Harte never had trusted that sort of blind confidence. Usually, it was a mask for ignorance, and in his experience, both were dangerous.

Everywhere, shadows lurked, rustling in doorways and curling against the walls of the buildings. Occasionally, one of the shadows would bring fire to its fingertips. A flicker of flame would come to life, the puff of smoke enwreathing a briefly illuminated face, and then the night would go dark again.

It isn't magic, Harte reminded himself. Just a simple flare of a match, the mundane glow from the flickering tip of a cigarette.

This close to the river, Harte could almost detect the scent of the water. On the other side lay everything he'd never been able to reach, an entire land that was more than the stinking streets and the day-after-day scrambling urgency of the city. A world where he could be something more than a rat in a trap.

But in the next breath, the scent of water was covered by the heaviness of axle grease and soot, the ripeness of days-old fish and oyster shells. A reminder that he still had a long way to go before he could be making plans about a different future.

Finally, they came to a long, unremarkable warehouse. Jack took a ring of keys from his coat and made quick work of the heavy padlocks on the wooden door. But before the last one clicked open, he turned to Harte. "You probably wouldn't even need a key, would you?" he asked, cocking his head to the side. Jack's face was covered by shadows, but his body had gone rigid, like he'd finally sobered up enough to comprehend what he was doing. To have second thoughts.

"I'm not a thief, Jack."

"I know that." Jack shifted uneasily. "But I'm taking a risk in showing you this. I think you'll understand, and I'm going to trust it'll interest you enough that I won't have to worry."

"Whether I'm interested or not, you don't have to worry about me. I don't want any trouble."

Jack frowned like he was puzzling over something. For a second Harte thought Jack would change his mind, so he pulled on a look of boredom and moderate impatience. "Look, I didn't ask you to bring me here, but can we get on with it already? I need to get back and check on Esta, so if we're not going in—"

"No," Jack said, giving himself a visible shake. "You've come all this way, you should see it. I want you to." He pushed the door inward. Beyond it, blank darkness waited, but Jack quickly lit a kerosene lamp near the door. "After you," he said.

In the center of the room, there was a large misshapen object covered by a cloth. With a smile lighting his face as much as the lamp, Jack drew the heavy tarp off and revealed something that could have been pulled from the pages of Jules Verne. The machine clearly wasn't complete yet, but Harte could make out the gist of it: a large central globe made from what looked like glass, which was surrounded by three concentrically ringed arms that glinted in the light.

It looked harmless enough, quiet and still as it was, but there was something about the machine that made Harte nervous.

"Amazing, isn't it?" Jack said, giving one of the great orbiting arms a push, which made all the others glide slowly through their separate rotations as well.

"What the hell is it?" Harte asked, trying to shake the sense of apprehension he had standing next to it.

"*This* is the future, Darrigan," Jack said, beaming.

"The future?" Harte eyed him doubtfully.

"Come here and take a look." Jack walked past Harte to a long worktable on the left side of the room. Various blueprints and maps were laid out in haphazard piles, anchored in place by drafting tools and angles. He motioned for Harte to join him.

Reluctant to get too close to the strange machine, Harte made his way around the outer edge of the room, to the table where Jack was standing. At the far end of it was a model, a small rectangular building with a single tower growing from its center. The tower was capped with an odd, onion-shaped roof that reminded Harte of a picture he'd seen once of a Russian church.

"What is all this?" Harte asked.

Jack pointed to the model of the building. "My uncle's building a larger version of this out on Long Island. It's going to be a wireless transmitter—Tesla's doing the design. When it's done, it will transmit telegraphs, maybe even pictures, through the air. My uncle believes it's going to revolutionize the world of business."

"You don't think it will?" Harte asked, responding to the tone in Jack's words.

"I think he's thinking too small and missing the point entirely," Jack said as he began shuffling through a pile of papers. "Here, look."

Jack smoothed out one of the crumpled sheets for Harte to inspect.

"It's the Philosopher's Hand," he said, glancing up at Jack before returning his focus to the paper. The image was familiar to Harte—he'd studied enough alchemy to recognize the symbol and knew what it stood for.

"Exactly. I knew you'd understand," Jack said, excitement lighting his eyes. "Five fingers for five distinct elements, the basis of all we know and understand about otherworldly power. Everyone who studies the occult arts knows that the elements are the key to unlocking the secrets of magic. If you isolate the individual elements, you can harness their energy and command them to bend to your will. But look what holds them together."

The image depicted a hand with its fingers spread wide, each tipped with a different symbol—a key, a crown, a lantern, a star, and the moon. In the open palm, the fish and the flame, the symbols for . . .

"Mercury," Harte said, tapping the center of the palm. "The element that transcends all others. Sometimes known as quicksilver."

"Or Aether," Jack added. "The same substance the baron was able to isolate, if you're right."

"What's your point, Jack?" Harte asked, unease crawling down his spine. Perhaps he'd played his game a little too well: Jack had not only taken the hook, he now seemed to be dragging him out to sea. "And what does this have to do with that machine? Or with the future?"

"Everything." Jack stopped short. "It has *everything* to do with the future. Every day, the world sends more and more of its filth to our shores. Among them, Mageus sneak into our city. Filthy. Uncivilized. *Dangerous.* Their very existence threatens our civilization and, as we've seen for ourselves, the safety of our property and our citizens. But this machine will change everything, Darrigan." He ran his finger over the tip of the tower's roofline. "It will put a stop to that threat once and for all."

"The Brink already keeps the Mageus in their place."

"Maybe that was true during a simpler time," Jack said. "When the Brink was created, there were far fewer coming here. It was enough to simply trap them on the island. But the numbers have been steadily increasing. There have been attempts to meet the growing threat, of course. Ellis Island, for instance, was supposed to keep Mageus from ever setting foot on our shores, but those measures haven't been enough. Devious as they are, more maggots slip through the inspectors every day. There are even reports that some have made it off the island and onto the mainland. That cannot stand. The Order knows something has to be done. They've been working on a plan to increase the Brink's reach, but what they're doing won't work."

"No?" Harte kept his eyes trained on the model of the building, feigning interest to cover his fear.

"Not as long as they're using old-fashioned ideas—old-fashioned magic—instead of modern science. And so long as they're thinking too small."

"The Brink is small?" Harte asked, trying to keep his voice even.

Grew nodded. "But my machine won't be. Consider this, Darrigan. Tesla's tower will revolutionize wireless transmission, true, but it's only the *beginning* of what could be done with it. With the kind of power this receiver can generate, it could make the Brink obsolete." He smoothed out the rumpled paper bearing the Philosopher's Hand again. "The Brink was created more than a century ago by a ritual manipulation of the elements through the Aether. It's old-fashioned alchemy: Five artifacts, each imbued with the power of one of the basic elements, were used to complete the ritual. Like this hand—all the elements are connected through the Aether, the palm. It creates a circuit of sorts. When a Mageus passes through it, their power unbalances that circuit, and whatever magic they possess is drawn toward the elemental energies of the Brink as it attempts to balance itself.

"The whole system is self-perpetuating, powered by the very feral magic it takes, which is why it's lasted for so long with very little maintenance. But the Aether is the key," Jack said eagerly. "There are two problems with the Brink, though. First, the power taken from any Mageus who tries to cross the Brink becomes part of the circuit, but we can't do anything more with that power. For all intents and purposes, it's lost. We can't *use* it." Jack eyed him. "That's a waste, don't you think?"

"Yes," Harte forced out, his stomach turning. "Quite."

"This machine would put an end to that. Instead of redistributing the power it harvests, it collects it and holds it separately."

"And the other problem?"

"The Brink is limited by its size. When it was first created, no one knew how quickly the city would grow or that the wilds of Brooklyn and beyond would become what they have. No one could have imagined how many people would come to our shores. No one imagined that they would come *despite* the Brink."

"Desperate people will do desperate things," Harte murmured. They would chance the Brink and commit themselves to living in a rattrap of a city because it was still better than the places they came from, places still ravaged by the hate spurred on during the Disenchantment. Because the hope for a different future was *that* powerful.

"It's not desperation, Darrigan. It's a complete disregard for our way of life. The Order is aware of this problem, of course. They were hoping to unveil their grand plan at the upcoming Conclave, when the entire Order gathers, but it isn't working. The original artifacts aren't powerful enough to expand the size of the Brink without making it unstable. Now they're trying to replicate the original creation of the Brink, all in the hope that perhaps they might be able to re-create it in other places, trap any Mageus that manage to avoid New York. That hasn't worked either." He shook his head, a mocking expression on his face. "But will the Inner Circle listen to me?"

"No?" Harte asked, trying to hide his hopefulness.

"Of course not. They're stuck in the past, and its weight is dragging them under. It will drag us *all* under." With a violent motion, Jack swept the papers off the table, causing them to flutter into the air and then settle onto the ground at Harte's feet. "They're so focused on containing the maggots, they don't realize it has never worked. They're like rats, the way their numbers seem to be growing. Like rats, they need to be *exterminated*, and when I get my machine working, that's exactly what we'll do." He walked over to it and ran his hand over the shining metal of one of the orbital arms. "Once this machine is installed in Tesla's single tower, it will have enough energy to clean a one-hundred-mile radius of any feral magic. *Much* more efficient than the old rituals. Imagine one of these in every major city. It would send a message—a warning—to any who would come to this country and try to turn us from our destiny."

"One hundred miles?" Harte asked, feeling almost faint. "You're sure?"

"The last time we tested it, the field it generated reached as far as Fulton Street, and that was only at a fraction of its capacity." Jack smiled slyly.

"Quite impressive," Harte said, but he thought of Tilly as he said it and felt sick. He hadn't realized what Jack capable of. He'd been goading him on, encouraging him, when he should have been paying more attention.

"It is, isn't it?" Jack agreed. "When I multiply what this machine is capable of by the power of Tesla's transmitter, we can easily wipe out all the feral magic in Manhattan, maybe even reach as far as Philadelphia and Boston. But unlike the Brink, the power this machine will generate once it's installed in Tesla's tower would be *usable*. Imagine it—feral magic eradicated, transformed into civilized power that could be used to guide and shape the future of this new century. Or . . . it could become a weapon unlike any the world has ever seen. This country could become even greater than the empires of Europe after the Disenchantment."

Harte didn't have any idea how to respond without giving away his true feelings. He hadn't realized that the Brink kept the power it took from Mageus, but to increase that danger?

If Jack succeeded, if the Order ever controlled such a machine, magic would be doomed *everywhere*, as would every single person with an affinity. If Jack was right about the machine's possibilities, Harte's plan to leave the city was pointless. If he didn't find a way to stop Jack, to destroy the machine, there wouldn't be anywhere to hide.

"You said the machine doesn't work?" he asked.

"No." Jack scraped his hand through his hair, frustrated. "Not yet, at least. I haven't found a way to stabilize the power that it collects. There's something about feral magic that isn't stable. The last one I built didn't last a week before it blew up and killed my machinist." His eyes were a little wild as they searched the silent metal, as though it would whisper its secrets if he waited long enough. "All the power it generated was lost."

Just like Tilly. The existence of the machine explained the strange boundary on Fulton Street, but if Tilly had died when the machine exploded . . . what did that mean about Dolph's plan to destroy the Brink?

"It's not the machine," Jack continued, not noticing Harte's dismay. "The design is flawless—I did it myself. The mechanism works perfectly when it's in motion. But after meeting your Miss Filosik, I've realized what I'm missing."

"You have?" Harte asked, not liking the sound of that one bit.

"It's the *Aether* I've been forgetting about."

"The Aether?" He could barely make himself say the word.

"Yes, of course! I don't know why it didn't occur to me before." Jack ran a trembling hand through his hair again, making himself look even more disheveled and unhinged. "Without isolating the Aether, the power would be unstable, unpredictable. In the Philosopher's Hand, Aether is what stabilizes the elements, so it might also stabilize the power this machine harvests. The problem is no one since the Last Magician has been able to isolate or produce it."

"The Last Magician?" Harte's head was still spinning. "I'm afraid I'm not sure who that is."

"No?" Jack's brows wrinkled in surprise, and an unwelcome wariness flashed in his eyes.

"At least not by that particular name," Harte amended. It felt as though everything were spinning out of control.

Jack studied him a moment longer. "The Last Magician was someone like us, devoted to studying the hermetic arts many centuries ago. It's rumored that he succeeded in ways others haven't since. Some of his breakthroughs helped to create the Brink."

"He was a member of the Order?"

"Not exactly, but the Order built upon his work. We have his journal, a record of all he'd learned and all he accomplished—a tome called the Ars Arcana. Arcanum, of course, being another name for the philosopher's stone."

"That can't be a coincidence," Harte said knowing that Jack could never, *never* get the Book. "You think this book will help you isolate Aether?"

"I do, but the Order keeps it under lock and key. Only the highest ranking members have access to it. I've been trying to take a look for months now, but I'm not a member of the Inner Circle. Now, that no longer matters." Jack smiled, an unholy excitement lighting his face. "If you're right about your Miss Filosik, I might not need to see those records. Not if we can get her to share her father's secrets with us."

Harte's mind raced to stay ahead of Jack. The machine changed everything. . . .

Harte suddenly remembered the old man's prediction, that he would somehow destroy the Book. He hadn't completely believed Esta, hadn't believed in the prediction. But now he understood, because he could see clearly what he had to do.

He needed the Book, now more than ever.

"You'd have to get her to trust you," Harte said as an idea struck him: If Jack was interested in Esta, if he was still on the hook, they could still run their game. If they could hold off Jack *and* get the Book, maybe he could still get out of the city. As soon as he was out, he would destroy the Book and any chance Jack or the Order had of finishing this machine.

He wouldn't be able to tell Esta until it was over. She didn't understand what was at stake, if not now with Jack, then someday with someone. And he knew that with her faith in the old man's words, he would never convince her that the Book was too dangerous to exist.

But that didn't mean she couldn't still help him.

When everything was done, when they were safe, maybe he'd be able to explain. Maybe she'd even forgive him.

And if she didn't?

He'd lived with worse.

"I'm sure that won't be a problem," Jack said with a devilish smile. "It's possible my machine could be working before the Conclave, as I planned."

"The Order won't have any choice but to recognize your genius," Harte told him, hiding his true feelings behind his most dazzling smile. Inside, he felt like he could barely breathe.

"And the maggots won't have a chance."

Harte nodded his agreement and clapped Jack on the back, but silently he vowed to do everything in his power to make sure that future never came to be.

A CHANGE OF HEART

It was nearly three in the morning before Harte finally got rid of Jack and made his way back home. He let himself into the apartment, expecting to find Esta already locked in his room. Or, more likely, wide-eyed and ready to throttle him for leaving her. After what Jack had shown him, though, he'd be happy to take his chances with her anger. He couldn't get away from the docks, and from that nightmare of a machine, fast enough. But when he lit the lamps, there was no sign she'd even been there.

He told himself he'd wait an hour and forced himself to sit, watching the clock on the side table as the seconds ticked by. By the time thirty-seven minutes had passed, he'd had enough. Grabbing his coat and hat, he headed out again to find her.

The streets had been long since cleared by the time he made it back to the Haymarket. Police barriers were up, and the front door of the dance hall had been boarded over. The smell of smoke still hung in the air. The sidewalks were mostly empty, but a boy was asleep in one of the doorways nearby, curled against the street. Harte tapped him gently to wake him. When the boy's eyes blinked open, angry at the disruption, Harte held up a dollar and watched the boy's eyes go wide.

"Did you see a woman in a gold-colored gown tonight?"

"I've seen lots of women," the boy said, straightening his soft cap and reaching for the money.

Harte pulled it away. "She was wearing a necklace with garnets and diamonds that looked like a collar. And black feathers in her hair."

"I might have seen her," the boy said, eyeing him.

"Where?"

"I think she was with everyone else they took off to the Tombs." The boy pulled the money from Harte's grip. "But they all looked the same, so maybe it wasn't her." He tucked the money into his shirt and turned back over.

The Tombs? A memory of a damp floor and a crowded room filled with rough hands rose to strangle him. It was his fault. He'd been so angry with her after her little stunt onstage that he'd purposely pushed her. He'd let her wander off. Then he'd left her behind.

He had to tell Dolph. They had to get Esta out before something happened to her. Because there were plenty of ways to die that didn't require being put six feet under. He should know.

The Strega was nearly empty by the time Harte got to the Bowery. Viola was wiping down the bar top when Harte walked in.

"We're closing," she said as he came through the door. When she recognized him, "Oh, it's you." She gave him a stern look. "Where's Esta?"

He looked around the barroom before waving her over. "I need to see Dolph," he said.

"He's not here."

"Where the hell is he?"

Viola shrugged. "He sometimes gets restless this time of night. He went out."

"Well, when will he be back? I need to talk to him."

"Who knows? He's been in a mood lately." She narrowed her eyes at him. "Where is our girl?"

Harte frowned. "That's what I need to talk with Dolph about."

In a flash, her knife was out and at his throat. He could feel the sharp bite of its tip pressing against his neck.

"What have you done with her?" Viola demanded.

"I haven't done anything with her," he said keeping his eyes steady on her, so she would know he wasn't lying. "But there was a raid on the Haymarket tonight. She might have been taken."

The tip of the knife pressed more firmly against his skin. "What do you mean, taken?"

"We were separated in the confusion, and she didn't come back to my apartment. She might have been taken to the Tombs. I need help to find out for sure, and to get her out if that's what happened."

"I *knew* I didn't like your too-pretty face." He felt the prick of the knife and then the heat of his own blood as a drop trickled down his neck.

Harte remained motionless, because he didn't want Viola to know exactly how nervous he was. Or for her knife to slice any deeper. "If you're going to kill me, get it over with already," he told her, all false bravado. "Otherwise, tell me where Dolph went so I can get her back."

She scowled at him a moment longer. "I really don't know," she said, pulling the knife back and wiping its bloody tip on her skirt. "The boy might. Dolph tells him things sometimes." She frowned as she glanced in Nibsy's direction. Then she eyed Harte. "You *will* get her back." It wasn't a question.

"That's the plan," he said, moving toward the place where Nibs sat, working out something in a notebook at one of the back tables.

"I need to find Dolph," he said, without any other greeting. "Now."

"He's out." The boy didn't bother to look up. "Should be back in a few hours."

"I don't have a few hours."

Nibs looked up then, but there wasn't any concern on his face. Only curiosity.

"It's Esta," Harte explained. "She got caught up in a raid. I think she's been taken to the Tombs."

The boy cocked his head to the side and peered through the thick lenses of his glasses. "Dolph did say you were meeting with Jack Grew tonight. Did you manage to hook him?"

Harte ran his fingers through his hair, frustration spiking in him. "Yeah, nearly."

"Nearly? Or for sure?"

"It doesn't matter," Harte snapped. "Jack can wait."

"Got under your skin, did she?" Nibs looked entirely too pleased with himself. "I thought she might."

"It's not that," he denied. But even as he said the words, he knew they were a lie.

"No?" Nibs asked, curious.

"No," Harte said, refusing to admit that Nibs was right. "We need her is all. We can't get the Book without her."

"Sure we can," Nibs told him with a shrug. "Pickpockets and thieves are a dime a dozen."

"Not like her they're not," he said, not realizing until the words were out that he actually *meant* them. "We have to get her out of there before something happens to her." Because he needed her, he told himself. Not for any other reason.

"Playing the white knight now, Darrigan? The role doesn't exactly suit you," he mocked. "Forget about the girl. Right now your job is to focus on Jack Grew. Esta will get out when she gets out. Or she won't. It doesn't really matter now."

"Of course it matters," Harte growled.

Nibs shook his head. "She already did what we needed her to do," he said. A taunting smile erased the innocent, guileless expression he usually wore as something shifted in his eyes. "She hooked you, didn't she?"

He had known all along that he'd been played, but somehow hearing it straight from Nibs, understanding that Esta was nothing more than a pawn for Dolph, had Harte's temper snapping. In an instant he had the boy out of his chair, pinned against the wall. He sensed Viola's watchfulness from across the room, but he didn't care.

Nibs didn't even blink.

"I'm not some stupid mark," Harte growled.

"That right there is your biggest weakness, Darrigan. You think you can't be played. But Esta proved you wrong, didn't she? I knew she would, almost from the second I saw her. She played you *beautifully*."

In that moment Harte didn't want anything but to make the boy pay for his words. All he saw was fire and blood and anger as he drove his fist into Nibsy's face. He heard the crack of bone and felt the sickening crunch. At the same time his magic flared, and he pushed every bit of his affinity at Nibs, digging deep below the boy's innocent-looking surface.

The shock of what he saw plowed into him like a prizefighter's fist. Harte had always known there had to be something more to the boy than his innocent-looking smile and soft-spoken temperament, but he'd never expected *this*. Dolph was too smart, too powerful—how had the boy tricked him? Tricked them all?

Shaken by what he'd seen, Harte released Nibsy's collar and let the boy fall to the floor. A moment later, though, he felt another jolt—the shocking impact of Viola's magic slamming against him. Gasping, he stumbled toward the wall, barely able to keep himself upright.

"We're fine," Nibs called, as he pulled himself to his feet. "Let him go, Vi. It was a simple misunderstanding."

Harte couldn't focus enough to see Viola's reaction, but a second later the hot power she'd shoved toward him dissipated, and he could breathe again. He kept one hand on the wall at first, because his legs were still shaking. Across the room, Viola was watching him with careful eyes.

"I would have let Viola kill you if I didn't still need you," Nibs said. "Don't ever forget that. When you stop being of use to me, you're a dead man."

Harte ignored the threat and lowered his voice so Viola couldn't hear. "You can't actually think what you're planning will work?"

Nibs dabbed at his nose with the back of his hand. "I think it already is."

"You'd betray your own kind? For what?" Harte said, his mind racing. "Dolph would *free* you. Hell, he has some do-gooder notion of freeing everyone."

"You don't actually believe that." Nibs shook his head, disgust shadowing his features. "Dolph is no saint—you know that. You've seen what he's capable of. You've seen what he'll do for power. He loved Leena more than he loved anyone, and he managed to use her, to break her."

"What the Order did to her wasn't his fault," Harte said, finally accepting that truth. Harte might have wanted to blame him still, but Dolph hadn't created the Brink. He hadn't been the one to push Leena over it.

"No, but the marks were." Nibs nodded. "How do you think the marks worked, Darrigan?"

"Ritual magic. You're not telling me anything I don't already know," Harte sneered, refusing to let Nibs goad him into attacking again. Not with Viola watching.

"So you know he used Leena's affinity to create them?" Nibsy's eyes were dancing. "Of course you didn't know that. No one knew that particular fact."

"Dolph never would have done that to Leena," Harte said, trying to sound more confident than he felt.

"Don't kid yourself. Leena had always been his protection. Her ability to block any Mageus within her sight from using their affinity against Dolph or his people kept him safe. But everything they worked together to build wasn't enough for him. So he did a ritual to bring the marks to life, but he used *her* affinity in it. It weakened her. It made her angry, too. She said she forgave him, but I'm not sure that was completely true." He tilted his head, thoughtful. "Maybe if he hadn't taken so much from her, she could have fought the Order. Maybe she wouldn't have died on the Brink."

"Everyone dies on the Brink," he said, not taking the bait.

Nibs inclined his head. "So I wonder why you would want to keep it up?"

"I've agreed to help Dolph, haven't I?" Harte said, unease creeping through him. *He couldn't know.* "We have a deal. You know that."

"I know what you've *told* Dolph. But I also know you're a talented liar, Darrigan." Nibs shook his head. "I know a lot of things. About you.

About Dolph. About how people work and the choices they'll make. You might say I have an affinity for it."

So that was his talent? The absolute sureness the kid seemed to have made his skin crawl. "You don't know shit."

"I know that Dolph is blinded by his need to put things to rights for Leena. To avenge her. But bringing down the Brink won't destroy the hate and suspicion that feeds the Order's power. It'll only be the opening shot of a war he's not ready to fight. Do you really think he'll simply give the power of the Book away when he realizes what we're truly up against? He couldn't even leave Leena what she already had."

Harte shifted uneasily. He didn't trust Nibs—not after what he'd seen in the boy's heart and mind—but what he was saying made a sick sort of sense. Still, he knew what Nibs intended. . . .

"So you'd take it upon yourself to undercut him? You'd take the Book's power for yourself? Use it to rule the Mageus who are left?"

"Saw that, did you?"

"I saw everything, Nibs."

"Then you know that you and I aren't so very different, Darrigan. We're both working against Dolph. Neither of us has any desire to destroy the Brink. Which is why we're going to keep working together. And in exchange, I'll give you what you want most—a way out of the city."

"Are you forgetting that you pledged Dolph your loyalty? When he finds out what you're planning, you're as good as dead."

"You mean because of the mark?" the boy asked, ripping back his sleeve to show the tattoo below the crook of his elbow. "I'll let you in on a little secret, Darrigan. When Dolph tried to save Leena, the Brink took his ability to control us. The marks are useless now."

It couldn't be true—and yet Dolph *had* agreed almost too easily to Harte's demand to refuse his mark. "Even if that's true, you're underestimating him."

"No, I think my estimates have been perfect. My estimations are *always* perfect." He gave a shrug that couldn't hide his smugness.

"Not so perfect. I bet you weren't estimating that you'd have a broken nose tonight."

Nibs frowned, but he didn't argue. "All that matters is that Dolph's done everything I've expected him to do so far. And so have you."

"Not anymore. I'm out," Harte said, backing away. "I don't want any part in what you're planning. You might need me, but I don't need you."

Nibs laughed. Blood dripped down his lips and chin as he talked, but he didn't seem to notice it. "You don't understand, do you? There *isn't* any way out for you, Darrigan. You're in this to the end."

"Like hell I am."

Nibs took a step toward him. "What do you think you're going to do? I know what you've been planning all along. You think you'll take the Book and run, don't you? Leave us all trapped in here while you find freedom. But let me ask you one question—do you have any idea where your mother is right now?"

Harte froze. "What does that matter?"

"You tell me."

"After what she did to me, she can rot for all I care," Harte said stiffly, but panic was already roiling in his stomach.

"Oh, that's good," Nibs said, clapping slowly. "Quite the performance. If you hadn't asked Dolph to hide her from Kelly, I might even have believed you just now. But she's your soft spot, Darrigan. Always has been. Dolph knew that. It's why he sent Kelly after you."

"Dolph wouldn't work with Kelly."

"To get you, he would. He *did*. It was my suggestion, and it's worked out *beautifully*. They made a little trade—Dolph's secrets for Kelly's lackey. And you reacted exactly as he expected you to." He licked his lips. "Dolph's still too tied up with Kelly to bother giving me any trouble, but you ran right into his snare. The fact is you *do* care what happens to that mother of yours, and as long as you won't cut her loose, the string she has you on is always going to be your noose."

"You have no idea what you're talking about," Harte spat. If he could just get close enough to Nibs to touch him again without Viola noticing . . .

But she was still watching, and he had a feeling that if he did anything else to Nibs, she'd be in the mood to kill first and ask questions later.

"You know, Dolph had me take care of getting her situated. She likes opium, doesn't she, your mother?" Nibs stepped closer to Harte and smiled, his teeth stained red from the blood. "You're not out. And you won't breathe a word of our little conversation here to anyone. Not unless you want me to make sure your mother's out too. I can make sure she gets all the poppy she wants. Not to kill her. Not right away, at least. But there are worse things than dying, aren't there?"

Harte reached for him again, but this time the boy dodged away. "No, I don't think so. I know you can do more than read minds, Darrigan. I don't think I want you to touch me again."

"The only reason I'd touch you is to kill you," he growled.

"You're welcome to try. No one's been able to yet. I'm always three steps ahead of them, and I always will be." Nibs gave him a threatening look. "Go get Morgan's nephew. I want that book, or I'll make sure that everything you hold dear is destroyed. Your name. Your mother. Even your girl."

"I don't care."

"Let's not waste our time with lies, Darrigan. Get out of here before I tell Viola you need to be taken out." He smiled, satisfied. "She'll believe me, you know. They all will, because I'm one of them. And you *never* will be."

Harte took a step back, a war rioting inside him. All of his careful plans were crumbling around him. But then he thought of Esta, stuck in that dank, vermin-infested prison. Esta, who could steal anything. He could never tell her all of what he planned, but with her help, it just might work.

"You've overplayed your hand, Nibs."

"No," the boy said with a lurid smile. "You only think I have."

THE THREAD UNRAVELS

Viola was still washing glasses behind the bar when Dolph returned, tired and frustrated. He walked over to the bar, and she poured him two fingers of whiskey without his asking.

"You look worse than when you left."

Dolph stared at the drink, but he didn't take it. "I wasn't out for my health. Kelly's up to something. His boys cut up three of ours tonight."

"I thought you'd worked out something with him," Viola said with a frown.

He ignored the implied question. "He has some bigger game going. Even Jianyu is having trouble figuring out what it is." He took the glass in his hand and rubbed his thumb over its smooth surface.

"I could try to find out for you?"

"No," he said, and when she scowled at him, he explained, "It's not that I don't trust you to handle yourself, but I don't need Kelly to know we're worried." She continued to frown down at where her blades were resting on the bar top. He'd upset her, but she didn't argue.

That silence almost bothered him more. She'd been too quiet ever since Tilly's death. He told himself it was natural, expected, but with everything else going on, he wasn't sure if maybe there was something more happening with her.

"Jianyu return yet?" he asked.

"No, but Darrigan came in not long ago. Said that Esta had been picked up at the Haymarket. He was looking for you, but he had words with Nibs and then went storming off."

"Is that right?" Dolph eyed the boy at the back of the barroom. "About what?"

"You'd need to talk to Nibs."

The boy was sitting at his usual table in the back of the bar, poring over the nightly ledgers. His glasses were perched over a swollen nose and his right eye had already turned a painful-looking purple-green.

"I didn't know you were taking up prizefighting," Dolph said, easing himself into his usual chair.

"Not on purpose," Nibs said, glancing up. "Darrigan did it."

"Oh?"

"I might have pushed him too far when I reminded him that the Book was more important than the girl."

"Viola mentioned something about Esta getting herself arrested in the raid tonight. Do we need to send someone?"

"Darrigan will get her out," Nibs said. "He seems to be even more tied up with her than we planned."

"That's good, isn't it?" Dolph asked. "It's exactly what I wanted. Maybe if he's attached to her, he won't do anything stupid."

"Unless she's tied up with him, too." Nibs made another mark in his book.

"That would be a problem?"

"It would be if they started getting ideas," Nibs said with a frown. "We wouldn't want them going off on their own and cutting us out."

The boy was always figuring, always planning. It was a skill that Dolph had prized, back when he'd had the means to control Nibs. Back when taking his mark meant taking an oath of loyalty. But now that the marks were dead and useless, and Nibsy knew, Dolph was starting to wonder how much faith he should put in the boy whose plans rarely went awry.

Looking at Nibsy's broken nose and battered face, though, Dolph dismissed that thought almost as quickly as it had come to him. He was getting too paranoid. After all, the boy had taken a hit from Darrigan for him—a direct one, from the looks of it. That had to mean something.

He'd talk to the girl and make sure things were progressing. It wouldn't hurt to remind her what she stood to lose.

"Any news yet about what caused the raid?" Dolph asked. "It's too much of a coincidence that after months of quiet, the police pick tonight of all nights."

"I haven't heard from Bridget yet, if that's what you're asking." Nibs glanced up at him. "It's strange, now that I think of it. Usually she sends word by now. You don't think she was the one to tip them off, do you?"

"I doubt it." Dolph frowned. "Bridget hates the Order and pretty much everyone else. She wouldn't have anything to gain by helping them."

"Then where did she disappear to?"

"I don't know," Dolph said, uneasy.

He understood what Nibs was suggesting, but Bridget Malone owed him too much to cross him. After all, Dolph had freed her from her violent drunk of a husband. He'd given Bridget a second chance and the freedom to build a new life, and she repaid him by sending him new talent before the other bosses found them. Most of their kind knew of the arrangement, and if a girl found herself in a bad situation, she knew to go to Bridget. He couldn't see what she would have to gain by starting the raid.

"Did you finish with your business?" Nibs asked, turning back to his ledgers. "I expected you back a while ago."

"There were problems with Kelly tonight. A gang of his attacked three of our boys. Beat them to a pulp—it'll be lucky if Higgins can walk after he heals."

Nibs peered up over the wire rims of his spectacles. "Did they cross into Kelly's turf?"

"Of course not," Dolph said. His people knew to be careful. "It happened on Elizabeth Street, not two blocks from here. Kelly's boys shouldn't have even been there."

"You sure it was Kelly's that did it?" Nibs asked.

Dolph nodded. "They carved the Five Pointer's mark into each of their cheeks. Even if they recover from the other wounds, that will leave a scar. They'll be marked now for life."

"I thought you said he was under control," Nibs said.

Dolph frowned. Things were changing, he thought to himself. *Too fast.* And for the first time since he'd started down this road, he wondered if he would be able to keep up. "I'll send Viola. She can take care of the ones who did it without any evidence."

Nibsy's brows went up. "Wouldn't it be better to let Kelly know? It might put him back in his place."

"No. Let him wonder. Let him worry about his weaknesses and who his enemies might be. The more uneasy he is, the more vulnerable he'll be," Dolph said, but even as he spoke, he couldn't help wondering how much he was talking about Paul Kelly and how much the words were a warning to himself.

THE TOMBS

Halls of Justice

The city's Halls of Justice, better known as the Tombs, were a layer cake of depravity. The top floors housed the petty criminals— pickpockets, green game runners, and other less violent offenders. The farther down you went into the building, the worse the prisoners became. By the time you reached the second floor, you were among robbers and murders, and the ground floor held the worst of all—runners for the local games, shyster lawyers, phony bondsmen, and of course the city's police, who were so deep in the pockets of Tammany that justice was only a word they tossed around like the latest dirty joke.

Harte had spent a night there not long after his mother left him. Locked in a cell with grown men, he'd been helpless to do more than survive the night huddled in the corner, fending off unwanted advances the only way he knew how—with magic. For that to work, though, he'd let them touch him, skin to skin.

He'd made it through that night, but he hadn't left unaffected. After that night, he'd understood *exactly* what people were capable of.

Even now, safe as he was, staring up at the ornately carved columns and window lintels designed to look like some ancient Egyptian burial chamber, he felt as soiled as the building's once-white facade. He could only imagine what was happening to Esta.

My fault. He'd pushed her to go into the dance hall, even when she'd clearly been worried. He'd goaded her over dinner—an act for Jack, but one he'd enjoyed a little too much because of what she'd done during the performance. And then he'd left her behind. Now, because of him, she was in the prison that still haunted his dreams. And he had no idea how to get her out.

But he needed her out. If he was going to stop Jack from finishing his machine, avoid the future Nibs had planned, *and* get around Dolph, he was going to need her help.

The night he'd spent behind the walls of the Tombs, he'd sworn to himself that he would never be put in a position where he was that helpless ever again, and for the most part he'd held himself to that. Until now. Somehow, in the span of one night, everything had gone ass over elbow.

He let out a string of curses under his breath that would have embarrassed a prison guard.

"I knew you had a rougher side underneath all that polish," an amused voice said from behind him.

Harte turned to find Esta dressed with a ragged coat covering her evening gown. Her hair had mostly fallen and the black feathers that had adorned it the night before were broken or tilted at haphazard angles. The shock of seeing her there, safe and whole, sent such a wave of relief crashing through him that, before he thought better of it, he had his arms around her, crushing her to him, barely conscious of how she was pushing away.

It was only the smell of the coat that brought him back to his senses. It reeked of sweat and onions and stale tobacco. As he let her go and took a step back so he could breathe, he felt suddenly aware of how impulsively he'd reacted to seeing her. How dangerous it would be to let himself forget everything that was at stake.

"What are you doing here?" she asked.

"I'm rescuing you," he said, knowing exactly how absurd the words were even as he spoke them. She was standing there, right in front of him. And now she was smiling. She clearly didn't need to be rescued. "How did you get out?"

"I told you that day you tried to lock me up with those stupid handcuffs of yours—there isn't a lock I can't crack."

He frowned, trying desperately to regain his footing. "That was a risk, using your affinity in there. Someone might have noticed," he said, cringing inwardly at how stupid he sounded.

"I didn't. Use my affinity, I mean. I'm good enough without it. Once I got out of the cell, I traded the necklace for this coat and then lifted this." She held up a visitor's pass. "They're not exactly the brightest bunch, you know?"

"Desperate people rarely are."

She wrinkled her nose slightly as she pulled the filthy coat tighter around her, completely hiding her dress. "Did you make any progress with Jack?"

That's all she has to say? "You aren't going to ask why I left you?"

She blinked at him, her brows bunching. "I didn't know you did."

"Yeah." Harte squared his shoulders, daring her to complain about his choice. "I went with Jack when the police raided the ballroom. He was interested, and I didn't want to lose him. I left you," he challenged.

Her brow furrowed, but only slightly. "That's good, if you got something from him."

It wasn't the response he expected. "It is?" She should have been angrier. She should have been furious with him for leaving her. He would have been.

But she never reacted in any predictable way. It was maddening.

She rolled her eyes. "I'm not some wilting violet, Harte. You should know that much about me by now. If the situation was reversed, I probably would have done the same."

"You would have, wouldn't you?" he said, reminding himself of all the reasons he shouldn't trust her.

"What?" she asked warily.

"Where did you go last night?" he asked. "When you left me with Jack."

"I told you, I had to powder my nose."

She played you beautifully. That was what Nibs had said. How much was she still playing him?

"You were gone long enough to powder your entire body," he said, crossing his arms over his chest. "Try again. And this time, try without the lies."

"You don't trust me? I thought we were past this."

He huffed out a sound of disbelief. "You don't trust me, either, or you'd tell me what took you so long to get back to us. Were you meeting someone?"

"I don't know what you're talking about," she said, and she turned to walk away, but he snagged her wrist and pulled her back.

"There's too much at stake for any more lies between us. I came here to rescue you today," he said softly, trying a different approach.

Her expression was closed off, distant. "I didn't need you to rescue me."

Frustration had him wanting to lash out at her, but he held it in. Kept himself calm. This was too important to make any misstep because of his ego. "That isn't the point. *I came.*"

"But why? You've been trying to get rid of me since Dolph sent me. This would have been a perfect opportunity."

"Because I can't do this without you. I need you to hook Jack, but I need to know whose side you're on."

"I'm with Dolph," she told him, her brows furrowing. "Just like you're supposed to be."

"Are you? Or are you with Nibsy?"

Her brow wrinkled. "He works for Dolph," she said. "Isn't that the same thing?"

"Sure." He rubbed his hand over his mouth, scratching at the growth of whiskers that were already beginning to itch. "You're right."

"Are you okay?"

"If we're going to pull this off, we need to be able to trust each other."

"You really came back for me?" she asked, tilting her head to one side, so that a single lock of her hair fell over her forehead and into her eyes.

"Yeah. I did," he said, keeping his hands tucked into his pockets so that he wouldn't reach for her, wouldn't brush that lock of hair aside just so he could feel it slip between his fingers.

He was still uneasy. But if he was going to get the Book and keep it away from Jack and Nibsy, he needed her. Especially now that he couldn't depend on anyone else. He just had to keep his heart locked up and his head on straight.

ANGLES AND EDGES

Harte's Apartment

Esta sat on the edge of Harte's porcelain tub, looking at the news clipping. She'd changed something, or she'd started to. The story of Dolph's arrest and death was still there, but it kept blurring, as though the words couldn't decide which future to pick. She thought she could *almost* make out another story floating just beneath the surface of the page, like another time waiting for her to slip through to it. But then she'd blink, and it would be gone.

In truth, she was only delaying the inevitable moment when she'd have to face Harte again. He'd come back for her, and she had no idea what to do with that.

Maybe she'd been going about things all wrong. Professor Lachlan said she had to stop the Magician, and she'd assumed that meant working against him. But her actual goal was to get the Book, and maybe to do that, it would be easier to work *with* him. Maybe they didn't have to be enemies.

Except in the end, she would still betray him, just as she would betray the rest.

There was nothing for it, though. No way around it. To finish her job, she needed the Book. If she took the Book, the rest of them would lose. It didn't—*couldn't*—matter that she'd come to think of them as friends. She already had friends—Dakari and Mari, even Logan. But Mari was gone because of a mistake she had made. And if she didn't do what she'd been sent here for, she could be sacrificing Dakari and Logan's futures as well as her own. There wasn't a way to save them all.

But she wasn't there to save them all, she reminded herself, even as she felt her throat go tight. She had a future to get back to, and as much as she had grown fond of this time, grown to respect and admire the people in it, she refused to regret what she had to do.

She pulled the plug and watched the grime of the night before swirl down the drain, right along with most of the confidence she'd managed to summon. *Suck it up,* she told herself as she pulled Harte's robe around her. What was done was done. A minute past too late wasn't the time to start having regrets.

When she stepped out of the steamy bathroom, Harte was on the sofa, waiting with a sullen expression. On the table next to him, a neat pile of orange peelings sat atop a handkerchief. She could practically hear him think, the way he was sitting there—his hand scratching at the day-old scruff on the edge of his jawline as his eyes stared off into space.

He was so deep in thought that he didn't seem to notice her until she settled herself next to him.

"Feel better?" he asked, looking up.

"Yes. Much." She tucked her legs up under her.

"Wouldn't you rather get dressed?" He looked troubled when his gaze drifted over the robe she was wearing. Almost nervous.

Fine with her. She'd take any advantage she could get.

"No, I'm good," she said, leaning back comfortably. "It feels *amazing* to be out of that corset."

He gave her another uneasy look but didn't say anything more. It felt to Esta like he was on the edge of making some decision but wasn't sure whether to jump.

So maybe she'd give him a little push.

"Thanks for coming back for me," she said softly, touching his hand.

Harte looked momentarily surprised, but then he pulled away from her and composed himself. "Don't think it means more than it does." He picked up the newspaper and made a pretense of looking over the front page. But his motions were stiff and it was clear his eyes weren't focusing on any headline. "I need you to get Jack. Otherwise, I would have happily let you rot in there."

"Then I guess it's a good thing I didn't need your help after all," she drawled, frustrated with his moodiness. This approach clearly wasn't working, so she got up from the couch. She'd regroup and figure out another way.

He caught her by the hand, gently this time. She could have pulled away, but instead she turned to look at him. There was an unreadable expression on his face that made her pause.

"Don't start telling yourself stories about me, Esta. I'm not some knight in shining armor."

"I never said you were."

"I don't have some hidden heart of gold. I'm a bastard, in every sense of the word."

He seemed to be trying to convince himself as much as her. "I never thought otherwise."

"I know how women are," he muttered.

She looked at him and saw him anew—the sadness in his eyes. The way he held himself as though he were bracing for a slap. "You don't know half of what you think you do," she said softly.

"I know more than you can imagine. I saw where believing too much in a man got my mother." His mouth went tight.

"I'm sorry—"

"Don't be. I should've died in a gutter somewhere before my twelfth birthday. I would have deserved it after what I did."

She couldn't stop herself from taking a step toward him. "What could you have possibly done to deserve that at only eleven years old?"

"I sent my father away," he said. He lifted his chin, like he was waiting for her judgment.

She shook her head, not understanding. "You were a child. How could you send a grown man anywhere he didn't want to go?"

He looked at her, his stormy eyes dark with some unspoken emotion.

"I can do more than get into your head to see what's there. Do you remember that day onstage? When Nibsy brought you to the theater the first time? I put a suggestion into your mind. I told you what I needed for you to do to make the effect work. I gave you a command, and you obeyed."

She frowned. "That's not how I remember things ending up."

His mouth turned down. "Yeah, well . . . you weren't in the cabinet at the end, like you were supposed to be, but you did everything else. And you forgot everything the second the door of the cabinet opened, just like I told you to."

It felt right to her, answered one question that had been looming. But it raised so many more. "You really ordered your father away?"

He nodded. "The only thing he spent more time doing than beating me and my mother was drinking. I wanted a break. I just wanted her to be happy again, so I told him to leave. He did."

"You tried to save her."

"He never came back. He left the city, or he tried to. But he didn't get much farther than the Brink." His eyes were flat, emotionless.

"You were only a child. You couldn't have known," she said, thinking about her own inability to control her affinity at that age. She'd always been too impulsive, but then it had been worse. Like the time she was with Dakari and saw a tourist with an open backpack in Central Park. He'd warned her against it, but she thought she could lift the wallet inside before anyone noticed. But she hadn't quite known how to hold the seconds for very long, and they caught her with her hand in the bag. It was only Dakari's quick thinking that got her away, but he was a black man in a city where stop and frisk was the rule of law. He ended up flat on the pavement, his arms wrenched behind him while she couldn't do more than stand by and watch, tears clogging her vision.

He ended up spending the night in a holding cell. She'd never forgotten that day. Dakari had lived to forgive her, but from the sound of things, Harte's father hadn't been so lucky.

"My mother didn't care. When she found out what I had done, what

I *could* do, she was horrified. She went after him. She *hated* me for what I'd done. She risked the Brink to find him."

"Oh, Harte . . ."

"She didn't get very far, but even getting that close changed her," he said, his voice flat and almost emotionless, like he was telling her someone else's story instead of his own.

"I *am* sorry."

"Don't be," he told her. "It made me stronger. It made me who I am."

They weren't so different, the two of them. They'd both been abandoned by their parents, but at least she'd had the Professor. He'd seen something in her worth saving, but Harte never had that. She still might not trust him, but she understood him. The drive that made him who he was, the determination to prove himself—the bone-deep need to belong somewhere—those were all things she knew very well.

She understood the hurt, too. The fear that there was something intrinsically wrong with you to make the people who were supposed to love you leave. The way that fear either hardened you or destroyed you. It had turned into a sort of armor for her, another weapon in her arsenal, and she suspected the same was true of Harte.

"Don't look at me like that." He narrowed his eyes.

"Like what?"

"Like you know something about me. It'll be easier for both of us if you can get it through your head right now that I don't need some girl to come along and fix me. Life's carved away any softness I might have had, and all that's left now are hard edges. That's all I'll ever be. That's all I ever *want* to be."

She studied him—the stiff shoulders, the tight jaw, and the stormy eyes that dared her to judge him, and she had the sudden urge to ruffle his feathers again. She wanted to see the boy she'd met in the basement of the theater, the rumpled boy whose eyes glowed with possibility instead of desperation. She wanted to throw him off so he'd lose that distant look, just for a moment. She wanted to see if she could.

"I'm not here to save you." She sat next to him again and felt a surge of satisfaction when his brows furrowed.

"No, you're not, are you?" he asked, looking at her with the strangest expression.

"Nope," she said truthfully, reaching up to run her fingers through his hair. "I wouldn't bother trying."

"You wouldn't?" He looked wary now, but he didn't retreat. He seemed frozen, almost mesmerized.

"Who said I want you to be anything but what you are? I like your angles and your edges," she told him, hoping he could hear the truth in her words. "I have plenty of my own, you know."

"I know," he said, his voice soft with a hint of hope and desperation.

She smiled at the nervousness in his eyes. "I'd slice right through anyone softer."

He stared at her for what felt like a lifetime, as though he was afraid to move. As though he was afraid not to. "You would, wouldn't you?"

She nodded. He smelled of oranges, and she could imagine what it would be like to close the distance between them and have a taste of his lips. Kissing Harte on purpose would be like everything else between them—a battle of wills. A clash of temper. An unspoken understanding that neither would back away or back down.

And then what?

The thought was like cold water. In the end, she'd have to take the Book from him, from Dolph as well, and leave them all here in this past to face their fates alone.

"This is a terrible idea," she murmured.

"I know," he said, leaning closer.

Nothing is more important than the job. Professor Lachlan's words echoed in her mind, reminding her of the last time she'd lost sight of what was important. Reminding her that she had another life, another set of responsibilities, waiting for her. Maybe she didn't need to fight Harte, but she couldn't let herself start believing there was any future possible for them. At least no future that didn't end in betrayal.

She pulled back, ignoring the way her throat had gone tight with something that felt too close to longing. But what she longed for—for him, for a rest from constantly being on guard, for a place to call her own—she wasn't sure. "We have too much at stake to muck everything up with this." She motioned between them.

The urgency had drained from his eyes, and she could no longer read the expression on his face as he pulled farther back from her. The space between them, which was no more than the length of her arms, suddenly felt impossible. "You're right."

"I'm sorry, Harte. I—"

"No," he said. "Don't. There's no need. We were caught up in a moment, that's all. I'm the one who should be apologizing. But we can't get caught up like that again." He got up from the couch and headed into the kitchen.

Still unnerved, she followed him. "So you said that last night went well with Jack?" she asked, her voice a bit higher than usual. Desperate to get things back on track.

"It did," he told her, pouring himself a glass of water. He seemed to want to keep the table between them. That was fine with her.

"And?"

He took a long drink of the water before he spoke. "The good news is that you were brilliant last night. Jack absolutely believes you're the lost heir. It'll be up to you to reel him in, but it shouldn't be hard. He's itching to prove himself, so he's primed to make mistakes.

"Jack will be at the show again tonight," Harte continued. "It's all arranged. All you have to do is pretend you're interested in him when he comes backstage after. Stroke his ego a little and let him dig his own grave. Just lead him on enough to get us an invitation to Khafre Hall. We'll need a reason for him to want us there, though."

She remembered the men behind the wall at the Haymarket. "I think I have an idea of how to do that."

"You do?"

She nodded. "I heard something at the Haymarket that might help us." He gave her a quizzical look, but she ignored the question in his eyes. "The Order has a big party coming up for the equinox. It would be a shame if their entertainment canceled on them, don't you think?"

His expression shifted. "That should be easy enough. I'll talk to Dolph—it'll keep him happy to be in on the action." Something like relief flashed in his usually stormy eyes, softening them. Suddenly he looked like the boy in the basement of the theater, the boy she'd wanted to know better.

The boy she'd eventually betray.

Her heart twisted, but she ignored it. The deception was necessary. It was like Professor Lachlan had taught her: Emotions were a trap. Nothing was more important than the job.

THE BALANCE OF POWER

Nearly a week later, Dolph Saunders watched from the window of Harte Darrigan's apartment as Jack Grew helped Esta out of an unremarkable carriage. The girl smiled up at Jack and allowed herself to be walked to the door, but once the pair was close to the building, Dolph could no longer see them.

"Are they back yet?" Nibs asked from the doorway to the kitchen.

"Esta is. She'll be up soon."

The rooms were large and airy, clean and comfortably furnished. The boy had done well, and he'd done it on his own. Dolph himself had never had the chance to create a life like this, but for a moment he imagined what it might have been like if he'd chosen another path. If Leena had married him, they could have built a life on lies, moving uptown and pretending to be a normal couple, a normal family.

But they had started down this path together, and now he wouldn't turn from it.

A few minutes later the girl let herself in. She startled—but only a little—when she saw him and Nibs waiting.

She took her time about removing her hat and cloak, placing them neatly on the rack by the door. "What are you two doing here?" she asked, turning back to him.

"Waiting for one of you to return," he said flatly. "We came to check on you."

"I didn't know you were into personal service," she said dryly. There was something brittle in her voice, and her expression was hard as flint. He had the unwelcome sense that something had changed for her, and

393

he wasn't sure why that bothered him. But he hadn't survived so long by ignoring his instincts.

"I'm not usually, but when I feel that people are hiding something from me, I'm willing to make exceptions."

"I'm not hiding anything. I've told him everything since you sent me over here," she said, nodding toward Nibs. "You could call him off, you know. I don't need him checking every day. Every other day might be a nice change."

Nibs gave her a wry grin. "And here I thought you were starting to like me."

"Enough," Dolph said before Esta could respond. He'd already seen the table in the kitchen piled with papers and maps, drawings and diagrams. They were farther than he'd suspected. "You're sure you've told him *everything*?" he asked, eyeing her.

"Yes, of course." She met his eyes, her expression calm and determined.

He waited for the lie, but he didn't sense it. Perhaps she was simply better at concealing her thoughts. She had the same straight-backed sense of her own abilities that she'd had the first night, and the air around her still tasted of desire and ambition. Dolph liked that about her, but it still worried him.

"Well?" he asked, dispensing with the pleasantries. "Show me."

"Everything's in the kitchen."

They followed her into the small room. Nibs took an orange from the bowl on the table as Esta leaned over a diagram of Khafre Hall and made a note on the western side of the building. Then she walked them both through everything—the four dinners she'd had with Jack, the way he seemed intent on boasting about his knowledge of the Order. It was clear he was trying to use his status to impress her and to take advantage of her, just as they'd expected.

"He's been bragging to Harte about how easily swayed I am by his pretty face and deep pockets," she told Dolph. "As if I don't know all his money comes from his family. I'd almost feel bad about the position he's going to be in when we're through with him if he weren't so insufferable."

"You've done well," Dolph said, glancing at Nibs. He'd left much of the details about their progress out of his reports. Someone was lying, but to his frustration, Dolph couldn't have said who it was. He'd trusted Nibs for so long, but the girl seemed sincere as well.

"The Mysterium has to be below this room," she said, pointing to a spot on the map.

"I thought the boiler room was there," Nibs said, turning the paper to get a better view.

"It is. But Jack mentioned something tonight that I think we can use." Her excitement was palpable. "The building goes deeper here than we thought." She pointed to a spot on the plans beneath Khafre Hall's central meeting room.

"You know that for sure?" Dolph asked.

"Pretty sure. Apparently, they picked this particular location for their headquarters on purpose. Something to do with the congruence of the elements." She glanced up at him with a puzzled look. "I don't really understand half of what Jack said, but the main point is that the whole place is built over one of the city's lost rivers. Something about making sure the elemental powers were balanced."

"You're sure about this?" Dolph felt some of his earlier concern about the girl receding.

"I'm positive. Jack was so anxious to make sure that I knew *he* understood all about the importance of aligning the elements, he practically drew me a map." She smiled up at him, and for a moment he had a thought of Leena.

Ridiculous. Esta looked nothing like her. But there was something in the way she carried herself, something about her confidence that tugged at memories best left buried. Maybe Viola had been right—he was too soft on her. He could only hope he wouldn't live to regret that.

"Does that change anything?" he asked Nibs.

The boy considered it. "If there's a river under there, we would have a second way in—or out. We'd have to account for that."

"Have you told Darrigan about this?" he asked Esta.

"Yes," a voice said from behind them. "*Have* you told Darrigan about this?"

AN INVITATION

"Harte—" Esta looked momentarily surprised—maybe even a little guilty—when she turned to find him watching from the doorway. It was the guilt in her expression that made him wary.

"This is cozy," he said, stepping into his kitchen. He hadn't planned on her being back from her date with Jack yet. She'd been staying out later and later every night, but he'd come home to spend some time in his apartment alone for once. He hadn't been prepared to find her bent over their notes with Dolph. And Nibs. Seeing the boy there, in his own apartment, made his vision go red and his every instinct go on high alert. But he kept himself under control. "Having a little meeting without me, are you?"

Her brows drew together. "We wouldn't be having it without you if you'd been here when I got back."

Maybe she was telling the truth. Maybe he could trust her—after all, Dolph was there too. But the way she'd managed to edge him out little by little had already been bothering him. And now to find her with Nibs . . . "You haven't been home this early in over a week. What am I supposed to do, sit around waiting? I had things to attend to at the theater," he said, his jaw tight.

She gave a derisive huff. "I'm sure you did."

"What's that supposed to mean?" he asked, stepping toward her.

"Nothing." She glared at him. "But you're not the one fending off Jack's constant pawing. I swear he's part octopus."

"You wouldn't have to fend him off if you'd let me come along." But for the last two nights, she'd insisted that Jack wanted to see her alone.

Esta thought they could get further if Jack believed he was getting the best of Harte by stealing his girl. Harte had agreed, reluctantly, but he couldn't help worrying that Esta had the advantage while he wasn't there. Whatever truce they might have come to, he had to remember that he couldn't fully trust her. No matter how much he might want to.

He smirked. "How far did he manage to get with you tonight?"

"You ass—" Her cheeks flushed.

"If you two are finished?" Dolph asked, impatience simmering behind his words.

"I'm not even close to finished," Harte told him, his eyes still steady on Esta. "What are you doing here anyway?"

"I came to check up on you," Dolph said, and there was a note of something in his voice that Harte had never heard before. That usual thread of confidence seemed to be worn away, near to breaking.

He looked at Dolph. "You don't need to check up on me," he said as he removed his coat and slung it on the back of a chair. "I'm keeping my word, like I said I would." He purposely ignored Nibs. There was no way he'd be able to keep up the ruse if he acknowledged the boy.

Dolph's icy gaze met his. "Are you?"

"Yes." Harte yanked his cravat loose and pulled at the collar of his starched shirt.

"Jianyu tells me that Paul Kelly was seen having drinks with Jack Grew. You wouldn't have had anything to do with that, would you?"

Nibs shifted, as though listening more intently to his answer.

Panic laced its fingers around Harte's throat, but he fought through it. "I'm not going back on my word," he said, answering the implied question rather than the stated one. But when Dolph didn't respond, only continued to pin him with that all-knowing stare of his, Harte added, "Kelly managed to get to Jack without my help."

"When was this?"

"The night of the Haymarket fiasco. I came to the Strega to tell you, but you were out."

"Yes," Dolph said. "I saw that you'd *talked* to Nibs."

"I didn't do anything he didn't have coming to him."

"There's no hard feelings, Darrigan. I shouldn't have goaded you when you were all worked up over Esta being arrested." Nibs gave Esta a small, almost-embarrassed smile that had Harte wanting to punch him again.

"You were worked up over me?" Esta asked, puzzled.

"Gave me quite the shiner," Nibs told her, the challenge clear in his tone.

"You punched him?"

"No one mentioned a meeting with Kelly," Dolph said with a low growl.

Harte ignored the other two and focused on Dolph. "The meeting with Kelly must have slipped my mind," he drawled. "Had to get your girl here out of jail since this one wasn't any help."

It was a gamble to throw that fact out there. . . . He probably shouldn't be poking at Nibs. If only he'd had more luck finding his mother. Once she was safe, it would be easy enough to tell Dolph everything he'd seen that night when his fist met Nibsy's face. But until he knew Nibs couldn't hurt her, he was basically muzzled.

"And after?" Dolph asked, his expression grim. "You had plenty of time to tell me."

"I've been a little busy since then," he said, gesturing to the evidence on the table between them. "Besides, didn't you tell me you'd taken care of Paul Kelly? I didn't think he was a problem anymore."

Dolph's jaw tensed, but he didn't respond. *Not a good sign.*

Harte took the momentary reprieve to change the course of the conversation. "What haven't you told me?" he asked Esta.

"Except for what I learned tonight, I've told you everything," she snapped.

"And when were you planning to tell me that?"

"As soon as I saw you, of course. But you got your knickers all in a twist over Dolph and Nibs being here and—"

"What was I supposed to think?" Seeing her with Dolph, not being included in whatever their conversation was—it had emphasized even more starkly how precarious his position was. He was playing them against each other, and if he wasn't careful, he'd end up trapped in the middle.

Esta glared at him. "You were supposed to shut up for a minute and put away that fragile male ego of yours so I could tell you what happened tonight."

"Fine." She was right, not that he'd admit it to her, especially not in front of Dolph, who seemed far too amused with the whole exchange. "So talk."

"As I was about to tell them—and would have told *you*, if you'd given me a second—remember how the Order is having something of a soiree to celebrate the spring equinox? It's in a week, and it seems their usual entertainment has become suddenly unavailable."

"A pity," Dolph said dramatically.

She glanced at Dolph. "Isn't it? But they've found themselves in need of someone at rather short notice. I suggested you, of course," she told Harte, pausing for dramatic effect and enjoying the anticipation in the boy's eyes.

"And?"

She pulled an embossed card from the handbag dangling from her wrist. "We've been invited to perform at Khafre Hall."

IV

THE HISTORY OF NOW

Esta could feel Harte's eyes on her in the darkness of the carriage.

Outside the window, the rain-drenched city passed by at a slow, steady pace. *I'll miss this,* she thought with a sudden pang of longing. This city was so different from hers, but it had become home just the same. She loved how it seemed to know it was on the cusp of greatness, as though it were simply waiting for the years to pass and reveal what it would become. Now that she had spent so many weeks walking those cobbled streets, she would always see *this* city there, beneath her own. At night, especially, she would never again need the help of Ishtar's Key to sense this time, this place, sitting just below the present. Just beyond her grasp.

Because there would be no returning. Once she had her stone, she *could* come back, but she knew already that once she left, she never would. There would be no reason to. She could look back on newspapers and reports like the clipping tucked securely in her bodice, but so many of the people she'd come to respect were invisible and unimportant to the men behind desks who wrote history.

She could not let that distract her, though. Against her skin, the waxen envelope with the news clipping reminded her that she had other responsibilities and another place to be. Whatever fondness Esta might have felt for this time, for this city, the news clipping reminded her that she had a duty to the future. She had to make sure that the past remained just as it should have been, or else who knew what her future might hold?

And the only way to do that was to make sure Harte didn't take the Book. To betray him—to betray all of them.

"Are you ready?" he asked, his voice soft.

"Of course," she told him, but she wasn't sure how much of a lie it was.

Not that it mattered anymore. Before the night was over, the Book and the stone would be hers, and she would be gone.

"It'll be fine," he said, his eyes steady. "Just like we practiced." He reached over and ran his fingers over her shoulders, rubbing lightly at the stiff muscles in her neck.

For a moment she felt only a strange, sudden wash of relief, as though all the tension between them, all the distrust and anger drained away with the tension in her muscles. And for a moment she allowed herself to feel real regret for what she was about to do. But no sooner did she let herself relax against the warmth of his fingertips than she also felt the heat of his magic.

She jerked away, her heart pounding in her chest. *I am such an idiot.* "Stay out of my head, Harte."

He stared at her, his expression unreadable until she turned away, wondering what he'd managed to see that had put that look on his face. Wondering what it meant for her careful plans.

They rode the rest of the way in a dangerous silence. She kept her eyes focused out the window, resolutely ignoring him and using the time to gather her thoughts. She could practically feel him watching her, but she refused to turn and give him anything else. There was too much riding on this night. Too much he could have discovered with that single touch.

The carriage came to a clattering stop. "We're here," he said, as though she couldn't see that for herself.

Harte got out of the carriage first and opened a large black umbrella before handing her down as well. Esta glanced up at the driver, Nibsy, who looked wet and miserable sitting in the drizzling rain. She gave him a nod that she hoped seemed confident. She wished she could apologize. After all, in the next two hours she'd betray him as well.

"It's time," Harte said.

She straightened her back and strengthened her resolve. Everything that had happened to her, everything she was, came down to this night. She knew that both Dolph and Harte wanted the Book. Both would try to take it for themselves.

And both would have to lose.

IN THE VIPER PIT

Khafre Hall

"I t's time," Harte said, sensing that Jack was already watching them from the covered portico, but Esta only stared at him with an unreadable expression. He would have been more comfortable to see rage in her eyes, but she was looking at him now with an emotion he couldn't place, and that worried him more than fury would have.

Maybe it had been a mistake to use his affinity on her one more time, but he had to know what he was in for. She'd been so reserved ever since Dolph had shown up unannounced at his apartment, doing everything by the book but never once letting him see what she was thinking. He'd hated it, the tiptoeing around each other. There had always been tension between them, a sense that they were both on different sides of the same game, but he felt like the game had been slipping away from him. And now he knew the truth.

He wished . . . He didn't know what he wished. That he hadn't seen the intentions behind those honey-colored eyes of hers? That he hadn't predicted her duplicity so easily? Or maybe, stupid as he was, he wished that he could stop himself from the inevitability of hurting her? But wishes were for children, and he'd grown up a long time ago. Only one of them could win this game, and it *had* to be him.

"You're going to have to talk to me eventually," he said. "Jack's going to notice if you don't. He'll suspect that something is wrong."

"Don't worry about me." Her expression was devoid of emotion. "I'll do my job. You just make sure to do yours."

Harte glanced back at Nibsy. The boy looked like a drowned rat sitting up in the driver's seat, but his eyes were steady and he wore an expression that warned not to cross him. Harte gave him a nod and pulled Esta's arm through his. She was stiff, clearly not wanting him to touch her. She looked afraid, not like someone who was planning to double-cross him before the night was through.

Looks could be deceiving, he thought to himself, ignoring the pang of regret he felt. *Let the games begin.*

Jack was waiting, nervous and jittery, with a glass of what was probably his usual whiskey already in his hand. He downed it and came to greet them. "Hell of a night, isn't it?" he said, sweat beading at his temples.

Harte extended his hand. "It was good of you to have us, Jack."

Next to him, Harte felt Esta transform. "Jack, *darling . . .*" She pulled herself away from him and held out both of her hands to greet Jack in her rolling accent. "I am *so* looking forward to meeting your friends."

Jack gave her a leering smile that made Harte clench his hands into fists. *She isn't for me,* he reminded himself.

"They're looking forward to meeting you as well," Jack told her, his voice carrying a note of something like lechery. Esta only smiled up at him.

Harte cleared his throat. "Did the equipment for our demonstration arrive?"

Jack didn't take his eyes from Esta. "This afternoon. It's all set up and ready for you."

"Good, good," Harte said, clapping Jack on the shoulder and giving him a bit of a shake. "Should we go in?"

Jack looked suddenly less sure, but he nodded and then led them through a short antechamber lit by torchlike sconces mounted to the wall. There, he gave their names to a man sitting in a caged room that reminded Harte of the ticket booth at the theater. After the man checked over his list and was satisfied, the click of a latch echoed and the wall directly in front of them began to part, allowing the golden glow of the room beyond to spill into the small space.

On the other side of the wall, the building was transformed. Gone were the wood-paneled walls and marble floors of the typical gentleman's club. Instead, walking through the opening in the wall was like stepping into an ancient Egyptian tomb. Gold glinted on the walls, highlighting borders of bright indigo and aquamarine symbols carved into sandstone pillars. Even with the size of the building, Harte hadn't expected anything like this. It was a room meant to inspire, to overwhelm, and Harte hated to admit that it had worked.

"Impressive, isn't it?" Jack said to Esta, who nodded and looked fairly awed herself.

She smiled at Jack, a secret smile that had Harte's stomach going sour. "It's as beautiful as you told me," she murmured.

"This way. We have your demonstration set up in the amphitheater."

They followed Jack to another receiving room. With jewel-toned silks capping the high ceiling, the room was reminiscent of Arabia. Palm trees claimed the walls, and a woman in a sparkling veiled dress performed a dance, gyrating her hips and torso as she snaked her way through the room. As they passed, her violet eyes met Harte's.

Good, he thought. At least that much was in place and going to plan.

The next hour was an interminable parade of the richest men in the city. They each took their turns looking him over as they greeted Esta. As they made their way through the room, Harte was well aware that everyone was watching, expecting him to make a mistake and betray his lack of breeding. He wouldn't give them the satisfaction. Tonight was his, and his alone.

"Well, well," a familiar voice said from just behind him. "Harte Darrigan. You have quite the busy social schedule these days, don't you?"

He stopped midstep, closing his eyes long enough to gather his wits—and his patience—as he forced his mouth into a smile. "Sam Watson," he began, turning to greet the reporter with his usual smile, but he stopped short when he saw who was on Sam's arm. "Evelyn?"

She was draped in black silk and had a satisfied gleam in her eye.

"Harte," she said, her voice smug. "What a lovely surprise." The way her mouth curled up told him to be on his guard. She wasn't any more surprised than she was a natural redhead.

"What are *you* doing here?" Harte asked. The room felt like it was spinning. Evelyn and Esta. Evelyn *here* with Sam Watson. At Khafre Hall. On the night when nothing could go wrong.

Looking him up and down, she smiled. "I could ask the same of you."

"I invited her," Sam said, wrapping an arm around her bare shoulder. "I'm covering the celebration tonight for the *Sun*."

"Are you?" Harte said. "First the Gala at the Met and now this? Why, Watson . . . you've turned into a society columnist."

Fury flashed through the reporter's eyes, but he managed to keep himself controlled. "I don't know, Darrigan. I have a feeling that, like the museum debacle, I'll get a better story than my editors were expecting tonight. Don't you?"

"I'm sure I wouldn't know," Harte said flatly, refusing to react to the clear challenge. "I'm just the floor show. Speaking of which, we should probably go prepare. If you'd excuse us?"

"Of course," Sam said pleasantly enough. "I'm looking forward to seeing what you can pull off tonight." He gave Harte a smile that was all teeth. "Until later?"

Harte gave him a noncommittal nod and then escorted Esta away, toward the doors of the amphitheater.

"What is she doing here?" Esta whispered, once they were far enough away.

"I don't know." But whatever Evelyn was doing, it was nothing good.

"We need to get out of here."

"She's a friend, Esta. She wouldn't do anything—"

Esta grabbed his arm, the first time she'd willingly touched him since the carriage ride. "She *knows*, Harte."

"What?" He shook his head in confusion.

"That day in the theater . . . when you were showing me the glass casket and she came to find you? I'd bet anything she heard you talking about the lost heir, about our plan with Jack."

His mouth felt suddenly dry. "You can't know that for sure. And besides, she's one of us. What would she have to gain by helping Jack?"

Esta pressed her lips together, impatience flashing in her eyes. "I don't know, but why is she *here*? Why tonight? You had to see that look of satisfaction in her eyes. She should be nervous being in a room filled with the Order—we are, and we have a team backing us up. No . . . She's planning something. Who's the man she's with?"

"Sam Watson. He's a reporter for the *New York Sun*."

"Sam Watson?" Her face drained of color.

"She and Sam go way back," Harte explained, making a show of smiling at the people passing with questioning eyes. "It's possible he looked her up because I teased him at the museum." But his instincts were screaming that Esta was right—Evelyn was up to something. And if she *did* know about the lost heir . . . After all the times he'd turned her down, and then after Esta humiliated her that day in his dressing room, she'd have plenty of reasons to hurt them. Especially if she got something out of it herself.

"You don't actually believe that, do you?"

"No," he admitted. "But she must be mad to come here tonight."

"But the payoff would be enormous," Esta said. "She wouldn't be the first Mageus to betray her kind in the hopes of a better life," she added, her expression unreadable. She seemed lost in thought and very, very far away from him.

"Are you okay?"

She blinked and, pressing her lips together, gave him a sure nod. "We should go. I can fake sick, and we'll keep Jack on the hook and try again some other time. It's too much of a risk with her here, *especially* if Evelyn knows."

They probably could get away with calling the whole thing off, but the Order wasn't the only thing Harte had to worry about. If they didn't go through with this, he didn't doubt that Nibs would take it as a reason to retaliate. Harte might be able to save himself tonight, but that would mean damning his mother . . . again.

"We've already tossed the dice," he said numbly. "And now we're just going to deal with where they've fallen."

"But—"

"Come on." He tucked her arm securely through his and led her into the cavernous space of the theater, all the while feeling like he was walking toward his certain doom.

A GOLDEN DAWN

The auditorium looked like one of the old movie palaces that people in Esta's own time were always trying to preserve. It was designed to look like an outdoor Roman amphitheater set under a canopy of sapphire blue. Long-limbed nude statues graced marble railings and towering columns. Above, instead of a ceiling, wisps of enchanted clouds plodded in a steady path across a star-studded sky.

Jack waved to them from the front of the room, near the stage, his expression anxious.

"Are you ready?" Harte murmured.

"Not even a little."

Evelyn knew what they were planning—Esta would stake her life on it—and nothing good could come from that. Especially with how she'd treated the other woman.

She could still fake sick or create some kind of diversion to get out of there. They didn't have to go through with this. They could leave, regroup. Try again when things were safer or more certain . . . But she knew instinctively it was too late for that. There was the news clipping tucked against her skin—the one with Sam Watson's name in the byline—to remind her what was at stake. If she ran now, she might never have another shot at the stone, so she allowed Harte to lead her through the crowd toward where Jack waited near the stage.

At least everyone was in a mood for celebration. The members of the Order and their bejeweled wives were floating on the rivers of champagne they'd been drinking during the cocktail hour, and laughter punctuated conversations all around them.

It's a good sign, she told herself. *It has to be.*

But she couldn't shake the feeling that she was hours, minutes away from knowing once and for all whether everything she'd done was enough. She would either succeed and be back in her own city by daybreak, or she'd—

No. She wouldn't even think about the alternative.

Jack seemed to have relaxed a little, though that might have had something to do with the glass of amber liquid in his hand. He led them backstage, where they would wait for their cue, and then he left them to take his own place in the audience.

From their vantage point, they could see the entire crowd as they took their seats and turned their pale faces to the man on the stage.

The men and the women in the audience didn't look like monsters. None of the crews of rough boys who patrolled the Bowery looking for Mageus were sitting in those seats. The silk-clad women, the tuxedoed men . . . she would wager that none had ever gotten their hands dirty in that way. Maybe they didn't know what the effects of the Order were. Maybe they didn't realize the pain and suffering the Order of Ortus Aurea caused for the people in the streets of lower Manhattan.

But the moment the High Princept—one of the highest-ranking members—stepped forward to speak, any charitable thought she might have been entertaining evaporated.

"As above," the High Princept called out, and the audience responded as one with the rest of the phrase, "so below."

"We gather tonight to celebrate the equinox, that time of balancing, of new birth, a reminder of our solemn duty to our people, to our way of life."

"I think I'm going to be sick," Esta whispered.

Harte shushed her, but his jaw was tight, his hands clenched in fists at his sides, so she had a feeling he felt the same.

"We gather together this night, brothers who have dedicated themselves to the principles of Reason and the project begun by our forefathers, pillars of the Enlightenment," the High Princept droned on. His tone and cadence made clear that this was a well-worn speech. "We stand on the shoulders of giants, and we build on what the founders of this great nation have accomplished. As the great thinker John Locke reminds us, no man's knowledge can go beyond his experience, and so we have made it our duty to immerse ourselves in experience, to push the boundaries of what is known about the Great Chain of Being, unlocking its secrets with our dedication and work."

The audience erupted into applause, and the speaker waited for it to subside, a small smile threatening at the corners of his mouth. The energy in the room was electric, but it wasn't the warmth of magic. Instead, the room was filled with the pulse of excitement that often runs through a mob before they explode into action: the sizzle of electrons, the tang of ozone, and the heady sense of righteousness that can only come from belief in purpose, no matter how insidious that belief may be. No matter the hate that might sustain itself from that darkly beating heart.

The Princept went on, buoyed by the crowd: "We have worked tirelessly for more than a century now to increase our knowledge for the good of our land, and this land owes our Order a great debt. Since its beginning, the Order of Ortus Aurea has continued the project of Enlightenment on these shores. But now we face an ever-growing threat. Hidden among those who would come to our shores with an innocent willingness to become part of our great nation is an undesirable element."

Someone in the crowd shouted out a slur, as the rest of the audience rustled. But the High Princept merely smiled benevolently.

"Yes. These Mageus come not with open hearts, willing to throw off the superstitions of their past, but with insidious intent. They hide in the shadows of our society, using their powers to take advantage of the innocent, set on the degradation of our standard of living and the debasement of our citizenry. It is against this element that we have worked tirelessly, for there is no cause more important than the character of our citizenship and the standard of living of our people.

"So let us join together to reaffirm our purpose and our dedication to this great land. Let us welcome all those who come to our shores willing to take up the mantle of democracy and Reason. But let us be always aware that there are those who pose a threat to our very way of life. For their power, uncontrolled and based not upon study and Reason but from uneducated impulse, is the antithesis of the foundations of democracy. Should their power be allowed to take root in this land, it would leave the once fertile soil of our nation barren and drained of promise.

"Let us recommit this day to our divine calling and prepare for a new dawn, a golden dawn of Reason and Science to balance against this danger in our midst. . . ."

"I'm definitely going to be sick," Esta whispered to Harte as the High Princept finished his speech to a thunderous round of applause from the audience. She'd known—of *course* she'd known—what the Order stood for, but to have to stand and face it, to pretend that the words weren't about her, about everyone she knew and cared for?

"Just focus on what we have to do," Harte told her. "Nothing else matters." He turned to her. "Block all of that out. You can't let them get into your head, especially not right now."

The High Princept raised his arms until the crowded amphitheater went quiet. "In celebration of this night, we have for your enjoyment a demonstration of the power of Reason . . . the very power our hallowed organization champions. May I present Mr. Darrigan, who has pulled himself up from obscurity through the study of the occult sciences, and his assistant, Miss von Filosik, daughter of the late baron, to whom the study of alchemy owes so much."

It was time. There was nowhere to go but out onto the stage. Harte offered his hand, and she placed her gloved palm in his as she pasted a brilliant smile on her face and allowed him to lead her onward into the glow of the footlights.

THE CARD SWITCH

If he hadn't spent so many years learning the delicate art of pretending, Harte might have hesitated. He might have felt weakened by the
onslaught of the Princept's speech, by the ragged anger simmering
in the room. But he'd lived on the edge of survival for so long that he
simply relied on the skills that had become instinct and took the stage
with his usual practiced flair. Esta, he could tell, was nervous. He could
sense the tension in her posture, and he could see the fear in her eyes.
He only hoped the footlights were too bright for the audience to see it
as well.

He launched into some of his better effects—the Indian needle trick
and a daring manipulation of fire, to start with. Then he gestured offstage
for their final demonstration of the evening, and the stagehands rolled out
a large, gleaming vault.

Esta looked at Harte, her eyes wide. Confused.

He knew what she was thinking. They had prepared all week for her
to perform the Glass Casket. They'd prepared for *her* to be the one who
stole the Book and the artifacts. But after what he'd learned from Nibsy,
he hadn't trusted her not to fall for the boy's innocent act like everyone
else. While they'd practiced, he'd made his own plans—a card switch on
a much larger scale. At first he had thought to protect her so she couldn't
be implicated when Dolph or Nibs found out what he'd done. But now
that he knew what she'd planned, he was glad he'd kept his secrets.

He gave her a wink that would look like little more than a playful
exchange to the audience, but he knew she would understand. *I'm a step
ahead of you.* Because he'd worked too long and had come too far to be

stopped by something as cliché as a pretty face now. And with the threat of Jack's machine, there was too much at risk.

Stepping to the front of the stage, Harte lifted his arm and saluted the audience. Never before had there been so much at stake in a performance. Never before had an audience been so dangerous. But having the odds stacked against him had never stopped him before, and it wouldn't stop him from doing what needed to be done now.

"Gentlemen . . . ?" He turned to the Princept who'd introduced him and the other high-ranking man at his side. "If you would come up and inspect this vault? Be thorough. Leave no doubt as to its durability."

"Actually," the Princept said, "we've arranged a little surprise for you." He gave a nod to someone offstage, and Sam Watson appeared with a set of chains and cuffs. Evelyn walked beside him, eating up the spotlight as she came closer to them.

Harte's throat went tight as Sam gave him a sharp-toothed smile that promised nothing good. But he kept his expression calm, indifferent, even as his mind raced with all the possibilities about how everything was about to go sour.

"We've all heard what you're capable of, Mr. Darrigan, so we hope you'll agree to a little challenge. Instead of using your own chains, I'm sure you wouldn't mind testing your abilities against the locks *we* provide. These cuffs were brought straight from the Halls of Justice, and all the locks and chains have been kept under my supervision until this moment to ensure they haven't been tampered with in any way. I trust that won't be a problem?"

"Of course not." Harte gave Sam his most charming smile, relieved. Handcuffs and chains were nothing to him. He'd made an art of escaping his whole life. If this was all they could throw at him, he could take it.

Esta, however, looked considerably less sure.

As they clapped him in the handcuffs and wrapped him in chains, the Princept checked over the safe, and when he was satisfied, he confirmed its integrity to the waiting crowd.

When they were finished securing him, Harte turned to the audience. "This safe is two-inch-thick steel with a double-bolt mechanism," he told the waiting crowd. "Once inside, a person would have ten minutes to escape before the air begins to thin. After twenty minutes, they would become light-headed and lose all sense of reason. At thirty minutes, they would begin to lose consciousness. At forty-five minutes, the air would run out." He paused dramatically, allowing the silence to settle over the audience. "To remain trapped so long would mean certain death . . . unless, of course, a person could manipulate the very matter of these bonds and free himself before that happens. Unless a person could command the very air to sustain him."

An interested murmuring rustled through the audience.

He ignored the unfamiliar weight of the handcuffs. "Gentlemen," he said, addressing the men who had chained him. "If you would be so kind as to lock me in?"

CHECKMATE

D olph Saunders stepped from the noise of The Devil's Own into the blessed, blessed silence of the night. He didn't waste time, but made his way swiftly along the empty street, sticking to the shadows. He had one more stop to make before he returned to the Strega to wait for news.

The cemetery was bathed in the wan light of the moon. He was only twenty-six, but he felt the aches of a much older man. He was weary, wrung out. Tired of the constant games. The constant need to be two steps ahead of the danger dogging at his heels.

If all went well tonight, those games would be at an end. One way or another.

"It's finished, Streghina. Tonight it will be done. *And you will be avenged,*" he added softly. Though he wasn't sure why, for surely the dead could hear what was in the deepest recesses of his worn and fractured heart.

He knelt at the foot of the grave Leena now shared with their child, the one she'd lost because of what he'd done, and prayed for her forgiveness. He prayed that what he was doing—his attempt to get the Book and to bring down the Brink and the Order once and for all—would make up for all he had done, but before he was finished, Dolph sensed that someone had entered the cemetery.

The intruder waited in the shadows near the gate, allowing Dolph the privacy of his audience with the dead, but Dolph could feel his impatience.

"What is it, Nibsy?" he said, speaking into the night. He didn't take his eyes from the grave as the boy approached him. "It can't already be done?" he asked, knowing that no good news would have come so soon.

"No, it's not. Not yet," Nibsy said.

The shot went off, shattering the night before Dolph even realized the boy was holding a gun, before he could turn and fight.

"But you are."

As Dolph slumped onto Leena's grave, everything fell into place.

In that instant, Dolph knew what he should have figured out long before but had been too willingly blind to see. Of course it had been Nibs, the very person who had guided his every decision after he lost Leena. The one who had known what the Brink took from him, who had suggested that he use Paul Kelly to pressure Harte.

Even before all of that, it was Nibs who had assured him that Leena would be safe. How deep had the boy's game gone? How blind had Dolph been in his willingness to trust?

He'd wanted an ace in his pocket and had chosen a serpent instead.

But the knowledge had come too late. He felt his heart beat once, twice more, and then the cold night faded as the world around him went dark.

A SECRET TOLD

Khafre Hall

The click of the heavy safe door swinging open echoed through the room. Esta could only watch as the men began to wrestle Harte into the massive safe. They'd rehearsed for this moment, and every single time, the rehearsal involved *her* getting into the Glass Casket. *Her* making her way into the Mysterium. *Her* finding the Book and the stone, and then *her* taking them, sifting through the layers of time and giving them to Professor Lachlan, where they belonged.

She'd been so stupid not to be prepared for him doing something like this, but she wouldn't go down without a fight.

"Wait!" she shouted, drawing the attention of the men to her. "A kiss for luck?"

The men exchanged glances before shrugging and stepping aside.

"She could have a key," Evelyn said. "You should check her to be sure."

But if Evelyn had thought to expose her, it didn't work. It took only a moment for Esta to open her mouth and demonstrate that she hadn't hidden a key or pick there, and then they let her by.

Harte's expression was stony as she approached him.

"Good luck, darling," she said, loud enough for anyone onstage to hear as she slid her arms around his neck and tilted her face toward him. As her lips came closer to his, she saw the question—the challenge—in his eye. And she pulled time still.

He gasped as the world went slow around him, his eyes wide with confusion, and then, with wonder. "So this is what you do," he murmured. "This is your affinity?"

"Shut up and focus," she snapped. "We don't have much time."

"It looks like we have all the time in the world," he said wryly as he nodded to the nearly frozen room around them.

"It's only slowed, not stopped completely. I won't be able to hold it indefinitely." She shook him a little. "What the *hell* are you doing?"

"I could ask the same of you," he said coldly. "But I already know."

Her stomach sank at the memory of his touch in the carriage. "I'm not the one switching the act up." But the words sounded weak, even to her.

"No?" he asked. "You weren't planning to take everything and leave us all holding the bag?

"You don't understand—"

"You told me the old man—your father—was dead, but that's not true, is it? You were going to take him the Book," he said, confirming her worst fears. "I'd started to trust you. *Everyone* trusted you."

"Maybe they shouldn't have." Her voice came out so much flatter, so much less confident than she'd intended.

Suddenly, she was painfully aware of the way the light slanted, the way the motes of dust hung suspended and unmoving around them in the beams of the footlights, like stars come to earth. She wanted to explain everything, tell him exactly why she needed the Book, but he was right. She'd take the Book back to Professor Lachlan like she was supposed to, but she couldn't lie to herself about what it meant for the people here.

"Nothing's more important than the job I have to do," she whispered, willing him to understand.

"I sure hope that's true." Harte's expression shuttered. "Because they'll go after Dolph, you know. They'll go after all those friends of yours."

"They'll go after them anyway. I *have to* take the Book. To protect it. *To protect them.* If I don't do this, they're dead—Dolph, Nibsy. Who knows who else."

His eyes went cold. "Is that all Nibsy gets out of your duplicity?"

"This doesn't have anything to do with him."

Harte laughed, a derisive huff of air that sounded as cracked and broken as the trust between them. "This has *everything* to do with him."

He wasn't making any sense, but she had to make him understand. She had to convince him. "If you take the Book now, every Mageus in this city will be lost."

"They're lost if I don't take the Book," he said, and he told her about the machine that Jack had built.

"Why didn't you tell me that morning?"

"Probably for the same reason you didn't you tell me the truth about the old man you called your father. You've never trusted me."

"And for good reason. Look at what you are doing! You're leaving me at the Order's mercy while you make off with the Book."

"You don't get it, do you? Nothing about this is meant to hurt you," he said, regret thick in his voice. "This was all just supposed to be misdirection, to take the suspicion away from you. I was going to come back for you. We were going to get out of the city together. Destroy the Book together. . . . Before I saw what I saw. Before I understood what you're planning."

Her chest tightened. "That's easy for you to say now."

"No, it's not. It's the hardest thing in the world to admit to what you gave up." He leaned his head toward her until their foreheads touched. "Unless you've changed your mind? Come with me. Help me destroy the Book. It's the only way to ensure the Mageus are safe from Jack and all those like him."

"I can't," she said, hating herself a little for how much she wanted to say yes. "Even if I wanted to, it would never work."

He pulled away from her, his expression stony from her rejection.

She ignored the hurt in his eyes, the anger in his expression. "This isn't about me," she whispered to him. "This is so much bigger than the two of us. Your life won't mean anything if you go through with this. If you take the Book, maybe you will keep Jack away from it, but you'll also condemn all of our kind to another century of the Order's control. You will condemn magic—and all Mageus with it—to a weakened half-life of existence. And it will *never* recover," she told him. "*We* will never recover. There is no walking away from this."

"You can't know that."

"I *do*. I've seen it. I've *lived* it. I know firsthand what the effect of your choices will do to our kind and to our world if you go through with this. But if you stop this now, maybe we can still fix things. Maybe we can change *everything*."

He looked at her, his stormy eyes testing her for the truth in her words. She knew they were unbelievable, but this was her only chance to finish what she'd started by coming here.

"You have to believe me." Esta took his face in her hands, feeling the cleanly shaven cheeks and the warmth of his skin beneath her fingers. "And *you* know how to see if I'm telling you the truth."

Someday, maybe she would share a kiss that was more than deception and manipulation. Someday, maybe she would press her lips against someone else's for no other reason than desire or aching want. *Maybe*.

But today was not that day.

She closed the distance between them, and at the very moment she pressed her lips against his, she let go of her hold on time. As the world spun back into motion, she put every piece of herself into the kiss, pulling him toward her, tangling her mouth against his, willing him to take what he would as she opened her mind to him. Because if he got the stone, if he took the Book and destroyed it, she would be lost. *Everything* would be lost.

His lips were impassive at first, and her stomach twisted with the understanding that he wouldn't take what she was offering. But then she felt the pulse of his magic, warm and now more familiar than it should have been. She didn't pull back or flinch away this time. Instead she bade him take all he would. His magic wrapped around her as his lips opened against hers, and she allowed herself to be laid bare, to risk everything for the chance that he wouldn't pursue this course he had set them on.

It was only when a smattering of applause came from the audience that she remembered where she was and what they were doing. She stepped back from him, her cheeks hot, but Harte's expression was impassive. Unreadable.

It doesn't matter if he believes me, she told herself. *All I have to do is slow time and I can get away—*

"Why don't you come stand with me, sweetheart?" Sam Watson said, taking her by the arm and pulling her away from the safe before she could do anything. He didn't release her arm, but he gave her a wink. "Best to make sure there's no question that your Mr. Darrigan doesn't have any assistance."

"Of course," she murmured, eyeing his hold on her arm. As long as he was touching her, she couldn't use her affinity, not without bringing him with her. She couldn't do anything about Harte or what he might have planned for the Book. All she could do was watch as they locked him into the safe and wait. And hope that what she'd told him had been enough.

THE MYSTERIUM

Still stunned by what Esta had shown him, Harte moved by instinct, pushing against the back of the vault to loosen the bolts there, adjusting his arms to slip free from the chains, all the while struggling to understand what he'd just seen.

What he'd found when he pushed into her mind was too unbelievable. Like something out of H. G. Wells. *She had to be lying.*

But he knew he would have been able to see the lie in her intentions, and no matter how he searched, there hadn't been one there. His head swirled with the strange images as he let himself out of the back of the safe, where Jianyu was already waiting, obscuring the view of anyone who might be watching. Together they moved to the back of the stage. When Harte saw the coast was clear for him to slip out into the hallway beyond, he gave Jianyu a nod to let him know he was good.

What he'd seen in Esta's mind changed nothing.

It changed everything.

As he came around the corner, he almost ran directly into Viola, who was hiding in the shadows. She was now dressed in black, looking every inch the assassin.

"Where's Esta?"

"On the stage, where she's supposed to be."

"This was not the plan."

He felt the searing energy of her magic a second before his head felt like it was being pressed in a vise. His vision started to blur, and he had the sense that at any moment everything could go black. "Dolph didn't tell you the whole plan," Harte said, fighting past the urge to scream from the pressure behind his eyes.

Viola raised a single arched brow in his direction, and a spike of pain shot through his chest. "Dolph trusts me."

"Dolph doesn't trust anyone right now," he gasped. "No one had the entire plan except me and him." Another bolt of pain rocketed through his chest, nearly making his legs give out. "It's better this way. They won't be able to accuse her of anything as long as she's standing on the stage with them. If they can't accuse her, they won't be able to trace it back to Dolph," he said, and the pressure eased a little. "Besides, she's not alone. Jianyu is there, isn't he? He'll make sure she gets out."

She lifted one of her knives to his throat. "I don't like this."

He met her glare head-on, fighting past the remaining pain. "We can argue about this, or we can finish what we came to do and get out of here."

Viola glared at him a moment longer, and then the pressure in his head eased completely, and he almost collapsed from the relief of it. "If you're lying to me, you won't make it out of this place alive."

She gave him a jerk of her head, and he followed her silently back through the Egyptian room. They stayed to the edges of the chamber, using the shadows of the great Egyptian gods to conceal themselves, until they came to the other side.

Gilded double doors carved with elaborate renderings of the tree of life marked the entrance to the Mysterium. If Jack had been correct, the passage behind those doors was available only to the Inner Circle, the highest and most exclusive members of the Order. Jack himself had never seen what lay beyond those doors, and if Harte had any say in it, he never would.

Viola dispatched the guard on the other side of the door before he could so much as lift a finger to sound an alarm. Once they were through, they found a wide hall that slanted downward, like a ramp. The floor was made of a polished black granite that reflected the light of the greenish lamps that hung from the walls, which were carved with gilded alchemical symbols. From where they were standing, they couldn't see the end of the hall. It passed downward, into the earth, and then cut to the right around a sharp corner.

Harte and Viola moved quickly, following the passage until it ended at a brass cage.

"Come on," Harte said, pulling the grated door of the elevator aside.

Viola hesitated. "You want me to get into that?"

"Unless you'd rather wait here." He climbed into the elevator's cage, and Viola, scowling at him, stepped warily into the small boxlike room.

Once she was in, he secured the gate and pressed the lever to make the elevator start its slow descent. The smooth granite turned to concrete and then bedrock as they continued down, rumbling into the depths of the building—into the very heart of the island itself.

"We should be ready for anything," he said, but when he glanced over, Viola already had her knives out.

When the elevator finally rattled to a stop at the bottom, Harte could hear water running nearby. The air was cool and damp. No one was waiting for them as they exited the elevator, but when they stepped out, they found another set of double doors, this time cast in iron and carved with mirror images of the Philosopher's Hand.

The closer they got to the doors, though, the more he could feel the cold energy that permeated them. Jack hadn't mentioned anything about protection on the Mysterium itself, but now that they were faced with entering it, Harte wasn't sure if they could.

"There's no way through that," he told Viola, feeling the sudden overwhelming reality that every risk he'd taken that night had been for nothing. "This isn't going to work. I need to get back onstage before—"

But Viola didn't seem bothered. She took a small item from an inner pocket and gestured toward the doors. "Dolph had a feeling we would find something like this."

"What is that?" he asked, eyeing the piece of pinkish stone she was holding. There was something carved on its surface, writing he couldn't make out.

"It's what we took from the museum—an amulet in the form of a seal. If Dolph's right, the inscription should break whatever protection this is."

As he motioned her forward, he wondered if it was the same piece Jack had been interested in. She held the object loosely between her index finger and thumb, and then she began rolling it over the door.

"To break false magic," Viola said, "you need to use false magic." She drew an intricate design of circles and concentric shapes onto the door, and as she worked, the seal left a glowing imprint of the markings from its surface. The markings began to swell and bleed over, until the entire door was alight with energy. All at once, the light broke, and the cold drained away from the space, until only the door was left.

Harte found himself immediately grateful that he hadn't turned Dolph over to the police as he'd considered after the Metropolitan burglary. Without the seal, they never would have gotten past those doors.

He gave a silent jerk of his head, and together he and Viola slipped cautiously into the Mysterium. On the other side of the doors, they found themselves in a cathedral-like chamber with a huge dome. The whole space was lit by the same otherworldly flames as the hallway above. A chemical reaction of some sort, he supposed.

The stepped farther into the room, toward a tall, square table in the middle. Its four legs stood atop round silver discs. On the center of it, a low golden bowl held a crystalline substance that looked neither liquid nor solid but seemed to glow from within. Next to the bowl lay a necklace with an enormous turquoise gem and a silver cuff he'd seen before—in the images Esta had given to him just minutes ago when she'd kissed him onstage.

It was yet another sign that he couldn't simply dismiss what she'd shown him. She couldn't have known what the cuff looked like unless everything she'd shown him was true.

Around the circumference of the room, five greenish lamps threw their eerie light up the curved stone walls, and three of the lamps had bodies lying in the pallid beam of their light, suspended in air as though on an invisible table.

"*Madonna*," Viola whispered, crossing herself. "I know these." She walked toward the nearest body, a man with graying hair and a thick beard. He was dressed in a white robe, his hands were crossed over his chest, and on his left index finger was a ring with a huge stone so clear it looked almost liquid. "This is Krzysztof Zeranski. He went missing a few weeks ago." She walked to the next body, a woman with light hair capped by a golden crown. She too was dressed in a white robe, and she too was unconscious. "Frieda Weber."

The final body was on the other side of the room, but even in the dim light, even from that distance, they could make out the vivid copper of Bridget Malone's curling hair. Viola walked over, her hand extended as though she could stop what had already happened. "No," she whispered, glancing back at Harte. "She disappeared the night of the Haymarket raid."

Bridget wasn't wearing a jewel, as the other two were. The blade of a dagger was plunged into her middle. "She's still breathing," Harte said, even as he knew that such a thing couldn't be. Not skewered by the knife as she was.

"But not bleeding."

"Should we help them?" Harte wondered out loud.

Viola shook her head. "I don't think there's anything to be done. We need to find the Book and get out of here." She walked over and examined the table. "I've seen these signs before," she said, pointing to the four discs the legs of the table rested on.

Harte frowned as he studied them. They were complex geometric designs—a pentagram inside of other shapes, all ringed by concentric circles. "I haven't."

"Dolph has a painting, one he took from the museum. This symbol is depicted there." She glanced up at him, her expression determined. "This is it."

As he looked around for some sign of the Book, he noticed that the entire floor of the chamber was a dazzlingly vivid mosaic of the tree of life made from precious stones. The branches sprouted from the central trunk, and at the end of each of the five limbs were five empty indentations in the floor. It was something of a puzzle, he realized—an enormous lock with a five-part key.

"I think we need to unlock it," he told her.

"Unlock what?"

"This image. The tree of life is an alchemical recipe. In alchemy, the pictures are symbols of elements or chemical reactions. I think the floor is a larger version of one. If we want to find the Book, I think we have to complete the formula." He looked around the room for some answer, and then he realized. "The cuff and the necklace—bring them over here."

He tried to fit the necklace and then the cuff into one of the indentations, but neither fit, so he moved on to the next and then the next, until he found the one that worked for the necklace. As the turquoise stone slid into place, its entire branch began to glow, as if the gemstones that formed it were lit from within. Then he repeated the process to find the spot for the cuff.

When the stone in the cuff clicked into place, he turned to Viola, who had been watching with a wary crease between her brows. "We need to get those as well," he said, meaning the jewels on the bodies at the edge of the room.

She frowned, but gave him a nod.

They approached Krzysztof first, but when Viola reached for the ring, she drew her hand back. "It feels like death. How are we supposed to get them?"

"As quickly as we can," he told her. "You still have that seal?"

She nodded and, understanding, traced it over Krzysztof's fingers and the ring.

"Let's give it a try," he said when the entire hand was aglow with the imprints from the seal. His fingers twitched as he readied himself. He could have used Esta right then, with her ability to lift any object in a blink, and for a heartbeat he regretted leaving her behind on that stage. But then he steadied himself and focused on what he needed to do.

The moment his finger touched the ring, he felt cold energy prickle along his fingertips, but he pulled it off as quickly as he could. As soon as it slipped free of Krzysztof's finger, the man's body fell lifeless to the floor. Viola cursed and crossed herself again, but Harte forced himself to keep moving. They were taking too long already.

"I'll work on this one. You do Frieda."

He found the location for the ring and then together they found the indent where the crown fit, before they turned to Bridget.

"We'll have to take out the knife," he realized. His stomach turned with the very thought of it. "You're better with knives than I am."

Viola only glared at him, so he traced the seal around the place where the knife was protruding from Bridget's stomach, and when he couldn't delay any longer, he grasped its garnet-encrusted hilt and pulled hard. He felt the resistance of flesh and muscle against the knife, heard the suck of her body as it released the metal. Bridget fell, deadweight, to the floor, and blood began to ooze from the wound.

Harte turned away before his stomach revolted and focused on the task at hand. There was one space left, and he had to insert the knife vertically, so its blade sank into the glittering floor. When the stone in its hilt finally clicked into place, the last branch lit and the entire floor began to shake. And then it began to move.

The altar in the center began to rise, floating on the silvery discs. Beneath it, a portion of the floor lifted as well, and as the thick column of the floor rose, Harte saw that the altar was actually the top of a much larger cabinet, and within the cabinet was a book.

They approached slowly, watchful in case the table above them was some kind of trap. The Book didn't look like anything special—it was small, no bigger than any of the ledgers Shorty used at the theater to keep track of ticket sales. The cover was crackled and dark with age, and it bore the same geometric design as the silver disks on the floor. Its pages hung out unevenly, as if the book had been added to over the years.

"That's it?"Viola asked, her voice laced with disgust. "All of this mess, all of this waste, and it's an ugly little thing?"

Harte reached his hand out slowly, waiting for some other trap. The moment his fingertips made contact with the cover, the green flames on the walls rose, flashing in a bright explosion of color that both he and Viola backed away from. Smoke filled the air, sickening and sweet and too familiar. *Opium.*

"We need to go," she said, reaching for the Book.

But Harte had not come so far to lose now. Before she could get the Book, he grabbed it.

The moment his fingers were around its cover, a hot, searing energy shot up his arm and into his chest, and his head was filled with the sounds of hundreds of voices. *Thousands of voices.* The noise lasted only a few seconds, but to Harte it felt like a never-ending barrage of screams and chants and voices in languages he didn't have words to describe. It felt as if time were standing still as they assaulted him, and then, just as quickly as they came, they were gone.

Or if not gone, they quieted. He could feel them still, inside of his head. Inside of *him.* They felt hungry.

He shook himself, trying to dismiss the last of the noise still whispering at the edges of his mind. He shouldn't have been able to understand the strange languages, but he understood what they were trying to tell him. Touching the Book felt like reading a person—all impressions and images—but stronger, clearer.

All at once he understood how wrong he had been about everything. How shortsighted they all had been to misunderstand so thoroughly. All at once he knew what had to be done.

"What is it?" Viola asked when he just stood there with the Book in his hands.

"Nothing," he said as he placed the Book in a bag and then went around the room to collect the other artifacts. "Let's go." He tucked the bag under his coat as the table began descending again. "I need to get back into the safe before they realize I'm gone or the whole thing is blown."

"I'll take that first," she said, holding him at knifepoint. He began to feel a sharp driving pressure inside his skull, Viola's way of warning him not to push.

He hesitated for a moment. But with voices still haunting his mind, urging him on, he knew what he was meant to do.

The opium smoke was growing thick in the room, but he wasn't sure how much it had affected her. He'd have to take his chances that it had weakened her enough for him to get away. Before she could make the pain in his head any worse, he threw the bag into the air, and when her eyes followed it, he attacked.

THE REVEAL

The minutes ticked by.

Ten.

Fifteen.

What's taking so long? Esta didn't doubt that Harte had a way out of the safe. She'd seen him do more difficult escapes before—at least the safe wasn't filled with water—but he wasn't a thief. Once Harte was out, she had no idea how he would be able to manage the rest on his own before the Order realized what was happening.

Twenty minutes.

The audience began to murmur expectantly. Esta forced herself to keep a pleasant, unworried smile pasted on her face, but she felt every pair of eyes in the audience focused on her.

"It's taking him quite a while," the High Princept said, his expression unsure.

She knew he was worried. It was one thing to play a harmless prank on a performer, but it was another to watch a man possibly dying onstage while you stood by doing nothing to help.

Sam Watson looked a little too pleased. He leaned over as though to whisper but spoke loud enough that anyone onstage could have heard him. "Perhaps the great Harte Darrigan isn't quite the master of the elements he claims to be?"

Across the stage, Evelyn smirked.

"I'm sure you're mistaken," Esta said, trying to pull away without much luck. "I have every faith he will succeed. He has command over forces far beyond your understanding."

But as the seconds ticked by, that faith began to falter.

At half an hour, the audience was shouting for them to open the safe and let the magician out, but Esta told them to wait. If there was any hope that giving up all her secrets had worked, she needed to give Harte time—to get the Book and the artifacts and to get back into the safe, so they could both escape together.

Across the stage, the High Princept was growing more agitated, and Evelyn was watching with her red mouth drawn into a smirk and her eyes bright with anticipation. A moment later she touched the High Princept on the arm and leaned over to whisper something into his ear.

The old man's eyes went curiously blank, and though he seemed completely calm, he barked for the vault to be opened. *Evelyn's doing.*

The audience went quiet as the combination was given and the large tumbler of the lock was rotated carefully. Esta tried to pull herself away from Sam Watson, who seemed to have a grip of steel. If she could just get away, she could slow time and find Harte. She could maybe even get him back into that safe before anyone understood what was happening.

But before she could find a way to disentangle herself from the reporter, the door swung open.

A gasp swept over the theater when the audience realized Harte was no longer in the safe.

"It's the girl!" Evelyn said, pointing at Esta as she came across the stage to where Sam still held on to her. "I told you, didn't I? I warned you they were up to something."

"So you did," Sam Watson said as he gripped her arm even more tightly and jerked her around to face the High Princept.

"This is all part of the effect . . . part of the act," Esta tried to tell them, but she couldn't keep the tremor out of her voice. "You simply have to close the safe and give him a chance to reappear."

"She's lying," Evelyn said, walking across the stage to where Sam Watson held Esta. "Harte Darrigan makes other people disappear. He never gives up the stage on his own. He's up to something, and she's helping him, just like I told you. She's no baron's daughter. It's all a con. I heard them myself. 'Here's to bringing down the Order.' Isn't that what you said?"

Esta shook her head, but she couldn't force out the words.

"Where's the magician?" the Princept snarled, so close to her face that she could smell the alcohol on his breath. "Where is Darrigan?"

"I don't know," she said honestly. Not that he would believe her. Not that *any* of them would believe her.

"Lock the entire building down," the High Princept shouted, his aged face turning an alarming shade of red. "I want every inch of this place searched until he's found. And you—" He pointed at Jack Grew, who was sitting white-faced and wide-eyed in the front row. "This is *your* fault. I won't forget that *you* were the one who brought them here." Then he turned to Sam Watson. "Take her to the safe room, and if you ever want a chance at full membership, do *not* let her get away."

The Princept stormed off down the steps, into the chaotic crowd, leaving Esta trapped by Sam Watson's strong grip. The theater had erupted into chaos.

She tried to shake off Watson, but every time she tried to maneuver, he countered it easily. Finally, he had her pinned, so she couldn't move.

"Please . . . this is a simple misunderstanding. I had nothing to do with him disappearing."

"Shut your lying mouth," Watson said, pulling her arms back until her joints screamed in pain. "You don't think I know you were a part of this too? I know you're one of them—" Before he could finish, Watson went stiff and released his hold on her. Suddenly, his head snapped backward, and then he buckled forward, doubling over and falling to the floor.

Esta stared, shocked. "Jianyu?" She didn't have time to react before Jianyu materialized before her.

"Come," he said, gesturing toward the back of the theater, where a large man stood in their way.

Jianyu put his arms up, ready, but she grabbed his hand instead and pulled at time. All around them, the movement in the room went slow. The frantic activity stilled. Men in tuxedos halted midstep as they tried to climb over one another, their faces portraits of rage and fear. Evelyn's overly painted face froze in its look of shocked surprise as she reached for Sam, who was now lying on the floor.

Jianyu's eyes went wide, and then he gave her a slow smile. "I see," he said, nodding with appreciation. "Come. We'll go together." She watched as he maneuvered the small disks in his hand and saw the shadow fall around them. "It's safer this way." Then he started to lead her in the direction of the rear of the stage.

"We have to stop Harte," she told him, pulling in the opposite direction. "He changed the act. He's going after the Book."

"I know," Jianyu said, refusing to go.

"You know?"

"It was all part of the plan." Jianyu gave her another tug, and she was confused enough that she let herself be pulled toward the room styled like an Egyptian tomb. When they found themselves back in that ornate chamber, she pulled him to a stop.

"I don't understand." All around them the building was silent, and the eyes of the enormous figures lining the walls seemed to watch them. "You *knew* he was going to switch the act on me?"

Jianyu nodded. "He came to Dolph with the idea a couple of days ago. He said he wanted to draw suspicion away from you."

"No, that's not right. It's another trick," she said, sure that it was only one more level of Harte Darrigan's game. It had to be.

"If it's a trick, Viola will dispense with him soon enough. Come."

She didn't trust Harte, but she knew what Viola could do, so Esta allowed Jianyu to lead her through the chaos of the building and out into the street.

Outside, the night was alive with confusion. Already she could hear the clanging sound of the fire brigades rushing toward them. There were flames lighting the western edge of the building, the dark smoke pouring out of broken windows. They used the confusion to dart away, toward the place where Dolph's carriage was waiting.

When they made it to the carriage, Nibs looked down at them from the driver's seat.

"Where's Darrigan?"

"He's not out yet?" Jianyu asked.

Nibs shook his head.

Esta's chest felt too tight to draw breath. All she'd shown him, and it hadn't been enough.

She heard the sound of footsteps coming toward them, and they all turned as one. For a heartbeat, hope flared in Esta's chest. For the space of a second, she expected to see Harte.

But it was Viola, dressed all in black and running toward them. "Go!" she shouted as a group of men stormed out the door behind her. She turned long enough to throw a knife back at them, hitting one in the throat so he crumpled to the street.

"But Darrigan—" Nibs said as Viola climbed into the cab.

"It doesn't matter. I have the Book," Viola told him.

"You're sure?" Nibs asked, his eyes flashing up to the building.

"I took care of him."

"What do you mean?" Esta asked, not wanting to really understand. But understanding just the same.

"He's gone, capisce?" She held up the bag. "We have what we came for." Viola slammed the door of the carriage.

Nibsy whipped the horses into action, and the carriage leaped away, leaving Harte Darrigan behind them.

Viola's eyes met Esta's. "I'm sorry," she said, and there was real regret, real pain in them. "I know the two of you had grown close, but I couldn't let him take this." Viola reached across the carriage and touched Esta's knee gently. "If there was another way—"

"I know," Esta told her truthfully. But she couldn't stop the burn of tears behind her eyes.

"You truly killed him?" Jianyu asked.

"He attacked me first."

Jianyu frowned. "Dolph trusted him."

Viola's eyes met his. "He shouldn't have."

Esta turned away from them both, pretending to stare out of the window of the carriage. Instead, she removed the clipping from the bodice of her dress. Despite everything that had gone wrong, it gave her some relief to see that it had returned to its original form.

No, Dolph never should have trusted Harte Darrigan, but at least he hadn't won. The past seemed to have been returned to its original path, and the Book was safe in Viola's care, which meant Esta still had a chance to complete the job she'd been sent to do.

She'd stolen from Viola and Dolph before. She could do it again.

She should have felt relieved, satisfied the job had been salvaged, so she didn't understand why the ache in her chest when she thought of Harte dead felt as though the night would swallow her whole.

MADNESS IN THE STREETS

Bella Strega

When they made it back to the Strega, Dolph was nowhere to be found.

"We should wait for him," Viola said when Nibs tried to take the bag she had carried from Khafre Hall. He tugged a bit harder, but Viola refused to relinquish it. "I give this to Dolph and no one else."

Nibs frowned. "Then I suppose we should send someone to fetch him."

No one expected that the bowler-hatted boys would return bearing his body instead.

They'd found Dolph shot in the back and already dead, lying across Leena's grave. The boys carried him in with a quiet solemnity that seemed at odds with the garish shirts and vests, and they placed him on the zinc bar top. Even in death, his skin nearly as pale as the flash of white in his hair, Dolph's very presence commanded the room.

The motley bunch of men and women he'd unified under his mark stood in an uneasy silence. There was no sign of the usual warmth of magic in the barroom. It had all but drained from the air, as though Dolph had taken it with him as he took his last breath, as though each of them understood that the one thing that had linked them was now gone, and in his absence—in the absence of the power of his mark—a new consensus would have to be negotiated.

"He'd want us to go on," Nibs said, his voice grave. "He'd want us to finish what we'd started."

Dolph's closest crew gathered around his usual table—Viola, Jianyu, and Nibs. Esta hung back at first, but Viola took her by the arm and escorted her back with the rest. Jianyu gave Nibs an encouraging look, and Nibs opened the bag and looked inside.

Esta knew from the way his expression changed that something was wrong. With shaking hands, he dumped the contents on the table. A few misshapen rocks. A small ledger bearing the theater's logo. And the dried peelings from an orange.

They all stared at the items in a horrified silence.

"No . . ." Nibsy shook his head as he pawed through the items, turning them over, examining them. "No!" he shouted, pushing them from the table with a vicious swipe of his arm. He turned on Viola. "This is *your* fault," he said. He had his finger in her face, and his expression was murderous. "You let this happen!"

Viola stared at the now empty table, shaking her head as though denying what they were all seeing. "*No*. I took the bag from him. I *killed* him."

"Are you sure about that?" Nibs' brows drew together.

"Certo! I know when I kill someone," she snarled, looking every bit like Nibs would be her next victim.

"Did he touch you?" Nibs asked.

"What? What are you talking about?"

"Did he *touch* you?" Nibs shouted. His face had turned a violent shade of red, and he was up in her face, so close that she could have bitten him.

Viola pushed him back and wiped his spittle from her face. "He fought me for the Book, so yes. He touched me. But he was dead a moment later."

"If he touched you, he could have altered your mind."

"What are you talking about? I *killed* him."

"It's what Darrigan does," Nibs sneered, shaking his head at her. "He can read minds, and he can put ideas into them as well. All it takes is a single touch, skin to skin. You probably wouldn't have even noticed."

"He's right," Esta said, numb with disbelief.

Viola shook her head. "No. It's not possible. There was opium—or something like it—a cloud of it filled the room when we took the Book from its place. There was no way Darrigan could have done anything, not before I killed him. My knives don't need magic to work."

"Where's the knife you used?" Nibs asked.

Viola pulled out Libitina, her favorite stiletto blade, and held it up.

"Where's his blood?"

"There should have been blood," Viola whispered.

"Darrigan was a stage magician, you imbecile. He trained himself to hold his breath longer than anyone should be able to. The opium wouldn't have affected him if he didn't breathe it."

"No . . . ," Viola whispered, shaking her head. As though she refused to believe that he'd tricked her so easily, that he'd destroyed everything.

Dolph was dead and the Order would hunt them, and they didn't have the Book.

Nibs only glared at her. "Then where's the Book? Where are the artifacts?"

Viola didn't have an answer.

But for Esta, the news was *that* much more devastating. She'd failed. Harte Darrigan—the *Magician*—had the Book, and he was gone.

So were the artifacts. So was her stone.

And so was any chance of her ever getting home.

It wasn't long after that things started to fall apart.

Before dawn broke the next day, an entire block of tenement buildings went up in flames. The fire brigades stayed away, but boys who wore the Five Point Gang's mark were seen at the edges of the crowd. Watching. Stopping any who tried to douse the fires or rescue their belongings. Their alliance with the mayor—and with the Order—seemed to be growing more complete.

Under Tammany Hall's protection, the members of Kelly's gang didn't hesitate to attack anyone they thought might be a threat. Fights broke out over innocent glances. Gunfire rained in the streets, catching anyone nearby in the crossfire.

No one in the Bowery was safe. Not as long as the Order was set on vengeance.

Of course, all the unrest was reported as more evidence of the threat the incoming masses of immigrants posed. After he wrote about the fire at Khafre Hall, Sam Watson turned his daily columns to denouncing the Mageus for the threat they posed to the city. Criminals, degenerates, and thieves were pouring across the borders, he argued, and nothing was being done. If they could destroy an institution as old and important as Khafre Hall, he reminded everyone, they could also threaten the country's very way of life.

Near Herald Square, ladies in feathered caps and gentlemen in white gloves pursed their lips and shook their heads as they *tsk-tsk*ed the plight of the mayor having to control such a threat. Above Houston, the people of Manhattan went on about their lives as usual, willfully ignoring the madness that raged in the streets below.

But the citizens of the areas around Five Points and the Bowery lived on the knifepoint of fear. They knew the madness wasn't their own doing. Everyone was running scared.

Everyone, it seemed, except Nibsy Lorcan, who had somehow stepped into the space left by Dolph Saunders with an ease that surprised Esta. No one had questioned it when Nibs began issuing orders while Dolph's body was still cooling on the bar. While everyone else had turned inward, becoming silent and wary with the irrevocable evidence of Dolph's death, Nibs seemed to have grown six inches overnight. He sat in Dolph's old seat like it had always been meant for him.

Too soon, she thought. And she couldn't help but remember Harte's words—*this has* everything *to do with him.*

No one else seemed to question Nibsy's rise, though. Or if they did, they were still too dazed with the shock of what had happened to care.

A week later, they were huddled in the kitchen of the Strega, away from the rest of Dolph's gang, when a trio of bowler-hatted boys came through the door. The four of them—Nibs, Viola, Jianyu, and Esta—turned as one, already bracing for something worse. The tallest of the three boys stepped forward to where Nibs was sitting and then gave a jerk of his head, like he wanted to speak to Nibs alone.

Nibs took the boy aside and listened intently, his nostrils flaring and his features going hard as the boy talked.

"What do you mean his mother's gone?" Nibs hissed loudly enough for the rest of the room to turn and watch.

"Just what I told you. They says you ordered her to be moved."

"To where?" Nibs asked, his face furious.

"They says they didn't know," the boy said with a shrug.

"Well, who took her?"

The boy hesitated, a look of confusion on his face. "They says *you* did."

Viola sent Esta a questioning look from across the table where they were sitting, but Esta shook her head. She didn't know what the boys were talking about. She glanced at Jianyu, but he was too busy watching Nibsy and the other boy with a quiet intensity.

"I didn't do any such thing," Nibs seethed, barely able to control the volume of his voice now.

"There's one more thing," the boy said. He held himself on guard, like he was about to dodge a punch.

"What?" Nibs' chest was heaving.

The boy held out a folded piece of paper. "They says I was supposed to give you this."

Nibs took the paper with a vicious swipe that had the boy startling back. "Get out," he barked, and he waited until the three boys left before he opened the message and read it. When he was done, he glanced up at Esta.

Both Jianyu and Viola straightened in their chairs.

"What?" she asked, not at all liking the look on Nibsy's face.

He handed her the paper without a word.

It was an advertising flyer. On it, the bold block letters proclaimed that the great Harte Darrigan would attempt the impossible by cheating death with a jump from the Brooklyn Bridge. And across the image of the bridge was a message scrawled in a familiar script: *If you want the Book, bring me the girl.*

"Harte Darrigan, it seems, isn't dead after all. Not yet, at least," Nibs said, meeting her eyes when she looked up from reading. "There's something I'm missing," he said, staring blindly into space. Thinking, no doubt. Making connections. Then his eyes rested on Esta. "I can't believe he didn't give you any indication of what he had planned."

Esta went on alert. Nibs had been watching her for two days now, and every time she caught him looking, it gave her an uneasy feeling. Like he saw something in her that he didn't like. "He used me the same as everyone," she said carefully. "If it looked like we were close, it was another part of his game."

"No . . ." Nibs stared at her, the expression in his eyes unreadable. "I don't think that's the case at all. You meant something to him."

She laughed, a cold, hard expulsion of air that she filled with every bit of her disdain. "I assure you, I meant nothing to him. Or maybe you forgot how he left me on that stage without any warning."

"So *you* say," Nibs said softly.

"So I know," she told him. "He left me in a room full of the Order's members. If it hadn't been for Jianyu, I'd still be there."

Nibs huffed out a laugh.

"She speaks truly," Jianyu said. "He left her without any protection. He had no way of knowing that I would be there, waiting. That was something Dolph had arranged."

Esta hesitated only a moment at the lie that had slipped so easily from Jianyu's lips. "See?" she snapped. It took everything she had in her not to glance at Jianyu. "Harte Darrigan can go to hell for all I care."

That much was true.

He'd left her. He'd betrayed them all, but he'd left *her*. And she hated herself for caring about that, for forgetting—even for a moment—why she was there, in that city. But it wasn't over yet. She would have one more chance to stop him from destroying the Book—one more chance to save them all.

She would not fail again.

ONE FINAL NIGHT

The Docks

Once night had cloaked the city, Harte watched the boat carrying the Order's artifacts glide from the docks, its engines off. When it was out of reach of the shoreline, the great boilers fired up, and the squat craft began to move faster, cutting a path through the starlight reflected in the dark water. He stayed where he was until the boat was no more than a dot on the horizon, knowing for certain now that he would never have the chance to make that trip, would never know what those other shores held in store.

Nibs Lorcan had overplayed his hand by warning Harte. It had taken some doing—late nights and secrets kept from Esta—but in the days leading up to the heist, Harte had managed to grease the right palms for word of where his mother might be. In the end it had been easy enough, especially with the right kind of touch.

Once he discovered she'd been stashed in a rank basement of a brothel near the docks, it had been hell to wait, but he knew he couldn't simply take her out of there without Nibs knowing. If Nibs had realized that he'd lost his leverage, he would never have let Harte near Khafre Hall or the Book. So he'd waited, unwilling to chance anything until the night of the heist, when it would be too late for Nibs to do anything to stop him.

But by the time Harte finally got to his mother, she'd been fed so much opium that it would be a miracle if she recovered at all. Still, he got her out, as he'd promised. As he gave the old couple who ran the brothel a stack of bills for their trouble, all he had to do was let his finger brush against their palms. It would have been hardly noticeable to them, especially with the way they were focused on the money, but a moment later they didn't remember him at all.

His mother was safe now, or as safe as she could be. Now he needed to turn himself to other things.

He'd been watching Jack's warehouse for two days. There'd been no sign of Jack, or anyone else, and Harte was finally confident that it was safe enough to chance approaching it. He couldn't finish things until he destroyed the machine and the plans to build another. After all, Harte Darrigan might be a bastard, he might be a double-crossing low-life scoundrel, but he wasn't so low as to leave a machine like that whole before he made his escape. Not when he knew the danger it posed to hundreds—maybe thousands—of innocent people.

It wouldn't be enough to stop Jack indefinitely, he knew, but it would set him back for a while. It would maybe even give the rest of them a fighting chance. Especially once Harte—and the Book with him—were gone.

First the machine. The wrench weighing down the pocket of his overcoat should do the trick. He'd destroy Jack's creation and send the whole damn place up in flames.

Then he'd go after Esta. He'd explain everything.

A shadow stirred near one of the low buildings at his back, and his every instinct came alert. No one could have known he was there. He'd taken every precaution, hidden his tracks twice over. There was no mistaking it, though—the feeling he had of being hunted.

"Who's there?" he called, but the soft lapping of the water was all he heard in reply. "I know someone's out there."

He waited, listening, but the feeling of being watched didn't go away.

"If you're thinking of killing me, I'd advise against it. If I'm dead, you'll never find out where I've put the things you're looking for," he said, not knowing if it was one of Dolph's crew or someone from the Order, and not really caring. Let them do the job for him for all he cared.

He hadn't lied—they'd never find the Book or the strange artifacts, not where he'd put them.

"Show yourself!" he called, his hand already wrapped around the wrench in his coat pocket. As though that would offer much protection.

Jianyu stepped into a shaft of moonlight. Maybe he should have been relieved that it wasn't Viola, but Harte still felt a tremor of fear run through him.

Let me explain, he wanted to say. But he didn't. Standing in the darkness near the water's edge was no place for pleading. He stood a little straighter instead.

"Did Dolph send you?" he asked, pretending a confidence he didn't feel.

"Dolph's dead," Jianyu told him, the flatness in his voice confirming his words.

"That's what I'd heard." He hadn't wanted to believe it, though.

"Shot in the back over Leena's grave," Jianyu said, even though Harte hadn't asked. He could almost feel the anger—and the anguish—in Jianyu's usually calm voice. "The night you betrayed us."

"I didn't betray Dolph," Harte said. "We had an arrangement, and I kept my word to him." But he knew when he'd heard whispers of Dolph's death that everything had gone south.

"Then where is the Book?"

"Safe," he said.

Jianyu's mouth turned down. "It would be safer with me."

"If it were with you, Nibs would have it, and we'd all be screwed."

Jianyu didn't say anything, simply continued to study him across the narrow stretch between them.

"I didn't kill Dolph," he said finally.

"If I thought you did, you'd be dead already."

He didn't trust Jianyu's too-calm demeanor. "If you didn't come to kill me, why *are* you here?"

"I'm here because Dolph is dead." He gave Harte an unreadable look and took a step closer. "But what we do from here . . . that is up to you."

FOOL ME ONCE

Jack's Apartment

J ack Grew was packing the last of his suitcases when the message came. An hour later, he would have been on a train bound to Cleveland and his new position as an assistant to the undersecretary of a refinery on the shores of Lake Erie. The message changed all that. Or at least put it on hold for the time being.

Jack held on to the folded slip of paper like a lifeline.

Not that he trusted Darrigan. No, he wouldn't be taken in by that charlatan again.

Daughter of Baron von Filosik? Like hell she was. He'd had people search Darrigan's apartment while the pair were putting on their little show at Khafre Hall, and they didn't find any sign of a trunk, or anything else that would indicate that the girl was who they said she was. The redhead had been right. They'd played him, and now Darrigan was going to pay.

I have the Book for you. Come alone, the message said.

Not a chance.

When Jack's carriage came to a stop at the foot of the bridge early the next day, he found a steady stream of people heading in the same direction. It looked as though the entire bridge had been closed down to the usual streetcar and carriage traffic, so he stopped a man to ask where they were headed. The man didn't seem to understand what Jack was saying, but he handed him a crumpled flyer.

Beneath the grease stains and wrinkles, Jack saw the image of the bridge and the smirking face of Harte Darrigan.

It shouldn't have surprised him that he was walking into a virtual circus, considering who he was dealing with. But if Darrigan thought to throw Jack off with this crowd, he was wrong. He'd learned his lesson, and now Darrigan would learn *his*.

He told his uncle—who had of course told the High Princept—about the note. The Order had taken everything from there.

Jack looked over his shoulder at the row of buildings lining the waterfront. He could just barely make out the glint of the sharpshooter's sight in a fourth-floor window. If anything went wrong, the Order wouldn't allow Darrigan to get away. If he tried to come back into the city, he was a dead man. If he tried to make it to the wilds of Brooklyn, Order patrols were already waiting. And if Jack himself happened to be in the line of fire . . . the High Princept had already made it clear that no one would care.

A suppressed shudder ran through him.

That wasn't going to happen. If anyone was going to kill that piece-of-shit magician, it was going to be him.

So Jack made his way with the rest of the crowd, following the long incline that led out over the shoreline and toward the soaring towers of the bridge. He took the entrance to the far right, one usually taken up by streetcars and trains. The farther he walked, the denser the crowd became, but this wasn't the refined crowd of Broadway. All around him, the clamoring of too many languages assaulted his ears. Guttural and brash, the voices were a noisy babble that made him feel as if *he* were the one who didn't belong.

It only served to make him angrier. After all, his family had practically built this city.

Still, the crowd would make it that much more difficult for the Order to deal with Darrigan. He pulled the brim of his hat low on his forehead and started on his way toward the arches of the first tower. The crowd had come to a stop there, a motley throng of humanity dressed in the gaudy satins and bright taffetas of people who didn't know better, people who bought their goods ready-made and three seasons out of fashion. And in the center of the teeming mass, as still as a rock in a current, was the magician.

ENDGAME

The Brooklyn Bridge

It was hard to even pretend confidence with a gun pressing into the small of her back, but Esta did what she could. She couldn't use her affinity, not with the grip the large boy had on her arm, but she could use the other magic Professor Lachlan had taught her when she was a girl. *Confidence is the key to any con. If they see you sweat, you're dead.*

The morning wind had kicked up by the time they made their way across the span of the bridge to the arches of the first tower that held the monstrous suspension cables aloft. With every step, she sensed what remained of Dolph's crew becoming more nervous, and who could blame them? Though the day was warm, there was a chill in the air. A cold, malicious energy that whispered of danger. A reminder that ahead was the end of the world for anyone with magic.

She hadn't been on this bridge since she was a child.

Now, the closer they got to that tower, the more she felt like the girl she'd once been. But Professor Lachlan wasn't there to help her, and she had a sinking feeling that if anyone carried her off the bridge this time, it would be because she was dead.

She straightened her spine, ignoring the kiss of the gun. She would get the Book and the stone from Darrigan, or she would die trying.

The boy pushed through the crowd, dragging her along, with Nibs following close behind. Viola was there too, somewhere, ready to step in if need be, as were Jianyu and a handful of Dolph's crew. All there to make sure that everything went their way, and to be certain that Harte Darrigan never came back into the city.

They made their way toward the front of the crowd. Each step was one closer to the cold currents of energy warning them of disaster and death. Eventually, they reached the point where she could see Harte, already warming the crowd up with some minor sleight of hand. When he looked up and saw her, an emotion she couldn't read—and one she didn't want to think too much about—flashed behind his eyes.

"Ladies and gentlemen," he announced. "I see my assistant has arrived." He held out his hand, as though nothing had happened between them. As though he'd never betrayed her, never left her for dead in a theater filled with the Ortus Aurea. "Esta, my dear?" When she didn't move, he asked the crowd to encourage her.

Applause surrounded them, and when she glanced at Nibs, for some indication of what she should do, she saw his indecision. His eyes were narrowed as he considered Harte, but then he gave a nod of his head. "If you try anything at all, you're dead," he told her.

She was sick of that particular threat. With a frustrated huff, she stepped toward Harte.

"I've missed you, sweetheart," he said, as he took her hand and made a show of kissing it for the audience.

"Funny," she replied, her eyes stinging with tears that had nothing to do with the breeze. "I haven't thought about you at all."

The audience close enough to hear roared their approval.

Harte had already removed his cloak. He handed it to her, and then he proceeded to remove his waistcoat as well. Before he could finish unbuttoning his vest, there was a disruption from deep within their numbers, and an uneasy murmuring rose within the crowd as a man made his way forward, gun drawn.

Harte's expression faltered just a little as he gave Jack Grew his most charming smile. "Jack! How good of you to make it."

"Give me the Book, Darrigan," Jack said, pointing the gun directly at his chest. "And the artifacts as well."

"You'll get them soon enough—"

"The Book!" he screamed, cocking back the hammer. "I will not allow you to make a fool of me again."

Harte's face went serious. "You're going to have to be patient, Jack. If you shoot me now, you'll never get what you came here for. So if you'd just lower that thing and—"

It felt like it all happened at once. She was on the bridge, and she was also standing in the hallway of Schwab's mansion. She was watching Harte about to be shot, and she was seeing Logan bleeding on the floor. Two moments, two places in time, but the same gunman. The same deadly weapon set to stop a beating heart.

She grabbed Harte and pulled time slow at the same moment that the gun went off, at the same moment that the bullet began traveling in its deadly path. And when she looked up, the bullet inched past them, so close they could feel its heat.

"I thought you hadn't missed me?" Harte said, close to her ear.

She realized that she was holding on to him maybe more tightly than she needed to. "Where's the Book?" she asked, not letting go as she backed away from him and the smell of oranges and Ivory soap.

"It's in my cloak." He indicated that she already held the cloak in her arms. "Along with your cuff."

"My cuff—" Her chest went tight.

"The one you showed me. The one you were after."

Around them, the world was silent. "And the rest?" she asked.

"Gone," he said, pushing a piece of hair out of her eye. "I sent them out of the city last night. By now they're on separate trains, heading to all the places I'll never go."

Her fingers tightened on the silky material of the cloak in her hands. "Why would you do that?"

"The Order can't have them, not with what Jack has planned. And I couldn't let Nibs get them either."

"Nibs?" He wasn't making any sense.

"He planned all of this from the beginning—Leena's death, Dolph going after the Book, even you—" He pressed his lips together. "He's the one who killed Dolph."

"No." She shook her head. "Dolph was shot the night of the heist. Nibs was with us."

"Was he?" Harte asked flatly. "Do you know for sure he was waiting outside Khafre Hall that entire time?"

"I can't believe he would . . . ," she started to say, but her words fell silent.

But it would explain so much about how tense the last couple of days had been at the Strega, about why Nibs had insisted on the gun against her back. "You were in the hall with us," she argued. "You can't know—"

"I know what he intended to do," Harte continued, his voice urgent. But he wouldn't look directly at her. "For all his ability to see how things will turn out, he wasn't expecting me to punch him that night you got taken to the Tombs."

She glanced back at Nibs, his face frozen in a sort of strangled fury, and she saw him suddenly in a different light. She'd been a fool not to see it all along.

"He's been pulling Dolph's strings the whole time. Dolph had no idea."

Esta shook her head again, wanting to deny everything he was telling her. It had to be more of his lies. "You should have warned Dolph."

"I couldn't," Harte said, not meeting her eyes. "Nibs had my mother, and I've already wronged her enough in my life. I couldn't do anything more to her. I thought I could work around Nibs. I thought I could get you out too, but things didn't go quite as I planned that night."

"You should have told me."

"I couldn't chance him finding out that you knew. The only way I could figure to get around him was to keep you working blind. There was too much at stake."

"You mean like Dolph's life?" she argued.

"I never meant for Dolph to die, but this was bigger than Dolph's life, Esta. He understood that. Nibs *cannot* get the Book. Do you understand me? He doesn't want to free the Mageus from the city. He wants to rule them. To use them—us—against the Sundren." His jaw clenched. "The Book's dangerous, Esta. It's not what you think—it's not what *any* of us thought. In the wrong hands, it would give someone devastating power. If Nibs were the one to control it, he'd be able to make himself more powerful than any Mageus who's ever lived. I can't imagine the devastation that would follow. No one would be safe."

"I can't . . ." The enormity of what he was saying felt unbelievable. "Why now? Why tell me all of this when it's too late to do anything?"

"Because it's not too late for you," he said. "I'm giving you a way out."

He took her hand and placed something heavy and smooth into her palm. *The cuff with her stone.* Immediately, she felt the warmth of it. The sureness of its power calling to her.

"Do what you need to do, but either way, get yourself out and take the Book with you. You can't let either Nibs or Jack get ahold of it. *Everything* depends upon that. Do you understand? Take it where they can't follow."

"But I—"

"Do you understand?" he demanded again.

"What about you?" she asked, still looking for the angle, the indication that this was all part of a larger game for him.

"I'm dead either way. The Book—it's not a normal book. It's like some sort of living thing." He grimaced, and then he met her eyes. The gray irises that had become so familiar to her were different now. She thought she could see something more than her own reflection in them, colors that she didn't have names for flashing in their depths. "When I touched it, I read it more easily than I can read a person. I've seen what's in there, and it's a part of me now. Even if you take the Book to where they can't reach it, the Order won't ever stop hunting me." He shook his head. "I can't risk that. If they see me jump and see me die, they won't have any reason to hunt you . . . or anyone else. You want to protect the people Dolph was protecting? This is the only way." He gave her a heartbreaking smile. "Whatever happens, the great Harte Darrigan won't soon be forgotten after what I do here today."

Her heart ached. *Yes, you will,* she knew. If he jumped from that bridge, no one would remember him in a week or a month, and definitely not over the years.

"So we bring down the Brink before that happens," she told him. "We free everyone right now and take the Order's power away from them." It wasn't the job she'd been sent to do, but it was what Professor Lachlan intended anyway, she reasoned.

"You don't understand. *None* of us do. The Brink isn't just a prison, Esta. It was built to *protect* magic. If it comes down, it won't free Mageus. Think about Tilly—when Jack's machine blew up, it took her life with it. Destroying the Brink would do the same thing. It would destroy any magic that it's taken, and when it does that, it would break everything connected to that magic. You, me, every Mageus who exists is connected to the old magic. When part of that dies, so will ours. And without our magic . . ." He couldn't finish.

She didn't have words to respond to him. It was too ridiculous and too big a lie to be believed. The Brink was what *killed* them, not what protected them.

"You can't expect me to believe that."

"I'm here, aren't I?" He swallowed hard, his mouth tight. "If the Book had offered me a way out of the city, don't you think I'd be gone? Do you really think I'd be here, in the middle of this circus otherwise? I *could* have used the Book to get through the Brink, but the magic in the Book is too powerful. The Brink itself might not have held. Jack told me how they made the Brink—connecting the elements through Aether. The Order has been trying to find a way to make it larger and more powerful, but Jack told me the connections through the Aether are too unstable. The Book might have been able to get me through, but that much magic could be enough to overload the circuit. And if that happens, it would be worse than any electrical outage."

"Because it would make magic go dark," she said, slowly putting the pieces together.

"Exactly. If I could have gotten out, I would have. I would have even taken you with me. But I can't risk destroying the circuit through the Aether. I'm still here because there's no way out without destroying the entire Brink, and to destroy it would be to threaten all magic. *All* Mageus. There's no way out for me, so I'm trusting you to help me finish this."

She stared at him, searching for the crack in the mask that would expose the lie in what he was telling her. But she did believe one thing—if there was a way out of the city, if there was a way through the Brink, Harte Darrigan *would* have taken it already.

But he hadn't.

Even now he was giving the Book to her and giving up the one thing he'd wanted from the beginning. If that wasn't enough to convince her, the fear in his stormy eyes was.

"Ready?" he asked.

"No," she said. There were a million other questions she needed to ask. There had to be another way. "I can't—"

He placed his fingers against her lips to stop her. "Let's finish this." He tore himself away from her grasp, and as he slipped away from her, she let go of time and the world began again.

When Harte didn't fall, Jack stood, too shocked to move, which gave the crowd time to wrestle the gun from his grasp. It took only a few moments more before he was arrested and dragged away, screaming and shouting all the while.

Once it was calm, Harte took his time removing his shirt. The muscles of his arms broadcast exactly how tense he was as he made a show of stripping for the public. The cool air raised gooseflesh on his bare shoulders, but his eyes were steady, calm.

"A kiss for luck, my dear?" he asked, his gray eyes determined.

When the crowd erupted with enthusiastic hoots, she couldn't deny him. She allowed him to put his mouth over hers, but this was not the kiss she'd wanted for herself that day in Harte's apartment. His lips were cool, as though he'd already been claimed by the water below, and there was nothing but a resigned determination in the quick brush of skin against skin, mouth against mouth.

She wasn't sure she trusted him, but to know he was about to die?

I can take him back with me, she thought in a sudden rush. To hell with everyone who might see them disappear.

Too soon, he pulled away from her, and the time for decisions had passed.

With a flourish, Harte mounted the railing. His eyes scanned the crowd, looked over them to the city beyond, and she thought she saw regret flash across his expression.

Nibs exploded from the crowd. "Stop him!"

Esta saw some of Dolph's boys move toward the railing where Harte stood, but before they could come any closer, police stormed the bridge. The crowd descended into confusion, surging in all directions to get away from the raised billy sticks and angry whistles of the police. In the confusion, she was pushed back from the railing, and from Harte.

There was no way to reach him. No way to turn him from what he meant to do. She'd saved the Book, but she couldn't save him.

Harte's eyes met hers. *Go!* he mouthed, and the air seemed to shimmer around him, the sun throwing up a glare as he let go of the cabled railing, and then he was gone.

Her heart seized. *Too late.*

She pushed through the crowd to the railing, where he'd disappeared. Below, there was no sign of him. She watched, waiting for him to surface or for some indication that he'd made it, but even as the crowd behind her was a riot of anger and confusion, the water was silent, holding its secrets as absolutely as a grave.

Esta didn't see Nibs coming for her through the crowd. She was too busy trying to breathe through the shock of what had just happened. But as she clung to Harte's cloak, she felt the hard outline of the Book. Her cuff was warm in her hand.

He hadn't betrayed her in the end. He'd given her exactly what she needed.

But before she could fully comprehend that he was well and truly gone, she felt someone grab her arm.

"Did he give it to you?" Nibs demanded, his pale face close to hers. "I know he told you where it is."

"What?" She tried to shake him off, but his hands gripped her arm painfully.

"Tell me," he said, pulling a snub-nosed pistol from his jacket and placing it under her chin. "Tell me or you can join him."

She couldn't breathe. She couldn't make sense of what was happening.

"Tell me what he did with the Book!" Nibsy said, his breath hot and sour on her face as the cool barrel of the gun pressed against her throat.

"I—" Esta knew in that moment that Harte had been right. She couldn't give it to him. She knew then that whatever happened, Nibs would never be worthy of the power it held. Her mind raced for some lie as she shifted the cloak against herself so he wouldn't feel the Book within its folds.

He clicked the hammer of the gun back, but before he could pull the trigger, his body went rigid and he gasped in pain. The gun fell from his hand, and he let go of his grip on Esta as he grabbed his leg.

Esta backed away from him and looked up to find Viola standing a few feet off, her face creased into a serious frown as she watched Nibs pull the silver knife from his thigh. She gave Esta a solemn nod, and then she was gone, melting into the crowd as though she'd never been there.

Only the feel of the cuff in her hand, warm and urgent and compelling, brought Esta to her senses. She gave in to the pull of Ishtar's Key, allowed the warmth of its energy to expand her until she could see the layers of time and history in that place—all the seconds to come that wouldn't have Harte Darrigan in them.

Nibs looked up at her, hate and anger twisting his features. He raised the gun, but it was too late. She'd found the layer of time she wanted, and she was gone.

A STARLESS SKY

Esta barely had time to dodge the semitruck as it sped past her. Gasping, she clung to the side of the roadway. The gusting air from the passing traffic lifted the hair around her face and whipped her skirts around her legs. It was night, but the glow of the city—*her* city— shattered the darkness. The gentle hum of automobiles replaced the clattering racket of cobbled streets and wooden wheels, and above her, she couldn't make out the stars.

Everything felt too fast. After weeks in a city that moved at the speed of a plodding horse or a rumbling elevated train, the flurry of cars and people felt like too much.

Harte's cloak was still in her arms, the Book still heavy within its folds. And if she just ignored the fact that it smelled like him, that combination of Ivory soap and the faint scent of oranges, she'd be fine.

She had to be fine. She still had work left to do.

She kept her head down and made the long walk back to Midtown, to the parking lot she'd left from, beneath the crown of the Empire State Building. For her, weeks had passed, but for this city, everything felt exactly the same. The summer night was warmer than the day in late March she'd left behind, and by the time she reached her destination, she was sweating from the heavy skirts and the pace she'd set.

As she rounded the corner, she stopped short and then retreated. The street where Dakari's car had once been was now blocked off, and a small crowd had formed. Shards of red from the lights of police cars bounced off the darkened windows of the surrounding buildings. From her vantage point, she couldn't see the street where Dakari had fallen, and she couldn't tell if he was still there.

Esta had tried to return to a few minutes after she originally left, just as Professor Lachlan had taught her. But after the walk from the bridge, she was too late. If they had Dakari . . . If he were injured or worse . . .

She had to fix this. She had to go back and save him.

Forcing herself to ignore the sounds of the sirens and the lights flashing around her, Esta focused on finding the layers of time. The stone in the cuff on her arm grew warm, but she ignored its heat and sifted through the moments, peeling back the minutes and seconds until she thought she was close to the instant the gunfire had erupted. She could almost see it—the lights from the police cars began to dim, their sirens fading into the quiet of the night before her original departure.

But just as she found that moment, the same sense of foreboding came over her that had made her body feel as if it were burning all those weeks ago, the night she left. The stone felt hot, like a branded warning against her skin. Just as it had before.

Something is wrong.

She took a deep breath, fighting against her own panic, struggling to make herself slip back to the seconds before Dakari was attacked, but this time, her instincts worked against her. With a gasping sob, she lost her hold on time, and the present—with all its light and noise—came flooding back. She bent over to steady herself, her heart pounding and her skin cold despite the warmth of the summer night. Despite the heat of the stone against her skin.

"No," she whispered, as though hearing her own voice would help her overcome her fear. But her voice sounded scared, shaken. It was too much of a coincidence for her to feel this way twice, but whether it had something to do with this particular moment, with the stone, or with something else, she didn't know. What she did know was that Dakari's life depended on her. She needed to try again, for Dakari's sake, but before she could, a hand grasped her by the shoulder and pulled her back as another hand covered the yelp of surprise that she would have otherwise let out.

"Shhhhh," a familiar voice said, close to her ear. "I'm going to let you go, but you need to keep quiet."

She turned to find Dakari standing behind her, but she couldn't do much more than open and close her mouth numbly, searching for the words that wouldn't come. "How did you . . ." she said finally, but she trailed off. She couldn't make sense of what she was seeing even as she felt the relief of having him there, whole and alive, before her.

He tore open his shirt, showing her the marred bulletproof vest beneath. "I'm always prepared, E." He rubbed at his chest, grimacing. "Though those gunshots are going to leave a bruise," he said.

Esta noticed the blood on his pants. "Dakari, your leg."

"I know, but I had to wait for you to get back. Now that you are, we should get out of here." In the distance she could already hear the scream of another siren bouncing off the buildings. "Come on," he said, lifting himself from the pavement. "You drive."

She caught the keys he tossed her.

"Maybe you could do that time thing you do? Get me back faster?" he asked.

"Right," she said, still so relieved to see him that she could hardly breathe. *He's not gone,* she thought as she pulled the seconds slow. "I thought you were dead." She helped him to the car, the city silent around them.

"Nah. I'm damn hard to kill." He patted his bulletproof vest again, wincing as he slid into the backseat with his injured leg propped in front of him.

"Who were those guys?" she asked as she took the driver's seat and glanced back in the rearview mirror.

A shadow crossed his expression. "Who knows?" he told her, but he didn't quite meet her eyes as he said it. "How long were you away this time?" he asked, tending to his leg as she started the car and began navigating through the strange tableau of a city gone nearly still.

"Weeks," she said, suddenly overwhelmed by the knowledge that they were all dead. Whatever had happened on that bridge, it was more than a hundred years later. Jianyu, Viola, the rest of the crew at the Strega, they'd all be dust in the grave by now. And she would never have the chance to say good-bye.

"Did you get it?" he asked, watching her with careful eyes in the rear-view mirror.

She nodded, and the relief that flashed across his face was so stark, it surprised her. Had he thought she wouldn't?

"The Professor'll be pleased."

"Maybe," she told him.

"What do you mean?" he asked, his brows drawn together in concern.

"I don't think we can destroy the Brink," she said, remembering everything Harte had told her. "Even if we could . . . I don't know if we *should*."

Dakari's expression was stern. "You don't mean that."

"I don't know anymore. I need to talk with Professor Lachlan. He'll know what to do."

Dakari didn't speak for a long moment. "You're right, E. You've been through a lot. Maybe you're not thinking straight. Let's just get back and we'll work it all out then." He wouldn't say anything else, but he kept eyeing her uneasily as she drove the final blocks to Orchard Street.

The exterior of the building on Orchard Street didn't look any different than it had when she left weeks ago, but then, why would it? For the people in her own time, she'd been gone only a few minutes. She looked up at the dark brick, seeing it through new eyes. It was an old tenement, and in the moonlight, with the lights out all around and the neighborhood quiet, it could have been a hundred years in the past. She could almost imagine walking the four blocks to Elizabeth Street and letting herself in through the Strega's back door. For a moment she imagined that the people she'd met there and come to admire weren't all dead and gone.

Dakari opened the front door and let them into the empty foyer. To Esta's relief, the foyer looked like it had before her mistakes at the Schwab mansion. It was, she hoped, a good sign—a sign that maybe she'd managed to fix her mistakes.

But it didn't feel like home anymore.

There was a clean, almost sterile quality to the place that felt wrong to her now. A building like this one should be teeming with life. There should be the sounds of children in the halls and the smells of five different apartments cooking dinner. But there had never been the sound of children in those hallways while she lived in them.

The door of 1A opened to reveal the true entrance of the building. Logan was waiting on the other side.

"You're up," Esta said, surprised to see him whole and healthy. "You're feeling okay?"

He frowned. "Why wouldn't I be?"

"You were shot," she told him, confused.

He glanced at Dakari. "I'm not sure what you're talking about."

Her stomach sank. "You were shot on the Schwab job. When I left, you weren't even conscious yet. . . ." Her words trailed off. "You don't remember being shot by the blond—by Jack?"

"There wasn't any blond," Logan said, looking at her as though she'd lost her mind. "There was you trying to save some serving girl and almost getting thrown out, but I don't remember any blond guy. And I definitely would have remembered being shot."

"Well, I'm glad to see you're okay."

He gave her another doubtful look. "The Professor's upstairs. He's waiting."

Dakari followed her into the elevator and pushed the button for the top floor.

"There really was a blond," she told him, needing him to believe her.

"Logan almost died. I brought him back. Something changed. Somehow things are different."

"Am I different?"

She glanced up at him. "No. I don't think so. You're still here."

He seemed surprised at that. "Where else would I be?"

"Nowhere," she said. "What about Mari?"

"She's probably in her workshop. What about her?"

She didn't have time to explain about Mari. The elevator was already coming to a stop, and Dakari was pulling back the gate and opening the door for her to step through.

I must have done something right. But the victory felt hollow when she thought of all the mistakes she'd made. When she thought of Harte Darrigan standing on the edge of that railing and willing her to go.

The Professor's library seemed mostly the same, but the piles were neater and there was something different in the way chairs and tables were organized. At the other end of the room, Professor Lachlan sat, peering through a large magnifying glass at the pages of an open book. He didn't look up, even though he must have heard the elevator arrive, but finished the passage he was reading and made a note in a notebook.

When he finally looked up, his eyes narrowed. "Do you have it?"

She held up the cloak. "Right here," she said.

"Good." He held out his hand. "Give it to me."

Esta hesitated. He seemed different. More distant, more demanding.

He's always been demanding, she reminded herself. Still, something felt wrong. For a moment she thought about trying to remove the Book from the inner pocket of the cloak herself, so that she didn't have to hand over both. It seemed wrong, somehow, to give this piece of Harte to anyone else, since it was all that was left of him.

"Esta?" Professor Lachlan asked, his jaw tense. "Give me the Book."

Dakari stepped up behind her. "Come on, E. Give the Professor the Book," he said softly, but there was a thread of steel in his voice he'd never used on her before.

Confused by their mood, she handed the cloak over without any further argument.

It took the Professor a moment to find the secret pocket, but rather than bothering with figuring out how to access it, he took out a small knife. There was nothing she could do but watch as he tore open the material and pulled out the Book.

It was smaller than she'd expected from the weight of the cloak. "That's it?" she asked, looking at the small, dark volume.

But she knew it was. On the cover was the symbol she recognized from the painting in Dolph's apartment and the book he'd shown her. She had no doubt that this small, unremarkable tome was the Ars Arcana, the Book that so many people had wanted. That so many people had died for.

Professor Lachlan's eyes were bright, eager. He ignored her disappointment as he ran his fingers over the symbol on the cover. "After all this time."

"Esta was telling me she doesn't think we should destroy the Brink," Dakari said.

"That's not what I said. And I was going to tell him myself." Esta glanced up at Dakari's flinty expression, and the feeling of unease she'd had since she walked into the building grew.

"What, *exactly*, were you going to tell me?" Professor Lachlan asked.

"It's about destroying the Brink. I don't think we can, not even with the Book," she said, swaying a little on her feet. She wanted nothing more than to collapse into the ancient sofa and tell him everything, but she had the sense that this was too important to relax.

"And what makes you think that?"

"Harte . . . I mean the Magician told me when he gave me the Book. He said destroying the Brink could destroy magic."

The Professor didn't look pleased. "And you believed him?"

"I don't know," she said honestly. "But I think we should be careful with that, and with the Brink. I think we should make sure we understand what we're doing."

"It's not your job to think about these things."

"I know. It's just . . . I thought you should know before you do anything."

The second hand on a clock ticked, the only sound in the silent library. "He got to you."

"No, it's not that," she told him, but she wasn't sure if she spoke the truth.

"He turned you," Professor Lachlan said, his voice flat and filled with disgust.

"*No.* I brought you the Book. I did my job."

Another long silence strangled the room. "Of course you did," he said, but the Professor didn't sound pleased. "I'm sure you're simply tired," he told her. "Overwrought. After all, I imagine you've been through quite an ordeal. Perhaps you should return to your room and rest."

"Maybe," she said. "It's been a long day." She gave a weak laugh. "It's been a long month."

"We can talk more about this tomorrow," Professor Lachlan told her, but his attention was already on the Book in his hands.

Esta turned back toward the elevator. She was halfway across the room when something caught her eye—a flash of silver in a shadowbox frame she didn't remember seeing there before. For a moment she looked at the art, not understanding what she was seeing, but then, all at once, she understood. "Those were Viola's," she told Professor Lachlan. Her stomach twisted at the sight of the slim stiletto blades crossed and mounted in the frame. There was no mistaking the deep *V*s cut into the exposed tangs of each. "How did you get them?"

"Excuse me?" Professor Lachlan asked.

She went over to the wall, to look closer at the knives. "How could you possibly have these?"

Professor Lachlan glanced at her. "I've had them for ages," he said. "Or don't you remember?" He gave Dakari a nod. "Perhaps it would be best if you escort her to her room?"

"I'm fine," Esta started to say, but Dakari was already at her side again.

"I'm sorry," he told her, his soft, dark eyes pained.

"What?" she asked, confused by his words. Before she understood what was happening, his arm snaked out to cage her against him and she felt the sharp bite of something in her biceps. "Dakari?"

She looked down at the place where the syringe was sticking into her upper arm, but her words already felt thick and the edge of her vision was already going black.

AN OLD FRIEND

Esta came to slowly, her head throbbing as she opened her eyes to find herself on the floor in a windowless room. She was still wearing a corset and long skirts, her clothing from the past, so at first she thought it had all been a bad dream. That she was still back in her narrow room above the Strega, but she could hear a siren in the distance, a wailing reminder that she was no longer with Dolph and the rest. She was home, but the ache in her arm where Dakari had jabbed her with the needle and the foggy numbness that filled her head wasn't the welcome she'd expected. Everything felt upside down.

She wasn't sure where she was, or if she was even still in Professor Lachlan's building. Her head was spinning as she pulled herself up and felt around the walls of the room, trying to find the door. She made it around the three corners of the small space before she found two seams where a door should have been, but there was no handle and no lock, only a smooth plate of metal over where the locking mechanism should be.

No matter how much she searched, she couldn't find any place to pick a lock or jimmy a hinge. It was a prison built for a thief.

It was a prison he'd built for her.

It could have been minutes or hours that she sat there in the darkness before she finally heard voices coming from the other side of the wall. She scuttled back and tried to focus enough to pull the seconds slow. But time slipped away from her—she couldn't find the spaces. She felt like she had in the basement of the Haymarket, unable to call on her affinity and at the mercy of whoever was coming for her.

The wall split open, and she blinked, shielding her eyes from the light of the hall. "Come on, E."

"Dakari? Is that you?" She wanted it to be him, but she also didn't know if she could trust him anymore.

A moment later he had hoisted her up onto still-shaky legs and was leading her out of the room.

"What's going on?" she asked him, and when he didn't answer, she tried to pull away. "Where are we going?"

He kept a tight hold on her, though, refusing to answer her questions as he half led, half dragged her down the hall toward the elevator.

"Why are you acting like this, Dakari? It's *me*. You know me." If she only had his knife, maybe she could have gotten through to him. But the knife was lost to the past, and if things didn't improve, she didn't know what her future held in store. "*Please*," she tried again.

He wouldn't look at her as pushed her gently into the elevator, and he kept hold of her the entire time the cage made its slow, rattling climb to the top. "Just answer his questions and do what he asks. Prove yourself to him, and it'll be fine. Everything can go back to how it should be."

But she doubted anything could ever go back to the way it had been before. Too much had changed.

When the elevator stopped at the library, Dakari led her forward. "Come on."

It was night, but she had no idea how long she'd been out of it with the drug they'd given her and no idea how much time had passed in the windowless prison they'd kept her in. The lights in the library were off, except for the small desk lamp that illuminated the Professor's face as he bent, serious and focused, over the Ars Arcana. Near him on the table were the five artifacts laid out in a straight line.

When he heard them approaching, he glanced up. "Are you feeling better?"

"You drugged me and locked me in a doorless room," she said, well aware she was pushing him. "What did I do to deserve that? I brought you the Book."

"You were also talking nonsense about the Brink being indestructible."

"I was only trying to warn you."

"Yes, and where did you get the information?"

"From Harte," she said, knowing how damning that sounded.

"Of course you did. Because you came to trust him, didn't you? It was exactly what I was afraid of happening. It's exactly why I gave you some incentive to return."

"An incentive?"

Professor Lachlan didn't so much as blink. "You're impulsive, but you're also predictable. I knew that if you believed Dakari's life was in danger, you'd be sure to return, no matter how you might have come to feel about those in the past."

She felt numb from more than the drug they'd given her now as the image of Dakari's body jerking from the impact of the bullets rose in her mind. He'd been wearing a vest, but those bullets hadn't been blanks. They'd torn through his legs. "You could have killed him!"

"His life was never in danger," the Professor said, dismissing her.

Esta glanced up at Dakari, but her old friend's expression was unreadable, his features closed off and distant. If he was upset or surprised by this news, his face didn't show it.

"You risked Dakari's life because you didn't trust me?" she pressed.

"I wouldn't have trusted anyone that much, but especially not you, impulsive girl that you are. So, no. I didn't trust that you wouldn't be swayed by Dolph Saunders or even the Magician. I couldn't trust that you wouldn't take one look into Harte Darrigan's pretty gray eyes, listen to his poor-little-boy-lost sob story, and decide to give him a chance. I gave myself some insurance. I gave you an incentive to return." He stared at her, his nostrils flaring from the exertion of his tirade.

With those words, something inside her clicked, and apprehension wrapped around her. "How did you know he had gray eyes?"

"What?" Professor Lachlan's face bunched in irritation.

"Harte Darrigan. You couldn't know what color his eyes were. Pictures wouldn't have shown you that."

His expression went slack, as though he realized the slip, but then a smile curved softly at his lips. "You always have been too observant for your own good."

Unease slinked through her. "You always told me that it made me a good thief."

"It did. But it also makes you a problem." Professor Lachlan spoke to Dakari. "If you'd secure her, I'll take it from here."

She knew it was coming, but she could still hardly believe what was happening when Dakari wrestled her into a chair and secured her arms and legs with rope.

"Just tell him the truth, E. If you're still with us, everything's gonna be okay."

"Dakari?" she pleaded, but it fell on deaf ears. He was already heading toward the elevator.

"You know, you were never supposed to come back here. None of this had to happen if you'd have just done what you should have. If you'd only given me the Book that day on the bridge—"

Esta turned back to meet Professor Lachlan's gaze. "How could I have given *you* the Book? That was a hundred years ago."

Professor Lachlan didn't speak at first, but there was something in his expression that made Esta's skin crawl. "Maybe you're not so very observant, after all. You don't recognize me, do you?" He frowned. "Have I really changed so much?"

"You look exactly the same as the last time I saw you," she said, confused by his question.

"A few weeks, a lifetime. Strange how similar two spans of time can be. I was right about you then. I've been right about you all along."

She saw then what maybe she should have seen before. "No . . ." He'd changed over the years, but beneath the age spots and wrinkles, beneath the tuft of white, thinning hair and the frailness, she thought she could see the boy he'd been. "Nibs?" she said, her voice barely working.

"I always hated that name," he told her.

"It can't be. You *can't* be him. That's impossible."

"It's *improbable*, not impossible. What's a century when you can find healers like Dakari to keep you whole?" Professor Lachlan gave Esta a chastising look. "What's a century when you're waiting for the key to your plans? I'm a patient man, Esta. You must know that much by now."

"You killed Dolph," she said. "He trusted you, and you killed him." She shook her head. "I don't understand—Dolph wanted to destroy the Brink. He wanted to bring down the Order. You were on the *same side*. There wasn't any reason to kill him."

Professor Lachlan—Nibs—sneered. "Dolph had some grand plan to destroy the Brink and free the Mageus in the city. But what would that have done? Started a war with the Sundren, a war we were too weak to win . . . at least with the Book in *his* hands."

"They were better hands than yours."

"He thought we needed the Book to gain our freedom, as though the Book of Mysteries, the most ancient and hallowed record of magic, was some simple grimoire he could use to break a wicked spell," Professor Lachlan scoffed. "He always was shaky on his Latin tenses. He misunderstood the message Leena sent him before the Order took her. I know, because she explained it to me when she gave me the note. . . . Not that I bothered to correct him. As long as he wanted to keep pursuing the Book, it worked for me, but I knew all along that it wasn't that the Book could free us, but that we could free *the Book* . . . And now I plan to do just that."

"But the Brink—"

Professor Lachlan waved off her protest. "I never cared about destroying the Brink. It never stopped me from doing the things I wanted to do. It can stay up for all I care. It's a mere nuisance compared to what the Ars Arcana contains," he told her, tapping the Book. "This isn't just a record of the most important magical developments throughout history. It is an object infused with the very *source* of magic. Whoever can unlock it controls it. And whoever controls it will have the whole world in their hands."

Esta remembered then what Harte had told her on the bridge—that no one had really understood the Ars Arcana's true nature. He'd been wrong. Nibs had known. Nibs had *always* known, and he'd manipulated them all.

"And you think you should have that power?" she asked, urging him on as she tried to think of some way out of the mess she'd walked right into.

"Why not me? The Order could barely touch the power these pages contain. They knew what the Book was capable of, which is why they kept it under lock and key. But they were never brave enough to actually use it. They'd been warned by the last person brave enough to attempt unlocking the Book's secrets and wielding its power after it nearly drove him mad."

"One of the Order?" she asked, realizing that she could just begin to feel the drug they gave her wearing off. She didn't know how long it would take before she could be free of it, but she might be able to wait it out. She needed to keep him distracted, to keep him talking. A little longer, and she could try to escape.

"One of their earliest founders," Professor Lachlan told her. "Most don't realize Isaac Newton started his career as an alchemist. Before he sat under any tree, he searched for the philosopher's stone—for a way to isolate quintessence. I've had a long time to learn about the Ars Arcana, a long time to learn about Newton's secrets. He got as far as creating the five artifacts by imbuing ancient objects from the five mystical dynasties with the power of Mageus whose affinities happened to align with the elements. But he stopped before he ever managed to unite them and use them to control the power of the Book. Historians believe that he had a nervous breakdown in 1693, but that wasn't what happened at all. It was the Book, and his breakdown was the result of attempting to control its power. After he recovered, he gave up alchemy and entrusted the Book to the Order for safekeeping."

"You always told me that elemental magic wasn't real magic," she argued, still reeling. "Or was that a lie, too?"

"It's not. Elemental magic *isn't* real magic. It requires breaking up the pieces of creation, dividing them and weakening them in order to control them. Real magic is about controlling the whole of creation, the spaces between the elements that make up the very fabric of existence. Mageus don't need the elements, but we can use them. We've always been able to use them. With the right rituals, the elements can be quite useful to augment natural power. It's what made the Order what it is. It's what made you what you are," he told her, lifting the cuff and examining it in the light of the desk lamp.

"The Order doesn't have real magic," she argued. She was feeling stronger now, but she had to keep him talking until she figured out how to escape. So she pressed on, taunting him with her disbelief. "They aren't Mageus. All the power they have is stolen."

He placed the cuff back onto the table before he looked at her. "That may be true now, but it wasn't always. The Order of the Ortus Aurea began as a front. Like so many of those so-called occult societies, it was formed so the richest, most influential Mageus could hide in plain sight. The Order is one of the oldest, though, and they were able to maintain their power even as the Disenchantment destroyed magic."

That news contradicted everything she'd ever been taught, everything she'd ever believed. "You're telling me that the members of the Order were once Mageus?"

"Of course they were. There's always been magic in the world, and at one time most people could put their finger on it, until they allowed themselves to forget. The Disenchantment helped with that. When the climate on the Continent grew too dangerous, the Mageus who could leave, did. They brought their little society to the New World, because they thought they could start fresh and they believed the new land was one where magic could take root. It didn't work, of course. Away from their homelands, after a few generations, their power had faded. So they used the secrets in these pages to create the Brink as a way to protect their magic.

"But they couldn't control it. What began as a way to build their power became a trap, and their magic continued to fade. A few generations more and the only magic they had left was the power they could steal through their experiments. The Brink was never intended as a weapon, but it became one well enough.

"By the time my family arrived in Manhattan, back in 1888, the Order had forgotten what they once were, what they'd come from. They feared the power that was coming to their shores, so they tried to eliminate it. They targeted the weak, the poor. Those who had no voice, no power to fight back. They killed my father because he tried to speak out, and then they hunted down my mother and brothers and sisters. I only got away because I was off working. An eleven-year-old, working at a factory just to put bread on the table.

"They had no idea what fear was, but they will. Newton knew that if anyone could finish what he started and control the Book's power, they'd be as powerful as a god, the last magician the world would ever know. Now that I have the Book and the stones, I can unlock the power of the Ars Arcana. I've been waiting a lifetime—more, really—for this moment."

"So do it already," she challenged. "You're standing here monologuing like some cartoon villain. If you have all the pieces, what are you waiting for?"

He smiled. A slow, creeping curve of his narrow lips. "I've been waiting for *you*, Esta."

"I won't help you."

"Oh, I think you will."

When he lifted himself from the chair and worked his way around the table to where she sat, she realized then that he didn't have his usual crutch. Instead, his hand rested on a cane topped with a silver Medusa head.

"That was Dolph's," she said through clenched teeth as anger flashed through her.

"Yes, it was. You might say he bequeathed it to me."

"More like you stole it."

"Mere semantics. All that matters now is that I've nearly won. Dolph Saunders didn't get the Book. Because of your work, Harte Darrigan didn't either."

Disgust rose in her throat. "I would *never* help you."

Professor Lachlan tipped his head to the side, his expression calm. "What makes you think you'll have any choice?"

THE IMPOSSIBLE CHOICE

Esta pulled against the ropes, desperate to loosen them enough to free herself. She wanted nothing more than to destroy the man in front of her. But the ropes holding her were too tight. They barely moved.

Professor Lachlan straightened. "You're only going to wear yourself out, and I'm nowhere near done with you."

"Funny, I'm more than finished with you," she spat.

He laughed as he made his way to the table that held the artifacts, scooping them up and bringing them to where she was still tied to the chair. "You certainly inherited your mother's fire, didn't you?"

Her voice sounded like gravel when she finally found it: "You knew my mother?"

Professor Lachlan took a moment to look her over, his cloudy eyes studying her. "Dressed like that, you look a bit like her, you know. Not much, but a little. Same eyes. Lighter hair." He placed the crown that held the Dragon's Eye on her head, so the cool metal lay snug against her forehead. "You're certainly impulsive like she was. Stubborn, too."

"You told me you found me in a park." Her own voice sounded very far away, and all around her, the room felt like a tunnel.

"I lied," he said, fastening the collar that held the Djinni's Star around her neck.

"Or maybe you're lying now."

"Am I?" He slid the ring with the clear agate called Delphi's Tear onto her left middle finger.

She could feel the warmth of the stones, but they didn't call to her, not like Ishtar's Key did. Professor Lachlan was still holding the cuff, and if he would just put it on her arm—if she could just fight past the drug in her system—maybe she could get away.

"You have to be lying." Because if he wasn't, then everything that Esta had ever believed about herself was also a lie.

"I'm surprised you didn't put it all together for yourself. You might be impulsive, maybe a bit overemotional, but I've never thought of you as stupid." He huffed out an amused laugh. "You didn't, though, did you?"

He studied her for a moment before he continued. "Actually, now that I look at you, you definitely have more of your father in you. I wonder why someone didn't notice the resemblance. Not that they would ever have put that together—not when everyone thought Dolph and Leena's child died at birth."

"Dolph?" she whispered.

"And Leena . . . who wasn't *quite* his wife." Professor Lachlan gave her a less-than-friendly pat on the cheek, but she didn't even feel the sting of his hand against her skin.

No.

Dolph Saunders couldn't be her father. She'd sat across from him countless times, had talked with him and argued with him. She would have known. When he bought her the knish from Schimmel's and told her what he wanted to do, wouldn't she have realized? When they brought his body in, pale and lifeless, and she had mourned with the others, wouldn't she have felt something—*anything*—that would have made her recognize who he was to her?

"That's not possible," she said through the tightness in her throat. "Dolph Saunders died more than a hundred years ago."

Professor Lachlan gave her a pitying look. "You *are* capable of traveling through time, aren't you?" He held up Ishtar's Key. "With the right equipment, that is."

"I would have remembered—"

"You were far too young to remember anything. You couldn't have been more than three when everything went wrong. After Darrigan took the Book and destroyed half of Khafre Hall, Tammany's patrols and the Order's influence made life a living hell in the Bowery—you know that now for yourself."

"No," she whispered, as though uttering that single syllable could change the truth that was staring her in the face. "I was there. He didn't have a child."

"He didn't *know* he had a child. Leena kept it from him after he betrayed her. He was so desperate back then to shore up his power that he didn't tell her he was dabbling in ritual magic. She didn't find out until it was too late that he'd taken some of her power and used it to turn his marks into weapons. The shock of it sent her into labor too early, and when you were born, she told everyone you'd died."

"How could she?"

"In those days, it was fairly easy. Fathers weren't all that involved. I think the real question you mean to ask is *why*." He shrugged. "Because it was clear from the beginning that you were something special, something rare and powerful, and she didn't trust that Dolph wouldn't use you as well."

"He never knew?" she asked, horrified that anyone could do such a thing.

"He never even saw you. She was desperate to protect you, and you should know well enough that desperate people are capable of terrible things. But they also make easy marks."

"She trusted you," Esta realized. It was the only way he could know.

Professor Lachlan nodded. "She needed an ally, and she believed in me. I don't think she ever intended to hide you for long, but lies have a tendency to take on lives of their own. We both knew your affinity was something different. Maybe once there had been others who could do what you can do, but they were hunted and eliminated during the Disenchantment. You were rare, even in 1902. An unexpected anomaly born from unexpected parents.

"It was easy enough to get her out of the way—Dolph believed me when I told him Leena would be fine going into Morgan's house. He was supposed to die that night as well, the stubborn bastard. But in the end it was easy enough to get rid of him, too."

"You killed them both," she whispered, still trying to process what he'd revealed. She was suddenly glad there was a chair holding her up, because she wouldn't have trusted her legs to do the job. "You lied to me about everything."

"I also saved you. Life is full of contradictions, isn't it?" All the amusement melted from his expression, and he leaned even closer. "By the end of the year, things had only gotten worse. Their Conclave was coming up, and the Order was growing increasingly desperate to find their artifacts. I knew if the raids got ahold of you, the Order would keep you. I couldn't risk losing you, so I did the only thing I could. I used Ishtar's Key to hide you."

He held up the cuff and examined the stone. This stone didn't have the crack bisecting its smooth surface. Even from that distance, Esta could feel its call.

"I'd experimented with it myself, and I knew it could be used to focus or amplify magical power, even if I wasn't completely sure what it would do for you. You were too small to have any control over your power, but I knew that if I got you scared enough, you'd use your affinity. So I locked you in a closet, and when you stopped crying, I opened the door to find you gone. Exactly as I'd hoped. Far out of the reach of the Order.

"They took me in, of course, and the interrogation wasn't an easy one. I didn't exactly walk away from it," he said, gesturing to his leg. "When I got back, the old woman I'd left watching the room said you'd never returned. I'd expected you to be back in minutes, maybe hours after the Order's men left." He frowned. "Ishtar's Key was more powerful than I'd realized, and you made me wait quite a while longer before you finally showed up. More than ninety years. But I was right in the end—it all worked out. I waited, and while I waited, I planned, and sure enough, you eventually appeared. As I knew you would."

"You *stole* me. You stole my entire life."

"I *made* you. I gave you a life you would never have had back then. And now you're going to repay the favor." He slipped the cuff onto her arm.

She could sense its heat, the call of its magic, but her blood still wasn't quite clear of whatever drug he'd given her, so she couldn't draw on it.

"Do you know what time is, Esta?" Professor Lachlan smiled when she didn't answer. "It's the substance that connects everything, the indefinable quality that transcends *everything*. It is the quintessence of existence—*Aether*. There was a reason I wanted you, a reason I saved you."

"Aether?" Esta asked, remembering Harte's words on the bridge.

He took the dagger, the one she'd stolen from Schwab's mansion that fateful night when everything had started to go wrong, and examined its tip. "It's a bit primitive, I know, but these things do tend to work better with a little blood."

Esta held herself steady, refusing to so much as flinch when the Professor approached her with the knife. Slowly, he traced it across her chest, just beneath her collarbone. She didn't even feel the bite of the blade. Her entire world had imploded—she'd betrayed her friends in the past and now she'd been betrayed by the only family she'd ever known. Everything she thought she knew about who she was or why she'd been saved was a lie. With everyone turned against her, she had no way out.

What was a little blood, a little pain in the face of all that?

When he was done, when her wound had started to feel hot, he tucked the knife into the bodice of her dress, so its blade was pointing down toward her belly and the Pharaoh's Heart lay flush against her skin.

"Aether connects all of the elements," he explained, "and so I will use your affinity to connect the stones. With them united, I'll be able to control the power of the Book."

"And what about me?" she said, hating the way her voice shook. "What happens to me?"

"I expect the same thing that happened to all the Mageus whose power was taken to create the original stones." He gave her an unreadable look. "You're just the vessel."

She tried to struggle against the ropes again, but with the dagger against her skin, she couldn't move without slicing herself to ribbons.

"Now, now. It'll only be a few more minutes." Professor Lachlan smiled softly then, and it wasn't the cold smile of Nibsy Lorcan, but instead was the smile Esta had grown up with, the smile she had craved so desperately as a child.

That betrayal sliced deeper than any wound the dagger could make.

But she lifted her chin. She would not let him know how afraid she was. The only thing she would allow him was her hate.

Professor Lachlan returned to the table and retrieved the Book. He ignored her as he flipped to a page he'd carefully marked, and then he began to read aloud.

At first it sounded like Latin, but as he droned on, the tenor of his voice changed, as though something had come over him, and she could no longer understand the individual words. As he chanted, the syllables grew more and more strange, until they no longer sounded like words, until his voice no longer sounded human, and as he chanted, the stones in the pieces of metal pressed against her skin began to grow warm. On and on he went, until time seemed to lose all meaning, until the heat from the stones felt as though it would burn straight through to her bones, until a strange wind had begun to swirl around the library, rustling the papers until it grew strong enough to send them into the air. Until the lights began to flicker. Until all at once, a terrible roaring filled her ears.

And then everything went dark.

The air in the room went still.

But Esta wasn't gone.

CONTINGENCIES

A flame flickered nearby, illuminating the deep wrinkles of Professor Lachlan's face as he approached her. "You're still alive," he said softly, like he was talking to himself more than her. "It didn't work."

"I can't say I'm all that sorry."

Professor Lachlan leaned close to her. "You will be." He used the intercom to tell Logan to check the breakers in the basement, and he began removing the artifacts from her one by one, beginning with her cuff. A moment later the lights flickered on again.

"Did you say one of the words wrong?" she asked, purposely poking at him.

"No. I said everything perfectly," he told her as he took the final artifact back. "I was afraid this might happen. I was afraid it had been too long."

"So your grand plan isn't going to work after all?" She didn't allow herself to hope. Not so long as she was still tied to the chair.

"Of course it will. There might not be enough magic left in the world for the ritual to work now, but there was before. So you'll take the Book back to the boy I once was, back to a world where magic still had power and I was still young enough to use it."

"Why would I ever do that?"

He studied her for a moment. "Because if you don't, you'll most likely disappear. If Ishtar's Key isn't in the past, I won't be able to give it to you as a child."

Her mind was racing. "Then I should have already disappeared," she challenged. "Me bringing Ishtar's Key back here, to this time, would have already changed my life. The date you gave me the stone would have already passed by now. Nibs—you—wouldn't have been able to give me the stone as a young girl, I wouldn't have grown up in this time, and we wouldn't be having this conversation."

"Unless you've already done it. I don't think this moment would change until you make the conscious decision to change the past." He smiled, clearly pleased with himself. "I've seen every connection, planned for every contingency. It's a particular *talent* of mine."

So that was Nibsy's power. No wonder he kept it such a secret.

Esta lifted her chin. "Maybe I'd rather disappear than let you win," she said. "Did you plan for that?"

"Actually, I did," he said. He walked to his desk and pressed a button. A moment later, the elevator rattled to life, the lift climbing toward them.

He pulled a gun from the drawer in his desk and aimed it directly at her. The barrel was tipped with a silencer.

"I won't help you unlock the power in that book," she said, pleased to hear that her voice didn't shake even if she did. "I'd rather die."

Professor Lachlan smiled. "I'm sure you would. But who would you be willing to sacrifice with you?"

The door to the elevator opened then. "You called, Professor?" Dakari said, stepping into the room.

"No!" she screamed, fighting against the ropes that held her. "Dakari, go—"

But it was too late. The gun went off, a soft clap followed by the louder sound of Dakari hitting the floor.

"No," she cried, and her eyes were already burning with tears. She was still fighting against the ropes, and against the truth of what had just happened.

Professor Lachlan walked to where she was sitting and jerked her chin up, forcing her to look at him. "It seems you have a choice after all. You can choose to fade away. Choose to disappear and never exist. Maybe it'll happen immediately. Maybe you'll have time to watch everyone you've ever cared for die, just as Dakari has. Logan. Mari. Her entire family you're so fond of. I'll bring them here for you, make sure you can see them plead for their lives before I kill them. So they can know it was you who signed their death warrant. Or you can do what I ask and take the Book back to my younger self."

"No," she whispered, shaking her head.

"You like to save people, don't you? Think of it—you could rewrite this future and give Dakari a new life in a world without the Order. A life that wouldn't end in a heap on my library floor. If you're very good, you might even convince my younger self to have mercy on Dolph's crew."

She couldn't stop the tears that ran down her face. She turned away from Professor Lachlan, unable to stomach him so close to her, and across the room Viola's knives glinted in the dim light.

Jianyu. Viola.

Maybe she couldn't save Dolph, but she could still save them. As long as she didn't give up, she could go back and try once more to change things.

"Fine," she said, keeping her eyes on Viola's knives, so Professor Lachlan wouldn't see the hate in her gaze. "I'll do it. But I will fight you every step of the way."

Professor Lachlan—Nibs—whoever he was—smiled. "I wouldn't expect anything less, girl, but know this: You're playing against a stacked deck. I've already considered everything you might do, and I've already accounted for all the outcomes. Fight all you want, but the future will be mine."

Professor Lachlan hadn't lied about being prepared. He'd accounted for what seemed like every contingency.

Logan had her by the arm to ensure she didn't use her affinity without taking him with her. The gun was just a precaution, they'd told her. In case she got any ideas. Not that she believed them. Once they were in the past, it would be easy enough for Logan to kill her.

They'd given her some sort of drug, timing it so that as they walked the six blocks to the park, it would wear off just enough to allow her to use Ishtar's Key to take Logan back to 1902. She wouldn't have a chance to get away before then, not without dealing with the gun.

She'd been given an exact date, one week after the day on the bridge. Once they were back, Logan had specific instructions about what to look for. If she tried to take him to any other time, he'd kill her. Or he'd injure her badly enough to make her want to cooperate.

Once they were back, the Strega would be an easy walk. There would be very little chance of her getting away, or for her to ruin Professor Lachlan's plans for them to deliver the Book and the stones. And once Nibs had them, there would be no stopping him.

To make things worse, she didn't really know Logan—not this version of Logan. She didn't have the same memories he did of their shared history, and all she could go on to predict how he would act was the hope that the intrinsic nature of a person was steady and stable no matter what trajectory their life took. He might have been a pain in the ass before, but he hadn't been evil. He wouldn't have purposely hurt someone. She could only hope that was still the case.

But she wasn't sure she believed it.

She kept her head down, her posture slouched, like the weight of the world—its past, present, and future—was on her shoulders. *Let them believe they've won,* she thought to herself. Let them think she was penned in. Even if she wasn't yet sure how she'd ever manage to get out.

The Professor looked at his watch, and when the time came that the medication would have been out of her system, he gave a stiff nod.

Logan jammed the gun harder into her back, a cue that she needed to start. But she still felt sluggish and numb from the lingering effects of the drug, so it was harder than usual to find the right moment, the exact time she was supposed to hit. She pushed down through the layers of years, until she felt the familiar pull of that time. Strange, she thought, for it to feel almost as if she were going home.

But Esta forced herself to ignore the sappy sentiment. It took everything she had to guide them to the moment she wanted. In the distance, the Freedom Tower—the city's one-fingered salute to the rest of the world—began to fade. The city dimmed around them and she felt that push-pull sensation, like she would fly apart and collapse in on herself all at once as she pulled them to the date she needed. The park receded and the city of yesterday began to materialize, and just as she was almost through, just before the present disappeared and the past was made real, Logan began to scream and tear at the bag he had strapped to his chest, the bag that contained the other artifacts and the Book.

Instinctively, she understood that this was the best chance she would have. She gave her arm a vicious twist, wrenching herself away from him, and Logan, who was still focused on the bag, let her go just as they landed hard on the damp cobbled streets of Old New York.

Her entire body was shaking with the effort it had taken to get away from him, and the cuff on her arm was warm. The neighborhood was eerily quiet for the middle of the day. In the distance, she heard the clanging of bells and smelled the heavy chemical smell of buildings burning.

Slipping through time always left Logan momentarily dizzied, and it did this time as well. He'd barely managed to pull the bag off and toss it away from himself when a group of darkly dressed boys came around the corner. *Five Pointers.*

Their eyes lit when they saw the two of them lying on the sidewalk, Logan still dazed from the trip, and their pace increased.

But before the boys could reach her, Esta pulled time slow and scooped the bag up. She brushed the grime of the streets from her dress, and with the world silent and still around her, she started to walk. She had somewhere she needed to be, a life she needed to save. She had to go back. She had to get to the bridge. Logan could fend for himself.

THE MAGICIAN

March 1902—The Brooklyn Bridge

The Magician stood at the edge of his world and took one last look at his city. Around him, chaos erupted on the bridge, but his eyes were on the only thing that mattered—Esta.

Go, he willed her. She had to take the Book where they would all be safe from it. She had to take *herself* there too, far away from Nibs or Jack or anyone else who might use her. *Including him.* If the Order ever found out what she was, what she could do . . .

Go.

But she wore the same stubborn expression he recognized from every other time he'd tried to get her to do something. *She wasn't leaving.* She wasn't getting away while she could. He'd expected her stubbornness, though, had known he would have to take the decision from her. It was only one step. A single step and it would all be over.

He closed his eyes and let himself feel the wind on his face one last time as he leaned into it—

And then he was falling, and the air around him pushed and pulled at him, pressing in on his body until he was so dizzy he thought he would vomit, his head pounding with an unnatural pressure. He fell and fell until he hit the ground in front of him, with something—someone—pinning him down.

He heard a soft, feminine moan, and the weight rolled off him.

"Jianyu?" Esta's voice came to him like a dream. "What are you doing here?"

It took him a second to find his voice, to make himself understand what he was seeing, but it was Esta. It was *really* Esta, not some dream of her. The bridge was empty and silent, and she was sprawled across Jianyu's back, looking more confused than he'd ever seen her. And he wasn't dead.

"He was helping me," Harte said, pulling himself up. He was still reeling from the shock of seeing her. The absolute wonder at being alive, when moments ago he'd thought Jianyu had decided to let him fall.

"Helping you?" She pulled herself off Jianyu, who lay unconscious on the ground. "Helping you do what?"

"Fake my own death." He swallowed uncomfortably when her expression seemed more angry than relieved.

Esta just stared at him with her eyes wide and a look of utter consternation on her face. It was maybe the first time he'd ever seen her at a loss for words.

"You're shaking," Harte said, touching her cheek with a trembling hand. Her skin was pale, her hair a mess around her face.

"I'm fine," she told him, but she didn't push him away. Then, all at once, her face crumpled. "You idiot," she said, slapping Harte. "You told me you were going to jump." Her voice was nearly manic, and her eyes were wild with unshed tears. "I thought you were dead," she cried, her voice cracking as her chin trembled.

"I'm not dead," he said softly, glad to hear his voice was so steady, considering how shaken he felt. He hadn't known for sure that Jianyu was going to be there, as they'd planned. When he'd leaned into the wind, Harte was forcing himself to put all his trust, his entire life, into someone else's hands.

She slapped him again, and he raised his arms to fend off the attack, but fell over instead, his head spinning from the motion. "Esta, stop!"

"You lied to me again!"

"I had to," he said, pulling himself upright again. He caught her hands, gently, so that she couldn't hit him again. "I needed you to get the Book away from Nibs and Jack, and I knew you wouldn't leave any other way."

But her expression didn't soften. Her golden eyes were still filled with fire. "You told me the Order would never stop hunting you."

"They won't."

Jianyu moaned nearby but hadn't yet come to.

"Then why?"

She seemed to have calmed down, so he released her hands. "I was going back to the city, to stop Nibs and the Order . . . to create a different future for you to return to."

Esta went still, her expression wary. "And I'm just supposed to believe you now?"

"He speaks truly," Jianyu added with a groan as he finally pulled himself upright. "We arranged everything after Dolph was found." He took a look around and seemed to realize finally that the bridge was empty. "What happened? Where did everyone go?" he asked, puzzled.

"They left hours ago," Esta explained.

"Hours?"

"For you, it would have felt like moments," Esta told him. "I thought I was just grabbing Harte. I didn't realize you were there too when I reached through."

Jianyu looked utterly perplexed. "Reached through?"

"Through time," she said. "I couldn't come all the way through. So I just kind of . . . pushed you past the moment you were in, to a different time." She rubbed at her arm, and pain flickered across her expression. "It's a long story."

Jianyu peered at Esta with confusion and no little amount of curiosity. "I would be most interested to hear your explanation."

"Later." Harte turned to Esta. "We had to make the Order and Nibs, *everyone*, believe that I was gone," he said, trying to explain. "Hell, you were supposed to believe it too. You were supposed to stay in your own time, when you'd be safe."

"There's no such thing as safe anymore," she said softly. Then she looked to Jianyu. "Does Viola know too? Was she in on this?"

"I thought the fewer who knew, the better. Easier to avoid suspicion around Nibs," Jianyu told her.

"Nibs," Esta said, her voice breaking.

Then she told them about Nibs and Professor Lachlan, about Dakari's death and Logan's betrayal.

"How did you ever get away?" Harte asked.

"I improvised." A small smile tugged at her lips. "And now I have this." She pulled the Book from the bag that she had slung across her body, but her eyes were still staring into its interior, and the color was draining from her face. "No."

"What?" he asked, wondering what could have put that look on her face after everything they'd been through.

She pulled out a charred piece of metal that looked strangely familiar. "Is that—?"

"They're gone," she whispered, dumping the contents of the bag onto the ground. The artifacts he'd stolen, all charred so badly they were nearly beyond recognition. "This happened before. When I came here the first time to find you. I showed you, remember?"

"Your cuff," Harte said, remembering the strange images that had flashed through his mind when she'd kissed him onstage. "What happened to them?"

"I don't know," she said. "But I wonder . . . I felt the same heat and pain when I reached to push you through as I'd felt the first time I came back. There must be something to the stones. They must not be able to exist in the same time as themselves."

Harte thought for a moment. "Nibs wouldn't have sent the stones back with this Logan character if he knew this would happen. He won't be able to get to them either. Not where I've put them. We're safe. It's over."

"It's not." She looked up at him, her expression unreadable. "Someday he will get them. He has before. We have to get the stones before he does."

"They seem to be beyond repair," Jianyu said, gesturing to the charred remains.

"Not these," Esta said. "The others." She met Harte's eyes. "The stones that should still be in *this* time."

"They're outside the city, and he's *inside*. He can't get out of the Brink."

"But they won't always be outside the city. Eventually they'll make their way back in. I know, because I've stolen every one of them before." She grabbed his arm. "And what's worse, Logan is here now. I left him lying on the sidewalk about a week from now. He's going to find Nibs, and he'll tell him everything that happens in the future. We can't let him have that information *and* the stones. We *have* to get to the stones before he does."

Harte frowned. "There's no way to get through the Brink without destroying it."

Her eyes were wide, her expression unreadable, but he could tell she was thinking, turning over ideas in her mind. And then something clicked, something shifted. "Maybe there is," she told him, sounding strangely calm.

"Esta, I've explained this . . ."

"I know. You told me that the Brink was like a circuit—that taking the Book through would short it out with the excess power. But there *are* ways to get through a circuit. There are ways to touch electricity. Look at the birds on the wires—you just can't be grounded."

He shook his head, not understanding. "Grounded?"

"Maybe grounded is the wrong word. But you're worried that the power of the Book would short out the Brink, right? We just need to keep the Book from disrupting the current of the Brink. Something Professor Lachlan—Nibs—told me might help. Aether and time are the same thing. Why can't we use my affinity for time to block the Book's power from disrupting the Aether of the Brink? Then it wouldn't overload the circuit, and maybe there wouldn't be any magical blackout."

"That might work," Jianyu said, his voice thoughtful. "It is not so different from what I do with light to disappear. I bend it around myself. If she could direct the Aether of the Brink around the Book instead of through it—"

"You don't understand, Esta. That won't work."

"Why not? If it's a circuit, then all we have to do is—"

He rested his hand on her arm, stopping her words. "It won't work because all that power isn't in the Book anymore." He swallowed hard, finally forcing himself to accept what he'd known ever since the voices had crashed into him in the Mysterium. "All that power is in *me.*"

Her mouth dropped open. "*In* you?"

He nodded, unable to speak. Because he wasn't sure how long he'd be able to live with it inside him, how long he'd be able to control it.

"So this is what you were hiding?" Jianyu asked, his voice dark.

He shifted, feeling vaguely guilty. Jianyu had risked so much to help him. "I told you everything I could."

"You should have told me *everything*," Jianyu said, his voice carrying a note of anger that Harte had never heard before, not even that night when Jianyu found him on the docks.

Esta shook her head. "It doesn't matter now. We need the stones."

He looked at her more closely then, with her hair falling down around her face and her clothes rumpled beyond repair. It was probably certain death for the both of them if he went along with her mad plan. But with the Book living inside of him, chipping away at him a little more every day, he already was a dead man. If her plan actually managed to work, maybe she could save them both. If not, he would happily take any number of minutes more he could in that crazy world, especially if they were minutes fighting with her.

"You'll need to find Viola and let her know what happened," she said to Jianyu. "We have some time before we catch up to when I left Logan. If you can keep him from getting to Nibs, that will buy us more. Because once Nibs knows that I'm back, he won't stop at anything to get the Book." She turned back to Harte, her eyes already shining with determination. "He won't know you didn't actually jump, and he won't know about the stones. That will give us an advantage, but even so, we're going to need every bit of luck to get this right."

"We're going to need a hell of a lot more than luck," he muttered, his head still swirling at everything that had happened, all that she wanted to do.

"I will find Viola, and together we can keep your friend from Nibs," Jianyu promised. "We'll give you all the time we can."

"But then what?" Harte said, still refusing to allow himself to hope.

"Then we unite the stones, take control of the Book's power," Esta said.

Harte frowned. "I'm not sure any one person should control it."

"I'm not either, but I'm not willing to let Nibs or the Order be the ones to make that decision," she said. "Are you?"

"I, for one, am not." Jianyu stood and offered his hand to help Harte to his feet. He handed Harte a parcel that he took from inside his own coat. "You go with Esta. I will see to things here."

Harte hesitated for a minute. "I owe you my thanks. For trusting me, even when I didn't deserve it. For helping me. You could have let me fall."

"I did it for Dolph," Jianyu said. "Do not forget your promise, and do not prove me a fool." And with a small bow of his head, he disappeared, leaving Harte and Esta alone on the bridge.

Harte watched the place where Jianyu had just been, and after a moment he unwrapped the parcel and put on the shirt that it contained.

"So you'll help me?" Esta asked as he buttoned the shirt. "You'll show me how to get through the Brink using the Book?"

It was no longer morning, Harte realized. The sun had just set and the whole skyline was aflame with the glow of twilight reflecting off the buildings. It looked like a city on fire, a dangerous and dazzling place.

He tucked in the shirt, straightened the sleeves. "You shouldn't have come back," he told her.

"I didn't have much of a choice," she said, and her golden eyes were clouded with pain.

"What you're asking me to do, what you're planning, it could be the death of us both."

"If we don't, it could be the death of *everyone*. Nibs cannot get those stones. The Order can't either."

"And what if we make everything worse?" The voices in his mind were louder now, humming their promises and threats. *They knew what she was. They wanted her.* He rubbed the back of his neck, a feeble attempt to subdue the thing that now lived inside of him.

"We still have to try."

He looked once more at that far side of the bridge, at the world he had come to believe he would never reach. *But Esta is back,* the voices whispered. So maybe, just maybe . . .

There was no talking her out of it, no turning her away from this course. And there was a part of him that didn't want to.

He held out his hand. "If you're ready?"

She looked up at his open palm and shook her head as she pulled herself to her feet. "Nice try."

But then she slipped her arm through his, and together they began walking toward the cold power of the Brink.

ACKNOWLEDGMENTS

~

This is a big book, and it took a lot of people to make it happen. Thanks go first and foremost to Michael Strother, who loved my pitch for this book and whose guidance made it so much better. I'm *so* grateful that Sarah McCabe was willing to adopt this behemoth and for her astute insights and support (even when the word count continued to grow). The entire team at Simon Pulse are my heroes for giving me the gift of more time to make it right and the gift of their support for this story. Craig Howell and Cliff Nielsen made *the most* amazing cover art, and I'm still blown away by the beautiful map Drew Willis designed. I could not be more indebted to the sharp eyes of Penina Lopez for her copyediting, to Valerie Shea for her proofreading, and to Clare McGlade for her cold read.

Thank you to all of the people who read early drafts: Kristen Lippert-Martin helped me solve a major plot issue and saved the book, Hope Cook's honest words helped me see mistakes I hadn't intended to make and saved the book, and Olivia Hinebaugh kept my spirits up when I felt like the whole project was pointless and saved the book. Kathryn Rose and Helene Dunbar also gave me essential insights to make this story stronger, and I'm grateful for their help.

Thanks to Flavia Brunetti, Guillaume Amphoux, and Christina Ketchum, who all assisted with some of the non-English phrases and words. Any mistakes are, of course, my own. The awesome people at the Lower East Side History Project were unbelievably helpful in walking me around the areas in this book and helping me find where everyone lived. They also give excellent dim sum recommendations.

I'm not sure what I would do without my rock star of an agent, Kathleen Rushall.

I should probably also thank Chris Cornell, who has no idea that his music was the soundtrack to writing this. Who knows why *Higher Truth* worked for 1902 New York, but it did.

To my family, who has lived with this book for as long as I have. It wasn't easy to write, which means there were times I wasn't easy to live with. To J, who makes it possible to run off to the city for research and never doubts that this is what I should be doing, and to H, and X, who are my hearts: I couldn't do any of this without their support, and I wouldn't want to.

Finally, like so many in this country, I'm the product of immigrants. A few years back I was looking at Ellis Island ship manifests, and I noticed that none of my great-grandmothers were listed as literate. I'm sure those women would have found me a strange creature with my fancy degrees and complete disinterest in housekeeping, but I hope they would be proud. After all, it was because of their sacrifices and determination that I find myself here, making a life out of the very words they came to this country unable to read. So for those women, and for all who came before, imperfect as they might have been, thank you.

LISA MAXWELL is the author of *Sweet Unrest, Gathering Deep,* and *Unhooked.* She grew up in Akron, Ohio, and has a PhD in English. She's worked as a teacher, scholar, bookseller, editor, and writer. When she's not writing books, she's a professor at a local college. She now lives near Washington, DC, with her husband and two sons. You can follow her on Twitter @LisaMaxwellYA or learn more about her upcoming books at Lisa-Maxwell.com.